THE NIBELUNGENLIED

Translated into Rhymed English Verse in the Metre of the Original

By George Henry Needler

Associate Professor of German in University College, Toronto

Ostara Publications

The Nibelungenlied
Translated into Rhymed English Verse in the Metre of the Original
Unknown Author
By George Henry Needler
Associate Professor of German in University College, Toronto

First published in English 1904.

This edition 2015
Ostara Publications
http://ostarapublications.com

Contents

I. The Nibelungen Saga

II. The Form of the Nibelungenlied

III. THE NIBELUNGENLIED

PREFACE

This translation of the Nibelungenlied is published with the simple purpose of placing one of the world's great epic poems within the reach of English readers. Translations are at best but poor substitutes for originals. A new translation of a poem implies also a criticism of those that have preceded it. My apology for presenting this new English version of the Nibelungenlied is that none of those hitherto made has reproduced the metrical form of the original. In the hope of making the outlines of the poem clearer for the modern reader, I have endeavored to supply in the Introduction a historical background by summing up the results of investigation into its origin and growth. The translation itself was begun many years ago, when I studied the original under Zarncke in Leipzig.

G. H. N.
University College, Toronto, September, 1904.

I. The Nibelungen Saga

1. Origin of the Saga

All the Aryan peoples have had their heroic age, the achievements of which form the basis of later saga. For the Germans this was the period of the Migrations, as it is called, in round numbers the two hundred years from 400 to 600, at the close of which we find them settled in those regions which they have, generally speaking, occupied ever since. During these two centuries kaleidoscopic changes had been taking place in the position of the various Germanic tribes. Impelled partly by a native love of wandering, partly by the pressure of hostile peoples of other race, they moved with astonishing rapidity hither and thither over the face of Europe, generally in conflict with one another or buffeted by the Romans in the west and south, and by the Huns in the east. In this stern struggle for existence and search for a permanent place of settlement some of them even perished utterly; amid the changing fortunes of all of them deeds were performed that fixed themselves in the memory of the whole people, great victories or great disasters became the subject of story and song.

We need only to recall such names as those of Ermanric and Theodoric to remind ourselves what an important part was played by the Germanic peoples of that Migration Period in the history of Europe. During it a national consciousness was engendered, and in it we have the faint beginnings of a national literature. Germanic saga rests almost entirely upon the events of these two centuries, the fifth and sixth. Although we get glimpses of the Germans during the four or five preceding centuries, none of the historic characters of those earlier times have been preserved in the national sagas.

With these sagas based on history, however, have been mingled in most cases primeval Germanic myths, possessions of the people from prehistoric times. A most conspicuous example of this union of mythical and originally historical elements is the Nibelungen saga, out of which grew in course of time the great national epic, the Nibelungenlied.

The Nibelungen saga is made up of two parts, on the one hand the mythical story of Siegfried and on the other the story, founded on historic fact, of the Burgundians. When and how the Siegfried myth arose it is impossible to say; its origin takes us back into the impenetrable mists of the unrecorded life of our Germanic forefathers, and its form was moulded by the popular poetic spirit. The other part of the saga is based upon the historic incident of the overthrow of the Burgundian kingdom by the Huns in the year 437.

This annihilation of a whole tribe naturally impressed itself vividly upon the imagination of contemporaries. Then the fact of history soon began to pass over into the realm of legend, and, from causes which can no longer be determined, this tradition of the vanished Burgundians became united with the mythical story of Siegfried. This composite Siegfried-Burgundian saga then became a common possession of the Germanic peoples, was borne with many of them to lands far distant from the place of its origin, and was further moulded by each according to its peculiar genius and surroundings. In the Icelandic Eddas, the oldest of which we have as they were written down in the latter part of the ninth century, are preserved the earliest records of the form it had taken among the northern Germanic peoples. Our Nibelungenlied, which is the chief source of our knowledge of the story as it developed in Germany, dates from about the year 1200.

These two versions, the Northern and the German, though originating in this common source, had diverged very widely in the centuries that elapsed between their beginning and the time when the manuscripts were written in which they are preserved. Each curtailed, re-arranged, or enlarged the incidents of the story in its own way. The character of the chief actors and the motives underlying what we may call the dramatic development assumed widely dissimilar forms.

The German Nibelungenlied may be read and appreciated as one of the world's great epic poems without an acquaintance on the part of the reader with the Northern version of the saga. In order, however, to furnish the setting for a few episodes that would in that case remain either obscure or colorless, and with a view to placing the readers of this translation in a position to judge better the deeper significance of the epic as the eloquent narrative of a thousand years of the life of the people among whom it grew, the broad outlines of the saga in its Northern form will be given here.

2. The Northern Form of the Saga

Starting at the middle of the fifth century from the territory about Worms on the Rhine where the Burgundians were overthrown, the saga soon spread from the Franks to the other Germanic peoples. We have evidence of its presence in northern Germany and Denmark. Allusions to it in the Anglo-Saxon poem, the *Wanderer*, of the seventh century and in the great Anglo-Saxon epic *Beowulf* of a short time later, show us that it had early become part of the national saga stock in England. Among the people of Norway and Iceland it took root and grew with particular vigor. Here, farthest away from its original home and least exposed to outward influences, it preserved on the whole most fully its heathen Germanic character, especially in its mythical part.

By a fortunate turn of events, too, the written record of it here is of considerably earlier date than that which we have from Germany. The Eddas, as the extensive collection of early Icelandic poems is called, are the fullest record of Germanic mythology and saga that has been handed down to us, and in them the saga of Siegfried and the Nibelungen looms up prominently. The earliest of these poems date from about the year 850, and the most important of them were probably written down within a couple of centuries of that time. They are thus in part some three centuries older than the German Nibelungenlied, and on the whole, too, they preserve more of the original outlines of the saga. By bringing together the various episodes of the saga from the Eddas and the Volsung saga, a prose account of the mythical race of the Volsungs, we arrive at the following narrative.

On their wanderings through the world the three gods Odin, Hönir, and Loki come to a waterfall where an otter is devouring a fish that it has caught. Loki kills the otter with a stone, and they take off its skin. In the evening they seek a lodging at the house of Hreidmar, to whom they show the skin. Hreidmar recognizes it as that of his son, whom Loki has killed when he had taken on the form of an otter. Assisted by his sons Fafnir

3

and Regin, Hreidmar seizes the three gods, and spares their lives only on the promise that they will fill the skin, and also cover it outwardly, with gold. Loki is sent to procure the ransom. With a net borrowed from the sea-goddess Ran he catches at the waterfall the dwarf Andvari in form of a fish and compels him to supply the required gold. Andvari tries to keep back a ring, but this also Loki takes from him, whereupon the dwarf utters a curse upon the gold and whosoever may possess it. The ransom is now paid to Hreidmar; even the ring must, on Hreidmar's demand, be given in order to complete the covering of the otter's skin. Loki tells him of the curse connected with the ownership of the gold. When Hreidmar refuses Fafnir and Regin a share in the treasure, he is killed by Fafnir, who takes possession of the hoard to the exclusion of Regin. In the form of a dragon Fafnir dwells on Gnita Heath guarding the hoard, while Regin broods revenge.

From Odin is descended King Volsung, who has a family of ten sons and one daughter. The eldest son is Sigmund, twin-born with his sister Signy. King Siggeir of Gautland sues for the hand of Signy, whom her father gives to Siggeir against her will. In the midst of King Volsung's hall stood a mighty oak-tree. As the wedding-feast is being held there enters a stranger, an old man with one eye, his hat drawn down over his face and bearing in his hand a sword. This sword he thrusts to the hilt into the tree, saying that it shall belong to him who can draw it out again; after which he disappears as he had come. All the guests try their strength in vain upon the sword, but Sigmund alone is able to draw it forth. He refuses to sell it to Siggeir for all his proffered gold. Siggeir plans vengeance. He invites Volsung and his sons to Gautland, and returns home thither with his bride Signy, who before going warns her father to be upon his guard.

At the appointed time King Volsung and his sons go as invited to Gautland. In spite of Signy's repeated warning he will not flee from danger, and falls in combat with Siggeir; his ten sons are taken prisoners, and placed in stocks in the forest. For nine successive nights a she-wolf comes and devours each night one of them, till only Sigmund remains. By the aid of Signy he escapes. The she-wolf, it was said, was the mother of Siggeir.

To Sigmund, who has hidden in a wood, Signy sends her eldest boy of ten years that Sigmund may test his courage and see if he is fit to be a helper in seeking revenge. Neither he, however, nor his younger brother stands the test. Signy sees that only a scion of the race of Volsung will suffice, and accordingly disguises herself and lives three days with Sigmund in the wood. From their union a son Sinfiotli is born, whom also, after ten years, she sends out to Sigmund. He stands every test of courage, and is trained by Sigmund, who thinks he is Siggeir's son.

Bent on revenge, Sigmund repairs with Sinfiotli to Siggeir's castle. After Sinfiotli has slain the king's two sons, he and Sigmund are overpowered and condemned to be buried alive. With Sigmund's sword, however, which Signy has managed to place in their hands, they cut their way out, then set fire to Siggeir's hall. Signy comes forth and reveals to Sigmund that Sinfiotli is their own son; and then, saying that her work of revenge is complete and that she can live no longer, she returns into the burning hall and perishes with Siggeir and all his race.

Sigmund now returns home and rules as a mighty king. He marries Borghild, who later kills Sinfiotli with a poisoned drink, and is cast away by Sigmund. He then marries Hjordis. Lyngvi, the son of King Hunding, was also a suitor and now invades Sigmund's land. The latter hews down many of his enemies, until an old man with one eye, in hat and dark cloak, interposes his spear, against which Sigmund's sword breaks in two. Sigmund falls severely wounded.

In the night Hjordis seeks the scene of the combat and finds Sigmund still alive. He refuses to allow her to heal his wounds, saying that Odin no longer wills that he swing the sword. He tells Hjordis to preserve carefully the pieces of the broken sword; the son she bears in her womb shall yet swing the sword when welded anew, and win thereby a glorious name. At dawn Sigmund dies. Hjordis is borne off by Vikings and, after the birth of her son, she becomes the wife of the Danish prince Alf.

The son of Hjordis was called Sigurd. He grew up a boy of wondrous strength and beauty, with eyes that sparkled brightly, and lived at the court of King Hjalprek, the father of Alf. Regin, the dwarfish brother of Fafnir, was his tutor. Regin welds together the pieces of the broken sword Gram, so sharp and strong that with it Sigurd cleaves Regin's anvil in twain. With men and ships that he has received from King Hjalprek Sigurd goes against the sons of Hunding, whom he slays, thereby avenging the death of his father. Regin has urged him to kill Fafnir and take possession of the hoard. On the Gnita Heath he digs a ditch from which, as the dragon Fafnir passes over it, he plunges the sword into his heart. The dying Fafnir warns him of the curse attached to the possession of the gold; also that Regin is to be guarded against. The latter bids him roast the heart of Fafnir. While doing so he burns his finger by dipping it in the blood to see if the heart is done, and to cool his finger puts it into his mouth. Suddenly he is able to understand the language of the birds in the wood. They warn him to beware of Regin, whom he straightway slays. The birds tell him further of the beautiful valkyrie Brynhild, who sleeps on the fire-encircled mountain awaiting her deliverer. Then Sigurd places Fafnir's hoard upon his steed Grani, takes with him also Fafnir's helm, and rides away to Frankenland. He sees a mountain encircled by a zone of fire, makes his way into it and beholds there, as he deems it, a man in full armor asleep. When he takes off the helmet he finds that it is a woman. With his sword he cuts loose the armor. The woman wakes and asks if it be the hero Sigurd who has awakened her. In joy that it is so, Brynhild relates to him how Odin had punished her by this magic sleep for disobedience, and how that she had yet obtained from him the promise that she should be wakened only by a hero who knew no fear. She now teaches Sigurd many wise runes, and tells him of harm to fear through love of her. In spite of all, however, Sigurd does not waver, and they swear an oath of mutual faithful love.

Next Sigurd comes to King Gjuki at the Rhine, and joins in friendship with him and his sons Gunnar and Hogni. Queen Grimhild gives Sigurd a potion which causes him to forget Brynhild and be filled with love for her own daughter Gudrun, whom he marries. Gunnar now seeks Brynhild for wife, and Sigurd goes with him on his wooing-journey. They come to the castle encircled by fire, where Brynhild lives. She will be wooed only by him who will ride to her through the flames. Gunnar tries in vain to do this, even when mounted on Sigurd's steed Grani. Sigurd and Gunnar then exchange shapes and the former spurs Grani through the flames. He calls himself Gunnar the son of Gjuki, and finally Brynhild consents to become his wife.

Three nights he shares her couch, but always his sharp sword lies between them. He takes the ring from her finger and places in its stead one from Fafnir's treasure. Then he exchanges form again with Gunnar, who is soon after wedded to Brynhild. Only now does Sigurd recollect the oath that he once swore to Brynhild himself.

One day Brynhild and Gudrun are bathing in the Rhine. A quarrel arises between them when Brynhild takes precedence of Gudrun by going into the water above her in the stream, saying that her husband is a braver and mightier man than Gudrun's. Gudrun retorts by revealing the secret that it was Sigurd in Gunnar's form, and not Gunnar himself, who rode through the flame, and in proof thereof shows her the ring taken by Sigurd from Brynhild's finger. Pale as death, Brynhild goes quietly home: Gunnar must die, she says in wrath. Sigurd tries to pacify her, even offering to desert Gudrun.

Now she will have neither him nor another, and when Gunnar appears she demands of him Sigurd's death. In spite of Hogni's protest Gunnar's stepbrother Gutthorm, who has not sworn blood-friendship with Sigurd, is got to do the deed. He is given the flesh of wolf and serpent to eat in order to make him savage. Twice Gutthorm goes to kill Sigurd, but cowers before the piercing glance of his eyes; at last he steals upon Sigurd asleep and thrusts his sword through him. The dying Sigurd hurls the sword after the fleeing murderer and cuts him in two. To Gudrun, who wakes from sleep by his side, he points to Brynhild as the instigator of the crime, and dies. Brynhild rejoices at the sound of Gudrun's wailing. Gudrun cannot find relief for her grief, the tears will not flow. Men and women seek to console her by tales of greater woes befallen them. But still Gudrun cannot weep as she sits by Sigurd's corpse. At last one of the women lifts the cloth from Sigurd's face and lays his head upon Gudrun's lap. Then Gudrun gazes on his blood-besmirched hair, his dimmed eyes, and breast pierced by the sword: she sinks down upon the couch and a flood of tears bursts at length from her eyes.

Brynhild now tells Gunnar that Sigurd had really kept faith with him on the wooing journey; but she will live with him no longer and pierces herself with a sword, after foretelling to Gunnar his future fate and that of Gudrun. In accord with her own request she is burned on one funeral-pyre with Sigurd, the sword between them as once before.

Atli,[1] king of the Huns, now seeks Gudrun for wife. She refuses, but Grimhild gives her a potion which causes her to forget Sigurd and the past, and then she becomes the wife of Atli. After Sigurd's death Gunnar had taken possession of the Niflungen hoard, and this Atli now covets. He treacherously invites Gunnar and the others to visit him, which they do in spite of Gudrun's warnings, first of all, however, sinking the hoard in the Rhine. On their arrival Atli demands of them the hoard, which, he says, belongs of right to Gudrun. On their refusal he attacks them. Hosts of fighters on both sides fall and in the end Gunnar and Hogni, the only two of their number remaining, are bound in fetters. Gunnar refuses Atli's command to reveal the hiding-place of the hoard, bidding them bring to him the heart of Hogni. They kill a servant and bring his heart to Gunnar; but Gunnar sees how it still quivers with fear, and knows it is not the heart of the fearless Hogni. Then the latter is really killed, and his heart is brought to Gunnar, who cries exultingly that now only the Rhine knows where the hoard lies hidden. In spite of Gudrun Atli orders that Gunnar be thrown into a den of serpents. With a harp communicated to him by Gudrun he pacifies them all but one, which stings him to the heart, and thus Gunnar dies. Gudrun is nominally reconciled with Atli, but in secret plans revenge for the death of her brothers. She kills Atli's two sons, gives him at a banquet their blood to drink and their hearts to eat. In the night she plunges a sword into his own heart, confesses herself to him as his murderer, and sets fire to the castle, in which Atli and all his remaining men are consumed.

---

1 That is, Attila; the Etzel of the Nibelungenlied.

3. The Saga as preserved in the Nibelungenlied

he saga as we find it in the German Nibelungenlied differs very widely in form and substance from the Northern version which has just been outlined, though the two have still enough points of similarity to indicate clearly a common origin. Each bears the stamp of the poetic genius of the people among whom it grew. Of all the sagas of the Germanic peoples none holds so prominent a place as the Nibelungen saga, and it may safely be said that the epic literature of the world, though offering poems of more refined literary worth, has none that are at the same time such valuable records of the growth of the poetic genius of two kindred peoples through many centuries of their early civilization as the Edda poems of this saga and the Nibelungenlied. It is impossible here to undertake a comparison of the two and point out in detail their parallelism and their respective significance as monuments of civilization; suffice it to indicate briefly the chief points of difference in the two stories, and note particularly those parts of the Nibelungenlied that have, as it were, suffered atrophy, and that point to earlier stages of the saga in which, as in the Northern version, they played a more important rôle.

First, as to the hoard. The Nibelungenlied knows nothing of its being taken by Loki from Andvari, of the latter's curse upon it, and how it came finally into the possession of Fafnir, the giant-dragon. Here it belongs, as we learn from Hagen's account (strophes 86-99), to Siegfried (Sigurd), who has slain the previous owners of it, Schilbung and Nibelung, and wrested it from its guardian the dwarf Alberich (Andvari). From this point onward its history runs nearly parallel in the two versions. After Siegfried's death it remains for a time with Kriemhild (Gudrun), is treacherously taken from her by Gunther (Gunnar) and Hagen (Hogni), and finally, before their journey to Etzel (Atli), sunk in the Rhine.

The protracted narrative of Sigurd's ancestry and his descent from Odin has no counterpart in the Nibelungenlied. Here we learn merely that Siegfried is the son of Siegmund. His father plays an entirely different part; and his mother's name is not Hjordis, as in the Edda, but Siegelind.

Of Siegfried's youth the Nibelungenlied knows very little. No mention is made of his tutelage to the dwarf smith Regin and preparation for the slaying of the dragon Fafnir. The account of him placed in the mouth of Hagen (strophes 86-501), how he won the hoard, the *tarnkappe*, and the sword Balmung, and slew the dragon, is evidently a faint echo of an earlier version of this episode, which sounds out of place in the more modern German form of the story. From the latter the mythical element has almost entirely vanished. It is worthy of note, moreover, that the very brief account of Siegfried's slaying of the dragon is given in the Nibelungenlied as separate from his acquisition of the hoard, and differs in detail from that of the Edda. Of Sigurd's steed Grani, his ride to Frankenland, and his awakening of Brynhild the Nibelungenlied has nothing to tell us. Through the account of Siegfried's assistance to Gunther in the latter's wooing of Brunhild (Adventures 6 and 7) shimmers faintly, however, the earlier tradition of the mythical Siegfried's awakening of the fire-encircled valkyrie. Only by our knowledge of a more original version can we explain, for example, Siegfried's previous acquaintance with Brunhild which the Nibelungenlied takes for granted but says nothing of. On this point of the relation between Sigurd and Brynhild it is difficult to form a clear account owing to the confusion and even contradictions that exist when the various Northern versions themselves are placed side by side. The name of the valkyrie whom Sigurd awakens from her magic sleep is not directly mentioned. Some of the accounts are based on the presupposition that she is one with the Brynhild whom Sigurd later wooes for Gunnar, while others either know nothing of the sleeping valkyrie or treat the two as separate personages. The situation in the Nibelungenlied is more satisfactorily explained by the theory that they were originally identical. But we see at once that the figure of Brunhild has here lost much of its original significance. It is her quarrel with Kriemhild (Gudrun) that leads to Siegfried's death, though the motives are not just the same in the two cases; and after the death of Siegfried she passes unaccountably from the scene.

But it is in the concluding part of the story—the part which, as we shall see, has its basis in actual history—that the two accounts diverge most widely. So strange, indeed, has been the evolution of the saga that the central character of it, Kriemhild (Gudrun) holds a diametrically opposite relation to her husband Etzel (Atli) at the final catastrophe in the two versions. In the Nibelungenlied as in the Edda the widowed

Kriemhild (Gudrun) marries King Etzel (Atli), her consent in the former resulting from a desire for revenge upon the murderers of Siegfried, in the latter from the drinking of a potion which takes away her memory of him; in the Nibelungenlied it is Kriemhild who treacherously lures Gunther and his men to their destruction unknown to Etzel, in the Edda the invitation comes from Atli, while Gudrun tries to warn them to stay at home; in the former Kriemhild is the author of the attack on the guests, in the latter Atli; in the former Kriemhild is the frenzied avenger of her former husband Siegfried's death upon her brother Gunther, in the latter Gudrun is the avenger of her brothers' death upon her husband Atli.

4. Mythical Element and Historical Element

sifting of the Nibelungen saga reveals a mythical element (the story of Siegfried) and a historical element (the story of the Burgundians and Etzel). How, when, and where these two elements were blended together must remain largely a matter of conjecture. This united central body received then from time to time accessions of other elements, some of them originally historical in character, some of them pure inventions of the poetic imagination.

The Siegfried myth is the oldest portion of the Nibelungen saga, and had already passed through a long period of development before its union with the story of the Burgundian kings. Like so many others of its kind, it is part of the spiritual equipment of our Germanic ancestors at the dawn of their recorded history. It grew gradually with the people themselves and has its counterpart among other peoples. Such myths are a record of the impressions made upon the mind of man by the mighty manifestations of the world of nature in which he lives; their formation may be likened to the unconscious impressions of its surroundings on the mind of the child. And just as the grown man is unable to trace back the formation of his own individuality to its very beginnings in infancy, so is it impossible for the later nation in its advanced stage to peer back beyond the dawn of its history. It is in the gloom beyond the dawn that such myths as this of Siegfried have their origin.

Though modern authorities differ greatly in their conjectures, it is generally agreed that the Siegfried story was in its original form a nature-myth. The young day slays the mist-dragon and awakens the sun-maiden that sleeps on the mountain; at evening he falls a prey to the powers of gloom that draw the sun down again beneath the earth. With this day-myth was probably combined the parallel myth of the changing seasons: the light returns in spring, slays the cloud-dragon, and frees the budding earth from the bonds of winter.[2]

In the course of time this nature-myth became transformed into a hero-saga; the liberating power of light was humanized into the person of the light-hero Siegfried. This stage of development had already been reached at the time of our earliest records, and the evidences point to the Rhine Franks, a West Germanic tribe settled in the fifth century in the country about Cologne, as the people among whom the transformation from nature-myth to hero-saga took place, for it is among them that the saga in its earliest form is localized. By the Rhine Siegfried is born, there he wins the Nibelungen hoard, and in Frankenland he finds the sleeping valkyrie. By the Rhine, too, he enters into service with the Nibelungen kings and weds their sister.

The Franks had as neighbors up-stream in the first half of the fifth century the Burgundians, an East Germanic tribe. These Burgundians, who were closely allied to the Goths, had originally dwelt in the Baltic region between the Vistula and the Oder, whence they had made their way south westward across Germany and settled in the year 413 in *Germania prima* on the west bank of the Rhine about Worms. Here a tragic fate was soon to overtake them. In the year 435 they had already suffered a reverse in a conflict with the Romans under Aëtius, and two years later, in 437, they were practically annihilated by the Huns. Twenty thousand of them, we are told, fell in battle, the remainder were scattered southward. Beyond the brief record by a contemporary, Prosper, we know but little of this event. It has been conjectured that the Huns were on this occasion acting as auxiliaries of Aëtius. At any rate it is fairly certain that Attila was not personally on the scene.

We can easily imagine what a profound impression this extinction of the Burgundians would produce upon the minds of their neighbors the Rhine Franks. Fact, too, would soon become mingled with fiction. This new feat was ascribed to Attila himself, already too well known as the scourge of Europe and the subduer of so many German tribes. A very few years later, however, fate was to subdue the mighty conqueror himself. With the great battle of Châlons in 451 the tide turned against him, and two years afterwards he died a mysterious death. The historian Jordanes of the sixth century relates that on the morning after Attila's wedding with a German princess named Ildico (Hildikô) he was found lying in bed in a pool of blood, having died of a hemorrhage. The mysteriousness of Attila's ending inspired his contemporaries with awe, and the popular fancy was not slow to clothe this event also in a dress of fiction. The attendant circumstances peculiarly favored such a process.

---

2 For the Siegfried saga in general see Symons in Paul's Grundriss der germanischen Philologie, 2d ed., vol. III, pp. 651-671.

Historians soon recorded the belief that Attila had perished at the hands of his wife, and it was only a step further for the imagination to find the motive for the deed in the desire of Hildikô to avenge the death of her German kinsmen who had perished through Attila. The saga of Attila's death is before long connected with the growing Burgundian saga, Hildikô becomes the sister of the Burgundian kings Gundahari, Godomar, and Gislahari, and her deed is vengeance taken upon Attila for his destruction of her brothers. As is seen at once from the outline I have already given (Chapter 2.) of the saga as we find it in the Edda, this is the stage of development it had reached when it began to find its way northward from the Rhine country to Norway and Iceland.

It is unnecessary here to record the speculations—for beyond speculations we cannot go—as to how the union of this historical saga of the Burgundians and Attila with the Siegfried saga took place. In the course of time, and naturally with greatest probability among the Rhine Franks who followed the Burgundians as occupants of *Germania prima*, the two were brought together, and the three Burgundian kings and their sister were identified with the three Nibelungen kings and their sister of the already localized Siegfried saga. It is also beyond the scope of this introduction to follow the course of the saga northward or to note its further evolution during its wanderings and in its new home until it was finally recorded in poetic form in the Edda. We have now to consider briefly the transformation it passed through in Germany between this date (about 500) and the time (about 1200) when it emerges in written record as the Nibelungenlied.

An account has already been given (Chapter 3.) of the chief features in which the Nibelungenlied differs from the Northern form. As we saw there, the mythical element of the Siegfried saga has almost entirely evaporated and the historical saga of the Burgundian kings and Attila has undergone a complete transformation. That the originally mythical and heathen Siegfried saga should dwindle away with the progress of civilization and under the influence of Christianity was but natural. The character of the valkyrie Brynhild who avenges upon Sigurd his infidelity to her, yet voluntarily unites herself with him in death, as heathen custom demanded, is no longer intelligible. She recedes into the background, and after Siegfried's death, though she is still living, she plays no further part. The Nibelungenlied found its final form on Upper German, doubtless Austrian, territory. Here alone was it possible that that greatest of all transformations could take place, namely, in the character of Attila. The Franks of the Rhine knew him only as the awe-inspiring conqueror who had annihilated their neighbors the Burgundians. In Austrian lands it was quite otherwise. Many Germanic tribes, particularly the East Goths, had fought under the banner of Attila, and in the tradition handed down from them he lived as the embodiment of wisdom and generosity. Here it was impossible that epic story should picture him as slaying the Burgundian kings through a covetous desire for their gold. The annihilation of the Burgundians is thus left without a motive. To supply this, Kriemhild's character is placed upon an entirely different basis. Instead of avenging upon Attila the death of her brothers the Burgundian kings, Kriemhild now avenges upon her brothers the slaying of her first husband Siegfried. This fundamental change in the character of Kriemhild has a deep ethical reason. To the ancient heathen Germans the tie of blood-relationship was stronger than that of wedlock, and thus in the original version of the story Attila's wife avenges upon him the death of her *brothers*; to the Christianized Germans of later times the marriage bond was the stronger, and accordingly from the altered motive Kriemhild avenges upon her brothers the slaying of her *husband*. In accordance, too, with this ethical transformation the scene of the catastrophe is transferred from Worms to Attila's court. Kriemhild now looms up as the central figure of the second half of the drama, while Etzel remains to the last ignorant of her designs for revenge.

This transformation of the fundamental parts of the saga was accompanied by another process, namely, the addition of new characters. Some of these are the product of the poetic faculty of the people or individuals who preserved and remoulded the story in the course of centuries, others are based upon history. To the former class belong the Margrave Ruediger, the ideal of gentle chivalry, and Volker the Fiddler-knight, doubtless a creation of the *spielleute*. To the second class belong Dietrich of Bern, in whom we see the mighty East Gothic king, Theodoric of Verona; also Bishop Pilgrim of Passau, a very late importation, besides several others in whom are perpetuated in more or less faint outline actual persons of history. This introduction of fresh characters from time to time as the saga grew has led to some strange anachronisms, which however are a disturbing element only to us readers of a modern day, who with sacrilegious hand lift the veil through which they were seen in a uniform haze of romance by the eye of the knights and ladies of seven centuries ago. *They* neither knew nor cared to know, for instance, that Attila was dead before Theodoric was born, and that Bishop Pilgrim flourished at Passau the trifling space of five hundred years later still.[3]

---

3 Attila lived from about 406 to 453; Theodoric, 475 to 526. Pilgrim was Bishop of Passau, 971 to 991.

II. The Nibelungenlied

1. The Manuscripts

Among the German epic poems of the Middle Ages the Nibelungenlied[4] enjoyed an exceptional popularity, as is evident from the large number of manuscripts—some thirty, either complete or fragmentary—that have been preserved from the centuries immediately following its appearance. Three are of prime importance as texts, namely, those preserved now in Munich, St. Gall, and Donaueschingen, and cited as A, B, and C respectively. Since the time when Lachmann, about a century ago, made the first scientific study of the poem, a whole flood of writings has been poured forth discussing the relative merits of these texts. Each in turn has had its claims advocated with warmth and even acrimony. None of these three principal manuscripts, however, offers the poem in its earliest form; they all point to a still earlier version. It is now generally admitted that the St. Gall manuscript (B), according

---

4 The closing strophe of MS. C calls the poem der *Nibelunge liet*, or Nibelungenlied, i.e. the lay of the Nibelungen, and this is the title by which it is commonly known. MSS. A and B have in the corresponding strophe *der Nibelunge nôt*, i.e. the 'need', 'distress', 'downfall' of the Nibelungen. In the title of the poem 'Nibelungen' is simply equivalent to 'Burgundians': the poem relates the downfall of the Burgundian kings and their people. Originally the Nibelungen were, as their name, which is connected with *nebel*, 'mist', 'gloom', signifies, the powers of darkness to whom the light-hero Siegfried fell a prey. After Siegfried obtains possession of the treasure the name Nibelungen is still applied to Alberich and the dwarfs who guard it and who are now Siegfried's vassals. Then after Siegfried's death the name is given to the Burgundians. It is a mistake to suppose that the name was applied in each case to those who became possessors of the hoard, for Siegfried himself is never so designated.

2. Stages in the Evolution of the Poem

Hand in hand with the discussion of the relative authenticity of the manuscripts went the consideration of another more important literary question,—the evolution of the poem itself. Even if we knew nothing of the history of the Nibelungen saga as revealed in the Edda and through other literary and historic sources, a reading of the poem would give us unmistakable hints that it is not, in its present form, a perfect literary unit. We detect inconsistencies in matter and inequalities of style that prove it to be a remodelling of material already existing in some earlier form. What, then, has been the history of its evolution? How did this primeval Siegfried myth, this historical saga of the Burgundians and Attila, first come to be part of the poetic stock of the German people? What was its earliest poetic form, and what series of transformations did it pass through during seven centuries of growth? These and many kindred questions present themselves, and the search for answers to them takes us through many winding labyrinths of the nation's contemporary history. Few products of German literature have so exercised and tantalized critics as the Nibelungenlied.

In this connection we have to remind ourselves that comparatively little of what must have been the large body of native poetry in Germany previous to the eleventh century has come down to us. Barely enough has been preserved to show the path of the nation's literary progress. Some of the important monuments have been saved by chance, while others of equal or perhaps greater value have been irrecoverably lost. The interest in the various incidents of the Nibelungen story was sufficient to keep it alive among the people and hand it down orally through many generations. If we could observe it as it passed from age to age we should doubtless see it undergoing continuous change according to the time and the class of the people that were the preservers of the native literature in its many ups and downs. Lachmann in the year 1816 was the first to bring scientific criticism to bear on the question of the Nibelungenlied and its origin. Applying to it the same methods as had recently been used by Wolf in his criticism of the Homeric poems, he thought he was able to discover as the basis of the complete epic a cycle of twenty separate *lieder*, ballads or shorter episodic poems, on the strength of which belief he went so far as to publish an edition of the poem in which he made the division into the twenty separate lays and eliminated those strophes (more than one third of the whole number) that he deemed not genuine. It is now generally admitted, however, that the pioneer of Nibelungen investigation fell here into over-positive refinements of literary criticism. Separate shorter poems there doubtless existed narrating separate episodes of the story, but these are no longer to be arrived at by a process of critical disintegration and pruning of the epic as we have it. An examination of the twenty *lieder* according to Lachmann's division convinces us that they are not separate units in the sense he conceived them to be. Though these twenty *lieder* may be based upon a number of earlier episodic poems, yet the latter already constituted a connected series. They were already like so many scenes of a gradually developing drama. Events were foreshadowed in one that were only fulfilled in another, and the incidents of later ones are often only intelligible on the supposition of an acquaintance with motives that originated in preceding ones. It is in this sense only, not according to Lachmann's overwrought theory, that we are justified in speaking of a *lieder cyclus*, or cycle of separate episodic poems, as the stage of the epic antecedent to the complete form in which we now have it. But beyond this cycle we cannot trace it back. How the mythical saga of Siegfried and the Nibelungen, and the story of the Burgundians and Attila, were first sung in alliterative lays in the Migration Period, how as heathen song they were pushed aside or slowly influenced by the spirit of Christianity, how with changing time they changed also their outward poetical garb from alliteration to rhyme and altered verse-form, till at last in the twelfth century they have become the cycle of poems from which the great epic of the Nibelungenlied could be constructed—of all this we may form a faint picture from the development of the literature in general, but direct written record of it is almost completely wanting.

3. Character of the Poem

The twelfth and thirteenth centuries witnessed far-reaching changes in the social and intellectual life of the German lands, the leading feature of which is the high development of all that is included under the name of chivalry. It is marked, too, by a revival of the native literature such as had not been known before, a revival which is due almost entirely to its cultivation by the nobility. From emperor down to the simple knight they were patrons of poetry and, what is most striking, nearly all the poets themselves belong to the knightly class. The drama has not yet begun, but in the field of epic and lyric there appear about the year 1200 poets who are among the greatest that German literature even down to the present time has to show. The epic poetry of that period, though written almost entirely by the knights, is of two distinct kinds according to its subject: on the one hand what is called the Court Epic, on the other hand the National, or Popular, Epic. The Court Epic follows for the most part French models and deals chiefly with the life of chivalry, whose ideals were embodied in king Arthur and his circle of knights; the National Epic drew its subjects from the national German saga, its two great products being the Nibelungenlied and the poem of Gudrun. Court Epic and National Epic are further distinct in form, the Court Epic being written in the rhymed couplets popularized in modern times in English by Sir Walter Scott, while the National Epic is composed in four-lined strophes.

Though we know the name and more or less of the life of the authors of the many court epics of the period, the name of the poet who gave the Nibelungenlied its final form has not been recorded. As we have seen, the poem is at bottom of a truly popular, national character, having its beginnings in mythology and early national history. For centuries the subject had been national property and connected with the name of no one individual. We have it now in the form in which it was remodelled to suit the taste of the court and the nobility, and like the court epic to be read aloud in castle hall. That it is written in four-lined strophes[5] and not in the usual rhymed couplets of the court epics is doubtless due to the fact that the former verse-form had already been used in the earlier ballads upon which it is based, and was simply taken over by the final moulder of the poem. This latter was probably a member of the nobility like the great majority of the epic poets of the time; he must at least have been well acquainted with the manners, tastes, sentiments, and general life of the nobility. Through him the poem was brought outwardly more into line with the literary ideals of the court circles. This shows itself chiefly in a negative way, namely, in the almost complete avoidance of the coarse language and farcical situations so common with the popular poet, the *spielmann*. Beyond this no violence is done to the simple form of the original. The style is still inornate and direct, facts still speak rather than words, and there is nothing approaching the refined psychological dissection of characters and motives such as we find in Wolfram von Eschenbach and the other court writers.

When we look to the inner substance we see that the ground ideals are still those of the original Germanic heroic age. The chief characters are still those of the first stages of the story—Siegfried, Brunhild, Gunther, Kriemhild, Hagen. The fundamental theme is the ancient theme of *triuwe*, unswerving personal loyalty and devotion, which manifests itself above all in the characters of Kriemhild and Hagen. Kriemhild's husband Siegfried is treacherously slain: her sorrow and revenge are the motives of the drama. Hagen's mistress has, though with no evil intent on Siegfried's part, received an insult to her honor: to avenge that insult is Hagen's absorbing duty, which he fulfils with an utter disregard of consequences. Over this their fundamental character the various persons of the story have received a gloss of outward conduct in keeping with the close of the twelfth century. The poet is at pains to picture them as models of courtly bearing, excelling in *höfscheit, zuht, tugent*. Great attention is paid to dress, and the preparation of fitting apparel for court festivities is described and re-described with wearisome prolixity. A cardinal virtue is *milte*, liberality in the bestowal of gifts. Courtesy toward women is observed with the careful formality of the age of the minnesingers. It was above all Siegfried, the light-hero of the original myth, whose character lent itself to an idealization of knighthood. Ruediger holds a like place in the latter part of the poem. In the evident pleasure with which the minstrel-knight Volker of the sword-fiddlebow is depicted, as well doubtless as in occasional gleams of broader humor, the hand of the minstrels who wrought on the story in its earlier ballad stages may be seen. And the whole poem, in keeping with its form in an age strongly

5 For description of the Nibelungen strophe see below, Chapter 7.

under church influence, has been tinged with the ideals of Christianity. Not only does the ordinary conversation of all the characters, including even the heathen Etzel, contain a great number of formal imprecations of God, but Christian institutions and Christian ethics come frequently into play. Mass is sung in the minster, baptism, marriage, burial are celebrated in Christian fashion, the devil is mentioned according to the Christian conception, we hear of priest, chaplain, and bishop, Christians are contrasted with heathen, and Kriemhild, in marrying Etzel, has a hope of turning him to Christianity. In Hagen's attempt to drown the chaplain whom the Burgundians have with them as they set out for the land of the Huns we have perhaps an expression of the conflict between the heathen and the Christian elements, possibly also a reflection of the traditional animosity of the *spielmann* to his clerical rival.

The Nibelungenlied and the Iliad of Homer have often been compared, but after all to no great purpose. The two epics are alike in having their roots deep in national origins, but beyond this we have contrasts rather than resemblances. The Iliad is a more varied and complete picture of the whole Greek world than the Nibelungenlied is of the German, its religious atmosphere has not been disturbed in the same way as that of the saga of early Germanic times projected several centuries into a later Christian age, and it possesses in every way a greater unity of sentiment. In the varied beauty of its language, its wealth of imagery, its depth of feeling and copiousness of incident the Iliad is superior to the Nibelungenlied with its language of simple directness, its few lyrical passages, its expression of feeling by deeds rather than by words. Homer, too, is in general buoyant, the Nibelungenlied is sombre and stern. And in one last respect the two epics differ most of all: the Iliad is essentially narrative and descriptive, a series of episodes; the Nibelungenlied is essentially dramatic, scene following scene of dramatic necessity and pointing steadily to a final and inevitable catastrophe.

4. Later Forms of the Saga

In the Northern Edda and in the German Nibelungenlied the Nibelungen saga found its fullest and most poetic expression. But these were not to be the only literary records of it. Both in Scandinavian lands and in Germany various other monuments, scattered over the intervening centuries, bear witness to the fact that it lived on in more or less divergent forms. The Danish historian Saxo Grammaticus of the latter part of the twelfth century has a reference to the story of Kriemhild's treachery toward her brothers.

About the year 1250 an extensive prose narrative, known as the Thidrekssaga, was written by a Norwegian from oral accounts given him by men from Bremen and Münster.

This narrative is interesting as showing the form the saga had taken by that date on Low German territory, and holds an important place in the history of the development of the saga.

It has much more to say of the early history of Siegfried than we find in the Nibelungenlied, and yet in the main outlines of the story of Kriemhild's revenge it corresponds with the German epic and not with the Northern Edda.

A chronicle of the island of Hven in the Sound, dating in its original form from the sixteenth century, as well as Danish ballads on the same island that have lived on into modern times, tell of Sivard (Siegfried), Brynhild, and also of Grimild's (Kriemhild's) revenge.

In Norway and Sweden traces of the saga have recently been discovered; while songs that are sung on the Faroe Islands, as an accompaniment to the dance on festive occasions, have been recorded, containing over six hundred strophes in which is related in more or less distorted form the Nibelungen story.

In Germany the two poems known as the *Klage* and *Hürnen Seyfrid* are the most noteworthy additional records of the Nibelungen saga, as offering in part at least independent material.

The *Klage* is a poem of over four thousand lines in rhymed couplets, about half of it being an account of the mourning of Etzel, Dietrich, and Hildebrand as they seek out the slain and prepare them for burial, the other half telling of the bringing of the news to Bechlaren, Passau, and Worms.

The poem was written evidently very soon after the Nibelungenlied, the substance of which was familiar to the author, though he also draws in part from other sources.

Compared with the Nibelungenlied it possesses but little poetic merit and is written with distinctly Christian sentiment which is out of harmony with the ground-tone of the Germanic tragedy.

The *Hürnen Seyfrid* is a poem of 179 four-lined strophes which is preserved only in a print of the sixteenth century, but at least a portion of whose substance reaches back in its original form to a period preceding the composition of the Nibelungenlied.

It is evidently, as we have it, formed by the union of two earlier separate poems, which are indeed to a certain extent contradictory of each other.

The first tells of the boyhood of Seyfrid (Siegfried) and his apprenticeship to the smith; how he slew many dragons, burned them, and smeared over his body with the resulting fluid horny substance (hence his name *hürnen*), which made him invulnerable; how he further found the hoard of the dwarf Nybling, and by service to King Gybich won the latter's daughter for his wife.

The second part tells how King Gybich reigned at Worms. He has three sons, Günther, Hagen, Gyrnot, and one daughter, Kriemhild. The latter is borne off by a dragon, but finally rescued by Seyfrid, to whom she is given in marriage.

The three brothers are jealous of the might and fame of Seyfrid, and after eight years Hagen slays him beside a cool spring in the Ottenwald. The poem *Biterolf*, written soon after the Nibelungenlied, and *Rosengarten* of perhaps a half-century later, represent Dietrich in conflict with Siegfried at Worms.

The famous shoemaker-poet Hans Sachs of Nuremberg in 1557 constructed a tragedy, *Der hörnen Sewfriedt*, on the story of Siegfried as he knew it from the *Hürnen Seyfrid* and the *Rosengarten*. A prose version of the *Hürnen Seyfrid*, with free additions and alterations, is preserved in the *Volksbuch vom gehörnten Sigfrid*, the oldest print of which dates from the year 1726.

Of the vast number of Fairy Tales, those most genuine creations of the poetic imagination of the people, in which live on, often to be sure in scarcely recognizable form, many of the myths and sagas of the nation's infancy, there are several that may with justice be taken as relics of the

Siegfried myth, for instance, The Two Brothers, The Young Giant, The Earth-Manikin, The King of the Golden Mount, The Raven, The Skilled Huntsman, and perhaps also the Golden Bird and The Water of Life;[6] though it would seem from recent investigations that Thorn-Rose or the Sleeping Beauty, is no longer to be looked upon as the counterpart of the sleeping Brynhild.

Finally, it is probable that several names in Germany and in Northern countries preserve localized memories of the saga.

---

6 These will be found in Grimm's Märchen as numbers 60, 90-93, 111, 57, and 97.

5. Poem and Saga in Modern Literature

Fundamentally different from the foregoing natural outgrowths of the Nibelungen saga are the modern dramas and poems founded upon it since the time of the romanticists at the beginning of the nineteenth century.[7] Nearly all of these have already vanished as so much chaff from the winnowing-mill of time: only two, perhaps, are now considered seriously, namely, Hebbel's *Die Nibelungen* and Richard Wagner's *Ring des Nibelungen*. Hebbel in his grandly conceived drama in three parts follows closely the story as we have it in our epic poem the Nibelungenlied, and the skill with which he makes use of its tragic elements shows his dramatic genius at its best.

But not even the genius of Hebbel could make these forms of myth and saga live again for us upon a modern stage, and the failure of this work with its wealth of poetic beauty and many scenes of highest dramatic effectiveness to maintain its place as an acting drama is sufficient evidence that the yawning gap that separates the sentiment of the modern world from that of the early centuries in which these sagas grew is not to be bridged over by the drama, however easy and indeed delightful it may be for us to allow ourselves to be transported thither to that romantic land upon the wings of epic story.

Wagner in his music-drama in three parts and prelude has followed in the main the saga in its Northern form[8] up to the death of Siegfried and Brunhild, but to the entire exclusion of the latter part of the story in which Atli (Etzel) figures; his work has accordingly hardly any connection with the Nibelungenlied here offered in translation. Only the

---

7 The curious will find a list of these in the introduction to Piper's edition, cited below, Chapter 7.
8 See above, Chapter 2.

pious loyalty of national sentiment can assign a high place in dramatic literature to Wagner's work with its intended imitation of the alliterative form of verse; while his philosophizing gods and goddesses are also but decadent modern representatives of their rugged heathen originals.

6. Modern German Translations

The language of the Nibelungenlied presents about the same difficulty to the German reader of to-day as that of our English Chaucer to us. Many translations into modern German have accordingly been made to render it accessible to the average reader without special study. In the year 1767 Bodmer in Zurich published a translation into hexameters of a portion of it, and since the investigations of Lachmann raised it to the position of a national epic of first magnitude many more have appeared, both in prose and verse. The best in prose is that by Scherr, of the year 1860. Of the metrical translations that by Simrock, which in its later editions follows pretty closely the text of MS. C, is deservedly the most popular and has passed through a great number of editions. Bartsch has also made a translation based on his edition of MS. B. These modern versions by Simrock and Bartsch reproduce best the metrical quality of the original strophe. Easily obtainable recent translations are those by Junghans (in Reclam's Universalbibliothek) of text C, and by Hahn (Collection Spemann) of text A.

7. English Translations[9]

Early in last century interest in the Nibelungenlied began to manifest itself in England. A synopsis of it, with metrical translation of several strophes, appeared in the year 1814 in Weber, Jamieson and Scott's "Illustrations of Northern Antiquities" (London and Edinburgh), in which, according to Lockhart, Sir Walter Scott's hand may perhaps be seen. Carlyle, laboring as a pioneer to spread a knowledge of German literature in England, contributed to the Westminster Review in 1831 his well-known essay on the Nibelungenlied which, though containing an additional mass of rather ill-arranged matter and now antiquated in many particulars, is still well worth reading for its enthusiastic account of the epic itself in the genuine style of the author. Carlyle here reproduces in metrical form a few strophes. He has said elsewhere that one of his ambitions was to make a complete English version of the poem. Since then an endless number of accounts of it, chiefly worthless, has appeared in magazines and elsewhere. The first attempt at a complete metrical translation was made in 1848 by Jonathan Birch, who however only reproduces Lachmann's twenty *lieder*, with some fifty-one strophes added on his own account. His version of the first strophe runs thus:

Legends of by-gone times reveal wonders and prodigies,
Of heroes worthy endless fame,—of matchless braveries,—
Of jubilees and festal sports,—of tears and sorrows great,—
And knights who daring combats fought:—the like I now relate.

In 1850 appeared William Nansom Lettsom's translation of the whole poem according to Braunfels' edition, with the opening strophe turned as follows:

In stories of our fathers high marvels we are told

---

9 For a complete list of these, also of magazine articles, etc., relating to the Nibelungenlied, see F. E. Sandbach, The *Nibelungenlied and Gudrun in England and America*, London, 1903.

Of champions well approved in perils manifold.
Of feasts and merry meetings, of weeping and of wail,
And deeds of gallant daring I'll tell you in my tale.

The next metrical rendering is that by A. G. Foster-Barham in the year 1887. His first strophe reads:

Many a wondrous story have the tales of old,
Of feats of knightly glory, and of the Heroes bold,
Of the delights of feasting, of weeping and of wail,
Of noble deeds of daring; you may list strange things in my tale.

In the year 1898 follows still another, by Alice Horton (edited by E. Bell). This latest translation is based on Bartsch's text of MS. B, and is prefaced by Carlyle's essay. First strophe:

To us, in olden legends, / is many a marvel told
Of praise-deserving heroes, / of labours manifold,
Of weeping and of wailing, / of joy and festival;
Of bold knights' battling shall you / now hear a wondrous tale.

Apart from the many faults of interpretation all of the metrical translations of the Nibelungenlied here enumerated are defective in one all-important respect: they do not reproduce the poem in its *metrical form*. Carlyle and other pioneers we may perhaps acquit of any intention of following the original closely in this regard. None of the translators of the complete poem, however, has retained in the English rendering what is after all the very essence of a poem,—its exact metrical quality. Birch has created an entirely different form of strophe in which all four lines are alike, each containing seven principal accents, with the cæsura, following the fourth foot. Lettsom makes the first serious attempt to reproduce the original strophe.

It is evident from the introduction to his translation (see p. xxvi) that he had made a careful study of its form, and he does in fact reproduce the first three lines exactly. Of the fourth line he says: "I have not thought it expedient to make a rule of thus lengthening the fourth lines of the stanzas, though I have lengthened them occasionally"(!). What moved him thus to deprive the stanza of its most striking feature—and one, moreover, that is easily preserved in English—he does not make clear. The versions of Foster-Barham and of Horton and Bell show the same disfigurement, the latter omitting the extra accent of the fourth line, as they say, "for the sake of euphony"(!).

It is just this lengthened close of each strophe that gives the Nibelungenlied its peculiar metrical character and contributes not a little to the avoidance of monotony in a poem of over two thousand strophes. In theory the form of the fourth line as it stands in the original is no more foreign to the genius of the English language than to that of modern German, and few of the many Germans giving a modernized version of the epic have been bold enough to lay sacrilegious hands upon it to shorten it.

A brief account of the Nibelungen strophe may not be out of place here, owing to the fact that its character has generally been misunderstood. The origin and evolution of the strophe have been the subject of much discussion, the results of which we need not pause to formulate here. As it appears in actual practice in our poem of about the year 1200, it was as follows: Each strophe consists of four long lines, the first line rhyming with the second, and the third with the fourth. The rhymes are masculine, that is, rhymes on the end syllable. Each line is divided by a clearly marked caesura into two halves; each half of the first three lines and the first half of the fourth line has three accented syllables, the second half of the fourth line has four accented syllables. The first half of each line ends in an unaccented syllabic—or, strictly speaking, in a syllable bearing a secondary accent; that is, each line has what is called a "ringing" caesura. The metrical character of the Nibelungen strophe is thus due to its fixed number of accented syllables. Of unaccented syllables the number may vary within certain limits. Ordinarily each accented syllable is preceded by an unaccented one; that is, the majority of feet are iambic. The unaccented syllable may, however, at times be wanting, or there may, on the other hand, be two or even three of them together. A characteristic of the second half of the last line is that there is very frequently no unaccented syllable between the second and the third accented ones. Among occasional variations of the normal strophe as here described may be mentioned the following: The end-rhyme is in a few instances feminine instead of masculine; while on the other hand the ending of the first half-lines is occasionally masculine instead of feminine, that is, the caesura is not "ringing." In a few scattered instances we find strophes that rhyme throughout in the caesura as well as at the end of lines;[10] occasionally the first and second lines, or still less frequently the third and fourth, alone have caesural rhyme.[11] Rhyming of the caesura may be regarded as accidental in most cases, but it is reproduced as exactly as possible in this translation.

In the original the opening strophe, which is altogether more regular than the average and is, moreover, one of the few that have also complete caesural rhyme, is as follows:

Uns ist in alten maeren / wunders vil geseit
von heleden lobebaeren, / von grôzer arebeit,
von fröuden, hochgezîten, / von weinen und von klagen,

---

10 Strophes 1, 17, 102, and possibly 841.
11 Strophes 18, 69, 103, 115, 129, 148, 177, 190, 198, 222, 231, 239, 293, 325, 345, 363, 485, 584, 703, 712, 859, 864, 894, 937, 1022, 1032, 1114, 1225, 1432, 1436, 1460, 1530, 1555, 1597,1855, 1909, 1944, 1956, 2133, 2200, 2206, 2338.

von küener recken strîten / muget ir nu wunder hoeren sagen.

Here the only place where the unaccented syllable is lacking before the accented is before *wunders* at the beginning of the second half of the first line. A strophe showing more typical irregularities is, for instance, the twenty-second:

In sînen besten zîten, / bî sînen jungen tagen,
man möhte michel wunder / von Sîvride sagen,
waz êren an im wüchse / und wie scoene was sîn lîp.
sît heten in ze minne / diu vil waetlîchen wîp.

Here the rhyme of the first and second lines is still masculine, *tagen* and *sagen* being pronounced *tagn* and *sagn*. The unaccented syllable is lacking, e.g., before the second accent of the second half of line two, also before the first and the third accent of the second half of line four. There are two unaccented syllables at the beginning (*Auftakt*) of the second half of line three. The absence of the unaccented syllable between the second and the third accent of the last half of the fourth line of a strophe, as here, is so frequent in the poem as to amount almost to a rule; it shows an utter misconception, or disregard, of its true character, nevertheless, to treat this last half-line as having only three accented syllables, as all translators hitherto have done.

THE NIBELUNGENLIED

FIRST ADVENTURE: Kriemhild's Dream

1

To us in olden story / are wonders many told
Of heroes rich in glory, / of trials manifold:
Of joy and festive greeting, / of weeping and of woe,
Of keenest warriors meeting, / shall ye now many a wonder know.

2

There once grew up in Burgundy / a maid of noble birth,
Nor might there be a fairer / than she in all the earth:
Kriemhild hight the maiden, / and grew a dame full fair,
Through whom high thanes a many / to lose their lives soon dooméd
were.

3

'Twould well become the highest / to love the winsome maid,
Keen knights did long to win her, / and none but homage paid.
Beauty without measure, / that in sooth had she,
And virtues wherewith many / ladies else adorned might be.

4

Three noble lords did guard her, / great as well in might,
Gunther and Gernot, / each one a worthy knight,
And Giselher their brother, / a hero young and rare.
The lady was their sister / and lived beneath the princes' care.

5

These lords were free in giving, / and born of high degree;
Undaunted was the valor / of all the chosen three.
It was the land of Burgundy / o'er which they did command,
And mighty deeds of wonder / they wrought anon in Etzel's land.

6

At Worms amid their warriors / they dwelt, the Rhine beside,
And in their lands did serve them / knights of mickle pride,
Who till their days were ended / maintained them high in state.
They later sadly perished / beneath two noble women's hate.

7

A high and royal lady, / Ute their mother hight,
Their father's name was Dankrat, / a man of mickle might.
To them his wealth bequeathed he / when that his life was done,
For while he yet was youthful / had he in sooth great honor won.

8

In truth were these three rulers, / as I before did say,
Great and high in power, / and homage true had they
Eke of knights the boldest / and best that e'er were known,
Keen men all and valiant, / as they in battle oft had shown.

9

There was of Tronje Hagen, / and of that princely line
His brother valiant Dankwart; / and eke of Metz Ortwein;
Then further the two margraves, / Gere and Eckewart;
Of Alzei was Volker, / a doughty man of dauntless heart.

10

Rumold the High Steward, / a chosen man was he,
Sindold and Hunold / they tended carefully
Each his lofty office / in their three masters' state,
And many a knight beside them / that I the tale may ne'er relate.

11

Dankwart he was Marshal; / his nephew, then, Ortwein
Upon the monarch waited / when that he did dine;
Sindold was Cup-bearer, / a stately thane was he,
And Chamberlain was Hunold, / masters all in courtesy.

12

Of the kings' high honor / and their far-reaching might,
Of their full lofty majesty / and how each gallant knight
Found his chiefest pleasure / in the life of chivalry,
In sooth by mortal never / might it full related be.

13

Amid this life so noble / did dream the fair Kriemhild
How that she reared a falcon, / in beauty strong and wild,
That by two eagles perished; / the cruel sight to see
Did fill her heart with sorrow / as great as in this world might be.

14

The dream then to her mother / Queen Ute she told,
But she could not the vision / than thus more clear unfold:

"The falcon that thou rearedst, / doth mean a noble spouse:
God guard him well from evil / or thou thy hero soon must lose."

15

"Of spouse, O darling mother, / what dost thou tell to me?
Without a knight to woo me, / so will I ever be,
Unto my latest hour / I'll live a simple maid,
That I through lover's wooing / ne'er be brought to direst need."

16

"Forswear it not so rashly," / her mother then replied.
"On earth if thou wilt ever / cast all care aside,
'Tis love alone will do it; / thou shalt be man's delight,
If God but kindly grant thee / to wed a right good valiant knight."

17

"Now urge the case, dear mother," / quoth she, "not further here.
Fate of many another / dame hath shown full clear
How joy at last doth sorrow / lead oft-times in its train.
That I no ruth may borrow, / from both alike I'll far remain."

18

Long time, too, did Kriemhild / her heart from love hold free,
And many a day the maiden / lived right happily,
Ere good knight saw she any / whom she would wish to woo.
In honor yet she wedded / anon a worthy knight and true.

19

He was that same falcon / she saw the dream within
Unfolded by her mother. / Upon her nearest kin,
That they did slay him later, / how wreaked she vengeance wild!
Through death of this one hero / died many another mother's child.

SECOND ADVENTURE: Siegfried

20

There grew likewise in Netherland / a prince of noble kind,
Siegmund hight his father, / his mother Siegelind—
Within a lordly castle / well known the country o'er,
By the Rhine far downward: / Xanten was the name it bore.

21

Siegfried they did call him, / this bold knight and good;
Many a realm he tested, / for brave was he of mood.
He rode to prove his prowess / in many a land around:
Heigh-ho! what thanes of mettle / anon in Burgundy he found!

22

In the springtime of his vigor, / when he was young and bold,
Could tales of mickle wonder / of Siegfried be told,
How he grew up in honor, / and how fair he was to see:
Anon he won the favor / of many a debonair lady.

23

As for a prince was fitting, / they fostered him with care:
Yet how the knightly virtues / to him native were!
'Twas soon the chiefest glory / of his father's land,
That he in fullest measure / endowed with princely worth did stand.

24

He soon was grown in stature / that he at court did ride.
The people saw him gladly, / lady and maid beside
Did wish that his own liking / might lead him ever there.
That they did lean unto him / the knight was soon right well aware.

25

In youth they let him never / without safe escort ride;
Soon bade Siegmund and Siegelind / apparel rich provide;
Men ripe in wisdom taught him, / who knew whence honor came.
Thus many lands and people / he won by his wide-honored name.

26

Now was he of such stature / that he could weapons bear:
Of what thereto he needed / had he an ample share.
Then to think of loving / fair maids did he begin,
And well might they be honored / for wooer Siegfried bold to win.

27

Then bade his father Siegmund / make known to one and all
That he with his good kinsmen / would hold high festival.
And soon were tidings carried / to all the neighboring kings;
To friends at home and strangers / steeds gave he and rich furnishin

28

Wherever they found any / who knight was fit to be
By reason of his kindred, / all such were courteously
Unto the land invited / to join the festal throng,
When with the prince so youthful / on them the knightly sword was
hung.

29

Of this high time of revelry / might I great wonders tell.
Siegmund and Siegelind / great honor won full well,
Such store of goodly presents / they dealt with generous hand,
That knights were seen full many / from far come pricking to their
land.

30

Four hundred lusty squires / were there to be clad
In knight's full garb with Siegfried. / Full many a beauteous maid
At work did never tire, / for dear they did him hold,
And many a stone full precious / those ladies laid within the gold,

31

That they upon the doublets / embroidered cunningly
Of those soon to be knighted: / 't was thus it had to be,
Seats bade the host for many / a warrior bold make right
Against the high midsummer, / when Siegfried won the name of knight.

32

Then went unto the minster / full many a noble knight
And gallant squires beside them. / The elder there with right
Did wait upon the younger, / as once for them was done.
They were all light-hearted, / in hope of pleasure every one.

33

God to praise and honor / they sang the mass' song;
There, too, were crowds of people, / a great and surging throng,
When after knightly custom / knighthood received they then,
In such a stately pageant / as scarce might ever be again.

34

They hastened where they found them / saddled many a steed;
In the court of Siegmund's castle / they tilted with such speed
That far the din resounded / through castle and through hall,
As in the play with clamor / did join the fiery riders all.

35

Well-tried old knights and youthful / met there in frequent clash,
There was sound of shattered lances / that through the air did crash,
And along before the castle / were splinters seen to fly
From hands of knights a many: / each with other there did vie.

36

The king he bade give over: / they led the chargers out:
There was seen all shattered / many a boss well-wrought,
And many a stone full costly / lay there upon the sward
From erstwhile shining shield-bands, / now broken in the jousting hard.

37

The guests all went thereafter / where seats for them were reared;
They by the choicest viands / from weariness were cheered,
And wine, of all the rarest, / that then in plenty flowed.
Upon both friends and strangers / were fitting honors rich bestowed.

38
In such merry manner / all day did last the feast.
Many a wandering minstrel / knew not any rest,
But sang to win the presents / dealt out with bounteous hand;
And with their praise was honored / far and wide King Siegmund's land.

39
The monarch then did order / Siegfried his youthful son
In fee give lands and castles, / as he erstwhile had done.
To all his sword-companions / he gave with such full hand,
That joyed they o'er the journey / they now had made unto that land.

40
The festival yet lasted / until the seventh day.
Siegelind after old custom / in plenty gave away
—For so her son she honored— / rich gifts of shining gold:
In sooth deserved she richly / that all should him in honor hold.

41
Never a wandering minstrel / was unprovided found:
Horses there and raiment / so free were dealt around,
As if to live they had not / beyond it one day more.
I ween a monarch's household / ne'er bestowed such gifts before.

42
Thus closed the merry feasting / in this right worthy way,
And 't was well known thereafter / how those good knights did say
That they the youthful hero / for king would gladly have;
But this nowise he wished for, / Siegfried the stately knight and brave.

43
While that they both were living, / Siegmund and Siegelind,
No crown their son desired, / —thereto he had no mind.
Yet would he fain be master / o'er all the hostile might
That in the lands around him / opposed the keen and fiery knight.

THIRD ADVENTURE: How Siegfried came to Worms

44
Seldom in sooth, if ever, / the hero's heart was sad.
He heard them tell the story, / how that a winsome maid
There lived afar in Burgundy, / surpassing fair to see:
Great joy she brought him later, / but eke she brought him misery.

45
Of her exceeding beauty / the fame spread far and near,

And of the thing, moreover, / were knights oft-times aware
How the maid's high spirit / no mortal could command:
The thing lured many a stranger / from far unto King Gunther's land.

46
Although to win her favor / were many wooers bent,
In her own heart would never / Kriemhild thereto consent
That any one amongst them / for lover she would have:
Still to her was he a stranger / to whom anon her troth she gave.

47
To true love turned his fancy / the son of Siegelind.
'Gainst his, all others' wooing / was like an idle wind:
Full well did he merit / a lady fair to woo,
And soon the noble Kriemhild / to Siegfried bold was wedded true.

48
By friends he oft was counselled, / and many a faithful man,
Since to think of wooing / in earnest he began,
That he a wife should find him / of fitting high degree.
Then spoke the noble Siegfried: / "In sooth fair Kriemhild shall it be,

49
"The noble royal maiden / in Burgundy that dwells,
For sake of all her beauty. / Of her the story tells,
Ne'er monarch was so mighty / that, if for spouse he sighed,
'Twere not for him befitting / to take the princess for his bride."

50
Unto King Siegmund also / the thing was soon made known.
His people talked about it, / whereby to him was shown
The Prince's fixéd purpose. / It grieved him sorely, too,
That his son intent was / the full stately maid to woo.

51
Siegelind asked and learned it, / the noble monarch's wife.
For her loved son she sorrowed / lest he should lose his life,
For well she knew the humor / of Gunther and his men.
Then gan they from the wooing / strive to turn the noble thane.

52
Then said the doughty Siegfried: / "O father dear to me,
Without the love of woman / would I ever be,
Could I not woo in freedom / where'er my heart is set.
Whate'er be said by any, / I'll keep the selfsame purpose yet."

53
"Since thou wilt not give over," / the king in answer said,
"Am I of this thy purpose / inwardly full glad,
And straightway to fulfil it / I'll help as best I can,
Yet in King Gunther's service / is many a haughty-minded man.

54

"And were there yet none other / than Hagen, warrior-knight,
He with such haughty bearing / is wont to show his might,
That I do fear right sorely / that sad our end may be,
If we set out with purpose / to win the stately maid for thee."

55

"Shall we by that be hindered?" / outspake Siegfried then;
"Whate'er in friendly fashion / I cannot obtain
I'll yet in other manner / take that, with sword in hand.
I trow from them I'll further / wrest both their vassals and their land."

56

"I grieve to hear thy purpose," / said Siegmund the king;
"If any one this story / unto the Rhine should bring,
Then durst thou never after / within that land be seen.
Gunther and Gernot, / —well known to me they long have been.

57

"By force, however mighty, / no man can win the maid,"
Spake King Siegmund further, / "to me hath oft been said.
But if with knightly escort / thither thou wilt ride,
Good friends—an have we any— / shall soon be summoned to thy side."

58

"No wish," then answered Siegfried, / "it ever was of mine,
That warrior knights should follow / with me unto the Rhine
As if arrayed for battle: / 'twould make my heart full sad,
To force in hostile manner / to yield to me the stately maid.

59

"By my own hand—thus only— / trust I to win my bride;
With none but twelve in company / to Gunther's land I'll ride.
In this, O royal father, / thy present help I pray."
Gray and white fur raiment / had his companions for the way.

60

Siegelind his mother / then heard the story too,
And grieved she was on hearing / what her dear son would do,
For she did fear to lose him / at hands of Gunther's men.
Thereat with heart full heavy / began to weep the noble queen.

61

Then came forth Sir Siegfried / where the queen he sought,
And to his weeping mother / thus gently spake his thought:
"No tear of grief thou shouldest / ever shed for me,
For I care not a tittle / for all the warriors that be.

62

"So help me on my journey / to the land of Burgundy,

And furnish such apparel / for all my knights and me,
As warriors of our station / might well with honor wear.
Then I in turn right truly / to thee my gratitude will swear."
63
"Since thou wilt not give over," / Siegelind then replied,
"My only son, I'll help thee / as fits thee forth to ride,
With the best apparel / that riders ever wore,
Thee and thy companions: / ye shall of all have goodly store."
64
Then bowed the youthful Siegfried / the royal dame before,
And said: "Upon the journey / will I take no more,
But twelve good knights only: / for these rich dress provide,
For I would know full gladly / how 't doth with Kriemhild betide."
65
Then sat at work fair women / by night and eke by day,
And rest indeed but little / from busy toil had they,
Until they had made ready / the dress Siegfried should wear.
Firm bent upon the journey, / no other counsel would he hear.
66
His father bade a costly / garb for him prepare,
That leaving Siegmund's country / he the same might wear.
For all their glittering breastplates / were soon prepared beside,
And helmets firmly welded, / and shining shields long and wide.
67
Then fast the day grew nearer / when they should thence depart.
Men and likewise women / went sorrowing in heart,
If that they should ever / see more their native land.
With full equipment laden / the sumpter horses there did stand.
68
Their steeds were stately, furnished / with trappings rich with gold;
It were a task all bootless / to seek for knights more bold
Than were the gallant Siegfried / and his chosen band.
He longed to take departure / straightway for Burgundian land.
69
Leave granted they with sadness, / both the king and queen,
The which to turn to gladness / sought the warrior keen,
And spake then: "Weep ye shall not / at all for sake of me,
Forever free from doubtings / about my safety may ye be."
70
Stern warriors stood there sorrowing, / —in tears was many a maid.
I ween their hearts erred nothing, / as sad forebodings said
That 'mongst their friends so many / thereby were doomed to die.
Good cause had they to sorrow / at last o'er all their misery.

71

Upon the seventh morning / to Worms upon the strand
Did come the keen knights riding. / Bright shone many a band
Of gold from their apparel / and rich equipment then;
And gently went their chargers / with Siegfried and his chosen men.

72

New-made shields they carried / that were both strong and wide
And brightly shone their helmets / as thus to court did ride
Siegfried the keen warrior / into King Gunther's land.
Of knights before was never / beheld so richly clad a band.

73

The points of their long scabbards / reached down unto the spur,
And spear full sharply pointed / bore each chosen warrior.
The one that Siegfried carried / in breadth was two good span,
And grimly cut its edges / when driven by the fearless man.

74

Reins with gold all gleaming / held they in the hand,
The saddle-bands were silken. / So came they to the land.
On every side the people / to gape at them began,
And also out to meet them / the men that served King Gunther ran.

75

Gallant men high-hearted, / knight and squire too,
Hastened to receive them, / for such respect was due,
And bade the guests be welcome / unto their master's land.
They took from them their chargers, / and shields as well from out the hand.

76

Then would they eke the chargers / lead forth unto their rest;
But straight the doughty Siegfried / to them these words addressed:
"Yet shall ye let our chargers / stand the while near by;
Soon take we hence our journey; / thereon resolved full well am I.

77

"If that be known to any, / let him not delay,
Where I your royal master / now shall find, to say,—
Gunther, king so mighty / o'er the land of Burgundy."
Then told him one amongst them / to whom was known where that might be:

78

"If that the king thou seekest, / right soon may he be found.
Within that wide hall yonder / with his good knights around
But now I saw him sitting. / Thither do thou repair,
And thou may'st find around him / many a stately warrior there."

79

Now also to the monarch / were the tidings told,
That within his castle / were knights arrived full bold,
All clad in shining armor / and apparelled gorgeously;
But not a man did know them / within the land of Burgundy.

80

Thereat the king did wonder / whence were come to him
These knights adventure seeking / in dress so bright and trim,
And shields adorned so richly / that new and mighty were.
That none the thing could tell him / did grieve him sorely to hear.

81

Outspake a knight then straightway, / Ortwein by name was he,
Strong and keen as any / well was he known to be:
"Since we of them know nothing, / bid some one quickly go
And fetch my uncle Hagen: / to him thou shalt the strangers show.

82

"To him are known far kingdoms / and every foreign land,
And if he know these strangers / we soon shall understand."
The king then sent to fetch him: / with his train of men
Unto the king's high presence / in stately gear went he then.

83

What were the king's good pleasure, / asked Hagen grim in war.
"In the court within my castle / are warriors from afar,
And no one here doth know them: / if them thou e'er didst see
In any land far distant, / now shalt thou, Hagen, tell to me."

84

"That will I do, 'tis certain."— / To a window then he went,
And on the unknown strangers / his keen eye he bent.
Well pleased him their equipment / and the rich dress they wore,
Yet ne'er had he beheld them / in land of Burgundy before.

85

He said that whencesoever / these knights come to the Rhine,
They bear a royal message, / or are of princely line.
"Their steeds are so bedizened, / and their apparel rare:
No matter whence they journey, / high-hearted men in truth they are."

86

Further then spake Hagen: / "As far as goes my ken,
Though I the noble Siegfried / yet have never seen,
Yet will I say meseemeth, / howe'er the thing may be,
This knight who seeks adventure, / and yonder stands so proud, is he.

87

"'Tis some new thing he bringeth / hither to our land.
The valiant Nibelungen / fell by the hero's hand,

Schilbung and Nibelung, / from royal sire sprung;
Deeds he wrought most wondrous / anon when his strong arm he swung.

88
"As once alone the hero / rode without company,
Found he before a mountain / —as hath been told to me—
With the hoard of Nibelung / full many stalwart men;
To him had they been strangers / until he chanced to find them then.

89
"The hoard of King Nibelung / entire did they bear
Forth from a mountain hollow. / And now the wonder hear,
How that they would share it, / these two Nibelung men.
This saw the fearless Siegfried, / and filled he was with wonder then.

90
"He came so near unto them / that he the knights espied,
And they in turn him also. / One amongst them said:
'Here comes the doughty Siegfried, / hero of Netherland.'
Since 'mongst the Nibelungen / strange wonders wrought his mighty hand.

91
"Right well did they receive him, / Schilbung and Nibelung,
And straight they both together, / these noble princes young,
Bade him mete out the treasure, / the full valorous man,
And so long time besought him / that he at last the task began.

92
"As we have heard in story, / he saw of gems such store
That they might not be laden / on wagons full five score;
More still of gold all shining / from Nibelungenland.
'Twas all to be divided / between them by keen Siegfried's hand.

93
"Then gave they him for hire / King Nibelung's sword.
And sooth to say, that service / brought them but small reward,
That for them there performed / Siegfried of dauntless mood.
His task he could not finish; / thereat they raged as were they wood.

94
"They had there of their followers / twelve warriors keen,
And strong they were as giants: / what booted giants e'en?
Them slew straightway in anger / Siegfried's mighty hand,
And warriors seven hundred / he felled in Nibelungenland

95
"With the sword full trusty, / Balmung that hight.
Full many a youthful warrior / from terror at the sight
Of that deadly weapon / swung by his mighty hand

Did render up his castle / and pledge him fealty in the land.

96

"Thereto the kings so mighty, / them slew he both as well.
But into gravest danger / through Alberich he fell,
Who thought for his slain masters / vengeance to wreak straightway,
Until the mighty Siegfried / his wrath with strong arm did stay.

97

"Nor could prevail against him / the Dwarf, howe'er he tried.
E'en as two wild lions / they coursed the mountainside,
Where he the sightless mantle[12] / from Alberich soon won.
Then Siegfried, knight undaunted, / held the treasure for his own.

98

"Who then dared join the struggle, / all slain around they lay.
Then he bade the treasure / to draw and bear away
Thither whence 'twas taken / by the Nibelungen men.
Alberich for his valor / was then appointed Chamberlain.

99

"An oath he had to swear him, / he'd serve him as his slave;
To do all kinds of service / his willing pledge he gave"—
Thus spake of Tronje Hagen— / "That has the hero done;
Might as great before him / was never in a warrior known.

100

"Still know I more about him, / that has to me been told.
A dragon, wormlike monster, / slew once the hero bold.
Then in its blood he bathed him, / since when his skin hath been
So horn-hard, ne'er a weapon / can pierce it, as hath oft been seen.

101

"Let us the brave knight-errant / receive so courteously
That we in nought shall merit / his hate, for strong is he.
He is so keen of spirit / he must be treated fair:
He has by his own valor / done many a deed of prowess rare."

102

The monarch spake in wonder: / "In sooth thou tellest right.
Now see how proudly yonder / he stands prepared for fight,
He and his thanes together, / the hero wondrous keen!
To greet him we'll go thither, / and let our fair intent be seen."

103

"That canst thou," out spake Hagen, / "well in honor do.
He is of noble kindred, / a high king's son thereto.
'Tis seen in all his bearing; / meseems in truth, God wot,

12 This is the *tarnkappe*, a cloak that made the wearer invisible, and also gave
him the strength of twelve men.

The tale is worth the hearing / that this bold knight has hither brought."

104

Then spake the mighty monarch: / "Be he right welcome here.
Keen is he and noble, / of fame known far and near.
So shall he be fair treated / in the land of Burgundy."
Down then went King Gunther, / and Siegfried with his men found he.

105

The king and his knights with him / received so well the guest,
That the hearty greeting / did their good will attest.
Thereat in turn the stranger / in reverence bowed low,
That in their welcome to him / they did such courtesy bestow.

106

"To me it is a wonder," / straightway spake the host,
"From whence, O noble Siegfried, / come to our land thou dost,
Or what here thou seekest / at Worms upon the Rhine."
Him the stranger answered: / "Put thou away all doubts of thine.

107

"I oft have heard the tiding / within my sire's domain,
How at thy court resided / —and know this would I fain—
Knights, of all the keenest, / —'tis often told me so—
That e'er a monarch boasted: / now come I hither this to know.

108

"Thyself have I heard also / high praised for knightly worth;
'Tis said a nobler monarch / ne'er lived in all the earth.
Thus speak of thee the people / in all the lands around.
Nor will I e'er give over / until in this the truth I've found.

109

"I too am warrior noble / and born to wear a crown;
So would I right gladly / that thou of me shouldst own
That I of right am master / o'er people and o'er land.
Of this shall now my honor / and eke my head as pledges stand.

110

"And art thou then so valiant / as hath to me been told,
I reck not, will he nill he / thy best warrior bold,
I'll wrest from thee in combat / whatever thou may'st have;
Thy lands and all thy castles / shall naught from change of masters save."

111

The king was seized with wonder / and all his men beside,
To see the manner haughty / in which the knight replied
That he was fully minded / to take from him his land.
It chafed his thanes to hear it, / who soon in raging mood did stand.

112

"How could it be my fortune," / Gunther the king outspoke,
"What my sire long ruled over / in honor for his folk,
Now to lose so basely / through any vaunter's might?
In sooth 'twere nobly showing / that we too merit name of knight!"

113

"Nowise will I give over," / was the keen reply.
"If peace through thine own valor / thy land cannot enjoy,
To me shall all be subject: / if heritage of mine
Through thy arm's might thou winnest, / of right shall all hence-forth
be thine.

114

"Thy land and all that mine is, / at stake shall equal lie.
Whiche'er of us be victor / when now our strength we try,
To him shall all be subject, / the folk and eke the land."
But Hagen spake against it, / and Gernot too was quick at hand.

115

"Such purpose have we never," / Gernot then said,
"For lands to combat ever, / that any warrior dead
Should lie in bloody battle. / We've mighty lands and strong;
Of right they call us master, / and better they to none belong."

116

There stood full grim and moody / Gernot's friends around,
And there as well amongst them / was Ortwein to be found.
He spake: "This mild peace-making / doth grieve me sore at heart,
For by the doughty Siegfried / attacked all undeserved thou art.

117

"If thou and thy two brothers / yourselves to help had naught,
And if a mighty army / he too had hither brought,
I trow I'd soon be able / to make this man so keen
His manner now so haughty / of need replace by meeker mien."

118

Thereat did rage full sorely / the hero of Netherland:
"Never shall be measured / 'gainst me in fight thy hand.
I am a mighty monarch, / thou a king's serving-knight;
Of such as thou a dozen / dare not withstand me in the fight."

119

For swords then called in anger / of Metz Sir Ortwein:
Son of Hagen's sister / he was, of Tronje's line.
That Hagen so long was silent / did grieve the king to see.
Gernot made peace between them: / a gallant knight and keen was he.

120

Spake he thus to Ortwein: / "Curb now thy wrathful tongue,
For here the noble Siegfried / hath done us no such wrong;
We yet can end the quarrel / in peace,—such is my rede—
And live with him in friendship; / that were for us a worthier deed."

121

Then spake the mighty Hagen: / "Sad things do I forebode
For all thy train of warriors, / that this knight ever rode
Unto the Rhine thus arméd. / 'Twere best he stayed at home;
For from my masters never / to him such wrong as this had come."

122

But outspake Siegfried proudly, / whose heart was ne'er dismayed:
"An't please thee not, Sir Hagen, / what I now have said,
This arm shall give example / whereby thou plain shall see
How stern anon its power / here in Burgundy will be."

123

"Yet that myself will hinder," / said then Gernot.
All his men forbade he / henceforth to say aught
With such unbridled spirit / to stir the stranger's ire.
Then Siegfried eke was mindful / of one most stately maid and fair.

124

"Such strife would ill befit us," / Gernot spake again;
"For though should die in battle / a host of valiant men
'Twould bring us little honor / and ye could profit none."
Thereto gave Siegfried answer, / good King Siegmund's noble son:

125

"Wherefore bides thus grim Hagen, / and Ortwein tardy is
To begin the combat / with all those friends of his,
Of whom he hath so many / here in Burgundy?"
Answer him they durst not, / for such was Gernot's stern decree.

126

"Thou shalt to us be welcome," / outspake young Giselher,
"And all thy brave companions / that hither with thee fare.
Full gladly we'll attend thee, / I and all friends of mine."
For the guests then bade they / pour out in store of Gunther's wine.

127

Then spake the stately monarch: / "But ask thou courteously,
And all that we call ours / stands at thy service free;
So with thee our fortune / we'll share in ill and good."
Thereat the noble Siegfried / a little milder was of mood.

128

Then carefully was tended / all their knightly gear,
And housed in goodly manner / in sooth the strangers were,

All that followed Siegfried; / they found a welcome rest.
In Burgundy full gladly / anon was seen the noble guest.

129

They showed him mickle honor / thereafter many a day,
And more by times a thousand / than I to you could say.
His might respect did merit, / ye may full well know that.
Scarce a man e'er saw him / who bore him longer any hate.

130

And when they held their pastime, / the kings with many a man,
Then was he ever foremost; / whatever they began,
None there that was his equal, / —so mickle was his might—
If they the stone were putting, / or hurling shaft with rival knight.

131

As is the knightly custom, / before the ladies fair
To games they turned for pastime, / these knights of mettle rare;
Then ever saw they gladly / the hero of Netherland.
But he had fixed his fancy / to win one fairest maiden's hand.

132

In all that they were doing / he'd take a ready part.
A winsome loving maiden / he bore within his heart;
Him only loved that lady, / whose face he ne'er had seen,
But she full oft in secret / of him spake fairest words, I ween.

133

And when before the castle / they sped in tournament,
The good knights and squires, / oft-times the maiden went
And gazed adown from casement, / Kriemhild the princess rare.
Pastime there was none other / for her that could with this compare.

134

And knew he she was gazing / whom in his heart he bore,
He joy enough had found him / in jousting evermore.
And might he only see her, / —that can I well believe—
On earth through sight none other / his eyes could such delight receive.

135

Whene'er with his companions / to castle court he went,
E'en as do now the people / whene'er on pleasure bent,
There stood 'fore all so graceful / Siegelind's noble son,
For whom in love did languish / the hearts of ladies many a one.

136

Eke thought he full often: / "How shall it ever be,
That I the noble maiden / with my own eyes may see,
Whom I do love so dearly / and have for many a day?
To me is she a stranger, / which sorely grieves my heart to say."

137
Whene'er the kings so mighty / rode o'er their broad domain,
Then of valiant warriors / they took a stately train.
With them abroad rode Siegfried, / which grieved those ladies sore:
—He too for one fair maiden / at heart a mickle burden bore.

138
Thus with his hosts he lingered / —'tis every tittle true—
In King Gunther's country / a year completely through,
And never once the meanwhile / the lovely maid did see,
Through whom such joy thereafter / for him, and eke such grief should be.

FOURTH ADVENTURE: How Siegfried fought with the Saxons

139
Now come wondrous tidings / to King Gunther's land,
By messengers brought hither / from far upon command
Of knights unknown who harbored / against him secret hate.
When there was heard the story, / at heart in sooth the grief was great.

140
Of these I now will tell you: / There was King Luedeger
From out the land of Saxons, / a mighty warrior,
And eke from land of Denmark / Luedegast the king:
Whene'er they rode to battle / went they with mighty following.

141
Come were now their messengers / to the land of Burgundy,
Sent forth by these foemen / in proud hostility.
Then asked they of the strangers / what tidings they did bring:
And when they heard it, straightway / led them to court before the king.

142
Then spake to them King Gunther: / "A welcome, on my word.
Who 'tis that send you hither, / that have I not yet heard:
Now shall ye let me know it," / spake the monarch keen.
Then dreaded they full sorely / to see King Gunther's angry mien.

143
"Wilt them, O king, permit us / the tidings straight to tell
That we now have brought thee, / no whit will we conceal,
But name thee both our masters / who us have hither sent:
Luedegast and Luedeger, / —to waste thy land is their intent.

144

"Their hate hast thou incurréd, / and thou shalt know in sooth
That high enraged against thee / are the monarchs both.
Their hosts they will lead hither / to Worms upon the Rhine;
They're helped by thanes full many— / of this put off all doubts of thine.

145

"Within weeks a dozen / their march will they begin;
And if thy friends be valiant, / let that full quick be seen,
To help thee keep in safety / thy castles and thy land:
Full many a shield and helmet / shall here be cleft by warrior's hand.

146

"Or wilt thou with them parley, / so let it quick be known,
Before their hosts so mighty / of warlike men come down
To Worms upon Rhine river / sad havoc here to make,
Whereby must death most certain / many a gallant knight o'ertake."

147

"Bide ye now the meanwhile," / the king did answer kind,
"Till I take better counsel; / then shall ye know my mind.
Have I yet warriors faithful, / from these I'll naught conceal,
But to my friends I'll straightway / these warlike tidings strange reveal."

148

The lordly Gunther wondered / thereat and troubled sore,
As he the message pondered / in heart and brooded o'er.
He sent to fetch grim Hagen / and others of his men,
And bade likewise in hurry / to court bring hither Gernot then.

149

Thus at his word his trusted / advisers straight attend.
He spake: "Our land to harry / foes all unknown will send
Of men a mighty army; / a grievous wrong is this.
Small cause have we e'er given / that they should wish us aught amiss."

150

"Our swords ward such things from us," / Gernot then said;
"Since but the fated dieth, / so let all such lie dead.
Wherefore I'll e'er remember / what honor asks of me:
Whoe'er hath hate against us / shall ever here right welcome be."

151

Then spake the doughty Hagen: / "Methinks 'twould scarce be good;
Luedegast and Luedeger / are men of wrathful mood.
Help can we never summon, / the days are now so few."
So spake the keen old warrior, / "'Twere well Siegfried the tidings knew."

152

The messengers in the borough / were harbored well the while,
And though their sight was hateful, / in hospitable style
As his own guests to tend them / King Gunther gave command,
Till 'mongst his friends he learnéd / who by him in his need would stand.

153

The king was filled with sorrow / and his heart was sad.
Then saw his mournful visage / a knight to help full glad,
Who could not well imagine / what 'twas that grieved him so.
Then begged he of King Gunther / the tale of this his grief to know.

154

"To me it is great wonder," / said Siegfried to the king,
"How thou of late hast changéd / to silent sorrowing
The joyous ways that ever / with us thy wont have been."
Then unto him gave answer / Gunther the full stately thane:

155

"'Tis not to every person / I can the burden say
That ever now in secret / upon my heart doth weigh:
To well-tried friends and steady / are told our inmost woes."
—Siegfried at first was pallid, / but soon his blood like fire up-rose.

156

He spake unto the monarch: / "To thee I've naught denied.
All ills that now do threaten / I'll help to turn aside.
And if but friends thou seekest, / of them the first I'll be,
And trow I well with honor / till death to serve thee faithfully."

157

"God speed thee well, Sir Siegfried, / for this thy purpose fair:
And though such help in earnest / thy arm should render ne'er,
Yet do I joy at hearing / thou art so true to me.
And live I yet a season, / right heartily repaid 'twill be.

158

"Know will I also let thee / wherefore I sorrowing stand.
Through messengers from my foemen / have tidings reached my land
That they with hosts of warriors / will ride my country o'er;
Such thing to us did never / thanes of any land before."

159

"Small cause is that for grieving," / said then Siegfried;
"But calm thy troubled spirit / and hearken to my rede:
Let me for thee acquire / honor and vantage too,
And bid thou now assemble / for service eke thy warriors true.

160

"And had thy mighty enemies / to help them now at hand

Good thanes full thirty thousand, / against them all I'd stand,
Had I but one good thousand: / put all thy trust in me."
Then answered him King Gunther: / "Thy help shall full requited be."
161
"Then bid for me to summon / a thousand of thy men,
Since I now have with me / of all my knightly train
None but twelve knights only; / then will I guard thy land.
For thee shall service faithful / be done alway by Siegfried's hand.
162
"Herein shall help us Hagen / and eke Ortwein,
Dankwart and Sindold, / those trusted knights of thine;
And with us too shall journey / Volker, the valiant man;
The banner he shall carry: / bestow it better ne'er I can.
163
"Back to their native country / the messengers may go;
They'll see us there right quickly, / let them full surely know,
So that all our castles / peace undisturbed shall have."
Then bade the king to summon / his friends with all their warriors brave.
164
To court returned the heralds / King Luedeger had sent,
And on their journey homeward / full joyfully they went.
King Gunther gave them presents / that costly were and good,
And granted them safe convoy; / whereat they were of merry mood.
165
"Tell ye my foes," spake Gunther, / "when to your land ye come,
Than making journeys hither / they better were at home;
But if they still be eager / to make such visit here,
Unless my friends forsake me, / cold in sooth shall be their cheer."
166
Then for the messengers / rich presents forth they bore,
Whereof in sooth to give them / Gunther had goodly store:
And they durst not refuse them / whom Luedeger had sent.
Leave then they took immediate, / and homeward joyfully they went.
167
When to their native Denmark / the messengers returned,
And the king Luedegast / the answer too had learned,
They at the Rhine had sent him, / —when that to him was told,
His wrath was all unbounded / to have reply in words so bold.
168
'Twas said their warriors numbered / many a man full keen:
"There likewise among them / with Gunther have we seen
Of Netherland a hero, / the same that Siegfried hight."

King Luedegast was grievéd, / when he their words had heard aright.

169

When throughout all Denmark / the tidings quick spread o'er,
Then in hot haste they summoned / helpers all the more,
So that King Luedegast, / 'twixt friends from far and near,
Had knights full twenty thousand / all furnished well with shield and spear.

170

Then too his men did summon / of Saxony Luedeger,
Till they good forty thousand, / and more, had gathered there,
With whom to make the journey / 'gainst the land of Burgundy.
—At home likewise the meanwhile / King Gunther had sent forth decree

171

Mighty men to summon / of his own and brothers twain,
Who against the foemen / would join the armed train.
In haste they made them ready, / for right good cause they had.
Amongst them must thereafter / full many a noble thane lie dead.

172

To march they quick made ready. / And when they thence would fare,
The banner to the valiant / Volker was given to bear,
As they began the journey / from Worms across the Rhine;
Strong of arm grim Hagen / was chosen leader of the line.

173

With them there rode Sindold / and eke the keen Hunold
Who oft at hands of Gunther / had won rewards of gold;
Dankwart, Hagen's brother, / and Ortwein beside,
Who all could well with honor / in train of noble warriors ride.

174

"King Gunther," spake then Siegfried, / "stay thou here at home;
Since now thy knights so gallant / with me will gladly come,
Rest thou here with fair ladies, / and be of merry mood:
I trow we'll keep in safety / thy land and honor as we should.

175

"And well will I see to it / that they at home remain,
Who fain would ride against thee / to Worms upon the Rhine.
Against them straight we'll journey / into their land so far
That they'll be meeker minded / who now such haughty vaunters are."

176

Then from the Rhine through Hesse / the hosts of knights rode on
Toward the land of Saxons, / where battle was anon.
With fire and sword they harried / and laid the country waste,
So that both the monarchs / full well the woes of war did taste.

177

When came they to the border / the train-men onward pressed.
With thought of battle-order / Siegfried the thanes addressed:
"Who now shall guard our followers / from danger in the rear?"
In sooth like this the Saxons / in battle worsted never were.

178

Then said they: "On the journey / the men shall guarded be
By the valiant Dankwart, / —a warrior swift is he;
So shall we lose the fewer / by men of Luedeger.
Let him and Ortwein with him / be chosen now to guard the rear."

179

Spake then the valiant Siegfried: / "Myself will now ride on,
And against our enemies / will keep watch in the van,
Till I aright discover / where they perchance may be."
The son of fair Queen Siegelind / did arm him then immediately.

180

The folk he left to Hagen / when ready to depart,
And as well to Gernot, / a man of dauntless heart.
Into the land of Saxons / alone he rode away,
And by his hand was severed / many a helmet's band that day.

181

He found a mighty army / that lay athwart the plain,
Small part of which outnumbered / all those in his own train:
Full forty thousand were they / or more good men of might.
The hero high in spirit / saw right joyfully the sight.

182

Then had eke a warrior / from out the enemy
To guard the van gone forward, / all arméd cap-a-pie.
Him saw the noble Siegfried, / and he the valiant man;
Each one straight the other / to view with angry mien began.

183

Who he was I'll tell you / that rode his men before,
—A shield of gold all shining / upon his arm he bore—
In sooth it was King Luedegast / who there the van did guard.
Straightway the noble Siegfried / full eagerly against him spurred.

184

Now singled out for combat / him, too, had Luedegast.
Then full upon each other / they spurred their chargers fast,
As on their shields they lowered / their lances firm and tight,
Whereat the lordly monarch / soon found himself in sorry plight.

185

After the shock their chargers / bore the knights so fast
Onward past each other / as flew they on the blast.

Then turned they deftly backward / obedient to the rein,
As with their swords contested / the grim and doughty fighters twain.
186
When Siegfried struck in anger / far off was heard the blow,
And flew from off the helmet, / as if 'twere all aglow,
The fiery sparks all crackling / beneath his hand around.
Each warrior in the other / a foeman worth his mettle found.
187
Full many a stroke with vigor / dealt eke King Luedegast,
And on each other's buckler / the blows fell thick and fast.
Then thirty men discovered / their master's sorry plight:
But ere they came to help him / had doughty Siegfried won the fight.
188
With three mighty gashes / which he had dealt the king
Through his shining breastplate / made fast with many a ring.
The sword with sharpest edges / from wounds brought forth the blood,
Whereat King Luedegast / apace fell into gloomy mood.
189
To spare his life he begged him, / his land he pledged the knight,
And told him straight moreover, / that Luedegast he hight.
Then came his knights to help him, / they who there had seen
How that upon the vanguard / fierce fight betwixt the twain had been.
190
After duel ended, / did thirty yet withstand
Of knights that him attended; / but there the hero's hand
Kept safe his noble captive / with blows of wondrous might.
And soon wrought greater ruin / Siegfried the full gallant knight.
191
Beneath his arm of valor / the thirty soon lay dead.
But one the knight left living, / who thence full quickly sped
To tell abroad the story / how he the others slew;
In sooth the blood-red helmet / spake all the hapless tidings true.
192
Then had the men of Denmark / for all their grief good cause,
When it was told them truly / their king a captive was.
They told it to King Luedeger, / when he to rage began
In anger all unbounded: / for him had grievous harm been done.
193
The noble King Luedegast / was led a prisoner then
By hand of mighty Siegfried / back to King Gunther's men,
And placed in hands of Hagen: / and when they did hear
That 'twas the king of Denmark / they not a little joyful were.

194
He bade the men of Burgundy / then bind the banners on.
"Now forward!" Siegfried shouted, / "here shall yet more be done,
An I but live to see it; / ere this day's sun depart,
Shall mourn in land of Saxons / full many a goodly matron's heart.

195
"Ye warriors from Rhineland, / to follow me take heed,
And I unto the army / of Luedeger will lead.
Ere we again turn backward / to the land of Burgundy
Helms many hewn asunder / by hand of good knights there shall be."

196
To horse then hastened Gernot / and with him mighty men.
Volker keen in battle / took up the banner then;
He was a doughty Fiddler / and rode the host before.
There, too, every follower / a stately suit of armor wore.

197
More than a thousand warriors / they there had not a man,
Saving twelve knights-errant. / To rise the dust began
In clouds along the highway / as they rode across the fields,
And gleaming in the sunlight / were seen the brightly shining shields.

198
Meanwhile eke was nearing / of Saxons a great throng,
Each a broadsword bearing / that mickle was and long,
With blade that cut full sorely / when swung in strong right hand.
'Gainst strangers were they ready / to guard their castles and their land.

199
The leaders forth to battle / led the warriors then.
Come was also Siegfried / with his twelve chosen men,
Whom he with him hither / had brought from Netherland.
That day in storm of battle / was blood-bespattered many a hand.

200
Sindold and Hunold / and Gernot as well,
Beneath their hands in battle / full many a hero fell,
Ere that their deeds of valor / were known throughout the host.
Through them must many a stately / matron weep for warrior lost.

201
Volker and Hagen / and Ortwein in the fight
Lustily extinguished / full many a helmet's light
With blood from wounds down flowing,— / keen fighters every one.
And there by Dankwart also / was many a mickle wonder done.

202
The knights of Denmark tested / how they could weapons wield.

Clashing there together / heard ye many a shield
And 'neath sharp swords resounding, / swung by many an arm.
The Saxons keen in combat / wrought 'mid their foes a grievous harm.
203
When the men of Burgundy / pressed forward to the fight,
Gaping wounds full many / hewed they there with might.
Then flowing down o'er saddle / in streams was seen the blood,
So fought for sake of honor / these valiant riders keen and good.
204
Loudly were heard ringing, / wielded by hero's hand,
The sharply-cutting weapons, / where they of Netherland
Their master followed after / into the thickest throng:
Wherever Siegfried led them / rode too those valiant knights along.
205
Of warriors from Rhine river / could follow not a one.
There could be seen by any / a stream of blood flow down
O'er brightly gleaming helmet / 'neath Siegfried's mighty hand,
Until King Luedeger / before him with his men did stand.
206
Three times hither and thither / had he the host cut through
From one end to the other. / Now come was Hagen too
Who helped him well in battle / to vent his warlike mood.
That day beneath his valor / must die full many a rider good.
207
When the doughty Luedeger / Siegfried there found,
As he swung high in anger / his arm for blows around
And with his good sword Balmung / knights so many slew,
Thereat was the keen warrior / filled with grief and anger too.
208
Then mickle was the thronging / and loud the broadswords clashed,
As all their valiant followers / 'gainst one another dashed.
Then struggled all the fiercer / both sides the fight to win;
The hosts joined with each other: / 'twas frightful there to hear the din.
209
To the monarch of the Saxons / it had been told before,
His brother was a captive, / which grieved his heart right sore.
He knew not that had done it / fair Siegelind's son,
For rumor said 'twas Gernot. / Full well he learned the truth anon.
210
King Luedeger struck so mighty / when fierce his anger rose,
That Siegfried's steed beneath him / staggered from the blows,
But forthwith did recover; / then straight his rider keen
Let all his furious mettle / in slaughter of his foes be seen.

211
There helped him well grim Hagen, / and Gernot in the fray,
Dankwart and Volker; / dead many a knight there lay.
Sindold and Hunold / and Ortwein, doughty thane,
By them in that fierce struggle / was many a valiant warrior slain.

212
Unparted in storm of battle / the gallant leaders were,
Around them over helmet / flew there many a spear
Through shield all brightly shining, / from hand of mighty thane:
And on the glancing armor / was seen full many a blood-red stain.

213
Amid the hurly-burly / down fell many a man
To ground from off his charger. / Straight 'gainst each other ran
Siegfried the keen rider / and eke King Luedeger.
Then flew from lance the splinters / and hurled was many a pointed spear.

214
'Neath Siegfried's hand so mighty / from shield flew off the band.
And soon to win the victory / thought he of Netherland
Over the valiant Saxons, / of whom were wonders seen.
Heigh-ho! in shining mail-rings / many a breach made Dankwart keen!

215
Upon the shining buckler / that guarded Siegfried's breast
Soon espied King Luedeger / a painted crown for crest;
By this same token knew he / it was the doughty man,
And to his friends he straightway / amid the battle loud began:

216
"Give o'er from fighting further, / good warriors every one!
Amongst our foes now see I / Siegmund's noble son,
Of netherland the doughty / knight on victory bent.
Him has the evil Devil / to scourge the Saxons hither sent."

217
Then bade he all the banners / amid the storm let down.
Peace he quickly sued for: / 'Twas granted him anon,
But he must now a hostage / be ta'en to Gunther's land.
This fate had forced upon him / the fear of Siegfried's mighty hand.

218
They thus by common counsel / left off all further fight.
Hacked full many a helmet / and shields that late were bright
From hands down laid they weary; / as many as there might be,
With stains they all were bloody / 'neath hands of the men of Burgundy.

219
Each whom he would took captive, / now they had won the fight.
Gernot, the noble hero, / and Hagen, doughty knight,
Bade bear forth the wounded. / Back led they with them then
Unto the land of Burgundy / five hundred stalwart fighting-men.

220
The knights, of victory cheated, / their native Denmark sought,
Nor had that day the Saxons / with such high valor fought,
That one could praise them for it, / which caused the warriors pain.
Then wept their friends full sorely / at home for those in battle slain.

221
For the Rhine then laden / they let their armor be.
Siegfried, the knight so doughty, / had won the victory
With his few chosen followers; / that he had nobly done,
Could not but free acknowledge / King Gunther's warriors every one.

222
To Worms sent Gernot riding / now a messenger,
And of the joyous tiding / soon friends at home were ware,
How that it well had prospered / with him and all his men.
Fought that day with valor / for honor had those warriors keen.

223
The messenger sped forward / and told the tidings o'er.
Then joyfully they shouted / who boded ill before,
To hear the welcome story / that now to them was told.
From ladies fair and noble / came eager questions manifold,

224
Who all the fair fortune / of King Gunther's men would know.
One messenger they ordered / unto Kriemhild to go.
But that was done in secret: / she durst let no one see,
For he was 'mongst those warriors / whom she did love so faithfully.

225
When to her own apartments / was come the messenger
Joyfully addressed him / Kriemhild the maiden fair:
"But tell me now glad tidings, / and gold I'll give to thee,
And if thou tell'st not falsely, / good friend thou'lt ever find in me.

226
"How has my good brother / Gernot in battle sped,
And how my other kinsmen? / Lies any of them dead?
Who wrought most deeds of valor? / —That shall thou let me know."
Then spake the messenger truly: / "No knight but did high valor show.

227
"But in the dire turmoil / rode rider none so well,
O Princess fair and noble, / since I must truly tell,

58

As the stranger knight full noble / who comes from Netherland;
There deeds of mickle wonder / were wrought by doughty Siegfried's
hand.

228
"Whate'er have all the warriors / in battle dared to do,
Dankwart and Hagen / and the other knights so true,
Howe'er they fought for honor, / 'twas naught but idle play
Beside what there wrought Siegfried, / King Siegmund's son, amid the
fray.

229
"Beneath their hands in battle / full many a hero fell,
Yet all the deeds of wonder / no man could ever tell,
Wrought by the hand of Siegfried, / when rode he 'gainst the foe:
And weep aloud must women / for friends by his strong arm laid low.

230
"There, too, the knight she loved / full many a maid must lose.
Were heard come down on helmet / so loud his mighty blows,
That they from gaping gashes / brought forth the flowing blood.
In all that maketh noble / he is a valiant knight and good.

231
"Many a deed of daring / of Metz Sir Ortwein wrought:
For all was evil faring / whom he with broadsword caught,
Doomed to die that instant, / or wounded sore to fall.
And there thy valiant brother / did greater havoc work than all

232
"That e'er in storm of battle / was done by warrior bold.
Of all those chosen warriors / let eke the truth be told:
The proud Burgundian heroes / have made it now right plain,
That they can free from insult / their country's honor well maintain.

233
"Beneath their hands was often / full many a saddle bare,
When o'er the field resounding / their bright swords cut the air.
The warriors from Rhine river / did here such victory win
That for their foes 'twere better / if they such meeting ne'er had seen.

234
"Keen the knights of Tronje / 'fore all their valor showed,
When with their stalwart followers / against their foes they rode;
Slain by the hand of Hagen / must knights so many be,
'Twill long be in the telling / here in the land of Burgundy.

235
"Sindold and Hunold, / Gernot's men each one,
And the valiant Rumold / have all so nobly done,
King Luedeger will ever / have right good cause to rue

That he against thy kindred / at Rhine dared aught of harm to do.

236

"And deeds of all most wondrous / e'er done by warrior keen
In earliest time or latest, / by mortal ever seen,
Wrought there in lusty manner / Siegfried with doughty hand.
Rich hostages he bringeth / with him unto Gunther's land.

237

"By his own strength subdued them / the hero unsurpassed
And brought down dire ruin / upon King Luedegast,
Eke on the King of Saxons / his brother Luedeger.
Now hearken to the story / I tell thee, noble Princess fair.

238

"Them both hath taken captive / Siegfried's doughty hand.
Hostages were so many / ne'er brought into this land
As to the Rhine come hither / through his great bravery."
Than these could never tidings / unto her heart more welcome be.

239

"With captives home they're hieing, / five hundred men or mo',
And of the wounded dying / Lady shalt thou know,
Full eighty blood-stained barrows / unto Burgundian land,
Most part hewn down in battle / beneath keen Siegfried's doughty hand.

240

"Who message sent defiant / unto the Rhine so late
Must now as Gunther's prisoners / here abide their fate.
Bringing such noble captives / the victors glad return."
Then glowed with joy the princess / when she the tidings glad did learn.

241

Her cheeks so full of beauty / with joy were rosy-red,
That passed he had uninjured / through all the dangers dread,
The knight she loved so dearly, / Siegfried with doughty arm.
Good cause she had for joying / o'er all her friends escaped from harm.

242

Then spake the beauteous maiden: / "Glad news thou hast told me,
Wherefor now rich apparel / thy goodly meed shall be,
And to thee shall be given / ten marks of gold as well."
'Tis thus a thing right pleasant / to ladies high such news to tell.

243

The presents rich they gave him, / gold and apparel rare.
Then hastened to the casement / full many a maiden fair,
And on the street looked downward: / hither riding did they see
Many a knight high-hearted / into the land of Burgundy.

244

There came who 'scaped uninjured, / and wounded borne along,
All glad to hear the greetings / of friends, a joyful throng.
To meet his friends the monarch / rode out in mickle glee:
In joying now was ended / all his full great anxiety.

245

Then did he well his warriors / and eke the strangers greet;
And for a king so mighty / 'twere nothing else but meet
That he should thank right kindly / the gallant men each one,
Who had in storm of battle / the victory so bravely won.

246

Then of his friends King Gunther / bade tidings tell straightway,
Of all his men how many / were fallen in the fray.
Lost had he none other / than warriors three score:
Then wept they for the heroes, / as since they did for many more.

247

Shields full many brought they / all hewn by valiant hand,
And many a shattered helmet / into King Gunther's hand.
The riders then dismounted / from their steeds before the hall,
And a right hearty welcome / from friends rejoicing had they all.

248

Then did they for the warriors / lodging meet prepare,
And for his guests the monarch / bade full well have care.
He bade them take the wounded / and tend them carefully,
And toward his enemies also / his gentle bearing might ye see.

249

To Luedeger then spake he: / "Right welcome art thou here.
Through fault of thine now have I / lost many friends full dear,
For which, have I good fortune, / thou shall right well atone.
God rich reward my liegemen, / such faithfulness to me they've shown."

250

"Well may'st thou thank them, truly," / spake then Luedeger;
"Hostages so noble / won a monarch ne'er.
For chivalrous protection / rich goods we offer thee,
That thou now right gracious / to us thy enemies shalt be."

251

"I'll grant you both your freedom," / spake the king again;
"But that my enemies surely / here by me remain,
Therefor I'll have good pledges / they ne'er shall quit my land,
Save at my royal pleasure." / Thereto gave Luedeger the hand.

252

Sweet rest then found the weary / their tired limbs to aid,

And gently soon on couches / the wounded knights were laid;
Mead and wine right ruddy / they poured out plenteously:
Than they and all their followers / merrier men there none might be.

254
Their shields all hacked in battle / secure were laid away;
And not a few of saddles / stained with blood that day,
Lest women weep to see them, / hid they too from sight.
Full many a keen rider / home came aweary from the fight.

254
The host in gentlest manner / did his guests attend:
The land around with stranger / was crowded, and with friend.
They bade the sorely wounded / nurse with especial care:
Whereby the knights high-hearted / 'neath all their wounds knew not despair.

255
Who there had skill in healing / received reward untold,
Silver all unweighéd / and thereto ruddy gold
For making whole the heroes / after the battle sore.
To all his friends the monarch / gave presents rich in goodly store.

256
Who there again was minded / to take his homeward way
They bade, as one a friend doth, / yet a while to stay.
The king did then take counsel / how to reward each one,
For they his will in battle / like liegemen true had nobly done.

257
Then outspake royal Gernot: / "Now let them homeward go;
After six weeks are over, / —thus our friends shall know—
To hold high feast they're bidden / hither to come again;
Many a knight now lying / sore wounded will be healed ere then.

258
Of Netherland the hero / would also then take leave.
When of this King Gunther / did tidings first receive,
The knight besought he kindly / not yet his leave to take:
To this he'd ne'er consented / an it were not for Kriemhild's sake.

259
A prince he was too noble / to take the common pay;
He had right well deserved it / that the king alway
And all his warriors held him / in honor, for they had seen
What by his arm in battle / bravely had accomplished been.

260
He stayed there yet a little / for the maiden's sake alone,
Whom he would see so gladly. / And all fell out full soon
As he at heart had wished it: / well known to him was she.

Home to his father's country / joyously anon rode he.
261
The king bade at all seasons / keep up the tournament,
And many a youthful rider / forth to the lists there went.
The while were seats made ready / by Worms upon the strand
For all who soon were coming / unto the Burgundian land.
262
In the meantime also, / ere back the knights returned,
Had Kriemhild, noble lady, / the tidings likewise learned,
The king would hold high feasting / with all his gallant men.
There was a mickle hurry, / and busy were fair maidens then
263
With dresses and with wimples / that they there should wear.
Ute, queen so stately, / the story too did hear,
How to them were coming / proud knights of highest worth.
Then from enfolding covers / were store of dresses rich brought forth.
264
Such love she bore her children / she bade rich dress prepare,
Wherewith adorned were ladies / and many a maiden fair,
And not a few young riders / in the land of Burgundy.
For strangers many bade she / rich garments eke should measured be.

FIFTH ADVENTURE: How Siegfried first saw Kriemhild

265
Unto the Rhine now daily / the knights were seen to ride,
Who there would be full gladly / to share the festive tide.
To all that thither journeyed / to the king to show them true,
In plenty them were given / steeds and rich apparel too.
266
And soon were seats made ready / for every noble guest,
As we have heard the story, / for highest and for best,
Two and thirty princes / at the festival.
Then vied with one another / to deck themselves the ladies all.
267
Never was seen idle / the young Prince Giselher:
The guests and all their followers / received full kindly were
By him and eke by Gernot / and their men every one.
The noble thanes they greeted / as ever 'tis in honor done.
268
With gold bright gleaming saddles / unto the land they brought,

Good store of rich apparel / and shields all richly wrought
Unto the Rhine they carried / to that high festival.
And joyous days were coming / for the woúnded warriors all.
269
They who yet on couches / lay wounded grievously
For joy had soon forgotten / how bitter death would be:
The sick and all the ailing / no need of pity had.
Anent the days of feasting / were they o'er the tidings glad,
270
How they should make them merry / there where all were so.
Delight beyond all measure, / of joys an overflow,
Had in sooth the people / seen on every hand:
Then rose a mickle joyance / over all King Gunther's land.
271
Full many a warrior valiant / one morn at Whitsuntide
All gorgeously apparelled / was thither seen to ride,
Five thousand men or over, / where the feast should be;
And vied in every quarter / knight with knight in revelry.
272
Thereof the host was mindful, / for he well did understand
How at heart right warmly / the hero of Netherland
Loved alone his sister, / though her he ne'er had seen,
Who praised for wondrous beauty / before all maidens else had been.
273
Then spake the thane so noble / of Metz Sir Ortwein:
"Wilt thou full be honored / by every guest of thine,
Then do them all the pleasure / the winsome maids to see,
That are held so high in honor / here in the land of Burgundy.
274
"What were a man's chief pleasure, / his very joy of life,
An 't were not a lovely maiden / or a stately wife?
Then let the maid thy sister / before thy guests appear."
—Brave thanes did there full many / at heart rejoice the rede to hear.
275
"Thy words I'll gladly follow," / then the monarch said,
And all the knights who heard him / ere thereat right glad.
Then told was Queen Ute / and eke her daughter fair,
That they with maids in waiting / unto the court should soon repair.
276
Then in well-stored wardrobes / rich attire they sought,
And forth from folding covers / their glittering dresses brought,
Armbands and silken girdles / of which they many had.
And zealous to adorn her / was then full many a winsome maid.

277
Full many a youthful squire / upon that day did try,
By decking of his person, / to win fair lady's eye;
For the which great good fortune / he'd take no monarch's crown:
They longed to see those maidens, / whom they before had never known.

278
For her especial service / the king did order then
To wait upon his sister / a hundred of his men,
As well upon his mother: / they carried sword in hand.
That was the court attendance / there in the Burgundian land.

279
Ute, queen so stately, / then came forth with her:
And with the queen in waiting / ladies fair there were,
A hundred or over, / in festal robes arrayed.
Eke went there with Kriemhild / full many a fair and winsome maid.

280
Forth from their own apartments / they all were seen to go:
There was a mickle pressing / of good knights to and fro,
Who hoped to win the pleasure, / if such a thing might be,
The noble maiden Kriemhild, / delight of every eye, to see.

281
Now came she fair and lovely, / as the ruddy sun of morn
From misty clouds emerging. / Straight he who long had borne
Her in his heart and loved her, / from all his gloom was freed,
As so stately there before him / he saw the fair and lovely maid.

282
Her rich apparel glittered / with many a precious stone,
And with a ruddy beauty / her cheeks like roses shone.
Though you should wish to do so, / you could not say, I ween,
That e'er a fairer lady / in all the world before was seen.

283
As in a sky all starlit / the moon shines out so bright,
And through the cloudlets peering / pours down her gentle light,
E'en so was Kriemhild's beauty / among her ladies fair:
The hearts of gallant heroes / were gladder when they saw her there.

284
The richly clad attendants / moved stately on before,
And the valiant thanes high-hearted / stood patiently no more,
But pressed right eager forward / to see the lovely maid:
In noble Siegfried's bosom / alternate joy and anguish swayed.

285
He thought with heart despairing, / "How could it ever be,

That I should win thy favor? / There hoped I foolishly.
But had I e'er to shun thee, / then were I rather dead."
And oft, to think upon it, / the color from his visage fled.
286
The noble son of Siegmund / did there so stately stand
As if his form were pictured / by good old master's hand
Upon a piece of parchment. / All who saw, confessed
That he of all good heroes / was the stateliest and the best.
287
The fair Kriemhild's attendants / gave order to make way
On all sides for the ladies, / and willing thanes obey.
To see their noble bearing / did every warrior cheer;
Full many a stately lady / of gentle manner born was there.
288
Then outspake of Burgundy / Gernot the valiant knight:
"To him who thus has helped thee / so bravely in the fight,
Gunther, royal brother, / shalt thou like favor show,
A thane before all others; / he's worthy of it well, I trow.
289
"Let then the doughty Siegfried / unto my sister go
To have the maiden's greetings, / —'twill be our profit so.
She that ne'er greeted hero / shall greet him courteously,
That thus the stately warrior / for aye our faithful friend may be."
290
The king's knights hastened gladly / upon his high command
And told these joyous tidings / to the prince of Netherland.
"It is the king's good pleasure / that thou to court shalt go,
To have his sister's greetings; / to honor thee 'tis ordered so."
291
Then was the thane full valiant / thereat soon filled with joy.
Yea, bore he in his bosom / delight without alloy
At thought that he should straightway / Ute's fair daughter see.
Siegfried anon she greeted / in courteous manner lovingly.
292
As she saw the knight high-hearted / there before her stand,
Blushed red and spake the maiden, / the fairest of the land:
"A welcome, brave Sir Siegfried, / thou noble knight and good."
As soon as he had heard it, / the hearty greeting cheered his mood.
293
Before her low he bended; / him by the hand took she,
And by her onward wended / the knight full willingly.
They cast upon each other / fond glances many a one,
The knight and eke the maiden; / furtively it all was done.

294
Whether he pressed friendly / that hand as white as snow
From the love he bore her, / that I do not know;
Yet believe I cannot / that this was left undone,
For straightway showed the maiden / that he her heart had fully won.

295
In the sunny summer season / and in the month of May
Had his heart seen never / before so glad a day,
Nor one so fully joyous, / as when he walked beside
That maiden rich in beauty / whom fain he'd choose to be his bride.

296
Then thought many a warrior: / "Were it likewise granted me
To walk beside the maiden, / just as now I see,
Or to lie beside her, / how gladly were that done!"
But ne'er a knight more fully / had gracious lady's favor won.

297
From all the lands far distant / were guests distinguished there,
But fixed each eye was only / upon this single pair.
By royal leave did Kriemhild / kiss then the stately knight:
In all the world he never / before had known so rare delight.

298
Then full of strange forebodings, / of Denmark spake the king:
"This full loving greeting / to many woe will bring,
—My heart in secret warns me— / through Siegfried's doughty hand.
God give that he may never / again be seen within my land."

299
On all sides then 'twas ordered / 'fore Kriemhild and her train
Of women make free passage. / Full many a valiant thane
With her unto the minster / in courtly way went on.
But from her side was parted / the full stately knight anon.

300
Then went she to the minster, / and with her many a maid.
In such rich apparel / Kriemhild was arrayed,
That hearty wishes many / there were made in vain:
Her comely form delighted / the eye of many a noble thane.

301
Scarce could tarry Siegfried / till mass was sung the while.
And surely did Dame Fortune / upon him kindly smile,
To him she was so gracious / whom in his heart he bore.
Eke did he the maiden, / as she full well deserved, adore.

302
As after mass then Kriemhild / came to the minster door,
The knight his homage offered, / as he had done before.

Then began to thank him / the full beauteous maid,
That he her royal brothers / did 'gainst their foes so nobly aid.
303
"God speed thee, Sir Siegfried," / spake the maiden fair,
"For thou hast well deservéd / that all these warriors are,
As it hath now been told me, / right grateful unto thee."
Then gan he cast his glances / on the Lady Kriemhild lovingly.
304
"True will I ever serve them," / —so spake the noble thane—
"And my head shall never / be laid to rest again,
Till I, if life remaineth, / have their good favor won.
In sooth, my Lady Kriemhild, / for thy fair grace it all is done."
305
Ne'er a day passed over / for a twelve of happy days,
But saw they there beside him / the maiden all did praise,
As she before her kinsmen / to court would daily go:
It pleased the thane full highly / that they did him such honor show.
306
Delight and great rejoicing, / a mighty jubilee,
Before King Gunther's castle / daily might ye see,
Without and eke within it, / 'mongst keen men many a one.
By Ortwein and by Hagen / great deeds and wondrous there were done.
307
Whate'er was done by any, / in all they ready were
To join in way right lusty, / both the warriors rare:
Whereby 'mongst all the strangers / they won an honored name,
And through their deeds so wondrous / of Gunther's land spread far the fame.
308
Who erstwhile lay sore wounded / now were whole again,
And fain would share the pastime, / with all the king's good men;
With shields join in the combat, / and try the shaft so long.
Wherein did join them many / of the merry-making throng.
309
To all who joined the feasting / the host in plenty bade
Supply the choicest viands: / so guarded well he had
'Gainst whate'er reproaches / could rise from spite or spleen.
Unto his guests right friendly / to go the monarch now was seen.
310
He spake: "Ye thanes high-hearted, / ere now ye part from me,
Accept of these my presents; / for I would willingly
Repay your noble service. / Despise ye not, I pray,

What now I will share with you: / 'tis offered in right grateful way."

311

Straightway they of Denmark / thus to the king replied:
"Ere now upon our journey / home again we ride,
We long for lasting friendship. / Thereof we knights have need,
For many a well-loved kinsman / at hands of thy good thanes lies
dead."

312

Luedegast was recovered / from all his wounds so sore,
And eke the lord of Saxons / from fight was whole once more.
Some amongst their warriors / left they dead behind.
Then went forth King Gunther / where he Siegfried might find.

313

Unto the thane then spake he: / "Thy counsel give, I pray.
The foes whom we hold captive / fain would leave straightway,
And long for lasting friendship / with all my men and me.
Now tell me, good Sir Siegfried, / what here seemeth good to thee.

314

"What the lords bid as ransom, / shall now to thee be told
Whate'er five hundred horses / might bear of ruddy gold,
They'd give to me right gladly, / would I but let them free."
Then spake the noble Siegfried: / "That were to do right foolishly.

315

"Thou shalt let them freely / journey hence again;
And that they both hereafter / shall evermore refrain
From leading hostile army / against thee and thy land,
Therefor in pledge of friendship / let each now give to thee the hand."

316

"Thy rede I'll gladly follow." / Straightway forth they went.
To those who offered ransom / the answer then was sent,
Their gold no one desired / which they would give before.
The warriors battle-weary / dear friends did yearn to see once more.

317

Full many a shield all laden / with treasure forth they bore:
He dealt it round unmeasured / to friends in goodly store;
Each one had marks five hundred / and some had more, I ween.
Therein King Gunther followed / the rede of Gernot, knight full keen.

318

Then was a great leave-taking, / as they departed thence.
The warriors all 'fore Kriemhild / appeared in reverence,
And eke there where her mother / Queen Ute sat near by.
Gallant thanes were never / dismissed as these so graciously.

319
Bare were the lodging-places, / when away the strangers rode.
Yet in right lordly manner / there at home abode
The king with friends around him, / full noble men who were.
And them now saw they daily / at court before Kriemhild appear.

320
Eke would the gallant hero / Siegfried thence depart,
The thing to gain despairing / whereon was set his heart.
The king was told the tidings / how that he would away.
Giselher his brother / did win the knight with them to stay.

321
"Whither, O noble Siegfried, / wilt thou now from us ride?
Do as I earnest pray thee, / and with these thanes abide,
As guest here with King Gunther, / and live right merrily.
Here dwell fair ladies many: / them will he gladly let thee see."

322
Then spake the doughty Siegfried: / "Our steeds leave yet at rest,
The while from this my purpose / to part will I desist.
Our shields once more take from us. / Though gladly home I would,
Naught 'gainst the fond entreaties / of Giselher avail me could."

323
So stayed the knight full gallant / for sake of friendship there.
In sooth in ne'er another / country anywhere
Had he so gladly lingered: / iwis it was that he,
Now whensoe'er he wished it, / Kriemhild the maiden fair could see.

324
'Twas her surpassing beauty / that made the knight to stay.
With many a merry pastime / they whiled the time away;
But love for her oppressed him, / oft-times grievously.
Whereby anon the hero / a mournful death was doomed to die.

SIXTH ADVENTURE: How Gunther fared to Isenland to Brunhild

325
Tidings unknown to any / from over Rhine now come,
How winsome maids a many / far yonder had their home.
Whereof the royal Gunther / bethought him one to win,
And o'er the thought the monarch / of full joyous mood was seen.

326
There was a queenly maiden / seated over sea,
Like her nowhere another / was ever known to be.

She was in beauty matchless, / full mickle was her might;
Her love the prize of contest, / she hurled the shaft with valiant knight.

327
The stone she threw far distant, / wide sprang thereafter too.
Who turned to her his fancy / with intent to woo,
Three times perforce must vanquish / the lady of high degree;
Failed he in but one trial, / forfeited his head had he.

328
This same the lusty princess / times untold had done.
When to a warrior gallant / beside the Rhine 'twas known,
He thought to take unto him / the noble maid for wife:
Thereby must heroes many / since that moment lose their life.

329
Then spake of Rhine the master: / "I'll down unto the sea
Unto Brunhild journey, / fare as 'twill with me.
For her unmeasured beauty / I'll gladly risk my life,
Ready eke to lose it, / if she may not be my wife."

330
"I counsel thee against it," / spake then Siegfried.
"So terrible in contest / the queen is indeed,
Who for her love is suitor / his zeal must dearly pay.
So shalt thou from the journey / truly be content to stay."

331
"So will I give thee counsel," / outspake Hagen there,
"That thou beg of Siegfried / with thee to bear
The perils that await thee: / that is now my rede,
To him is known so fully / what with Brunhild will be thy need."

332
He spake: "And wilt thou help me, / noble Siegfried,
To win the lovely maiden? / Do what now I plead;
And if in all her beauty / she be my wedded wife,
To meet thy fullest wishes / honor will I pledge and life."

333
Thereto answered Siegfried, / the royal Siegmund's son:
"Giv'st thou me thy sister, / so shall thy will be done,
—Kriemhild the noble princess, / in beauty all before.
For toils that I encounter / none other meed I ask thee more."

334
"That pledge I," spake then Gunther, / "Siegfried, in thy hand.
And comes the lovely Brunhild / thither to this land,
Thereunto thee my sister / for wife I'll truly give,
That with the lovely maiden / thou may'st ever joyful live."

335
Oaths the knight full noble / upon the compact swore,
Whereby to them came troubles / and dangers all the more,
Ere they the royal lady / brought unto the Rhine.
Still should the warriors valiant / in sorest need and sorrow pine.

336
With him carried Siegfried / that same mantle then,
The which with mickle trouble / had won the hero keen
From a dwarf in struggle, / Alberich by name.
They dressed them for the journey, / the valiant thanes of lofty fame.

337
And when the doughty Siegfried / the sightless mantle wore,
Had he within it / of strength as good a store
As other men a dozen / in himself alone.
The full stately princess / anon by cunning art he won.

338
Eke had that same mantle / such wondrous properties
That any man whatever / might work whate'er he please
When once he had it on him, / yet none could see or tell.
'Twas so that he won Brunhild; / whereby him evil since befell.

339
"Ere we begin our journey, / Siegfried, tell to me,
That we with fullest honor / come unto the sea,
Shall we lead warriors with us / down to Brunhild's land?
Thanes a thirty thousand / straightway shall be called to hand."

340
"Men bring we ne'er so many," / answered Siegfried then.
"So terrible in custom / ever is the queen,
That all would death encounter / from her angry mood.
I'll give thee better counsel, / thane in valor keen and good.

341
"Like as knights-errant journey / down the Rhine shall we.
Those now will I name thee / who with us shall be;
But four in all the company / seaward shall we fare:
Thus shall we woo the lady, / what fortune later be our share.

342
"Myself one of the company, / a second thou shalt be,
Hagen be the third one / —so fare we happily;
The fourth let it be Dankwart, / warrior full keen.
Never thousand others / dare in fight withstand us then."

343
"The tale I would know gladly," / the king then further said,
"Ere we have parted thither / —of that were I full glad—

What should we of apparel, / that would befit us well,
Wear in Brunhild's presence: / that shalt thou now to Gunther tell."

344
"Weeds the very finest / that ever might be found
They wear in every season / in Brunhild's land:
So shall we rich apparel / before the lady wear,
That we have not dishonor / where men the tale hereafter hear."

345
Then spake he to the other: / "Myself will go unto
My own loving mother, / if I from her may sue
That her fair tendant maidens / help that we be arrayed
As we may go in honor / before the high majestic maid."

346
Then spake of Tronje Hagen / with noble courtliness:
"Why wilt thou of thy mother / beg such services?
Only let thy sister / hear our mind and mood:
So shall for this our journey / her good service be bestowed."

347
Then sent he to his sister / that he her would see,
And with him also Siegfried. / Ere that such might be,
Herself had there the fair one / in rich apparel clad.
Sooth to tell, the visit / but little did displease the maid.

348
Then also were her women / decked as for them was meet.
The princes both were coming: / she rose from off her seat,
As doth a high-born lady / when that she did perceive,
And went the guest full noble / and eke her brother to receive.

349
"Welcome be my brother / and his companion too.
I'd know the story gladly," / spake the maiden so,
"What ye now are seeking / that ye are come to me:
I pray you straightway tell me / how 't with you valiants twain may be."

350
Then spake the royal Gunther: / "Lady, thou shall hear:
Spite of lofty spirits / have we yet a care.
To woo a maid we travel / afar to lands unknown;
We should against the journey / have rich apparel for our own."

351
"Seat thee now, dear brother," / spake the princess fair;
"Let me hear the story, / who the ladies are
That ye will seek as suitors / in stranger princes' land."
Both good knights the lady / took in greeting by the hand.

352
With the twain then went she / where she herself had sat,
To couches rich and costly, / in sooth believe ye that,
Wrought in design full cunning / of gold embroidery.
And with these fair ladies / did pass the time right pleasantly.

353
Many tender glances / and looks full many a one
Fondly knight and lady / each other cast upon.
Within his heart he bore her, / she was as his own life.
Anon the fairest Kriemhild / was the doughty Siegfried's wife.

354
Then spake the mighty monarch: / "Full loving sister mine,
This may we ne'er accomplish / without help of thine.
Unto Brunhild's country / as suitor now we fare:
'Tis fitting that 'fore ladies / we do rich apparel wear."

355
Then spake the royal maiden: / "Brother dear to me,
In whatsoever manner / my help may given be,
Of that I well assure you, / ready thereto am I.
To Kriemhild 'twere a sorrow / if any should the same deny.

356
"Of me, O noble brother, / thou shalt not ask in vain:
Command in courteous manner / and I will serve thee fain.
Whatever be thy pleasure, / for that I'll lend my aid
And willingly I'll do it," / spake the fair and winsome maid.

357
"It is our wish, dear sister, / apparel good to wear;
That shall now directing / the royal hand prepare;
And let thy maids see to it / that all is done aright,
For we from this same journey / turn not aside for word of wight."

358
Spake thereupon the maiden: / "Now mark ye what I say:
Myself have silks in plenty; / now send us rich supply
Of stones borne on bucklers, / so vesture we'll prepare."
To do it royal Gunther / and Siegfried both right ready were.

359
"And who are your companions," / further questioned she,
"Who with you apparelled / now for court shall be?"
"I it is and Siegfried, / and of my men are two,
Dankwart and Hagen, / who with us to court shall go.

360
"Now rightly what we tell thee, / mark, O sister dear:
'Tis that we four companions / for four days may wear

Thrice daily change of raiment / so wrought with skilful hand
That we without dishonor / may take our leave of Brunhild's land."
361
After fair leave-taking / the knights departed so.
Then of her attendants / thirty maids to go
Forth from her apartments / Kriemhild the princess bade,
Of those that greatest cunning / in such skilful working had.
362
ks that were of Araby / white as the snow in sheen,
And from the land of Zazamank / like unto grass so green,
With stones of price they broidered; / that made apparel rare.
Herself she cut them, Kriemhild / the royal maiden debonair.
363
Fur linings fashioned fairly / from dwellers in the sea
Beheld by people rarely, / the best that e'er might be,
With silken stuffs they covered / for the knights to wear.
Now shall ye of the shining / weeds full many a wonder hear.
364
From land of far Morocco / and eke from Libya
Of silks the very finest / that ever mortal saw
With any monarch's kindred, / they had a goodly store.
Well showed the Lady Kriemhild / that unto them good will she bore.
365
Since they unto the journey / had wished that so it be,
Skins of costly ermine / used they lavishly,
Whereon were silken pieces / black as coal inlaid.
To-day were any nobles / in robes so fashioned well arrayed.
366
From the gold of Araby / many a stone there shone.
The women long were busy / before the work was done;
But all the robes were finished / ere seven weeks did pass,
When also trusty armor / for the warriors ready was.
367
When they at length were ready / adown the Rhine to fare,
A ship lay waiting for them / strong built with mickle care,
Which should bear them safely / far down unto the sea.
The maidens rich in beauty / plied their work laboriously.
368
Then 'twas told the warriors / for them was ready there
The finely wrought apparel / that they were to wear;
Just as they had wished it, / so it had been made;
After that the heroes / there by the Rhine no longer stayed.

369

To the knights departing / went soon a messenger:
Would they come in person / to view their new attire,
If it had been fitted / short and long aright.
'Twas found of proper measure, / and thanked those ladies fair each knight.

370

And all who there beheld them / they must needs confess
That in the world they never / had gazed on fairer dress:
At court to wear th' apparel / did therefore please them well.
Of warriors better furnished / never could a mortal tell.

371

Thanks oft-times repeated / were there not forgot.
Leave of parting from them / the noble knights then sought:
Like thanes of noble bearing / they went in courteous wise.
Then dim and wet with weeping / grew thereat two shining eyes.

372

She spake: "O dearest brother, / still here thou mightest stay,
And woo another woman— / that were the better way—
Where so sore endangered / stood not thus thy life.
Here nearer canst thou find thee / equally a high-born wife."

373

I ween their hearts did tell them / what later came to pass.
They wept there all together, / whatever spoken was.
The gold upon their bosoms / was sullied 'neath the tears
That from their eyes in plenty / fell adown amid their fears.

374

She spake: "O noble Siegfried, / to thee commended be
Upon thy truth and goodness / the brother dear to me,
That he come unscathed / home from Brunhild's land."
That plighted the full valiant / knight in Lady Kriemhild's hand.

375

The mighty thane gave answer: / "If I my life retain,
Then shall thy cares, good Lady, / all have been in vain.
All safe I'll bring him hither / again unto the Rhine,
Be that to thee full sicker." / To him did the fair maid incline.

376

Their shields of golden color / were borne unto the strand,
And all their trusty armor / was ready brought to hand.
They bade their horses bring them: / they would at last depart.
—Thereat did fairest women / weep with sad foreboding heart.

377

Down from lofty casement / looked many a winsome maid,

As ship and sail together / by stirring breeze were swayed.
Upon the Rhine they found them, / the warriors full of pride.
Then outspake King Gunther: / "Who now is here the ship to guide?"
378
"That will I," spake Siegfried; / "I can upon the flood
Lead you on in safety, / that know ye, heroes good;
For all the water highways / are known right well to me."
With joy they then departed / from the land of Burgundy.
379
A mighty pole then grasped he, / Siegfried the doughty man,
And the ship from shore / forth to shove began.
Gunther the fearless also / himself took oar in hand.
The knights thus brave and worthy / took departure from the land.
380
They carried rich provisions, / thereto the best of wine
That might in any quarter / be found about the Rhine.
Their chargers stood in comfort / and rested by the way:
The ship it moved so lightly / that naught of injury had they.
381
Stretched before the breezes / were the great sail-ropes tight,
And twenty miles they journeyed / ere did come the night,
By fair breezes favored / down toward the sea.
Their toil repaid thereafter / the dauntless knights full grievously.
382
Upon the twelfth morning, / as we in story hear,
Had they by the breezes / thence been carried far,
Unto Castle Isenstein / and Brunhild's country:
That to Siegfried only / was known of all the company.
383
As soon as saw King Gunther / so many towers rise
And eke the boundless marches / stretch before his eyes,
He spake: "Tell me, friend Siegfried, / is it known to thee
Whose they are, the castles / and the majestic broad country?"
384
Thereto gave answer Siegfried: / "That well to me is known:
Brunhild for their mistress / do land and people own
And Isenstein's firm towers, / as ye have heard me say.
Ladies fair a many / shall ye here behold to-day.
385
"And I will give you counsel: / be it well understood
That all your words must tally / —so methinks 'twere good.
If ere to-day is over / our presence she command,
Must we leave pride behind us, / as before Brunhild we stand.

386
"When we the lovely lady / 'mid her retainers see,
Then shall ye, good companions, / in all your speech agree
That Gunther is my master / and I his serving-man:
'Tis thus that all he hopeth / shall we in the end attain."
387
To do as he had bidden / consented straight each one,
And spite of proudest spirit / they left it not undone.
All that he wished they promised, / and good it proved to be
When anon King Gunther / the fair Brunhild came to see.
388
"Not all to meet thy wishes / do I such service swear,
But most 'tis for thy sister, / Kriemhild the maiden fair;
Just as my soul unto me / she is my very life,
And fain would I deserve it / that she in truth become my wife."

SEVENTH ADVENTURE: How Gunther won Brunhild

389
The while they thus did parley / their ship did forward glide
So near unto the castle / that soon the king espied
Aloft within the casements / many a maiden fair to see.
That all to him were strangers / thought King Gunther mournfully.
390
He asked then of Siegfried, / who bare him company:
"Know'st thou aught of the maidens, / who the same may be,
Gazing yonder downward / upon us on the tide?
Howe'er is named their master, / minded are they high in pride."
391
Then spake the valiant Siegfried: / "Now thither shalt thou spy
Unseen among the ladies, / then not to me deny
Which, wert thou free in choosing, / thou'dst take to be thy queen."
"That will I do," then answered / Gunther the valiant knight and keen.
392
"I see there one among them / by yonder casement stand,
Clad in snow-white raiment: / 'tis she my eyes demand,
So buxom she in stature, / so fair she is to see.
An I were free in choosing, / she it is my wife must be."
393
"Full well now in choosing / thine eyes have guided thee:
It is the stately Brunhild / the maiden fair to see,

That doth now unto her / thy heart and soul compel."
All the maiden's bearing / pleased the royal Gunther well.

394

But soon the queen commanded / from casement all to go
Of those her beauteous maidens: / they should not stand there so
To be gazed at by the strangers. / They must obey her word.
What were the ladies doing, / of that moreover have we heard.

395

Unto the noble strangers / their beauty they would show,
A thing which lovely women / are ever wont to do.
Unto the narrow casements / came they crowding on,
When they spied the strangers: / that they might also see, 'twas done.

396

But four the strangers numbered, / who came unto that land.
Siegfried the doughty / the king's steed led in hand:
They saw it from the casements, / many a lovely maid,
And saw the willing service / unto royal Gunther paid.

397

Then held he by the bridle / for him his gallant steed,
A good and fair-formed charger, / strong and of noble breed,
Until the royal Gunther / into the saddle sprung.
Thus did serve him Siegfried: / a service all forgot ere long.

398

Then his own steed he also / led forth upon the shore.
Such menial service had he / full seldom done before,
That he should hold the stirrup / for monarch whomsoe'er.
Down gazing from the casements / beheld it ladies high and fair.

399

At every point according, / the heroes well bedight
—Their dress and eke their chargers / of color snowy white—
Were like unto each other, / and well-wrought shield each one
Of the good knights bore with him, / that brightly glimmered in the sun.

400

Jewelled well was saddle / and narrow martingale
As they rode so stately / in front of Brunhild's Hall,
And thereon bells were hanging / of red gold shining bright.
So came they to that country, / as fitting was for men of might,

401

With spears all newly polished, / with swords, well-made that were
And by the stately heroes / hung down unto the spur:
Such bore the valiant riders / of broad and cutting blade.
The noble show did witness / Brunhild the full stately maid.

402

With him came then Dankwart / and Hagen, doughty thane.
The story further telleth / how that the heroes twain
Of color black as raven / rich attire wore,
And each a broad and mighty / shield of rich adornment bore.

403

Rich stones from India's country / every eye could see,
Impending on their tunics, / sparkle full brilliantly.
Their vessel by the river / they left without a guard,
As thus the valiant heroes / rode undaunted castleward.

404

Six and fourscore towers / without they saw rise tall,
Three spacious palaces / and moulded well a hall
All wrought of precious marble / green as blade of grass,
Wherein the royal Brunhild / with company of fair ladies was.

405

The castle doors unbolted / were flung open wide
As out toward them / the men of Brunhild hied
And received the strangers / into their Lady's land.
Their steeds they bade take over, / and also shield from out the hand.

406

Then spake a man-in-waiting: / "Give o'er the sword each thane,
And eke the shining armor."— / "Good friend, thou ask'st in vain,"
Spake of Tronje Hagen; / "the same we'd rather wear."
Then gan straightway Siegfried / the country's custom to declare.

407

"'Tis wont within this castle, / —of that be now aware—
That never any stranger / weapons here shall bear.
Now let them hence be carried: / well dost thou as I say."
In this did full unwilling / Hagen, Gunther's man, obey.

408

They bade the strangers welcome / with drink and fitting rest.
Soon might you see on all sides / full many knights the best
In princely weeds apparelled / to their reception go:
Yet did they mickle gazing / who would the keen new-comers know.

409

Then unto Lady Brunhild / the tidings strange were brought
How that unknown warriors / now her land had sought,
In stately apparel / come sailing o'er the sea.
The maiden fair and stately / gave question how the same might be.

410

"Now shall ye straight inform me," / spake she presently,
"Who so unfamiliar / these warrior knights may be,

That within my castle / thus so lordly stand,
And for whose sake the heroes / have hither journeyed to my land."

411

Then spake to her a servant: / "Lady, I well can say
Of them I've ne'er seen any / before this present day:
Be it not that one among them / is like unto Siegfried.
Him give a goodly welcome: / so is to thee my loyal rede.

412

"The next of the companions / he is a worthy knight:
If that were in his power / he well were king of might
O'er wide domains of princes, / the which might reach his hand.
Now see him by the others / so right majestically stand.

413

"The third of the companions, / that he's a man of spleen,
—Withal of fair-formed body, / know thou, stately Queen,—
Do tell his rapid glances / that dart so free from him.
He is in all his thinking / a man, I ween, of mood full grim.

414

"The youngest one among them / he is a worthy knight:
As modest as a maiden, / I see the thane of might
Goodly in his bearing / standing so fair to see,
We all might fear if any / affront to him should offered be.

415

"How blithe soe'er his manner, / how fair soe'er is he,
Well could he cause of sorrow / to stately woman be,
If he gan show his anger. / In him may well be seen
He is in knightly virtues / a thane of valor bold and keen."

416

Then spake the queen in answer: / "Bring now my robes to hand.
And is the mighty Siegfried / come unto this land,
For love of me brought thither, / he pays it with his life.
I fear him not so sorely / that I e'er become his wife."

417

So was fair Brunhild / straightway well arrayed.
Then went with her thither / full many a beauteous maid,
A hundred good or over, / bedight right merrily.
The full beauteous maidens / would those stranger warriors see.

418

And with them went the warriors / there of Isenland,
The knights attending Brunhild, / who bore sword in hand,
Five hundred men or over. / Scarce heart the strangers kept
As those knights brave and seemly / down from out the saddle leapt.

419
When the royal lady / Siegfried espied,
Now mote ye willing listen / what there the maiden said.
"Welcome be thou, Siegfried, / hither unto this land.
What meaneth this thy journey, / gladly might I understand."
420
"Full mickle do I thank thee, / my Lady, high Brunhild,
That thou art pleased to greet me, / noble Princess mild,
Before this knight so noble, / who stands before me here:
For he is my master, / whom first to honor fitting were.
421
"Born is he of Rhineland: / what need I say more?
For thee 'tis highest favor / that we do hither fare.
Thee will he gladly marry, / an bring that whatsoe'er.
Betimes shalt thou bethink thee: / my master will thee never spare.
422
"For his name is Gunther / and he a mighty king.
If he thy love hath won him, / more wants he not a thing.
In sooth the king so noble / hath bade me hither fare:
And gladly had I left it, / might I to thwart his wishes dare."
423
She spake: "Is he thy master / and thou his vassal art,
Some games to him I offer, / and dare he there take part,
And comes he forth the victor, / so am I then his wife:
And be it I that conquer, / then shall ye forfeit each his life."
424
Then spake of Tronje Hagen: / "Lady, let us see
Thy games so fraught with peril. / Before should yield to thee
Gunther my master, / that well were something rare.
He trows he yet is able / to win a maid so passing fair."
425
"Then shall ye try stone-putting / and follow up the cast,
And the spear hurl with me. / Do ye naught here in haste.
For well may ye pay forfeit / with honor eke and life:
Bethink ye thus full calmly," / spake she whom Gunther would for wife.
426
Siegfried the valiant / stepped unto the king,
And bade him speak out freely / his thoughts upon this thing
Unto the queen so wayward, / he might have fearless heart.
"For to well protect thee / from her do I know an art."
427
Then spake the royal Gunther: / "Now offer, stately Queen,

What play soe'er thou mayest. / And harder had it been,
Yet would I all have ventured / for all thy beauty's sake.
My head I'll willing forfeit / or thyself my wife I'll make."

428

When therefore the Queen Brunhild / heard how the matter stood
The play she begged to hasten, / as indeed she should.
She bade her servants fetch her / therefor apparel trim,
A mail-coat ruddy golden / and shield well wrought from boss to rim.

429

A battle-tunic silken / the maid upon her drew,
That in ne'er a contest / weapon piercéd through,
Of skins from land of Libya, / and structure rare and fine;
And brilliant bands embroidered / might you see upon it shine.

430

Meanwhile were the strangers / jibed with many a threat;
Dankwart and Hagen, / their hearts began to beat.
How here the king should prosper / were they of doubtful mood,
Thinking, "This our journey / shall bring us wanderers naught of good."

431

le did also Siegfried / the thane beyond compare,
Before 'twas marked by any, / unto the ship repair,
Where he found his sightless mantle[13] / that did hidden lie,
And slipped into 't full deftly: / so was he veiled from every eye.

432

Thither back he hied him / and found great company
About the queen who ordered / what the high play should be.
There went he all in secret; / so cunningly 'twas done,
Of all around were standing / perceived him never any one.

433

The ring it was appointed / wherein the play should be
'Fore many a keen warrior / who the same should see.
More than seven hundred / were seen their weapons bear,
That whoso were the victor / they might sure the same declare.

434

Thither was come Brunhild; / all arméd she did stand
Like as she were to combat / for many a royal land;
Upon her silken tunic / were gold bars many a one,
And glowing 'mid the armor / her flesh of winsome color shone.

435

Then followed her attendants / and with them thither brought
At once a shield full stately, / of pure red gold 'twas wrought,

13 See strophe 97, note.

With steel-hard bands for facings, / full mickle 'twas and broad,
Wherewith in the contest / would guard herself the lovely maid.

436
To hold the shield securely / a well-wrought band there was,
Whereon lay precious jewels / green as blade of grass.
Full many a ray their lustre / shot round against the gold.
He were a man full valiant / whom this high dame should worthy hold.

437
The shield was 'neath the boss-point, / as to us is said,
Good three spans in thickness, / which should bear the maid.
Of steel 'twas wrought so richly / and had of gold such share,
That chamberlain and fellows / three the same scarce could bear.

438
When the doughty Hagen / the shield saw thither brought,
Spake the knight of Tronje, / and savage was his thought:
"Where art thou now, King Gunther? / Shall we thus lose our life!
Whom here thou seekst for lover, / she is the very Devil's wife."

439
List more of her apparel; / she had a goodly store.
Of silk of Azagang / a tunic made she wore,
All bedight full richly; / amid its color shone
Forth from the queen it covered, / full many a sparkling precious stone.

440
Then brought they for the lady, / large and heavy there,
As she was wont to hurl it, / a sharply-pointed spear;
Strong and massive was it, / huge and broad as well,
And at both its edges / it cut with devastation fell.

441
To know the spear was heavy / list ye wonders more:
Three spears of common measure / 'twould make, and something o'er.
Of Brunhild's attendants / three scarce the same could bear.
The heart of noble Gunther / thereat began to fill with fear.

442
Within his soul he thought him: / "What pickle am I in?
Of hell the very Devil, / how might he save his skin?
Might I at home in Burgundy / safe and living be,
Should she for many a season / from proffered love of mine be free."

443
Then spake Hagen's brother / the valiant Dankwart:
"In truth this royal journey / doth sorely grieve my heart.
We passed for good knights one time: / what caitiff's death, if we
Here in far-off country / a woman's game are doomed to be!

444

"It rueth me full sorely / that I came to this land.
And had my brother Hagen / his good sword in hand,
And had I mine to help him, / a bit more gently then,
A little tame of spirit, / might show themselves all Brunhild's men.

445

"And know it of a certain / to lord it thus they'd cease;
E'en though oaths a thousand / I'd sworn to keep the peace,
Before that I'd see perish / my dear lord shamefully,
Amid the souls departed / this fair maid herself should be."

446

"Well should we unhampered / quit at last this land,"
Spake his brother Hagen, / "did we in armor stand,
Such as we need for battle, / and bore we broadswords good:
'Twould be a little softened, / this doughty lady's haughty mood."

447

Well heard the noble maiden / what the warriors spoke.
Back athwart her shoulder / she sent a smiling look:
"Now thinks he him so valiant, / so let them arméd stand;
Their full keen-edged broadswords / give the warriors each in hand."

448

When they their swords received, / as the maiden said,
The full valiant Dankwart / with joy his face grew red.
"Now play they what them pleaseth," / cried the warrior brave;
"Gunther is yet a freeman, / since now in hand good swords we have."

449

The royal Brunhild's prowess / with terror was it shown.
Into the ring they bore her / in sooth a ponderous stone,
Great and all unwieldy, / huge it was and round:
And scarce good knights a dozen / together raised it from the ground.

450

To put this was her custom / after trial with the spear.
Thereat the men of Burgundy / began to quake with fear.
"Alack! Alack!" quoth Hagen, / "what seeks the king for bride?
Beneath in hell 'twere better / the Devil had her by his side!"

451

On her white arms the flowing / sleeves she backward flung,
Then with grasp of power / the shield in hand she swung,
And spear poised high above her. / So did the contest start.
Gunther and Siegfried / saw Brunhild's ire with falling heart.

452

And were it not that Siegfried / a ready help did bring,
Surely then had perished / beneath her hand the king.

There went he unperceived / and the king's hand did touch.
Gunther at his cunning / artifice was troubled much.

453
"What is that hath touched me?" / thought the monarch keen.
Then gazed he all around him: / none was there to be seen.
A voice spake: "Siegfried is it, / a friend that holds thee dear.
Before this royal maiden / shall thy heart be free from fear.

454
"Thy shield in hand now give me / and leave it me to bear,
And do thou rightly mark thee / what thou now shalt hear.
Now make thyself the motions, / —the power leave to me."
When he did know him rightly, / the monarch's heart was filled with glee.

455
"Now secret keep my cunning, / let none e'er know the same:
Then shall the royal maiden / here find but little game
Of glory to win from thee, / as most to her is dear.
Behold now how the lady / stands before thee void of fear."

456
The spear the stately maiden / with might and main did wield,
And huge and broad she hurled it / upon the new-made shield,
That on his arm did carry / the son of Siegelind;
From the steel the sparks flew hissing / as if were blowing fierce the wind.

457
The mighty spear sharp-pointed / full through the shield did crash,
That ye from off the mail-rings / might see the lightning flash.
Beneath its force they stumbled, / did both those men of might;
But for the sightless mantle / they both were killed there outright.

458
From mouth of the full doughty / Siegfried burst the blood.
Full soon he yet recovered; / then seized the warrior good
The spear that from her strong arm / thus his shield had rent,
And back with force as came it / the hand of doughty Siegfried sent.

459
He thought: "To pierce the maiden / were but small glory earned,"
And so the spear's sharp edges / backward pointing turned;
Against her mail-clad body / he made the shaft to bound,
And with such might he sent it / full loud her armor did resound.

460
The sparks as if in stormwind / from mail-rings flew around.
So mightily did hurl it / the son of Siegmund
That she with all her power / could not the shaft withstand.

In sooth it ne'er was speeded / so swiftly by King Gunther's hand.
461
But to her feet full sudden / had sprung Brunhild fair.
"A shot, O noble Gunther, / befitting hero rare."
She weened himself had done it, / and all unaided he,
Nor wot she one far mightier / was thither come so secretly.
462
Then did she go full sudden, / wrathful was her mood,
A stone full high she heaved / the noble maiden good,
And the same far from her / with might and main she swung:
Her armor's mail-rings jingled / as she herself thereafter sprung.
463
The stone, when it had fallen, / lay fathoms twelve from there,
And yet did spring beyond it / herself the maiden fair.
Then where the stone was lying / thither Siegfried went:
Gunther feigned to move it, / but by another arm 'twas sent.
464
A valiant man was Siegfried / full powerful and tall.
The stone then cast he farther, / and farther sprang withal.
From those his arts so cunning / had he of strength such store
That as he leaped he likewise / the weight of royal Gunther bore.
465
And when the leap was ended / and fallen was the stone,
Then saw they ne'er another / but Gunther alone.
Brunhild the fair maiden, / red grew she in wrath:
Siegfried yet had warded / from royal Gunther surest death.
466
Unto her attendants / she spake in loud command,
When she saw 'cross the circle / the king unvanquished stand.
"Come hither quick, my kinsmen, / and ye that wait on me;
Henceforth unto Gunther / shall all be pledged faithfully."
467
Then laid the knights full valiant / their swords from out the hand;
At feet 'fore mighty Gunther / from Burgundian land
Offered himself in service / full many a valiant knight.
They weened that he had conquered / in trial by his proper might.
468
He gave her loving greeting, / right courteous was he.
Then by the hand she took him, / the maiden praiseworthy,
In pledge that all around him / was his to have and hold.
Whereat rejoiced Hagen / the warrior valorous and bold.
469
Into the spacious palace / with her thence to go

Bade she the noble monarch. / When they had done so,
Then still greater honors / unto the knight were shown.
Dankwart and Hagen, / right willingly they saw it done.

470
Siegfried the valiant, / by no means was he slow,
His sightless mantle did he / away in safety stow.
Then went he again thither / where many a lady sat.
He spake unto the monarch— / full cunningly was done all that:

471
"Why bidest thus, my master? / Wilt not the play begin,
To which so oft hath challenged / thee the noble queen?
Let us soon have example / what may the trial be."
As knew he naught about it, / did the knight thus cunningly.

472
Then spake the queen unto him: / "How hath this ever been,
That of the play, Sir Siegfried, / nothing thou hast seen,
Wherein hath been the victor / Gunther with mighty hand?"
Thereto gave answer Hagen / a grim knight of Burgundian land.

473
Spake he: "There dost thou, Lady, / think ill without a cause:
By the ship down yonder / the noble Siegfried was,
The while the lord of Rhineland / in play did vanquish thee:
Thus knows he nothing of it," / spake Gunther's warrior courteously.

474
"A joy to me these tidings," / the doughty Siegfried spoke,
"That so thy haughty spirit / is brought beneath the yoke,
And that yet one there liveth / master to be of thine.
Now shalt thou, noble maiden, / us follow thither to the Rhine."

475
Then spake the maiden shapely: / "It may not yet be so.
All my men and kindred / first the same must know.
In sooth not all so lightly / can I quit my home.
First must I bid my trusty / warriors that they hither come."

476
Then bade she messengers / quickly forth to ride,
And summoned in her kindred / and men from every side.
Without delay she prayed them / to come to Isenstein,
And bade them all be given / fit apparel rare and fine.

477
Then might ye see daily / 'twixt morn and eventide
Unto Brunhild's castle / many a knight to ride.
"God wot, God wot," quoth Hagen, / "we do an evil thing,
To tarry here while Brunhild / doth thus her men together bring.

478

"If now into this country / their good men they've brought
—What thing the queen intendeth / thereof know we naught:
Belike her wrath ariseth, / and we are men forlorn—
Then to be our ruin / were the noble maiden born."

479

Then spake the doughty Siegfried: / "That matter leave to me.
Whereof thou now art fearful, / I'll never let it be.
Ready help I'll bring thee / hither unto this land,
Knights of whom thou wotst not / till now I'll bring, a chosen band.

480

"Of me shalt thou ask not: / from hence will I fare.
May God of thy good honor / meanwhile have a care.
I come again right quickly / with a thousand men for thee,
The very best of warriors / hitherto are known to me."

481

"Then tarry not unduly," / thus the monarch said.
"Glad we are full fairly / of this thy timely aid."
He spake: "Till I come to thee / full short shall be my stay.
That thou thyself hast sent me / shalt thou unto Brunhild say."

EIGHTH ADVENTURE: How Siegfried fared to his Knights, the Nibelungen

482

Thence went then Siegfried / out through the castle door
In his sightless mantle / to a boat upon the shore.
As Siegmund's son doth board it / him no mortal sees;
And quickly off he steers it / as were it wafted by the breeze.

483

No one saw the boatman, / yet rapid was the flight
Of the boat forth speeding / driven by Siegfried's might.
They weened that did speed it / a swiftly blowing wind:
No, 'twas Siegfried sped it, / the son of fairest Siegelind.

484

In that one day-time / and the following night
Came he to a country / by dint of mickle might,
Long miles a hundred distant, / and something more than this:
The Nibelungen were its people / where the mighty hoard was his.

485

Alone did fare the hero / unto an island vast
Whereon the boat full quickly / the gallant knight made fast.

Of a castle then bethought him / high upon a hill,
And there a lodging sought him, / as wayworn men are wont to still.
486
Then came he to the portals / that locked before him stood.
They guarded well their honor / as people ever should.
At the door he gan a-knocking, / for all unknown was he.
But full well 'twas guarded, / and within it he did see
487
A giant who the castle / did guard with watchful eye,
And near him did at all times / his good weapons lie.
Quoth he: "Who now that knocketh / at the door in such strange wise?"
Without the valiant Siegfried / did cunningly his voice disguise.
488
He spake: "A bold knight-errant / am I; unlock the gate.
Else will I from without here / disturbance rare create
For all who'd fain lie quiet / and their rest would take."
Wrathful grew the Porter / as in this wise Siegfried spake.
489
Now did the giant valorous / his good armor don,
And placed on head his helmet; / then the full doughty man
His shield up-snatched quickly / and gate wide open swung.
How sore was he enraged / as himself upon Siegfried he flung!
490
'How dared he thus awaken / brave knights within the hall?'
The blows in rapid showers / from his hand did fall.
Thereat the noble stranger / began himself to shield.
For so a club of iron / the Porter's mighty arm did wield,
491
That splinters flew from buckler, / and Siegfried stood aghast
From fear that this same hour / was doomed to be his last,
So mightily the Porter's / blows about him fell.
To find such faithful warder / did please his master Siegfried well.
492
So fiercely did they struggle / that castle far within
And hall where slept the Nibelungen / echoed back the din.
But Siegfried pressed the Porter / and soon he had him bound.
In all the land of Nibelungen / the story soon was bruited round.
493
When the grim sound of fighting / afar the place had filled,
Alberich did hear it, / a Dwarf full brave and wild.
He donned his armor deftly, / and running thither found
This so noble stranger / where he the doughty Porter bound.

494
Alberich was full wrathy, / thereto a man of power.
Coat of mail and helmet / he on his body wore,
And in his hand a heavy / scourge of gold he swung.
Where was fighting Siegfried, / thither in mickle haste he sprung.

495
Seven knobs thick and heavy / on the club's end were seen,
Wherewith the shield that guarded / the knight that was so keen
He battered with such vigor / that pieces from it brake.
Lest he his life should forfeit / the noble stranger gan to quake.

496
The shield that all was battered / from his hand he flung;
And into sheath, too, thrust he / his sword so good and long.
For his trusty chamberlain / he did not wish to slay,
And in such case he could not / grant his anger fullest sway.

497
With but his hands so mighty / at Alberich he ran.
By the beard then seized he / the gray and aged man,
And in such manner pulled it / that he full loud did roar.
The youthful hero's conduct / Alberich did trouble sore.

498
Loud cried the valiant steward: / "Have mercy now on me.
And might I other's vassal / than one good hero's be,
To whom to be good subject / I an oath did take,
Until my death I'd serve thee." / Thus the man of cunning spake.

499
Alberich then bound he / as the giant before.
The mighty arm of Siegfried / did trouble him full sore.
The Dwarf began to question: / "Thy name, what may it be?"
Quoth he: "My name is Siegfried; / I weened I well were known to thee."

500
"I joy to hear such tidings," / Dwarf Alberich replied.
"Well now have I found thee / in knightly prowess tried,
And with goodly reason / lord o'er lands to be.
I'll do whate'er thou biddest, / wilt thou only give me free."

501
Then spake his master Siegfried: / "Quickly shalt thou go,
And bring me knights hither, / the best we have to show,
A thousand Nibelungen, / to stand before their lord."
Wherefore thus he wished it, / spake he never yet a word.

502
The giant and Alberich / straightway he unbound.

Then ran Alberich quickly / where the knights he found.
The warriors of Nibelung / he wakened full of fear.
Quoth he: "Be up, ye heroes, / before Siegfried shall ye appear."

503
From their couches sprang they / and ready were full soon,
Clothed well in armor / a thousand warriors boon,
And went where they found standing / Siegfried their lord.
Then was a mickle greeting / courteously in act and word.

504
Candles many were lighted, / and sparkling wine he drank.
That they came so quickly, / therefor he all did thank.
Quoth he: "Now shall ye with me / from hence across the flood."
Thereto he found full ready / the heroes valiant and good.

505
Good thirty hundred warriors / soon had hither pressed,
From whom were then a thousand / taken of the best.
For them were brought their helmets / and what they else did need.
For unto Brunhild's country / would he straightway the warriors lead.

506
He spake: "Ye goodly nobles, / that would I have you hear,
In full costly raiment / shall ye at court appear,
For yonder must there see us / full many a fair lady.
Therefore shall your bodies / dight in good apparel be."

507
Upon a morning early / went they on their way.
What host of brave companions / bore Siegfried company!
Good steeds took they with them / and garments rich to wear,
And did in courtly fashion / unto Brunhild's country fare.

508
As gazed from lofty parapet / women fair to see,
Spake the queen unto them: / "Knows any who they be,
Whom I see yonder sailing / upon the sea afar?
Rich sails their ships do carry, / whiter than snow they are."

509
Then spake the king of Rhineland: / "My good men they are,
That on my journey hither / left I lying near.
I've sent to call them to me: / now are they come, O Queen."
With full great amazing / were the stately strangers seen.

510
There saw they Siegfried / out on the ship's prow stand
Clad in costly raiment, / and with him his good band.
Then spake Queen Brunhild: / "Good monarch, let me know,
Shall I go forth to greet them, / or shall I greetings high forego?"

511

He spake: "Thou shalt to meet them / before the palace go,
So that we see them gladly / they may surely know."
Then did the royal lady / fulfil the king's behest.
Yet Siegfried in the greeting / was not honored with the rest.

512

Lodgings were made ready / and their armor ta'en in hand.
Then was such host of strangers / come into that land,
On all sides they jostled / from the great company.
Then would the knights full valiant / homeward fare to Burgundy.

513

Then spake Queen Brunhild: / "In favor would I hold
Who might now apportion / my silver and my gold
To my guests and the monarch's, / for goodly store I have."
Thereto an answer Dankwart, / Giselher's good warrior, gave:

514

"Full noble royal Lady, / give me the keys to hold.
I trow I'll so divide it," / spake the warrior bold,
"If blame there be about it, / that shall be mine alone."
That he was not a niggard, / beyond a doubt he soon had shown.

515

When now Hagen's brother / the treasure did command,
So many a lavish bounty / dealt out the hero's hand,
Whoso mark did covet, / to him was given such store
That all who once were poor men / might joyous live for evermore.

516

In sooth good pounds a hundred / gave he to each and all.
A host in costly raiment / were seen before the hall,
Who in equal splendor / ne'er before were clad.
When the queen did hear it, / verily her heart was sad.

517

Then spake the royal lady: / "Good King, it little needs,
That now thy chamberlain / of all my stately weeds
Leave no whit remaining, / and squander clean my gold.
Would any yet prevent it, / him would I aye in favor hold.

518

"He deals with hand so lavish, / in sooth doth ween the thane
That death I've hither summoned; / but longer I'll remain.
Eke trow I well to spend all / my sire hath left to me."
Ne'er found queen a chamberlain / of such passing generosity.

519

Then spake of Tronje Hagen: / "Lady, be thou told,
That the king of Rhineland / raiment hath and gold

So plenteous to lavish / that we may well forego
To carry with us homeward / aught that Brunhild can bestow."
520
"No; as high ye hold me," / spake the queen again,
"Let me now have filled / coffers twice times ten
Of gold and silken raiment, / that may deal out my hand,
When that we come over / into royal Gunther's land."
521
Then with precious jewels / the coffers they filled for her.
The while her own chamberlain / must be standing near:
For no whit would she trust it / unto Giselher's man.
Whereat Gunther and Hagen / heartily to laugh began.
522
Then spake the royal lady: / "To whom leave I my lands?
First must they now be given / in charge from out our hands."
Then spake the noble monarch: / "Whomsoe'er it pleaseth thee,
Bid him now come hither, / the same we'll let our Warden be."
523
One of her highest kindred / near by the lady spied,
—He was her mother's brother— / to him thus spake the maid:
"Now be to thee entrusted / the castles and eke the land,
Until that here shall govern / Gunther the king by his own hand."
524
Trusty knights two thousand / from her company
Chose she to journey with her / unto Burgundy,
Beyond those thousand warriors / from Nibelungenland.
They made ready for the journey, / and downward rode unto the strand.
525
Six and eighty ladies / led they thence with her,
Thereto good hundred maidens / that full beauteous were.
They tarried no whit longer, / for they to part were fain.
Of those they left behind them, / O how they all to weep began!
526
In high befitting fashion / quitted she her land:
She kissed of nearest kindred / all who round did stand.
After fair leave-taking / they went upon the sea.
Back to her father's country / came never more that fair lady.
527
Then heard you on the journey / many a kind of play:
Every pleasant pastime / in plenty had they.
Soon had they for their journey / a wind from proper art:
So with full great rejoicing / did they from that land depart.

528
Yet would she on the journey / not be the monarch's spouse:
But was their pleasant pastime / reserved for his own house
At Worms within his castle / at a high festival,
Whither anon full joyous / came they with their warriors all.

NINTH ADVENTURE: How Siegfried was sent to Worms

529
When that they had journeyed / full nine days on their way,
Then spake of Tronje Hagen: / "Now hear what I shall say.
We tarry with the tidings / for Worms upon the Rhine.
At Burgundy already / should now be messengers of thine."

530
Then outspake King Gunther: / "There hast thou spoken true.
And this selfsame journey, / none were so fit thereto
As thyself, friend Hagen. / So do thou now ride on.
This our high court journey, / none else can better make it known."

531
Thereto answered Hagen: / "Poor messenger am I.
Let me be treasure-warden. / Upon the ships I'll stay
Near by the women rather, / their guardian to be,
Till that we bring them safely / into the land of Burgundy.

532
"Now do thou pray Siegfried / that he the message bear,
For he's a knight most fitting / this thing to have in care.
If he decline the journey, / then shalt thou courteously,
For kindness to thy sister, / pray that he not unwilling be."

533
He sent for the good warrior / who came at his command.
He spake: "Since we are nearing / home in my own land,
So should I send a message / to sister dear of mine
And eke unto my mother, / that we are nigh unto the Rhine.

534
"Thereto I pray thee, Siegfried, / now meet my wish aright,"
Spake the noble monarch: / "I'll ever thee requite."
But Siegfried still refused it, / the full valiant man,
Till that King Gunther / sorely to beseech began.

535
He spake: "Now bear the message, / in favor unto me
And eke unto Kriemhild / a maiden fair to see,

That the stately maiden / help me thy service pay."
When had heard it Siegfried, / ready was the knight straightway.

536
"Now what thou wilt, command me: / 'twill not be long delayed.
This thing will I do gladly / for sake of that fair maid.
Why should I aught refuse her, / who all my heart hath won?
What thou for her commandest, / whate'er it be 'twill all be done."

537
"Then say unto my mother, / Ute the queen,
That we on our journey / in joyous mood have been.
Let know likewise my brothers / what fortune us befell.
Eke unto all our kinsmen / shalt thou then merry tidings tell.

538
"Unto my fair sister / shalt thou all confide.
From me bring her fair compliment / and from Brunhild beside,
And eke unto our household / and all my warriors brave.
What my heart e'er did strive for, / how well accomplished it I have!

539
"And say as well to Ortwein / nephew dear of mine
That he do bid make ready / at Worms beside the Rhine.
And all my other kindred, / to them made known shall be,
With Brunhild I am minded / to keep a great festivity.

540
"And say unto my sister, / when that she hath learned
That I am to my country / with many a guest returned,
She shall have care to welcome / my bride in fitting way.
So all my thoughts of Kriemhild / will be her service to repay."

541
Then did Sir Siegfried / straightway in parting greet
High the Lady Brunhild, / as 'twas very meet,
And all her company; / then toward the Rhine rode he.
Nor in this world a better / messenger might ever be.

542
With four and twenty warriors / to Worms did he ride.
When soon it was reported / the king came not beside,
Then did all the household / of direst news have dread:
They feared their royal master / were left in distant country dead.

543
Then sprang they from the saddle, / full high they were of mood.
Full soon before them Giselher / the prince so youthful stood,
And Gernot his brother. / How quickly then spake he,
When he the royal Gunther / saw not in Siegfried's company:

544
"Be thou welcome, Siegfried. / Yet shalt thou tell to me,
Why the king my brother / cometh not with thee.
Brunhild's prowess is it / hath taken him, I ween;
And so this lofty wooing / hath naught but our misfortune been."

545
"Now cease such ill foreboding. / To you and friends hath sent
My royal companion / his good compliment.
Safe and sound I left him; / myself did he command
That I should be his herald / with tidings hither to your land.

546
"Quickly shall ye see to it, / how that it may be,
That I the queen and likewise / your fair sister see.
From Gunther and Brunhild / the message will I tell
That hath now been sent them: / the twain do find them passing well."

547
Then spake the youthful Giselher: / "So shalt thou go to her:
Here dost thou on my sister / a favor high confer.
In sooth she's mickle anxious / how't with my brother be.
The maid doth see thee gladly, / —of that will I be surety."

548
Then outspake Sir Siegfried: / "If serve her aught I can,
That same thing most willing / in truth it shall be done.
Who now will tell the ladies / I would with them confer?"
Then was therein Giselher / the stately knight his messenger.

549
Giselher the valiant / unto his mother kind
And sister spake the tidings / when he the twain did find:
"To us returned is Siegfried, / the hero of Netherlands
Unto the Rhine he cometh / at my brother Gunther's command.

550
"He bringeth us the tidings / how't with the king doth fare.
Now shall ye give permission / that he 'fore you appear.
He'll tell the proper tidings / from Isenland o'er the main."
Yet mickle sad forebodings / did trouble still the ladies twain.

551
They sprang for their attire / and donned it nothing slow.
Then bade they that Siegfried / to court should thither go.
That did he right willing / for he gladly them did see.
Kriemhild the noble maiden / spake to him thus graciously.

552
"Welcome be, Sir Siegfried, / thou knight right praiseworthy.
Yet where may King Gunther / my noble brother be?

It is through Brunhild's prowess, / I ween, he is forlorn.
Alack of me, poor maiden, / that I into this world was born!"
553
The valiant knight then answered: / "Give me news-bringer's meed
Know ye, fairest ladies, / ye weep without a need.
I left him well and happy, / that would I have you know;
They two have sent me hither / to bear the tidings unto you.
554
"And offer thee good service / both his bride and he,
My full noble lady, / in love and loyalty.
Now give over weeping, / for straight will they be here."
They had for many a season / heard not a tale to them so dear.
555
With fold of snow-white garment / then her eyes so bright
Dried she after weeping. / She gan thank the knight
Who of these glad tidings / had been the messenger.
Then was a mickle sorrow / and cause of weeping ta'en from her.
556
She bade the knight be seated, / which he did willingly.
Then spake the lovely maiden: / "It were a joy to me,
Could I the message-bringer / with gold of mine repay.
Thereto art thou too high-born; / I'll serve thee then in other way."
557
"If I alone were ruler," / spake he, "o'er thirty lands,
Yet gifts I'd take right gladly, / came they from thy fair hands."
Then spake the virtuous maiden: / "In truth it shall be so."
Then bade she her chamberlain / forth for message-money go.
558
Four and twenty armlets / with stones of precious kind,
These gave she him for guerdon. / 'Twas not the hero's mind,
That he himself should keep them: / he dealt them all around
Unto her fair attendants / whom he within the chamber found.
559
Of service, too, her mother / did kindly offer make.
"Then have I more to tell you," / the keen warrior spake:
"Of what the king doth beg you, / when comes he to the Rhine.
Wilt thou perform it, lady, / then will he e'er to thee incline.
560
"The noble guests he bringeth, / —this heard I him request,
That ye shall well receive them; / and furthermore his hest,
That ye ride forth to meet him / 'fore Worms upon the strand.
So have ye from the monarch / faithfully his high command."

561
Then spake the lovely maiden: / "Full ready there am I.
If I in aught can serve him, / I'll never that deny.
In all good faith and kindness / shall it e'er be done."
Then deeper grew her color / that from increase of joy she won.

562
Never was royal message / better received before.
The lady sheer had kissed him, / if 'twere a thing to dare.
From those high ladies took he / his leave in courteous wise.
Then did they there in Burgundy / in way as Siegfried did advise.

563
Sindold and Hunold / and Rumold the thane
In truth were nothing idle, / but wrought with might and main
To raise the sitting-places / 'fore Worms upon the strand.
There did the royal Steward / busy 'mid the workers stand.

564
Ortwein and Gere / thought longer not to bide,
But sent unto their kinsmen / forth on every side.
They told of festive meeting / there that was to be;
And deck themselves to meet them / did the maidens fair to see.

565
The walls throughout the palace / were dight full richly all,
Looking unto the strangers; / and King Gunther's hall
Full well with seats and tables / for many a noble guest.
And great was the rejoicing / in prospect of the mighty feast.

566
Then rode from every quarter / hither through the land
The three monarchs' kinsmen, / who there were called to hand,
That they might be in waiting / for those expected there.
Then from enfolding covers / took they store of raiments rare.

567
Some watchers brought the tidings / that Brunhild's followers were
Seen coming riding hither. / Then rose a mickle stir
Among the folk so many / in the land of Burgundy.
Heigh-ho! What valiant warriors / alike on both parts might you see!

568
Then spake the fair Kriemhild: / "Of my good maidens, ye
Who at this reception / shall bear me company,
From out the chests now seek ye / attire the very best.
So shall praise and honor / be ours from many a noble guest."

569
Then came the knights also / and bade bring forth to view
The saddles richly furnished / of ruddy golden hue,

That ladies fair should ride on / at Worms unto the Rhine.
Better horse-equipment / could never artisan design.
570
Heigh-ho! What gold all glancing / from the steeds there shone!
Sparkled from their bridles / full many a precious stone.
Gold-wrought stools for mounting / and shining carpets good
Brought they for the ladies: / joyous were they all of mood.
571
Within the court the heroes / bedight with trappings due
Awaited noble maidens, / as I have told to you.
A narrow band from saddle / went round each horse's breast,
Its beauty none could tell you: / of silk it was the very best.
572
Six and eighty ladies / came in manner meet
Wearing each a wimple. / Kriemhild there to greet
They went, all fair to look on, / in shining garments clad.
Then came eke well apparelled / full many a fair and stately maid.
573
Four and fifty were they / of the land of Burgundy,
And they were eke the noblest / that ever you might see.
Adorned with shining hair-bands / the fair-haired maids came on.
What now the king desired, / that most carefully was done.
574
Made of stuffs all costly, / the best you might desire,
Before the gallant strangers / wore they such rich attire
As well did fit the beauty / of many amid the throng.
He sure had lost his senses, / who could have wished them any wrong.
575
Of sable and of ermine / many a dress was worn.
Arms and hands a many / did they full well adorn
With rings o'er silken dresses / that there did clothe them well.
Of all the ready-making / none might ever fully tell.
576
Full many a well-wrought girdle / in long and costly braid
About the shining garments / by many a hand was laid
On dress of precious ferrandine / of silk from Araby.
And full of high rejoicing / were those maids of high degree.
577
With clasps before her bosom / was many a fair maid
Laced full beauteously. / She might well be sad,
Whose full beaming color / vied not with weeds she wore.
Such a stately company / ne'er possessed a queen before.

578
When now the lovely maidens / attired you might see,
Soon were those beside them / should bear them company,
Of warriors high-hearted / a full mickle band.
And with their shields they carried / full many an ashen shaft in hand.

TENTH ADVENTURE: How Brunhild was received at Worms

579
On yonder side Rhine river / they saw a stately band,
The king and host of strangers, / ride down unto the strand,
And also many a lady / sitting on charger led.
By those who should receive them / was goodly preparation made.

580
Soon they of Isenland / the ship had entered then,
And with them Siegfried's vassals / the Nibelungen men;
They strained unto the shore / with untiring hand
When they beheld the monarch's / friends upon the farther strand.

581
Now list ye eke the story / of the stately queen,
Ute, how at her bidding / ladies fair were seen
Forth coming from the castle / to ride her company.
Then came to know each other / full many a knight and fair lady.

582
The Margrave Gere / but to the castle gate
The bridle held for Kriemhild; / the keen Siegfried did wait
Thenceforward upon her. / She was a beauteous maid.
Well was the knight's good service / by the lady since repaid.

583
Ortwein the valiant / Queen Ute rode beside,
And many a knight full gallant / was stately lady's guide.
At such a high reception, / that may we say, I ween,
Was ne'er such host of ladies / in company together seen.

584
With show of rider's talent / the tilt was carried on,
For might the knights full gallant / naught fitting leave undone,
As passed down to the river / Kriemhild the lady bright.
Then helped was many a lady / fair from charger to alight.

585
The king had then come over / and many a stranger too.
Heigh-ho! What strong shafts splintered / before the ladies flew!

Many a shaft go crashing / heard you there on shield.
Heigh-ho! What din of costly / arms resounded o'er the field.
586
The full lovely maidens / upon the shore did stand,
As Gunther with the strangers / stepped upon the land;
He himself did Brunhild / by the hand lead on.
Then sparkled towards each other / rich dress and many a shining stone.
587
Then went Lady Kriemhild / with fullest courtesy due,
To greet the Lady Brunhild / and her retinue.
And saw ye each the head-band / with fair hand move aside
When they kissed each other: / high courtesy did the ladies guide.
588
Then spake the maiden Kriemhild, / a high-born lady she:
"Unto this our country / shalt thou right welcome be,
To me and to my mother / and each true friend of mine,
That we here have with us." / Then each did unto each incline.
589
Within their arms the ladies / oft-times clasped each other.
Like this fond reception / heard ye of ne'er another,
As when both the ladies / there the bride did greet,
Queen Ute and her daughter; / oft-times they kissed her lips so sweet.
590
When all of Brunhild's ladies / were come upon the strand,
Then was there taken / full fondly by the hand
By the warriors stately / many a fair lady.
Before the Lady Brunhild / the train of fair maids might ye see.
591
Before their greetings ended / a mickle time was gone,
For lips of rosy color / were kissed there, many a one.
Long stood they together, / the royal ladies high,
And so to look upon them / pleased many a noble warrior's eye.
592
Then spied with probing eye, too, / who before did hear
That till then was never / aught beheld so fair,
As those two royal ladies: / they found it was no lie.
In all their person might ye / no manner of deceit espy.
593
Who there could spy fair ladies / and judge of beauty rare,
They praised the wife of Gunther / that she was passing fair;
Yet spake again the wise men / who looked with keener gaze,
They rather would to Kriemhild / before Brunhild award the praise.

594
Then went unto each other / maid and fair lady.
Full many a fair one might ye / in rich adornment see.
There stood rich tents a many, / silken great and small,
Wherewith in every quarter / 'fore Worms the field was covered all.

595
Of the king's high kindred / a mighty press there was.
Then bade they Brunhild / and Kriemhild on to pass,
And with them all the ladies, / where they in shade might be.
Thither did bring them warriors / of the land of Burgundy.

596
When now the strangers also / on horse sat every one,
Plenteous knightly tilting / at shield was there begun.
Above the field rose dust-clouds, / as had the country been
All in flames a-burning; / who bore the honors there was seen.

597
Looked on full many a maiden / as the knights did sport them so.
Meseemeth that Sir Siegfried / full many a to-and-fro
Did ride with his good followers / along 'fore many a tent.
With him of Nibelungen / a thousand stately men there went.

598
Then came of Tronje Hagen, / whom the king did send;
He bade in pleasing manner / the tourney have an end,
Before in dust be buried / all the ladies fair.
And ready to obey him / soon the courteous strangers were.

599
Then spake Sir Gernot: / "Now let the chargers stand,
Until the air is cooler, / for we must be at hand
As escort for fair ladies / unto the stately hall;
And will the king take saddle, / so let him find you ready all."

600
When now the sound of tourney / o'er all the field was spent,
Then went for pleasant pastime / 'neath many a lofty tent
The knights unto the ladies, / and willing thither hied.
And there they passed the hours / till such time as they thence should
ride.

601
Just before the evening / when the sun was in the west,
And the air grew cooler, / no longer did they rest,
But both knights and ladies / unto the castle passed.
And eyes in loving glances / on many a beauteous maid were cast.

602
By hand of goodly warrior / many a coat was rent,

For in the country's custom / they tourneyed as they went,
Until before the palace / the monarch did dismount.
They tended fairest ladies / as knights high-spirited are wont.
603
After fairest greeting / the queens did part again.
Dame Ute and her daughter, / thither passed the twain
With train of fair attendants / unto a hall full wide.
Din of merrymaking / heard ye there on every side.
604
Arranged were sitting-places / where the king would be
With his guests at table. / By him might ye see
Standing the fair Brunhild. / She wore a royal crown
In the monarch's country, / the which might well such mistress own.
605
Seats for all the people / at many a spacious board
There were, as saith the story, / where victuals rich were stored.
How little there was lacking / of all that makes a feast!
And by the monarch saw ye / sitting many a stately guest.
606
The royal host's attendants / in basins golden red
Carried water forward. / And should it e'er be said
By any that a better / service did receive
Ever guests of monarch, / I never could such thing believe.
607
Before the lord of Rhineland / with water was waited on,
Unto him Sir Siegfried, / as fitting was, had gone;
He called to mind a promise / that made by him had been
Ere that the Lady Brunhild / afar in Isenland he'd seen.
608
He spake: "Thou shalt bethink thee / what once did plight thy hand,
If that the Lady Brunhild / should come unto this land,
Thou'dst give to me thy sister. / Where now what thou hast sworn?
In this thy wooing journey / not small the labor I have borne."
609
Then to his guest the monarch: / "Well hast thou minded me,
And by this hand shall never / false word plighted be.
To gain thy wish I'd help thee / in the way as best I know."
Bidden then was Kriemhild / forth unto the king to go.
610
With her full beauteous maidens / unto the Hall she passed.
Then sprang the youthful Giselher / adown the steps in haste
"Bid now these many maidens / wend their way again;
None but my sister only / unto the king shall enter in."

611

Then led they Kriemhild thither / where the king was found,
With him were knights full noble / from many a land around.
Within that Hall so spacious / she waited the king's behest,
What time the Lady Brunhild / betook her likewise to the feast.

612

Then spake the royal Gunther: / "Sister mine full fair,
Redeem the word I've given, / an hold'st thou virtue dear.
Thee to a knight I plighted: / An tak'st thou him to man,
Thereby my wish full truly / unto the warrior hast thou done."

613

Then spake the noble maiden: / "Brother full dear to me,
Not long shalt thou entreat me. / In truth I'll ever be
Obedient to thy bidding; / that shall now be done,
And him I'll take full gladly, / my Lord, whom thou giv'st me for man."

614

Before those fair eyes' glances / grew Siegfried's color red.
The knight to Lady Kriemhild / his service offeréd.
Within a ring together / then were led the twain,
And they asked the maiden, / if she to take the knight were fain.

615

Upon her face not little / was the modest glow;
Nathless to joy of Siegfried / did fortune will it so,
That the maiden would not / refuse the knight her hand.
Eke swore his wife to make her / the noble king of Netherland.

616

When he to her had plighted, / and eke to him the maid,
Siegfried to embrace her / nothing more delayed,
But clasped in arms full fondly / and oft the lady fair,
And stately knights were witness / how that he kissed the princess there.

617

When that the maids attendant / from thence had ta'en their leave,
In place of honor seated / Siegfried might ye perceive
And by him fairest Kriemhild; / and many a knight at hand
Was seen of the Nibelungen / at Siegfried's service ready stand.

618

There too was Gunther seated / and with him Queen Brunhild.
At sight of Kriemhild sitting / by Siegfried was she filled
With anger such as never / before her heart did swell:
She wept, and tears in plenty / adown her shining face there fell.

619

Then spake who ruled the country: / "What aileth, lady mine,

That so thou let'st be dimméd / thine eyes that brightly shine?
Be straight of joyous spirit, / for now at thy command
My land and my good castles / and host of stately warriors stand."
620
"Good cause to me for weeping," / spake the lady fair.
"For sake of this thy sister / sorrow now I bear,
Whom here behold I seated / by one that serveth thee.
That must forever grieve me, / shall she thus dishonored be."
621
Then answered her King Gunther: / "But for the nonce be still.
At other time more fitting / the thing to thee I'll tell,
Wherefore thus my sister / to Siegfried I did give.
And truly with the hero / may she ever joyous live."
622
She spake: "Her name and beauty / thus lost it grieveth me.
An knew I only whither, / from hence I'd surely flee,
This night nor e'er hereafter / to share thy royal bed,
Say'st thou not truly wherefore / Kriemhild thus hath Siegfried wed."
623
Then spake the noble monarch: / "Then unto thee be known
That he as stately castles, / lands wide as I, doth own.
And know thou that full surely / a mighty monarch he;
Wherefore the fairest maiden / I grant him thus his wife to be."
624
Whate'er the king did tell her, / sad was she yet of mood.
Then hastened from the tables / full many a warrior good,
And jousted that the castle / walls gave back the din.
Amid his guests the monarch / waiting longingly was seen.
625
He deemed 'twere better lying / beside his fair lady.
Of thinking on that plaisance / his mind he could not free,
And what her love would bring him / before the night be past;
He many a glance full tender / upon the Lady Brunhild cast.
626
The guests they bade give over / in joust who combated,
For that with spouse new-wedded / the monarch would to bed.
Leaving then the banquet, / there together met
Kriemhild and Brunhild: / their bitter hate was silent yet.
627
At hand were their attendants; / they longer tarried not,
And chamberlains full lordly / lights for them had brought.
Then parted eke the followers / of the monarchs twain,
And bearing Siegfried company / went full many a worthy thane.

628

The lords were both come thither / where that they should lie.
As each one bethought him / of loving victory
To win o'er winsome lady, / merry he grew of mood.
The noble Siegfried's pastime / it was beyond all measure good.

629

As there Sir Siegfried / by fair Kriemhild lay
And to the maid devoted / himself in such fond way
As noble knight beseemeth, / they twain to him were one,
And not a thousand others / had he then ta'en for her alone.

630

I'll tell you now no further / how he the lady plied,
But list ye first the story / what Gunther did betide
By Lady Brunhild lying. / In sooth the noble thane
By side of other ladies / a deal more happily had lain.

631

Withdrawn were now attendants, / man and also maid;
Not long to lock the chamber / within the king delayed.
He weened to have good pleasure / of that fair lady,
Yet was the time still distant / when that she his wife should be.

632

In gown of whitest linen / unto the bed she passed.
Then thought the knight full noble: / "Now have I here at last
All that I e'er desired / as long as I can tell."
Perforce her stately beauty / did please the monarch passing well.

633

That they should shine more dimly / he placed the lights aside,
Then where did lie the lady / the thane full eager hied.
He placed himself a-nigh her, / his joy right great it was,
As in his arms the monarch / the winsome maid did there embrace.

634

A loving plaisance had he / with vigor there begun
If that the noble lady / had let the same be done.
She then did rage so sorely / that grieved was he thereat;
He weened to find who loved him, / —instead he found him naught
but hate.

635

Spake she: "Good knight and noble, / from this thing give o'er.
That which thou here hast hope of, / it may be nevermore.
A maid I still will keep me / —well mayest thou know that—
Until I learn that story." / Gunther wrathy grew thereat.

636

Her gown he wrought to ruin / to win her maidenhead.

Whereat did seize a girdle / the full stately maid,
A strong and silken girdle / that round her sides she wore,
And with the same the monarch / she soon had brought to pains full
sore.

637

His feet and his hands also, / together bound she all,
Unto a nail she bore him / and hung him on the wall.
Him who disturbed her sleeping / in his love she sorely let,
And from her mighty prowess, / he full nigh his death had met.

638

Then gan he to entreat her, / who master late had been.
"From these my bonds now loose me, / my full noble queen.
Nor trow I e'er, fair lady, / victor o'er thee to be,
And henceforth will I seldom / seek to lie thus nigh to thee."

639

She recked not how 'twere with him, / as she full softly lay.
There hung he, will he nill he, / the night through unto day,
Until the light of morning / through the windows shone.
Could he e'er boast of prowess, / small now the measure he did own.

640

"Now tell me, lordly Gunther, / wert thou thereat so sad,
If that in bonds should find thee" / —spake the fairest maid—
"Thy royal men-in-waiting, / bound by lady's hand?"
Then spake the knight full noble: / "Thou should'st in case most evil
stand.

641

"Eke had I little honor / therefrom," continued he.
"For all thy royal honor / let me then go to thee.
Since that my fond embracements / do anger thee so sore,
With these my hands I pledge thee / to touch thy garment nevermore."

642

Then she loosed him straightway / and he once more stood free.
To the bed he went as erstwhile / where rested his lady.
But far from her he laid him / and well he now forebore
To stir the lady's anger / by touching e'en the gown she wore.

643

At length came their attendants / who garments fresh did bring,
Whereof was ready for them / good store on that morning.
Yet merry as his folk were, / a visage sad did own
The lord of that proud country, / for all he wore that day a crown.

644

As was the country's custom, / a thing folk do of right,
Gunther and Brunhild / presently were dight

To go unto the minster / where the mass was sung.
Thither eke came Siegfried, / and in their trains a mighty throng.
645
As fitted royal honor / for them was thither brought
The crown that each should carry / and garments richly wrought.
There were they consecrated; / and when the same was done,
Saw ye the four together / happy stand and wearing crown.
646
There was knighted many a squire, / —six hundred or beyond—
In honor of the crowning, / that shall ye understand.
Arose full great rejoicing / in the land of Burgundy
As hand of youthful warrior / did shatter shaft right valiantly.
647
Then sat in castle casement / maidens fair to see,
And many a shield beneath them / gleamed full brilliantly.
Yet himself had sundered / from all his men the king;
Though joyous every other, / sad-visaged stood he sorrowing.
648
He and the doughty Siegfried, / how all unlike their mood!
Well wist the thing did grieve him / that noble knight and good.
He went unto the monarch / and straight addressed him so:
"This night how hast thou fared? / In friendship give thou me to know."
649
To his guest the king gave answer: / "Than shame and scathe I've naught.
The devil's dam I surely / into my house have brought.
When as I thought to have her / she bound me like a thrall;
Unto a nail she bore me / and hung me high upon the wall.
650
"There hung I sore in anguish / the night through until day
Ere that she would unbind me, / the while she softly lay!
And hast thou friendly pity / know then the grief I bear."
Then spake the doughty Siegfried: / "Such grieves me verily to hear.
651
"The which I'll show thee truly, / wilt thou me not deny.
I'll bring it that to-night she / so near to thee shall lie
That she to meet thy wishes / shall tarry nevermore."
Thereat rejoice did Gunther / to think perchance his trials o'er.
652
Then further spake Sir Siegfried: / "With thee 'twill yet be right.
I ween that all unequal / we twain have fared this night.
To me thy sister Kriemhild / dearer is than life;
Eke shall the Lady Brunhild / be yet this coming night thy wife."

109

653
"I'll come unto thy chamber / this night all secretly,"
Spake he, "and wrapped in mantle / invisible I'll be,
That of this my cunning / naught shall any know;
And thy attendants shalt thou / bid to their apartments go.

654
"The lights I'll all extinguish / held by each page in hand,
By the which same token / shalt thou understand
I present am to serve thee. / I'll tame thy shrewish wife
That thou this night enjoy her, / else forfeit be my caitiff life."

655
"An thou wilt truly leave me" / —answered him the king—
'My lady yet a maiden, / I joy o'er this same thing.
So do thou as thou willest; / and takest thou her life,
E'en that I'll let pass o'er me, / —to lose so terrible a wife."

656
"Thereto," spake then Siegfried, / "plight I word of mine,
To leave her yet a maiden. / A sister fair of thine
Is to me before all women / I ever yet have seen."
Gunther believed right gladly / what had by Siegfried plighted been.

657
Meanwhile the merry pastime / with joy and zest went on.
But all the din and bustle / bade they soon be done,
When band of fairest ladies / would pass unto the hall
'Fore whom did royal chamberlains / bid backward stand the people all.

658
The chargers soon and riders / from castle court were sped.
Each of the noble ladies / by bishop high was led,
When that before the monarchs / they passed to banquet board,
And in their train did follow / to table many a stately lord.

659
There sat the king all hopeful / and full of merriment;
What him did promise Siegfried, / thereon his mind was bent.
To him as long as thirty / did seem that single day;
To plaisance with his lady, / thither turned his thought alway.

660
And scarce the time he bided / while that the feast did last.
Now unto her chamber / the stately Brunhild passed,
And for her couch did Kriemhild / likewise the table leave.
Before those royal ladies / what host ye saw of warriors brave!

661
Full soon thereafter Siegfried / sat right lovingly

With his fair wife beside him, / and naught but joy had he.
His hand she clasped full fondly / within her hand so white,
Until—and how she knew not— / he did vanish from her sight.
662
When she the knight did fondle, / and straightway saw him not,
Unto her maids attendant / spake the queen distraught:
"Meseemeth a mickle wonder / where now the king hath gone.
His hands in such weird fashion / who now from out mine own hath drawn?"
663
Yet further not she questioned. / Soon had he hither gone
Where with lights were standing / attendants many a one.
The same he did extinguish / in every page's hand;
That Siegfried then was present / Gunther thereby did understand.
664
Well wist he what he would there; / so bade he thence be gone
Ladies and maids-in-waiting. / And when that was done,
Himself the mighty monarch / fast did lock the door:
Two bolts all wrought securely / he quickly shoved the same before.
665
The lights behind the curtains / hid he presently.
Soon a play was started / (for thus it had to be),
Betwixt the doughty Siegfried / and the stately maid:
Thereat was royal Gunther / joyous alike and sad.
666
Siegfried there laid him / by the maid full near.
Spake she: "Let be, now, Gunther, / an hast thou cause to fear
Those troubles now repeated / which befell thee yesternight."
And soon the valiant Siegfried / through the lady fell in sorry plight.
667
His voice did he keep under / and ne'er a word spake he.
Intently listened Gunther, / and though he naught could see,
Yet knew he that in secret / nothing 'twixt them passed.
In sooth nor knight nor lady / upon the bed had mickle rest.
668
He did there as if Gunther / the mighty king he were,
And in his arms he pressed her, / the maiden debonair.
Forth from the bed she hurled him / where a bench there stood,
And head of valiant warrior / against a stool went ringing loud.
669
Up sprang again undaunted / the full doughty man,
To try for fortune better. / When he anew began
Perforce to curb her fury, / fell he in trouble sore.

I ween that ne'er a lady / did so defend herself before.
670
When he would not give over, / up the maid arose:
"My gown so white thou never / thus shalt discompose.
And this thy villain's manner / shall sore by thee be paid,
The same I'll teach thee truly," / further spake the buxom maid.
671
Within her arms she clasped him, / the full stately thane,
And thought likewise to bind him, / as the king yestreen,
That she the night in quiet / upon her couch might lie.
That her dress he thus did rumple, / avenged the lady grievously.
672
What booted now his prowess / and eke his mickle might?
Her sovereignty of body / she proved upon the knight;
By force of arm she bore him, / —'twixt wall and mighty chest
(For so it e'en must happen) / him she all ungently pressed.
673
"Ah me!"—so thought the hero— / "shall I now my life
Lose at hand of woman, / then will every wife
Evermore hereafter / a shrewish temper show
Against her lord's good wishes, / who now such thing ne'er thinks to
do."
674
All heard the monarch meanwhile / and trembled for the man.
Sore ashamed was Siegfried, / and a-raging he began.
With might and main he struggled / again to make him free,
Ere which to sorest trouble / 'neath Lady Brunhild's hand fell he.
675
Long space to him it seeméd / ere Siegfried tamed her mood.
She grasped his hand so tightly / that 'neath the nails the blood
Oozéd from the pressure, / which made the hero wince.
Yet the stately maiden / subdued he to obedience since.
676
Her unrestrainéd temper / that she so late displayed,
All overheard the monarch, / though ne'er a word he said.
'Gainst the bed did press her Siegfried / that aloud she cried,
Ungentle was the treatment / that he meted to the bride.
677
Then grasped she for a girdle / that round her sides she wore,
And thought therewith to bind him; / but her limbs and body o'er
Strained beneath the vigor / that his strong arm displayed.
So was the struggle ended / —Gunther's wife was vanquishéd.
678

She spake: "O noble monarch, / take not my life away.
The harm that I have done thee / full well will I repay.
No more thy royal embraces / by me shall be withstood,
For now I well have seen it, / thou canst be lord o'er woman's mood."
679
From the couch rose Siegfried, / lying he left the maid,
As if that he would from him / lay his clothes aside.
He drew from off her finger / a ring of golden sheen
Without that e'er perceivéd / his practice the full noble queen.
680
Thereto he took her girdle / that was all richly wrought:
If from wanton spirit / he did it, know I not.
The same he gave to Kriemhild: / the which did sorrow bear.
Then lay by one another / Gunther and the maiden fair.
681
Hearty were his embraces / as such king became:
Perforce must she relinquish / her anger and her shame.
In sooth not little pallid / within his arms she grew,
And in that love-surrender / how waned her mighty prowess too!
682
Then was e'en she not stronger / than e'er another bride;
He lay with fond embraces / the beauteous dame beside.
And had she struggled further, / avail how could it aught?
Gunther, when thus he clasped her, / such change upon her strength
had wrought.
683
And with right inward pleasure / she too beside him lay
In warmest love embracings / until the dawn of day!
Meantime now had Siegfried / departure ta'en from there,
And was full well receivéd / by a lady debonair.
684
Her questioning he avoided / and all whereon she thought,
And long time kept he secret / what he for her had brought,
Until in his own country / she wore a royal crown;
Yet what for her he destined, / how sure at last it was her own.
685
Upon the morn was Gunther / by far of better mood
Than he had been before it; / joy thus did spread abroad
'Mid host of knights full noble / that from his lands around
To his court had been invited, / and there most willing service found.
686
The merry time there lasted / until two weeks were spent,
Nor all the while did flag there / the din of merriment

And every kind of joyance / that knight could e'er devise;
With lavish hand expended / the king thereto in fitting wise.
687
The noble monarch's kinsmen / upon his high command
By gifts of gold and raiment / told forth his generous hand,
By steed and thereto silver / on minstrel oft bestowed.
Who there did gift desire / departed thence in merry mood.
688
All the store of raiment / afar from Netherland,
The which had Siegfried's thousand / warriors brought to hand
Unto the Rhine there with them, / complete 'twas dealt away,
And eke the steeds well saddled: / in sooth a lordly life led they.
689
Ere all the gifts so bounteous / were dealt the guests among,
They who would straightway homeward / did deem the waiting long.
Ne'er had guests of monarch / such goodly gifts before;
And so as Gunther willed it / the merry feast at last was o'er.

ELEVENTH ADVENTURE: How Siegfried came home with his Wife

690
When that now the strangers / all from thence were gone,
Spake unto his followers / noble Siegmund's son:
"We shall eke make ready / home to my land to fare."
Unto his spouse was welcome / such news when she the same did hear.
691
She spake unto her husband: / "When shall we hence depart?
Not hastily on the journey / I pray thee yet to start.
With me first my brothers / their wide lands shall share."
Siegfried yet it pleased not / such words from Kriemhild to hear.
692
The princes went unto him / and spake they there all three:
"Now know thou well, Sir Siegfried, / for thee shall ever be
In faithfulness our service / ready while yet we live."
The royal thanes then thanked he / who thus did proof of friendship give.
693
"With thee further share we," / spake young Giselher,
"The lands and eke the castles / by us that ownéd are.
In wide lands whatsoever / we rule o'er warriors brave,
Of the same with Kriemhild / a goodly portion shalt thou have.

694

Then spake unto the princes / the son of Siegmund
When he their lofty purpose / did rightly understand:
"God grant your goodly heritage / at peace may ever be,
And eke therein your people. / The spouse in sooth so dear to me."

695

"May well forego the portion / that ye to her would give.
For she a crown shall carry, / if to such day I live,
And queen more rich than any / that lives she then must be.
What else to her ye offer, / therein I'll meet you faithfully."

696

Then spake the Lady Kriemhild: / "If wealth thou wilt not choose,
Yet gallant thanes of Burgundy / shalt thou not light refuse.
They're such as monarch gladly / would lead to his own land.
Of these shall make division / with me my loving brothers' hand."

697

Thereto spake noble Gernot: / "Now take to please thy mind.
Who gladly will go with thee / full many here thou'lt find.
Of thirty hundred warriors / we give thee thousand men
To be thy royal escort." / Kriemhild did summon then

698

Hagen of Tronje to her / and Ortwein instantly:
And would they and their kinsmen / make her good company?
To hear the same did Hagen / begin to rage full sore.
Quoth he: "E'en royal Gunther / may thus bestow us nevermore.

699

"Other men that serve thee, / let them follow thee;
Thou know'st the men of Tronje / and what their pledges be:
Here must we by the monarchs / in service true abide;
Hereto as them we followed, / so shall we henceforth keep their side."

700

And so the thing was ended: / to part they ready make.
A high and noble escort / did Kriemhild to her take,
Maidens two and thirty / and five hundred men also.
In Lady Kriemhild's company / the Margrave Eckewart did go.

701

Leave took they all together, / squire and also knight,
Maidens and fair ladies, / as was their wont aright.
There parted they with kisses / and eke with clasp of hand:
Right merrily they journeyed / forth from royal Gunther's land.

702

Their friends did give them escort / upon the way full far.
Night-quarters at every station / they bade for them prepare,

Where they might wish to tarry / as on their way they went.
Then straightway was a messenger / unto royal Siegmund sent,

703
To him and Siegelind bearing / thereof the joyful sign
That his son was coming / from Worms upon the Rhine
And with him Ute's daughter, / Kriemhild the fair lady.
As this could other message / nevermore so welcome be.

704
"Well is me!" quoth Siegmund, / "that I the day have known,
When the fair Lady Kriemhild / here shall wear a crown.
Thus higher shall my kingdom / stand in majesty.
My son the noble Siegfried / here himself the king shall be."

705
Then dealt the Lady Siegelind / velvet red in store,
Silver and gold full heavy / to them the news that bore:
She joyed to hear the story / that there her ear did greet.
Then decked themselves her ladies / all in rich attire meet.

706
'Twas told, with Siegfried coming / whom they did expect.
Then bade they sitting-places / straightway to erect,
Where he before his kinsmen / a crown in state should wear.
Then men of royal Siegmund / forward rode to meet him there.

707
Was e'er more royal greeting, / news have I not to hand,
As came the knights full noble / into Siegmund's land.
There the royal Siegelind / to Kriemhild forth did ride
With ladies fair a many, / and followed gallant knights beside

708
Out a full day's journey / to welcome each high guest.
And little with the strangers / did they ever rest
Until into a castle / wide they came once more,
The same was called Xanten, / where anon a crown they wore.

709
With smiling lips Dame Siegelind / —and Siegmund eke did this—
To show the love they bore her / full oft did Kriemhild kiss,
And eke the royal Siegfried: / far was their sorrow gone.
And all the merry company, / good welcome had they every one.

710
The train of strangers bade they / 'fore Siegmund's Hall to lead,
And maidens fair a many / down from gallant steed
Helped they there dismounting. / Full many a man was there
To do them willing service / as was meet for ladies fair.

711

How great soe'er the splendor / erstwhile beside the Rhine,
Here none the less was given / raiment yet more fine,
Nor were they e'er attired / in all their days so well.
Full many a wonder might I / of their rich apparel tell.

712

How there in state resplendent / they sat and had full store,
And how each high attendant / gold-broidered raiment wore,
With stones full rare and precious / set with skill therein!
The while with care did serve them / Siegelind the noble queen.

713

Then spake the royal Siegmund / before his people so:
"To every friend of Siegfried / give I now to know
That he before these warriors / my royal crown shall wear."
And did rejoice that message / the thanes of Netherland to hear.

714

His crown to him he tendered / and rule o'er wide domain
Whereof he all was master. / Where'er did reach his reign
Or men were subject to him / bestowed his hand such care
That evil-doers trembled / before the spouse of Kriemhild fair.

715

In such high honor truly / he lived, as ye shall hear,
And judged as lofty monarch / unto the tenth year,
What time his fairest lady / to him a son did bear.
Thereat the monarch's kinsmen / filled with mickle joyance were.

716

They soon the same did christen / and gave to him a name,
Gunther, as hight his uncle, / nor cause was that for shame:
Grew he but like his kinsmen / then happy might he be.
As well he did deserve it, / him fostered they right carefully.

717

In the selfsame season / did Lady Siegelind die,
When was full power wielded / by Ute's daughter high,
As meet so lofty lady / should homage wide receive.
That death her thus had taken / did many a worthy kinsman grieve.

718

Now by the Rhine yonder, / as we likewise hear,
Unto mighty Gunther / eke a son did bear
Brunhild his fair lady / in the land of Burgundy.
In honor to the hero / Siegfried naméd eke was he.

719

The child they also fostered / with what tender care!
Gunther the noble monarch / anon did masters rare

Find who should instruct him / a worthy man to grow.
Alas! by sad misfortune / to friends was dealt how fell a blow!
720
At all times the story / far abroad was told,
How that in right worthy / way the warriors bold
Lived there in Siegmund's country / as noble knights should do.
Likewise did royal Gunther / eke amid his kinsmen true.
721
Land of the Nibelungen / Siegfried as well did own,
—Amid his lofty kindred / a mightier ne'er was known—
And Schilbung's knights did serve him, / with all that theirs had been.
That great was thus his power / did fill with joy the knight full keen.
722
Hoard of all the greatest / that hero ever won,
Save who erstwhile did wield it, / now the knight did own,
The which before a mountain / he seized against despite,
And for whose sake he further / slew full many a gallant knight.
723
Naught more his heart could wish for; / yet had his might been less,
Rightly must all people / of the high knight confess,
One was he of the worthiest / that e'er bestrode a steed.
Feared was his mickle prowess, / and, sooth to say, thereof was need.

TWELFTH ADVENTURE: How Gunther bade Siegfried to the Feast

724
Now all time bethought her / royal Gunther's wife:
"How now doth Lady Kriemhild / lead so haughty life?
In sooth her husband Siegfried / doth homage to us owe,
But now full long unto us / little service he doth show."
725
That in her heart in secret / eke she pondered o'er.
That they were strangers to her / did grieve her heart full sore,
And so seldom sign of service / came from Siegfried's land.
How it thus was fallen, / that she fain would understand.
726
She probed then the monarch, / if the thing might be,
That she the Lady Kriemhild / once again might see.
She spake it all in secret / whereon her heart did dwell;
The thing she then did speak of / pleased the monarch passing well.

727
"How might we bring them hither" / —spake the mighty king—
"Unto this my country? / 'Twere ne'er to do, such thing.
They dwell too distant from us, / the quest I fear to make."
Thereto gave answer Brunhild, / and in full crafty wise she spake:

728
"How high soe'er and mighty / king's man were ever one,
Whate'er should bid his master, / may he not leave undone."
Thereat did smile King Gunther, / as such words spake she:
Ne'er bade he aught of service, / oft as Siegfried he did see.

729
She spake: "Full loving master, / as thou hold'st me dear,
Help me now that Siegfried / and thy sister fair
Come to this our country, / that them we here may see;
In sooth no thing could ever / unto me more welcome be.

730
"Thy sister's lofty bearing / and all her courtesy,
Whene'er I think upon it, / full well it pleaseth me,
How we did sit together / when erst I was thy spouse!
Well in sooth with honor / might she the valiant Siegfried choose."

731
She pleaded with the monarch / so long till answered he:
"Know now that guests none other / so welcome were to me.
To gain thy wish 'tis easy: / straight messengers of mine
To both shall message carry, / that hither come they to the Rhine."

732
Thereto the queen gave answer: / "Now further shalt thou say,
When thou them wilt summon, / or when shall be the day
That our dear friends come hither / unto our country.
Who'll bear thy message thither, / shalt thou eke make known to me."

733
"That will I," spake the monarch. / "Thirty of my men
Shall thither ride unto them." / The same he summoned then,
And bade them with the message / to Siegfried's land to fare.
They joyed as gave them Brunhild / stately raiment rich to wear.

734
Then further spake the monarch: / "Ye knights from me shall bring
This message, nor withhold ye / of it anything,
Unto the doughty Siegfried / and eke my sister fair:
In the world could never any / to them a better purpose bear.

735
"And pray them both that hither / they come unto the Rhine.
With me will e'er my lady / such grace to pay combine,

Ere turn of sun in summer / he and his men shall know
That liveth here full many / to them would willing honor show.
736
"Unto royal Siegmund / bear greeting fair from me,
That I and my friends ever / to him well-minded be.
And tell ye eke my sister / she shall no wise omit
Hither to friends to journey: / ne'er feast could better her befit."
737
Brunhild and Ute / and ladies all at hand,
They sent a fairest greeting / unto Siegfried's land
To winsome ladies many / and many a warrior brave.
With godspeed from the monarch / and friends the messengers took leave.
738
They fared with full equipment: / their steeds did ready stand
And rich were they attired: / so rode they from that land
They hastened on the journey / whither they would fare;
Escort safe the monarch / had bidden eke for them prepare.
739
Their journey had they ended / e'er three weeks were spent.
At the Nibelungen castle, / whither they were sent,
In the mark of Norway / found they the knight they sought,
And weary were the horses / the messengers so far had brought.
740
Then was told to Siegfried / and to Kriemhild fair
How knights were there arrivéd / who did raiment wear
Like as in land of Burgundy / of wont the warriors dressed.
Thereat did hasten Kriemhild / from couch where she did lying rest.
741
Then bade eke to a window / one of her maids to go.
She saw the valiant Gere / stand in the court below,
And with him his companions, / who did thither fare.
To hear such joyous tidings, / how soon her heart forgot its care.
742
She spake unto the monarch: / "Look now thitherward
Where with the doughty Gere / stand in the castle yard
Whom to us brother Gunther / adown the Rhine doth send!"
Thereto spake doughty Siegfried: / "With greeting fair we'll them attend."
743
Then hastened their retainers / all the guests to meet,
And each of them in special / manner then did greet
The messengers full kindly / and warmest welcome bade.

Siegmund did likewise / o'er their coming wax full glad.

744

In fitting way was harbored / Gere and his men,
And steeds in charge were taken. / The messengers went then
Where beside Sir Siegfried / the Lady Kriemhild sat.
To court the guests were bidden, / where them did greeting fair await.

745

The host with his fair lady, / straightway up stood he,
And greeted fairly Gere / of the land of Burgundy
And with him his companions / King Gunther's men also.
Gere, knight full mighty, / bade they to a settle go.

746

"Allow that first the message / we give ere sit we down;
The while we'll stand, though weary / upon our journey grown.
Tidings bring we to you / what greetings high have sent
Gunther and Brunhild / who live in royal fair content.

747

"Eke what from Lady Ute / thy mother now we've brought.
The youthful Giselher / and also Sir Gernot
And best among thy kinsmen / have sent us here to thee:
A fairest greeting send they / from the land of Burgundy."

748

"God give them meed," spake Siegfried; / "Good will and faith withal
I trow full well they harbor, / as with friends we shall;
Likewise doth eke their sister. / Now further shall ye tell
If that our friends belovéd / at home in high estate do dwell.

749

"Since that we from them parted / hath any dared to do
Scathe to my lady's kinsmen? / That shall ye let me know.
I'll help them ever truly / all their need to bear
Till that their enemies / have good cause my help to fear."

750

Then spake the Margrave / Gere, a knight full good:
"In all that maketh knighthood / right proud they stand of mood.
Unto the Rhine they bid you / to high festivity:
They'd see you there full gladly, / thereof may ye not doubtful be.

751

"And bid they eke my Lady / Kriemhild that she too,
When ended is the winter, / thither come with you.
Ere turn of sun in summer / trust they you to see."
Then spake the doughty Siegfried: / "That same thing might hardly be."

752
Thereto did answer Gere / of the land of Burgundy:
"Your high mother Ute / hath message sent by me,
Likewise Gernot and Giselher, / that they plead not in vain.
That you they see so seldom / daily hear I them complain.

753
"Brunhild my mistress / and all her company
Of fair maids rejoice them; / if the thing might be
That they again should see you, / of merry mood they were."
Then joy to hear the tidings / filled the Lady Kriemhild fair.

754
Gere to her was kinsman. / The host did bid him rest,
Nor long were they in pouring / wine for every guest.
Thither came eke Siegmund / where the strangers he did see,
And in right friendly manner / spake to the men of Burgundy:

755
"Welcome be, ye warriors, / ye Gunther's men, each one.
Since that fair Kriemhild / Siegfried my son
For spouse did take unto him, / we should you ofter see
Here in this our country, / an ye good friends to us would be."

756
They spake, whene'er he wished it, / full glad to come were they.
All their mickle weariness / with joy was ta'en away.
The messengers were seated / and food to them they bore,
Whereof did Siegfried offer / unto his guests a goodly store.

757
Until nine days were over / must they there abide,
When did at last the valiant / knights begin to chide
That they did not ride thither / again unto their land.
Then did the royal Siegfried / summon his good knights to hand.

758
He asked what they did counsel: / should they unto the Rhine?
"Me unto him hath bidden / Gunther, friend of mine,
He and his good kinsmen, / to high festivity.
Thither went I full gladly, / but that his land so far doth lie.

759
"Kriemhild bid they likewise / that she with me shall fare.
Good friends, now give ye counsel / how we therefor prepare.
And were it armies thirty / to lead in distant land,
Yet must serve them gladly / evermore Siegfried's hand."

760
Then answer gave his warriors. / "An't pleaseth thee to go
Thither to the festival, / we'll counsel what thou do.

Thou shalt with thousand warriors / unto Rhine river ride.
So may'st thou well with honor / in the land of Burgundy abide."
761
Then spake of Netherland / Siegmund the king:
"Will ye to the festival, / why hide from me the thing!
I'll journey with you thither, / if it not displeasing be,
And lead good thanes a hundred / wherewith to swell your company."
762
"And wilt thou with us journey, / father full dear to me,"
Spake the valiant Siegfried, / "full glad thereat I'll be.
Before twelve days are over / from these my lands I fare."
To all who'd join the journey / steeds gave they and apparel rare.
763
When now the lofty monarch / was minded thus to ride
Bade he the noble messengers / longer not to bide,
And to his lady's kinsmen / to the Rhine a message sent,
How that he would full gladly / join to make them merriment.
764
Siegfried and Kriemhild, / this same tale we hear,
To the messengers gave so richly / that the burden could not bear
Their horses with them homeward, / such wealth in sooth he had.
The horses heavy-laden / drove they thence with hearts full glad.
765
Siegfried and Siegmund / their people richly clad.
Eckewart the Margrave, / straightway he bade
For ladies choose rich clothing, / the best that might be found,
Or e'er could be procuréd / in all Siegfried's lands around.
766
The shields and the saddles / gan they eke prepare,
To knights and fair ladies / who with them should fare
Lacked nothing that they wished for, / but of all they were possessed.
Then to his friends led Siegfried / many a high and stately guest.
767
The messengers swift hasted / homeward on their way,
And soon again came Gere / to the land of Burgundy.
Full well was he receivéd, / and there dismounted all
His train from off their horses / before the royal Gunther's Hall.
768
Old knights and youthful squires / crowded, as is their way,
To ask of them the tidings. / Thus did the brave knight say:
"When to the king I tell them / then shall ye likewise hear."
He went with his companions / and soon 'fore Gunther did appear.

769
Full of joy the monarch / did from the settle spring;
And did thank them also / for their hastening
Brunhild the fair lady. / Spake Gunther eagerly:
"How now liveth Siegfried, / whose arm hath oft befriended me?"

770
Then spake the valiant Gere: / "Joy o'er the visage went
Of him and eke thy sister. / To friends was never sent
A more faithful greeting / by good knight ever one,
Than now the mighty Siegfried / and his royal sire have done."

771
Then spake unto the Margrave / the noble monarch's wife:
"Now tell me, cometh Kriemhild? / And marketh yet her life
Aught of the noble bearing / did her erstwhile adorn?"
"She cometh to thee surely," / Gere answer did return.

772
Ute straightway the messengers / to her did command.
Then might ye by her asking / full well understand
To her was joyous tidings / how Kriemhild did betide.
He told her how he found her, / and that she soon would hither ride.

773
Eke of all the presents / did they naught withhold,
That had given them Siegfried: / apparel rich and gold
Displayed they to the people / of the monarchs three.
To him were they full grateful / who thus had dealt so bounteously.

774
"Well may he," quoth Hagen, / "of his treasure give,
Nor could he deal it fully, / should he forever live:
Hoard of the Nibelungen / beneath his hand doth lie.
Heigh-ho, if came it ever / into the land of Burgundy!"

775
All the king's retainers / glad they were thereat,
That the guests were coming. / Early then and late
Full little were they idle, / the men of monarchs three.
Seats builded they full many / toward the high festivity.

776
The valiant knight Hunold / and Sindold doughty thane
Little had of leisure. / Meantime must the twain,
Stands erect full many, / as their high office bade.
Therein did help them Ortwein, / and Gunther's thanks therefor they
had.

777
Rumold the High Steward / busily he wrought

Among them that did serve him. / Full many a mighty pot,
And spacious pans and kettles, / how many might ye see!
For those to them were coming / prepared they victuals plenteously.

THIRTEENTH ADVENTURE: How they fared to the Feast

778
Leave we now the ardor / wherewith they did prepare,
And tell how Lady Kriemhild / and eke her maidens fair
From land of Nibelungen / did journey to the Rhine.
Ne'er did horses carry / such store of raiment rich and fine.

779
Carrying-chests full many / for the way they made ready.
Then rode the thane Siegfried / with his friends in company
And eke the queen thither / where joy they looked to find.
Where now was high rejoicing / they soon in sorest grief repined.

780
At home behind them left they / Lady Kriemhild's son
That she did bear to Siegfried / —'twas meet that that be done.
From this their festive journey / rose mickle sorrow sore:
His father and his mother / their child beheld they never more.

781
Then eke with them thither / Siegmund the king did ride.
Had he e'er had knowledge / what should there betide
Anon from that high journey, / such had he never seen:
Ne'er wrought upon dear kindred / might so grievous wrong have been.

782
Messengers sent they forward / that the tidings told should be.
Then forth did ride to meet them / with gladsome company
Ute's friends full many / and many a Gunther's man.
With zeal to make him ready / unto his guests the king began.

783
Where he found Brunhild sitting, / thither straight went he.
"How receivéd thee my sister, / as thou cam'st to this country?
Like preparations shalt thou / for Siegfried's wife now make."
"Fain do I that; good reason / have I to love her well," she spake.

784
Then quoth the mighty monarch: / "The morn shall see them here.
Wilt thou go forth to meet them, / apace do thou prepare,
That not within the castle / their coming we await.

Guests more welcome never / greeted I of high estate."
785
Her maidens and her ladies / straight did she command
To choose them rich apparel, / the best within the land,
In which the stately company / before the guests should go.
The same they did right gladly, / that may ye full surely know.
786
Then eke to offer service / the men of Gunther hied,
And all his doughty warriors / saw ye by the monarch's side.
Then rode the queen full stately / the strangers forth to meet,
And hearty was the welcome / as she her loving guests did greet.
787
With what glad rejoicings / the guests they did receive!
They deemed that Lady Kriemhild / did unto Brunhild give
Ne'er so warm a welcome / to the land of Burgundy.
Bold knights that yet were strangers / rejoiced each other there to see.
788
Now come was also Siegfried / with his valiant men.
The warriors saw ye riding / thither and back again,
Where'er the plain extended, / with huge company.
From the dust and crowding / could none in all the rout be free.
789
When the monarch of the country / Siegfried did see
And with him also Siegmund, / spake he full lovingly:
"Be ye to me full welcome / and to all these friends of mine.
Our hearts right glad they shall be / o'er this your journey to the Rhine."
790
"God give thee meed," spake Siegmund, / a knight in honor grown.
"Since that my son Siegfried / thee for a friend hath known,
My heart hath e'er advised me / that thee I soon should see."
Thereto spake royal Gunther: / "Joy hast thou brought full great to
me."
791
Siegfried was there receivéd, / as fitted his high state,
With full lofty honors, / nor one did bear him hate.
There joined in way right courteous / Gernot and Giselher:
I ween so warm a welcome / did they make for strangers ne'er.
792
The spouse of each high monarch / greeted the other there.
Emptied was many a saddle, / and many a lady fair
By hero's hand was lifted / adown upon the sward.
By waiting on fair lady / how many a knight sought high reward!

793
So went unto each other / the ladies richly dight;
Thereat in high rejoicing / was seen full many a knight,
That by both the greeting / in such fair way was done.
By fair maidens standing / saw ye warriors many a one.

794
Each took the hand of other / in all their company;
In courteous manner bending / full many might ye see
And loving kisses given / by ladies debonair.
Rejoiced the men of Gunther / and Siegfried to behold them there.

795
They bided there no longer / but rode into the town.
The host bade to the strangers / in fitting way be shown,
That they were seen full gladly / in the land of Burgundy.
High knights full many tilting / before fair ladies might ye see.

796
Then did of Tronje Hagen / and eke Ortwein
In high feats of valor / all other knights outshine.
Whate'er the twain commanded / dared none to leave undone;
By them was many a service / to their high guests in honor shown.

797
Shields heard ye many clashing / before the castle gate
With din of lances breaking. / Long in saddle sate
The host and guests there with him, / ere that within they went.
With full merry pastime / joyfully the hours they spent.

798
Unto the Hall so spacious / rode the merry company.
Many a silken cover / wrought full cunningly
Saw ye beyond the saddles / of the ladies debonair
On all sides down hanging. / King Gunther's men did meet them there.

799
Led by the same the strangers / to their apartments passed.
Meanwhile oft her glances / Brunhild was seen to cast
Upon the Lady Kriemhild, / for she was passing fair.
In lustre vied her color / with the gold that she did wear.

800
Within the town a clamor / at Worms on every hand
Arose amid their followers. / King Gunther gave command
To Dankwart his Marshal / to tend them all with care.
Then bade he fitting quarters / for the retinue prepare.

801
Without and in the castle / the board for all was set:
In sooth were never strangers / better tended yet.

Whatever any wished for / did they straightway provide:
So mighty was the monarch / that naught to any was denied.
802

To them was kind attention / and all good friendship shown.
The host then at the table / with his guests sat him down.
Siegfried they bade be seated / where he did sit before.
Then went with him to table / full many a stately warrior more.
803

Gallant knights twelve hundred / in the circle there, I ween,
With him sat at table. / Brunhild the lofty queen
Did deem that never vassal / could more mighty be.
So well she yet was minded, / she saw it not unwillingly.
804

There upon an evening, / as the king with guests did dine,
Full many a rich attire / was wet with ruddy wine,
As passed among the tables / the butlers to and fro.
And great was their endeavor / full honor to the guests to show.
805

As long hath been the custom / at high festivity
Fit lodging there was given / to maid and high lady.
From whence soe'er they came there / they had the host's good care;
Unto each guest was meted / of fitting honors fullest share.
806

When now the night was ended / and came forth the dawn,
From chests they carried with them, / full many a precious stone
Sparkled on costly raiment / by hand of lady sought.
Stately robes full many / forth to deck them then they brought.
807

Ere dawn was full appeared, / before the Hall again
Came knights and squires many, / whereat arose the din
E'en before the matins / that for the king were sung.
Well pleased was the monarch / at joust to see the warriors young.
808

Full lustily and loudly / many a horn did blare,
Of flutes and eke of trumpets / such din did rend the air
That loud came back the echo / from Worms the city wide.
The warriors high-hearted / to saddle sprung on every side.
809

Arose there in that country / high a jousting keen
Of many a doughty warrior / whereof were many seen,
Whom there their hearts more youthful / did make of merry mood;
Of these 'neath shield there saw ye / many a stately knight and good.
810

There sat within the casements / many a high lady
And maidens many with them, / the which were fair to see.
Down looked they where did tourney / many a valiant man.
The host with his good kinsmen / himself a-riding soon began.
811
Thus they found them pastime, / and fled the time full well;
Then heard they from the minster / the sound of many a bell.
Forth upon their horses / the ladies thence did ride;
Many a knight full valiant / the lofty queens accompanied.
812
They then before the minster / alighted on the grass.
Unto her guests Queen Brunhild / yet well-minded was.
Into the spacious minster / they passed, and each wore crown.
Their friendship yet was broken / by direst jealousy anon.
813
When the mass was ended / went they thence again
In full stately manner. / Thereafter were they seen
Joyous at board together. / The pleasure full did last,
Until days eleven / amid the merry-making passed.

FOURTEENTH ADVENTURE: How the Queens Berated Each Other

814
Before the time of vespers / arose a mickle stir
On part of warriors many / upon the courtyard there.
In knightly fashion made they / the time go pleasantly;
Thither knights and ladies / went their merry play to see.
815
There did sit together / the queens, a stately pair,
And of two knights bethought them, / that noble warriors were.
Then spake the fair Kriemhild: / "Such spouse in sooth have I,
That all these mighty kingdoms / might well beneath his sceptre lie."
816
Then spake the Lady Brunhild: / "How might such thing be?
If that there lived none other / but himself and thee,
So might perchance his power / rule these kingdoms o'er;
The while that liveth Gunther, / may such thing be nevermore."
817
Then again spake Kriemhild: / "Behold how he doth stand
In right stately fashion / before the knightly band,
Like as the bright moon beameth / before the stars of heaven.

In sooth to think upon it / a joyous mood to me is given."
818
Then spake the Lady Brunhild: / "How stately thy spouse be,
Howe'er so fair and worthy, / yet must thou grant to me
Gunther, thy noble brother, / doth far beyond him go:
In sooth before all monarchs / he standeth, shalt thou truly know."
819
Then again spake Kriemhild: / "So worthy is my spouse,
That I not have praised him / here without a cause.
In ways to tell full many / high honor doth he bear:
Believe well may'st thou, Brunhild, / he is the royal Gunther's peer."
820
"Now guard thee, Lady Kriemhild, / my word amiss to take,
For not without good reason here / such thing I spake.
Both heard I say together, / when them I first did see,
When that erstwhile the monarch / did work his royal will o'er me,
821
And when in knightly fashion / my love for him he won,
Then himself said Siegfried / he were the monarch's man.
For liegeman thus I hold him, / since he the same did say."
Then spake fair Lady Kriemhild: / "With me 'twere dealt in sorry way.
822
"And these my noble brothers, / how could they such thing see,
That I of their own liegeman / e'er the wife should be?
Thus will I beg thee, Brunhild, / as friend to friend doth owe,
That thou, as well befits thee, / shalt further here such words forego."
823
"No whit will I give over," / spake the monarch's spouse.
"Wherefore should I so many / a knight full valiant lose,
Who to us in service / is bounden with thy man?"
Kriemhild the fair lady / thereat sore to rage began.
824
"In sooth must thou forego it / that he should e'er to thee
Aught of service offer. / More worthy e'en is he
Than is my brother Gunther, / who is a royal lord.
So shalt thou please to spare me / what I now from thee have heard.
825
"And to me is ever wonder, / since he thy liegeman is,
And thou dost wield such power / over us twain as this,
That he so long his tribute / to thee hath failed to pay.
'Twere well thy haughty humor / thou should'st no longer here display."
826
"Too lofty now thou soarest," / the queen did make reply.

"Now will I see full gladly / if in such honor high
This folk doth hold thy person / as mine own it doth."
Of mood full sorely wrathful / were the royal ladies both.
827
Then spake the Lady Kriemhild: / "That straightway shall be seen.
Since that thou my husband / dost thy liegeman ween,
To-day shall all the followers / of both the monarchs know,
If I 'fore wife of monarch / dare unto the minster go.
828
"That I free-born and noble / shalt thou this day behold,
And that my royal husband, / as now to thee I've told,
'Fore thine doth stand in honor, / by me shall well be shown.
Ere night shalt thou behold it, / how wife of him thou call'st thine own
829
To court shall lead good warriors / in the land of Burgundy.
And ne'er a queen so lofty / as I myself shall be
Was seen by e'er a mortal, / or yet a crown did wear."
Then mickle was the anger / that rose betwixt the ladies there.
830
Then again spake Brunhild: / "Wilt thou not service own,
So must thou with thy women / hold thyself alone
Apart from all my following, / as we to minster go."
Thereto gave answer Kriemhild: / "In truth the same I fain will do."
831
"Now dress ye fair, my maidens," / Kriemhild gave command.
"Nor shall shame befall me / here within this land.
An have ye fair apparel, / let now be seen by you.
What she here hath boasted / may Brunhild have full cause to rue."
832
But little need to urge them: / soon were they richly clad
In garments wrought full deftly, / lady and many a maid.
Then went with her attendants / the spouse of the monarch high;
And eke appeared fair Kriemhild, / her body decked full gorgeously,
833
With three and forty maidens, / whom to the Rhine led she,
All clad in shining garments / wrought in Araby.
So came unto the minster / the maidens fair and tall.
Before the hall did tarry / for them the men of Siegfried all.
834
The people there did wonder / how the thing might be,
That no more together / the queens they thus did see,
And that beside each other / they went not as before.
Thereby came thanes a many / anon to harm and trouble sore.

835
Here before the minster / the wife of Gunther stood.
And good knights full many / were there of merry mood
With the fair ladies / that their eyes did see.
Then came the Lady Kriemhild / with a full stately company.

836
Whate'er of costly raiment / decked lofty maids before,
'Twas like a windy nothing / 'gainst what her ladies wore.
The wives of thirty monarchs / —such riches were her own—
Might ne'er display together / what there by Lady Kriemhild shown.

837
Should any wish to do so / he could not say, I ween,
That so rich apparel / e'er before was seen
As there by her maidens / debonair was worn:
But that it grievéd Brunhild / had Kriemhild that to do forborne.

838
There they met together / before the minster high.
Soon the royal matron, / through mickle jealousy,
Kriemhild to pass no further, / did bid in rage full sore:
"She that doth owe her homage / shall ne'er go monarch's wife before."

839
Then spake the Lady Kriemhild / —angry was her mood:
"An could'st thou but be silent / that for thee were good.
Thyself hast brought dishonor / upon thy fair body:
How might, forsooth, a harlot / ever wife of monarch be?"

840
"Whom mak'st thou now a harlot?" / the king's wife answered her.
"That do I thee," spake Kriemhild, / "for that thy body fair
First was clasped by Siegfried, / knight full dear to me.
In sooth 'twas ne'er my brother / won first thy maidenhead from thee.

841
"How did thy senses leave thee? / Cunning rare was this.
How let his love deceive thee, / since he thy liegeman is?
And all in vain," quoth Kriemhild, / "the plaint I hear thee bring."
"In sooth," then answered Brunhild, / "I'll tell it to my spouse the king."

842
"What reck I of such evil? / Thy pride hath thee betrayed,
That thou deem'st my homage / should e'er to thee be paid.
Know thou in truth full certain / the thing may never be:
Nor shall I e'er be ready / to look for faithful friend in thee."

843
Thereat did weep Queen Brunhild: / Kriemhild waited no more,

But passed into the minster / the monarch's wife before,
With train of fair attendants. / Arose there mickle hate,
Whereby eyes brightly shining / anon did grow all dim and wet.
844
However God they worshipped / or there the mass was sung,
Did deem the Lady Brunhild / the waiting all too long,
For that her heart was saddened / and angry eke her mood.
Therefore anon must suffer / many a hero keen and good.
845
Brunhild with her ladies / 'fore the minster did appear.
Thought she: "Now must Kriemhild / further give me to hear
Of what so loud upbraideth / me this free-tongued wife.
And if he thus hath boasted, / amend shall Siegfried make with life."
846
Now came the noble Kriemhild / followed by warrior band.
Then spake the Lady Brunhild: / "Still thou here shalt stand.
Thou giv'st me out for harlot: / let now the same be seen.
Know thou, what thus thou sayest / to me hath mickle sorrow been."
847
Then spake the Lady Kriemhild: / "So may'st thou let me go.
With the ring upon my finger / I the same can show:
That brought to me my lover / when first by thee he lay."
Ne'er did Lady Brunhild / know grief as on this evil day.
848
Quoth she: "This ring full precious / some hand from me did steal,
And from me thus a season / in evil way conceal:
Full sure will I discover / who this same thief hath been."
Then were the royal ladies / both in mood full angry seen.
849
Then gave answer Kriemhild: / "I deem the thief not I.
Well hadst thou been silent, / hold'st thou thine honor high.
I'll show it with this girdle / that I around me wear,
That in this thing I err not: / Siegfried hath lain by thee full near."
850
Wrought of silk of Nineveh / a girdle there she wore,
That of stones full precious / showed a goodly store.
When saw it Lady Brunhild / straight to weep gan she:
Soon must Gunther know it / and all the men of Burgundy.
851
Then spake the royal matron: / "Bid hither come to me
Of Rhine the lofty monarch. / Hear straightway shall he
How that his sister / doth my honor stain.
Here doth she boast full open / that I in Siegfried's arms have lain."

852

The king came with his warriors, / where he did weeping find
His royal spouse Brunhild, / then spake in manner kind:
"Now tell me, my dear lady, / who hath done aught to thee?"
She spake unto the monarch: / "Thy wife unhappy must thou see.

853

"Me, thy royal consort, / would thy sister fain
Rob of all mine honor. / To thee must I complain:
She boasts her husband Siegfried / hath known thy royal bed."
Then spake the monarch Gunther: / "An evil thing she then hath said."

854

"I did lose a girdle: / here by her 'tis worn,
And my ring all golden. / That I e'er was born,
Do I rue full sorely / if thou wardest not from me
This full great dishonor: / that will I full repay to thee."

855

Then spake the monarch Gunther: / "Now shall he come near,
And hath he such thing boasted, / so shall he let us hear:
Eke must full deny it / the knight of Netherland."
Then straight the spouse of Kriemhild / hither to bring he gave command.

856

When that angry-minded / Siegfried them did see,
Nor knew thereof the reason, / straightway then spake he:
"Why do weep these ladies? / I'd gladly know that thing,
Or wherefore to this presence / I am bidden by the king."

857

Then spake the royal Gunther: / "Sore grieveth me this thing:
To me my Lady Brunhild / doth the story bring,
How that thereof thou boastest / that her fair body lay
First in thy embraces: / this doth thy Lady Kriemhild say."

858

Thereto gave answer Siegfried: / "An if she thus hath said,
Full well shall she repent it / ere doth rest my head:
Before all thy good warriors / of that I'll make me free,
And swear by my high honor / such thing hath ne'er been told by me."

859

Then spake of Rhine the monarch: / "That shalt thou let us see.
The oath that thou dost offer, / if such performéd be,
Of all false accusation / shalt thou delivered stand."
In ring to take their station / did he the high-born thanes command.

860

The full valiant Siegfried / in oath the hand did give.

Then spake the lordly monarch: / "Well now do I perceive
How thou art all blameless, / of all I speak thee free;
What here maintains my sister, / the same hath ne'er been done by thee."
861
Thereto gave answer Siegfried: / "If gain should e'er accrue
Unto my spouse, that Brunhild / from her had cause to rue,
Know that to me full sorely / 'twould endless sorrow be."
Then looked upon each other / the monarchs twain right graciously.
862
"So should we govern women," / spake the thane Siegfried,
"That to leave wanton babble / they should take good heed.
Forbid it to thy wife now, / to mine I'll do the same.
Such ill-becoming manner /in sooth doth fill my heart with shame."
863
No more said many a lady / fair, but thus did part.
Then did the Lady Brunhild / grieve so sore at heart,
That it must move to pity / all King Gunther's men.
To go unto his mistress / Hagen of Tronje saw ye then.
864
He asked to know her worry, / as he her weeping saw.
Then told she him the story. / To her straight made he vow,
That Lady Kriemhild's husband / must for the thing atone,
Else henceforth should never / a joyous day by him be known.
865
Then came Ortwein and Gernot / where they together spake,
And there the knights did counsel / Siegfried's life to take.
Thither came eke Giselher, / son of Ute high.
When heard he what they counselled, / spake he free from treachery:
866
"Ye good knights and noble, / wherefore do ye that?
Ne'er deserved hath Siegfried / in such way your hate,
That he therefor should forfeit / at your hands his life.
In sooth small matter is it / that maketh cause for woman's strife."
867
"Shall we rear race of bastards?" / Hagen spake again:
"Therefrom but little honor / had many a noble thane.
The thing that he hath boasted / upon my mistress high,
Therefor my life I forfeit, / or he for that same thing shall die."
868
Then spake himself the monarch: / "To us he ne'er did give
Aught but good and honor: / let him therefore live.
What boots it if my anger / I vent the knight upon?

Good faith he e'er hath shown us, / and that full willingly hath done."
869
Then outspake of Metz / Ortwein the thane:
"In sooth his arm full doughty / may bring him little gain.
My vengeance full he'll suffer, / if but my lord allow."
The knights—nor reason had they— / against him mortal hate did vow.
870
None yet his words did follow, / but to the monarch's ear
Ne'er a day failed Hagen / the thought to whisper there:
If that lived not Siegfried, / to him would subject be
Royal lands full many. / The king did sorrow bitterly.
871
Then did they nothing further: / soon began the play.
As from the lofty minster / passed they on their way,
What doughty shafts they shattered / Siegfried's spouse before!
Gunther's men full many / saw ye there in rage full sore.
872
Spake the king: "Now leave ye / such mortal enmity:
The knight is born our honor / and fortune good to be.
Keen is he unto wonder, / hath eke so doughty arm
That, were the contest open, / none is who dared to work him harm."
873
"Naught shall he know," quoth Hagen. / "At peace ye well may be:
I trow the thing to manage / so full secretly
That Queen Brunhild's weeping / he shall rue full sore.
In sooth shall he from Hagen / have naught but hate for evermore."
874
Then spake the monarch Gunther: / "How might such thing e'er be?"
Thereto gave answer Hagen: / "That shalt thou hear from me.
We'll bid that hither heralds / unto our land shall fare,
Here unknown to any, / who shall hostile tidings bear.
875
"Then say thou 'fore the strangers / that thou with all thy men
Wilt forth to meet the enemy. / He'll offer service then
If that thus thou sayest, / and lose thereby his life,
Can I but learn the story / from the valiant warrior's wife."
876
The king in evil manner / did follow Hagen's rede,
And the two knights, ere any / man thereof had heed,
Had treachery together / to devise begun.
From quarrel of two women / died heroes soon full many a one.

FIFTEENTH ADVENTURE: How Siegfried was Betrayed

877
Upon the fourth morning / two and thirty men
Saw ye to court a-riding. / Unto King Gunther then
Were tidings borne that ready / he should make for foe—
This lie did bring to women / many, anon full grievous woe.

878
Leave had they 'fore the monarch's / presence to appear,
There to give themselves out / for men of Luedeger,
Him erstwhile was conquered / by Siegfried's doughty hand
And brought a royal hostage / bound unto King Gunther's land.

879
The messengers he greeted / and to seat them gave command.
Then spake one amongst them: / "Allow that yet we stand
Until we tell the tidings / that to thee are sent.
Know thou that warriors many / on thee to wreak their hate are bent.

880
"Defiance bids thee Luedegast / and eke Luedeger
Who at thy hands full sorely / erstwhile aggrievéd were:
In this thy land with hostile / host they'll soon appear."
To rage begin the monarch / when such tidings he did hear.

881
Those who did act thus falsely / they bade to lodge the while.
How himself might Siegfried / guard against such guile
As there they planned against him, / he or ever one?
Unto themselves 'twas sorrow / great anon that e'er 'twas done.

882
With his friends the monarch / secret counsel sought.
Hagen of Tronje / let him tarry not.
Of the king's men yet were many / who fain would peace restore:
But nowise would Hagen / his dark purpose e'er give o'er.

883
Upon a day came Siegfried / when they did counsel take,
And there the knight of Netherland / thus unto them spake:
"How goeth now so sorrowful / amid his men the king?
I'll help you to avenge it, / hath he been wronged in anything."

884
Then spake the monarch Gunther: / "Of right do I lament,
Luedegast and Luedeger / have hostile message sent:
They will in open manner / now invade my land."

The knight full keen gave answer: / "That in sooth shall Siegfried's hand,

885
"As doth befit thy honor, / know well to turn aside.
As erstwhile to thy enemies, / shall now from me betide:
Their lands and eke their castles / laid waste by me shall be
Ere that I give over: / thereof my head be surety.

886
"Thou and thy good warriors / shall here at home abide,
And let me with my company / alone against them ride.
That I do serve thee gladly, / that will I let them see;
By me shall thy enemies, / —that know thou— full requited be."

887
"Good tidings, that thou sayest," / then the monarch said,
As if he in earnest / did joy to have such aid.
Deep did bow before him / the king in treachery.
Then spake Sir Siegfried: / "Bring that but little care to thee."

888
Then serving-men full many / bade they ready be:
'Twas done alone that Siegfried / and his men the same might see.
Then bade he make them ready / the knights of Netherland,
And soon did Siegfried's warriors / for fight apparelled ready stand.

889
"My royal father Siegmund, / here shalt thou remain,"
Spake then Sir Siegfried. / "We come full soon again
If God but give good fortune, / hither the Rhine beside;
Here shalt thou with King Gunther / full merrily the while abide."

890
Then bound they on the banners / as they thence would fare.
Men of royal Gunther / were full many there,
Who naught knew of the matter, / or how that thing might be:
There with Siegfried saw ye / of knights a mickle company.

891
Their helms and eke their mail-coats / bound on horse did stand:
And doughty knights made ready / to fare from out that land.
Then went of Tronje Hagen / where he Kriemhild found
And prayed a fair leave-taking, / for that to battle they were bound.

892
"Now well is me, such husband / I have," Kriemhild said,
"That to my loving kindred / can bring so potent aid,
As my lord Siegfried / doth now to friends of me.
Thereby," spake the high lady, / "may I full joyous-minded be.

893
"Now full dear friend Hagen, / call thou this to mind,
Good-will I e'er have borne thee, / nor hate in any kind.
Let now therefrom have profit / the husband dear to me.
If Brunhild aught I've injured / may't not to him requited be.

894
"For that I since have suffered," / spake the high lady.
"Sore punishment hath offered / therefor the knight to me.
That I have aught e'er spoken / to make her sad of mood,
Vengeance well hath taken / on me the valiant knight and good."

895
"In the days hereafter shall ye / be reconciled full well.
Kriemhild, belovéd lady, / to me shalt thou tell
How that in Siegfried's person / I may service do to thee.
That do I gladly, lady, / and unto none more willingly."

896
"No longer were I fearful," / spake his noble wife,
"That e'er in battle any / should take from him his life,
Would he but cease to follow / his high undaunted mood:
Secure were then forever / the thane full valiant and good."

897
"Lady," spake then Hagen, / "an hast thou e'er a fear
That hostile blade should pierce him, / now shalt thou give to hear
With what arts of cunning / I may the same prevent.
On horse and foot to guard him / shall ever be my fair intent."

898
She spake: "Of my kin art thou, / as I eke of thine.
In truth to thee commended / be then dear spouse of mine,
That him well thou guardest / whom full dear I hold."
She told to him a story / 'twere better had she left untold.

899
She spake: "A valorous husband / is mine, and doughty too.
When he the worm-like dragon / by the mountain slew,
In its blood the stately / knight himself then bathed,
Since when from cutting weapons / in battle is he all unscathed.

900
"Nathless my heart is troubled / when he in fight doth stand,
And full many a spear-shaft / is hurled by hero's hand,
Lest that I a husband / full dear should see no more.
Alack! How oft for Siegfried / must I sit in sorrow sore!

901
"On thy good-will I rest me, / dear friend, to tell to thee,
And that thy faith thou fully / provest now to me,

Where that my spouse may smitten / be by hand of foe.
This I now shall tell thee, / and on thy honor this I do.

902
"When from the wounded dragon / reeking flowed the blood,
And therein did bathe him / the valiant knight and good,
Fell down between his shoulders / full broad a linden leaf.
There may he be smitten; / 'tis cause to me of mickle grief.'

903
Then spake of Tronje Hagen: / "Upon his tunic sew
Thou a little token. / Thereby shall I know
Where I may protect him / when in the fight we strain."
She weened to save the hero, / yet wrought she nothing save his bane.

904
She spake: "All fine and silken / upon his coat I'll sew
A little cross full secret. / There, doughty thane, shalt thou
From my knight ward danger / when battle rageth sore,
And when amid the turmoil / he stands his enemies before."

905
"That will I do," quoth Hagen, / "lady full dear to me."
Then weenéd eke the lady / it should his vantage be,
But there alone did Kriemhild / her own good knight betray.
Leave of her took Hagen, / and joyously he went away.

906
The followers of the monarch / were all of merry mood.
I ween that knight thereafter / never any could
Of treachery be guilty / such as then was he
When that Queen Kriemhild / did rest on his fidelity.

907
With his men a thousand / upon the following day
Rode thence Sir Siegfried / full joyously away.
He weened he should take vengeance / for harm his friends did bear.
That he might view the tunic / Hagen rode to him full near.

908
When he had viewed the token / sent Hagen thence away
Two of his men in secret / who did other tidings say:
How that King Gunther's country / had nothing now to fear
And that unto the monarch / had sent them royal Luedeger.

909
'Twas little joy to Siegfried / that he must turn again
Ere for the hostile menace / vengeance he had ta'en.
In sooth the men of Gunther / could scarce his purpose bend.
Then rode he to the monarch, / who thus began his thanks to lend:

910

"Now God reward thee for it, / my good friend Siegfried,
That thou with mind so willing / hast holpen me in need.
That shall I e'er repay thee, / as I may do of right.
To thee before all other / friends do I my service plight.

911

"Now that from battle-journey / free we are once more,
So will I ride a-hunting / the wild bear and the boar
Away to the Vosges forest, / as I full oft have done."
The same had counselled Hagen, / the full dark and faithless man.

912

"To all my guests here with me / shall now be told
That we ride forth at daybreak: / themselves shall ready hold,
Who will join the hunting; / will any here remain
For pastime with fair ladies, / the thing behold I eke full fain."

913

Then outspake Sir Siegfried / as in manner due:
"If that thou rid'st a-hunting, / go I gladly too.
A huntsman shalt thou grant me / and good hound beside
That shall the game discover; / so with thee to the green I'll ride."

914

Straightway spake the monarch: / "Wilt thou but one alone?
And wilt thou, four I'll grant thee, / to whom full well is known
The forest with the runways / where most the game doth stray,
And who unto the camp-fires / will help thee back to find thy way."

915

Unto his spouse then rode he, / the gallant knight and bold.
Full soon thereafter Hagen / unto the king had told
How he within his power / would have the noble thane:
May deed so dark and faithless / ne'er by knight be done again!

SIXTEENTH ADVENTURE: How Siegfried was slain

916

Gunther and Hagen, / the knights full keen,
Proposed with evil forethought / a hunting in the green:
The boar within the forest / they'd chase with pointed spear,
And shaggy bear and bison. / —What sport to valiant men more dear?

917

With them rode also Siegfried / happy and light of heart:
Their load of rich refreshments / was made in goodly part.

Where a spring ran cooling / they took from him his life,
Whereto in chief had urged them / Brunhild, royal Gunther's wife.
918
Then went the valiant Siegfried / where he Kriemhild found;
Rich hunting-dress was laden / and now stood ready bound
For him and his companions / across the Rhine to go.
Than this a sadder hour / nevermore could Kriemhild know.
919
The spouse he loved so dearly / upon the mouth he kissed.
"God grant that well I find thee / again, if so He list,
And thine own eyes to see me. / 'Mid kin that hold thee dear
May now the time go gently, / the while I am no longer near."
920
Then thought she of the story / —but silence must she keep—
Whereof once Hagen asked her: / then began to weep
The princess high and noble / that ever she was born,
And wept with tears unceasing / the valiant Siegfried's wife forlorn.
921
She spake unto her husband: / "Let now this hunting be.
I dreamt this night of evil, / how wild boars hunted thee,
Two wild boars o'er the meadow, / wherefrom the flowers grew red.
That I do weep so sorely / have I poor woman direst need.
922
"Yea, do I fear, Sir Siegfried, / something treacherous,
If perchance have any / of those been wronged by us
Who might yet be able / to vent their enmity.
Tarry thou here, Sir Siegfried: / let that my faithful counsel be."
923
Quoth he: "I come, dear lady, / when some short days are flown.
Of foes who bear us hatred / here know I never one.
All of thine own kindred / are gracious unto me,
Nor know I aught of reason / why they should other-minded be."
924
"But nay, belovéd Siegfried, / thy death I fear 'twill prove.
This night I dreamt misfortune, / how o'er thee from above
Down there fell two mountains: / I never saw thee more.
And wilt thou now go from me, / that must grieve my heart full sore."
925
The lady rich in virtue / within his arms he pressed,
And with loving kisses / her fair form caressed.
From her thence he parted / ere long time was o'er:
Alas for her, she saw him / alive thereafter nevermore.

926

Then rode from thence the hunters / deep within a wold
In search of pleasant pastime. / Full many a rider bold
Followed after Gunther / in his stately train.
Gernot and Giselher, / —at home the knights did both remain.

927

Went many a horse well laden / before them o'er the Rhine,
That for the huntsmen carried / store of bread and wine,
Meat along with fishes / and other victualling,
The which upon his table / were fitting for so high a king.

928

Then bade they make encampment / before the forest green
Where game was like to issue, / those hunters proud and keen,
Who there would join in hunting, / on a meadow wide that spread.
Thither also was come Siegfried: / the same unto the king was said.

929

By the merry huntsmen / soon were watched complete
At every point the runways. / The company then did greet
Siegfried the keen and doughty: / "Who now within the green
Unto the game shall guide us, / ye warriors so bold and keen?"

930

"Now part we from each other," / answered Hagen then,
"Ere that the hunting / we do here begin!
Thereby may be apparent / to my masters and to me
Who on this forest journey / of the hunters best may be.

931

"Let then hounds and huntsmen / be ta'en in equal share,
That wheresoever any / would go, there let him fare.
Who then is first in hunting / shall have our thanks this day."
Not longer there together / did the merry hunters stay.

932

Thereto quoth Sir Siegfried: / "Of dogs have I no need,
More than one hound only / of trusty hunting breed
For scenting well the runway / of wild beast through the brake.
And now the chase begin we!" / —so the spouse of Kriemhild spake.

933

Then took a practised hunter / a good tracking-hound,
That did bring them where they / game in plenty found,
Nor kept them long awaiting. / Whate'er did spring from lair
Pursued the merry huntsmen, / as still good hunters everywhere.

934

As many as the hound started / slew with mighty hand
Siegfried the full doughty / hero of Netherland.

So swiftly went his charger / that none could him outrun;
And praise before all others / soon he in the hunting won.

935
He was in every feature / a valiant knight and true.
The first within the forest / that with his hand he slew
Was a half-grown wild-boar / that he smote to ground;
Thereafter he full quickly / a wild and mighty lion found.

936
When it the hound had started, / with bow he shot it dead,
Wherewith a pointed arrow / he had so swiftly sped
That the lion after / could forward spring but thrice.
All they that hunted with him / cried Siegfried's praise with merry voice.

937
Soon fell a prey unto him / an elk and bison more,
A giant stag he slew him / and huge ure-oxen four.
His steed bore him so swiftly / that none could him outrun;
Of stag or hind encountered / scarce could there escape him one.

938
A boar full huge and bristling / soon was likewise found,
And when the same bethought him / to flee before the hound,
Came quick again the master / and stood athwart his path.
The boar upon the hero / full charged straightway in mickle wrath.

939
Then the spouse of Kriemhild, / with sword the boar he slew,
A thing that scarce another / hunter had dared to do.
When he thus had felled him / they lashed again the hound,
And soon his hunting prowess / was known to all the people round.

940
Then spake to him his huntsmen: / "If that the thing may be,
So let some part, Sir Siegfried, / of the forest game go free;
To-day thou makest empty / hillside and forest wild."
Thereat in merry humor / the thane so keen and valiant smiled.

941
Then they heard on all sides / the din, from many a hound
And huntsmen eke the clamor / so great was heard around
That back did come the answer / from hill and forest tree—
Of hounds had four-and-twenty / packs been set by hunter free.

942
Full many a forest denizen / from life was doomed to part.
Each of all the hunters / thereon had set his heart,
To win the prize in hunting. / But such could never be,
When they the doughty Siegfried / at the camping-place did see.

943
Now the chase was ended, / —and yet complete 'twas not.
All they to camp who wended / with them thither brought
Skin of full many an animal / and of game good store.
Heigho! unto the table / how much the king's attendants bore!

944
Then bade the king the noble / hunters all to warn
That he would take refreshment, / and loud a hunting-horn
In one long blast was winded: / to all was known thereby
That the noble monarch / at camp did wait their company.

945
Spake one of Siegfried's huntsmen: / "Master, I do know
By blast of horn resounding / that we now shall go
Unto the place of meeting; / thereto I'll make reply."
Then for the merry hunters / blew the horn right lustily.

946
Then spake Sir Siegfried: / "Now leave we eke the green."
His charger bore him smoothly, / and followed huntsmen keen.
With their rout they started / a beast of savage kind,
That was a bear untaméd. / Then spake the knight to those behind

947
"For our merry party / some sport will I devise.
Let slip the hound then straightway, / a bear now meets my eyes,
And with us shall he thither / unto the camp-fire fare.
Full rapid must his flight be / shall he our company forbear."

948
From leash the hound was loosened, / the bear sprang through the brake,
When that the spouse of Kriemhild / did wish him to o'ertake.
He sought a pathless thicket, / but yet it could not be,
As bruin fondly hoped it, / that from the hunter he was free.

949
Then from his horse alighted / the knight of spirit high,
And gan a running after. / Bruin all unguardedly
Was ta'en, and could escape not. / Him caught straightway the knight,
And soon all unwounded / had him bound in fetters tight.

950
Nor claws nor teeth availed him / for aught of injury,
But bound he was to saddle. / Then mounted speedily
The knight, and to the camp-fire / in right merry way
For pastime led he bruin, / the hero valiant and gay.

951
In what manner stately / unto the camp he rode!

He bore a spear full mickle, / great of strength and broad.
A sword all ornamented / hung down unto his spur,
And wrought of gold all ruddy / at side a glittering horn he wore.

952
Of richer hunting-garments / heard I ne'er tell before.
Black was the silken tunic / that the rider wore,
And cap of costly sable / did crown the gallant knight.
Heigho, and how his quiver / with well-wrought hands was rich bedight!

953
A skin of gleaming panther / covered the quiver o'er,
Prized for its pleasant odor. / Eke a bow he bore,
The which to draw if ever / had wished another man,
A lever he had needed: / such power had Siegfried alone.

954
Of fur of costly otter / his mantle was complete,
With other skins embroidered / from head unto the feet.
And 'mid the fur all shining, / full many a golden seam
On both sides of the valiant / huntsman saw ye brightly gleam.

955
Balmung, a goodly weapon / broad, he also wore,
That was so sharp at edges / that it ne'er forbore
To cleave when swung on helmet: / blade it was full good.
Stately was the huntsman / as there with merry heart he rode.

956
If that complete the story / to you I shall unfold,
Full many a goodly arrow / did his rich quiver hold
Whereof were gold the sockets, / and heads a hand-breadth each.
In sooth was doomed to perish / whate'er in flight the same did reach.

957
Pricking like goodly huntsman / the noble knight did ride
When him the men of Gunther / coming thither spied.
They hasted out to meet him / and took from him his steed,
As bruin great and mighty / by the saddle he did lead.

958
When he from horse alighted / he loosed him every band
From foot and eke from muzzle. / Straight on every hand
Began the dogs a howling / when they beheld the bear.
Bruin would to the forest: / among the men was mickle stir.

959
Amid the clamor bruin / through the camp-fires sped:
Heigho, how the servants / away before him fled!
O'erturned was many a kettle / and flaming brands did fly:

Heigho, what goodly victuals / did scattered in the ashes lie!
960
Then sprang from out the saddle / knights and serving-men.
The bear was wild careering: / the king bade loosen then
All the dogs that fastened / within their leashes lay.
If this thing well had ended, / then had there passed a merry day.
961
Not longer then they waited / but with bow and eke with spear
Hasted the nimble hunters / to pursue the bear,
Yet none might shoot upon him / for all the dogs around.
Such clamor was of voices / that all the mountain did resound.
962
When by the dogs pursuéd / the bear away did run,
None there that could o'ertake him / but Siegfried alone.
With his sword he came upon him / and killed him at a blow,
And back unto the camp-fire / bearing bruin they did go.
963
Then spake who there had seen it, / he was a man of might.
Soon to the table bade they / come each noble knight,
And on a smiling meadow / the noble company sat.
Heigho, with what rare victuals / did they upon the huntsmen wait!
964
Ne'er appeared a butler / wine for them to pour.
Than they good knights were never / better served before,
And had there not in secret / been lurking treachery,
Then were the entertainers / from every cause of cavil free.
965
Then spake Sir Siegfried: / "A wonder 'tis to me,
Since that from the kitchen / so full supplied are we,
Why to us the butlers / of wine bring not like store:
If such the huntsman's service / a huntsman reckon me no more.
966
"Meseems I yet did merit / some share of courtesy."
The king who sat at table / spake then in treachery:
"Gladly shall be amended / wherein we're guilty so.
The fault it is of Hagen, / he'd willing see us thirsting go."
967
Then spake of Tronje Hagen: / "Good master, hear me say,
I weened for this our hunting / we did go to-day
Unto the Spessart forest: / the wine I thither sent.
Go we to-day a-thirsting, / I'll later be more provident."
968
Thereto replied Sir Siegfried: / "Small merit here is thine.

Good seven horses laden / with mead and sparkling wine
Should hither have been conducted. / If aught the same denied,
Then should our place of meeting / have nearer been the Rhine beside."

969
Then spake of Tronje Hagen: / "Ye noble knights and bold,
I know here nigh unto us / a spring that's flowing cold.
Be then your wrath appeaséd, / and let us thither go."
Through that same wicked counsel / came many a thane to grievous woe.

970
Sore was the noble Siegfried / with the pangs of thirst:
To bid them rise from table / was he thus the first.
He would along the hillside / unto the fountain go:
In sooth they showed them traitors, / those knights who there did counsel so.

971
On wagons hence to carry / the game they gave command
Which had that day been slaughtered / by Siegfried's doughty hand.
He'd carried off the honors, / all who had seen did say.
Hagen his faith with Siegfried / soon did break in grievous way.

972
When now they would go thither / to where the linden spread,
Spake of Tronje Hagen: / "To me hath oft been said,
That none could follow after / Kriemhild's nimble knight
Or vie with him in running: / would that he'd prove it to our sight!"

973
Then spake of Netherland / bold Siegfried speedily:
"That may ye well have proof of, / will ye but run with me
In contest to the fountain. / When that the same be done,
To him be given honor / who the race hath fairly won."

974
"Now surely make we trial," / quoth Hagen the thane.
Thereto the doughty Siegfried: / "I too will give you gain,
Afore your feet at starting / to lay me in the grass."
When that he had heard it, / thereat how joyous Gunther was!

975
And spake again the warrior: / "And ye shall further hear:
All my clothing likewise / will I upon me wear,
The spear and shield full heavy / and hunting-dress I'll don."
His sword as well as quiver / had he full quickly girded on.

976
Doffed they their apparel / and aside they laid it then:
Clothed in white shirts only / saw you there the twain.

Like unto two wild panthers / they coursed across the green:
Yet first beside the fountain / was the valiant Siegfried seen.

977

No man in feats of valor / who with him had vied.
The sword he soon ungirded / and quiver laid aside,
The mighty spear he leanéd / against the linden-tree:
Beside the running fountain / stood the knight stately to see.

978

To Siegfried naught was lacking / that doth good knight adorn.
Down the shield then laid he / where did flow the burn,
Yet howsoe'er he thirsted / no whit the hero drank
Before had drunk the monarch: / therefor he earned but evil thank.

979

There where ran clear the water / and cool from out the spring,
Down to it did bend him / Gunther the king.
And when his thirst was quenchéd / rose he from thence again:
Eke the valiant Siegfried, / how glad had he done likewise then.

980

For his courtesy he suffered. / Where bow and sword there lay,
Both did carry Hagen / from him thence away,
And again sprang quickly thither / where the spear did stand:
And for a cross the tunic / of the valiant knight he scanned.

981

As there the noble Siegfried / to drink o'er fountain bent,
Through the cross he pierced him, / that from the wound was sent
The blood nigh to bespatter / the tunic Hagen wore.
By hand of knight such evil / deed shall wrought be nevermore.

982

The spear he left projecting / where it had pierced the heart.
In terror as that moment / did Hagen never start
In flight from any warrior / he ever yet had found.
Soon as the noble Siegfried / within him felt the mighty wound,

983

Raging the knight full doughty / up from the fountain sprang,
The while from 'twixt his shoulders / stood out a spearshaft long.
The prince weened to find there / his bow or his sword:
Then in sooth had Hagen / found the traitor's meet reward.

984

When from the sorely wounded / knight his sword was gone,
Then had he naught to 'venge him / but his shield alone.
This snatched he from the fountain / and Hagen rushed upon,
And not at all escape him / could the royal Gunther's man.

985
Though he nigh to death was wounded / he yet such might did wield
That out in all directions / flew from off the shield
Precious stones a many: / the shield he clave in twain.
Thus vengeance fain had taken / upon his foe the stately thane.
986
Beneath his hand must Hagen / stagger and fall to ground.
So swift the blow he dealt him, / the meadow did resound.
Had sword in hand been swinging, / Hagen had had his meed,
So sorely raged he stricken: / to rage in sooth was mickle need.
987
Faded from cheek was color, / no longer could he stand,
And all his might of body / soon complete had waned,
As did a deathly pallor / over his visage creep.
Full many a fairest lady / for the knight anon must weep.
988
So sank amid the flowers / Kriemhild's noble knight,
While from his wound flowed thickly / the blood before the sight.
Then gan he reviling / —for dire was his need—
Who had thus encompassed / his death by this same faithless deed.
989
Then spake the sorely wounded: / "O ye base cowards twain,
Doth then my service merit / that me ye thus have slain?
To you I e'er was faithful / and so am I repaid.
Alas, upon your kindred / now have ye shame eternal laid.
990
"By this deed dishonored / hereafter evermore
Are their generations. / Your anger all too sore
Have ye now thus vented / and vengeance ta'en on me.
With shame henceforth be parted / from all good knights' company."
991
All the hunters hastened / where he stricken lay,
It was in sooth for many / of them a joyless day.
Had any aught of honor, / he mourned that day, I ween,
And well the same did merit / the knight high-spirited and keen.
992
As there the king of Burgundy / mourned that he should die,
Spake the knight sore wounded: / "To weep o'er injury,
Who hath wrought the evil / hath smallest need, I trow.
Reviling doth he merit, / and weeping may he well forego."
993
Thereto quoth grim Hagen: / "Ye mourn, I know not why:
This same day hath ended / all our anxiety.

Few shall we find henceforward / for fear will give us need,
And well is me that from his / mastery we thus are freed."

994
"Light thing is now thy vaunting," / did Siegfried then reply.
"Had I e'er bethought me / of this thy infamy
Well had I preservéd / 'gainst all thy hate my life.
Me rueth naught so sorely / as Lady Kriemhild my wife.

995
"Now may God have mercy / that to me a son was born,
That him alack!, the people / in times to come shall spurn,
That those he nameth kinsmen / have done the murderer's deed.
An had I breath," spake Siegfried, / "to mourn o'er this I well had need."

996
Then spake, in anguish praying, / the hero doomed to die:
"An wilt thou, king, to any / yet not good faith deny,
In all the world to any, / to thee commended be
And to thy loving mercy / the spouse erstwhile was wed to me.

997
"Let it be her good fortune / that she thy sister is:
By all the princely virtues, / I beg thee pledge me this.
For me long time my father / and men henceforth must wait:
Upon a spouse was never / wrought, as mine, a wrong so great."

998
All around the flowers / were wetted with the blood
As there with death he struggled. / Yet not for long he could,
Because the deadly weapon / had cut him all too sore:
And soon the keen and noble / knight was doomed to speak no more.

999
When the lords perceivéd / how that the knight was dead,
Upon a shield they laid him / that was of gold full red,
And counsel took together / how of the thing should naught
Be known, but held in secret / that Hagen the deed had wrought.

1000
Then spake of them a many: / "This is an evil day.
Now shall ye all conceal it / and all alike shall say,
When as Kriemhild's husband / the dark forest through
Rode alone a-hunting, / him the hand of robber slew."

1001
Then spake of Tronje Hagen: / "Myself will bring him home.
In sooth I reck but little / if to her ears it come,
Who my Lady Brunhild / herself hath grieved so sore.
It maketh me small worry, / an if she weep for evermore."

SEVENTEENTH ADVENTURE: How Kriemhild mourned for Siegfried, and How he was Buried

1002
There till the night they tarried / and o'er the Rhine they went.
By knights in chase might never / more evil day be spent;
For the game that there they hunted / wept many a noble maid.
In sooth by many a valiant / warrior must it since be paid.

1003
Of humor fierce and wanton / list now and ye shall hear,
And eke of direst vengeance. / Hagen bade to bear
Siegfried thus lifeless, / of the Nibelung country,
Unto a castle dwelling / where Lady Kriemhild found might be.

1004
He bade in secret manner / to lay him there before
Where she should surely find him / when she from out the door
Should pass to matins early, / ere that had come the day.
In sooth did Lady Kriemhild / full seldom fail the hour to pray.

1005
When, as was wont, in minster / the bell to worship bade,
Kriemhild, fair lady, wakened / from slumber many a maid:
A light she bade them bring her / and eke her dress to wear.
Then hither came a chamberlain / who Siegfried's corse found waiting there.

1006
He saw him red and bloody, / all wet his clothing too.
That it was his master, / in sooth no whit he knew.
On unto the chamber / the light in hand he bore,
Whereby the Lady Kriemhild / did learn what brought her grief full sore.

1007
When she with train of ladies / would to the minster go,
Then spake the chamberlain: / "Pause, I pray thee now:
Here before thy dwelling / a noble knight lies slain."
Thereat gan Lady Kriemhild / in grief unmeasured sore to plain.

1008
Ere yet that 'twas her husband / she did rightly find,
Had she Hagen's question / begun to call to mind,
How might he protect him: / then first did break her heart,

For all her joy in living / did with his death from her depart.
1009
Unto the earth then sank she / ere she a word did say,
And reft of all her pleasure / there the fair lady lay.
Soon had Kriemhild's sorrow / all measure passed beyond:
She shrieked, when past the swooning, / that did the chamber all resound.
1010
Then spake her attendants: / "What if't a stranger were?"
From out her mouth the heart-blood / did spring from anguish sore.
Then spake she: "It is Siegfried / my husband, other none:
This thing hath counselled Brunhild, / and Hagen's hand the deed hath done."
1011
The lady bade them lead her / where did lie the knight,
And his fair head she raiséd / with her hand full white.
Red though it was and bloody / she knew him yet straightway,
As all forlorn the hero / of Nibelungenland there lay.
1012
Then cried the queen in anguish, / whose hand such wealth might wield:
"O woe is me for sorrow! / Yet is not thy shield
With blow of sword now battered, / but murdered dost thou lie.
And knew I who hath done it, / by my counsel should he die."
1013
All of her attendants / did weep and wail enow
With their belovéd mistress, / for filled they were with woe
For their noble master / whom they should see no more.
For anger of Queen Brunhild / had Hagen wrought revenge full sore.
1014
Then spake Kriemhild sorrowing: / "Hence now the message take,
And all the men of Siegfried / shall ye straightway awake.
Unto Siegmund likewise / tell ye my sorrow deep,
If that he will help me / for the doughty Siegfried weep."
1015
Then ran straightway a messenger / and soon he found at hand,
Siegfried's valiant warriors / of Nibelungenland.
Of joy he all bereft him / with tale that he did bear,
Nor would they aught believe it / till sound of weeping met their ear.
1016
The messenger came eke quickly / where the king did lie,
Yet closed was not in sleeping / the monarch Siegmund's eye:
I ween his heart did tell him / the thing that there had been,

And that his dear son living / might nevermore by him be seen.

1017

"Awake, awake, Lord Siegmund. / Hither hath sent for thee
Kriemhild my mistress. / A wrong now beareth she,
A grief that 'fore all others / unto her heart doth go:
To mourn it shalt thou help her, / for sorely hast thou need thereto."

1018

Up raised himself then Siegmund. / He spake: "What may it be
Of wrong that grieveth Kriemhild, / as thou hast told to me?"
The messenger spake weeping: / "Now may I naught withhold:
Know thou that of Netherland / Siegfried brave lies slain and cold."

1019

Thereto gave answer Siegmund: / "Let now such mocking be
And tale of such ill tidings / —an thou regardest me—
As that thou say'st to any / now he lieth slain:
An were it so, I never / unto my end might cease to plain."

1020

"Wilt thou now believe not / the tidings that I bear,
So may'st thyself the Lady / Kriemhild weeping hear,
And all of her attendants, / that Siegfried lieth dead."
With terror filled was Siegmund: / whereof in very sooth was need.

1021

He and his men a hundred / from their beds they sprang,
Then snatched in hand full quickly / swords both sharp and long,
And toward the sound of weeping / in sorrow sore did speed.
There came a thousand warriors / eke of the valiant knight Siegfried.

1022

When they heard the women weeping / in such sore distress
Thought some, strict custom keeping, / we first must don our dress.
In sooth for very sorrow / their wits no more had they,
For on their hearts a burden / of grief full deep and heavy lay.

1023

Then came the monarch Siegmund / where he Kriemhild espied.
He spake: "Alack that ever / to this country I did ride!
Who in such wondrous manner, / and while good friends are near,
Hath of my child bereft me / and thee of spouse thou hold'st so dear?"

1024

"Ah, might I him discover," / spake the lady high,
"Evermore would mercy / I to him deny.
Such meed of vengeance should he / at my hands receive
That all who call him kinsman / reason good should have to grieve."

1025

Siegmund the monarch / in arms the knight did press,

And of his friends there gathered / so great was the distress,
That from the mighty wailing / palace and wide hall
And Worms the city likewise / with sound of woe re-echoed all.
1026
None was who aught might comfort / the wife of Siegfried there.
They drew the knight's attire / from off his body fair,
From wounds the blood, too, washed they / and laid him on the bier.
Then from all his people / a mighty wailing might ye hear.
1027
Then outspake his warriors / of Nibelungenland:
"Until he be avengéd / rest shall not our hand.
He is within this castle / who the deed hath done."
Then rushed to find their weapons / Siegfried's warriors every one.
1028
The knights of chosen valor / with shields did thither throng,
Eleven hundred warriors, / that did to train belong
Of Siegmund the monarch. / That his son lay dead,
Would he wreak dire vengeance, / whereof in very sooth was need.
1029
Yet knew they not whom should they / beset in battle then,
If it were not Gunther / and with him his men
With whom their lord Siegfried / unto the hunting rode.
Yet filled with fear was Kriemhild / when she beheld how armed they stood.
1030
How great soe'er her sorrow / and stern the grief she bore,
Yet for the Nibelungen / feared she death full sore
From her brother's warriors, / and bade them hold their wrath.
She gave them kindly warning / as friend to friend beloved doth.
1031
Then spake she rich in sorrow: / "What thing beginnest thou,
Good my lord Siegmund? / This case thou dost not know.
In sooth hath here King Gunther / so many a valiant knight,
Lost are ye all together, / will ye the thanes withstand in fight."
1032
With shields upraised they ready / for the fight did stand.
But the queen full noble / did straightway give command
To those high knights, and prayed them, / their purpose to give o'er.
That she might not dissuade them, / in sooth to her was sorrow sore.
1033
Spake she thus: "Lord Siegmund, / thou shalt this thing let be
Until more fitting season. / Seek will I e'er with thee
Full to avenge my husband. / Who him from me hath ta'en,

An I shall know him guilty, / in me shall surely find his bane.

1034
"Of warriors proud and mighty / are many here by Rhine,
Therefore will I advise not / the struggle to begin.
For one that we can muster / good thirty men have they;
As unto us their dealing, / God them requite in equal way.

1035
"Here shall ye bide with me / and help my grief to bear;
Soon as dawns the morning, / ye noble knights and rare,
Help me my loved husband / prepare for burial."
"That shall be done full willing," / spake the doughty warriors all.

1036
To you could never any / full the wonder say,
Of knights and noble ladies, / so full of grief were they,
That the sound of wailing / through the town was heard afar,
Whereat the noble burghers / hastily did gather there.

1037
With the guests they mourned together, / for sore they grieved as well.
What was the guilt of Siegfried / none to them might tell,
Wherefore the knight so noble / thus his life should lose.
Then wept with the high ladies / many a worthy burgher's spouse.

1038
Smiths they bade a casket / work full hastily
All of gold and silver / that great and strong should be.
They bade them fast to weld it / with bands of steel full good.
Then saw ye all the people / stand right sorrowful of mood.

1039
Now the night was over, / for day, they said, drew near.
Then bade the noble lady / unto the minster bear
Siegfried her lord full lovéd / for whom she mourned so.
Whoe'er was friend unto him, / him saw ye weeping thither go.

1040
As they brought him to the minster / bells full many rung.
On every hand then heard ye / how priests did chant their song.
Thither with his followers / came Gunther the king
And eke the grim knight Hagen / where was sound of sorrowing.

1041
He spake: "Full loving sister, / alack for grief to thee,
And that from such great evil / spared we might not be!
Henceforth must we ever / mourn for Siegfried's sake."
"That do ye without reason," / full of woe the lady spake.

1042
"If that ye grievéd for it, / befallen were it not.

For say I may full truly, / me had ye all forgot
There where I thus was parted / from my husband dear.
Would it God," spake Kriemhild, / "that done unto myself it were!"

1043
Fast they yet denied it. / Kriemhild spake again:
"If any speak him guiltless, / let here be seen full plain.
Unto the bier now shall he / before the people go;
Thus the truth full quickly / may we in this manner know."

1044
It is a passing wonder / that yet full oft is seen,
Where blood-bespotted slayer / beside slain corse hath been,
That from the wounds come blood-drops, / as here it eke befell.
Thereby the guilt of Hagen / might they now full plainly tell.

1045
Now ran the wounds all bloody / like as they did before.
Who erstwhile wept full sorely / now wept they mickle more.
Then spake the monarch Gunther: / "To thee the truth be known:
Slain hath he been by robbers, / nor is this deed by Hagen done."

1046
"Of these same robbers," spake she, / "full well I understand.
God give that yet may vengeance / wreak some friendly hand.
Gunther and Hagen, / yourselves have done this deed."
Then looked for bloody conflict / the valiant thanes that served Siegfried.

1047
Then spake unto them Kriemhild: / "Now bear with me my need."
Knights twain came likewise hither / and did find him dead,—
Gernot her brother / and the young Giselher.
With upright hearts then joined they / with the others grief to share.

1048
They mourned for Kriemhild's husband / with hearts all full of woe.
A mass should then be chanted: / to the minster forth did go
Man and child and woman / gathered from every side.
E'en they did likewise mourn him / who little lost that Siegfried died.

1049
Gernot and Giselher spake: / "O Sister dear,
Now comfort thee in sorrow, / for death is ever near.
Amends we'll make unto thee / the while that we shall live."
In the world might never any / unto her a comfort give.

1050
His coffin was made ready / about the middle day.
From off the bier they raised him / whereupon he lay.
But yet would not the lady / let him be laid in grave.

Therefor must all the people / first a mickle trouble have.

1051

In a shroud all silken / they the dead man wound.

I ween that never any / that wept not might be found.

There mournéd full of sorrow / Ute the queen full high

And all of her attendants / that such a noble knight did die.

1052

When did hear the people / how they in minster sung,

And that he there lay coffined, / came then a mickle throng:

For his soul's reposing / what offerings they bore!

E'en amid his enemies / found he of good friends a store.

1053

Kriemhild the poor lady / to her attendants spake:

"Let them shun no trouble / to suffer for my sake,

Who to him are friendly-minded / and me in honor hold;

For the soul of Siegfried / meted be to them his gold."

1054

Child so small there was not, / did it but reason have,

But offering carried thither. / Ere he was laid in grave,

More than a hundred masses / upon the day they sung,

Of all the friends of Siegfried / was gathered there a mickle throng.

1055

When were the masses over, / the folk departed soon.

Then spake the Lady Kriemhild: / "Leave ye me not alone

To pass the night in watching / by this chosen thane now dead,

With whose passing from me / all my joy of life hath fled.

1056

"Three days and three nights further / shall he lie on bier,

Until my heart find quiet / that weeps for spouse so dear.

God perchance commandeth / that death eke me do take:

That were for me poor Kriemhild / fit end of all my woe to make."

1057

Then of the town the people / went to their homes again.

Priests and monks yet bade she / longer there remain,

And all the hero's followers / who willing served alway.

They watched a night all gruesome, / and full of toil was eke the day.

1058

Meat and drink forgetting / abode there many a one.

If any were would take it / 'twas unto all made known,

That have they might in plenty: / thus did provide Siegmund.

Then for the Nibelungen / did trouble and sore need abound.

1059

The while the three days lasted / —such the tale we hear—

All who could join the chanting, / mickle must they bear
There of toil and trouble. / What gifts to them they bore!
Rich were seen full many / who did suffer need before.
1060
As many poor as found they / who themselves had naught,
By them yet an offering / bade they there be brought,
Of gold of Siegfried's treasure. / Though he no more might live,
Yet for his soul's reposing / marks many thousand did they give.
1061
Land of fruitful income / bestowed Kriemhild around,
Wheresoever cloisters / and worthy folk were found.
Silver and apparel / to the poor she gave in store,
And in good manner showed she / that truest love to him she bore.
1062
Upon the third morning / at the mass' tide
Was there beside the minster / filled the church-yard wide
With country-folk a-weeping / that came from far and near:
In death they yet did serve him / as is meet for friend full dear.
1063
And so it hath been told us, / ere these four days were o'er,
Marks full thirty thousand, / yea, in sooth, and more,
For his soul's reposing / to the poor were given there:
The while that lay all broken / his life and eke his body fair.
1064
When ended was the service / and full the masses sung,
In unrestrained sorrow / there the flock did throng.
They bade that from the minster / he to the grave be borne.
Them that fain had kept him / there beheld ye weep and mourn.
1065
Thence full loud lamenting / did the people with him pass.
Unmoved there never any / nor man nor woman was.
Ere that in grave they laid him / chanted they and read.
What host of priests full worthy / at his burial were gatheréd!
1066
Ere that the wife of Siegfried / was come unto the grave,
With water from the fountain / full oft her face they lave,
So struggled with her sorrow / the faithful lady fair.
Great beyond all measure / was the grief that she did bear.
1067
It was a mickle wonder / that e'er her life she kept.
Many a lady was there / that helped her as she wept.
Then spake the queen full noble: / "Ye men that service owe
To Siegfried, as ye love me, / now to me a mercy show.

1068

"Upon this sorrow grant ye / the little grace to me
That I his shining visage / yet once more may see."
So filled she was with anguish / and so long time she sought,
Perforce they must break open / the casket all so fairly wrought.

1069

Where she did see him lying / they then the lady led.
With hand full white and spotless / raised she his fair head;
Then kissed she there all lifeless / the good and noble knight,—
And wept so that for sorrow / ran blood from out her eyes so bright.

1070

Mournful was the parting / that then did rend the twain.
Thence away they bore her, / nor might she walk again,
But in a swoon did senseless / the stately lady lie.
In sooth her winsome body / for sorrow sore was like to die.

1071

When they the knight full noble / now in the grave had laid,
Beheld ye every warrior / beyond all measure sad
That with him was come hither / from Nibelung country.
Full seldom joyous-hearted / might ye royal Siegmund see.

1072

And many were among them / that for sorrow great
Till three days were over / did nor drink nor eat.
Yet might they not their bodies / long leave uncared-for so:
For food they turned from mourning / as people still are wont to do.

EIGHTEENTH ADVENTURE: How Siegmund fared Home Again

1073

Then went royal Siegmund / where he Kriemhild found.
Unto the queen spake he: / "Home must we now be bound.
We ween that guests unwelcome / here are we by the Rhine.
Kriemhild, belovéd lady, / come now to country that is mine.

1074

"Though from us hath been taken / by foul traitor's hand
Thy good spouse and noble / here in stranger land,
Thine be it not to suffer: / good friend thou hast in me
For sake of son belovéd: / thereof shalt thou undoubting be.

1075

"Eke shalt thou have, good lady, / all the power to hold,
The which erstwhile hath shown thee / Siegfried the thane full bold.

The land and the crown likewise, / be they thine own to call,
And gladly eke shall serve thee / Siegfried's doughty warriors all."
1076
Then did they tell the servants / that they thence would ride,
And straight to fetch the horses / these obedient hied.
'Mid such as so did hate them / it grieved them more to stay:
Ladies high and maidens / were bidden dress them for the way.
1077
When that for royal Siegmund / stood ready horse and man,
Her kinsmen Lady Kriemhild / to beseech began
That she from her mother / would still forbear to go.
Then spake the lofty lady: / "That might hardly yet be so.
1078
"How might I for ever / look with eyes upon
Him that to me, poor woman, / such evil thing hath done?"
Then spake the youthful Giselher: / "Sister to me full dear,
By thy goodness shalt thou / tarry with thy mother here."
1079
"Who in this wise have harmed thee / and so grieved thy heart,
Thyself may'st spurn their service: / of what is mine take part."
Unto the knight she answered: / "Such thing may never be.
For die I must for sorrow / when that Hagen I should see."
1080
"From need thereof I'll save thee, / sister full dear to me,
For with thy brother Giselher / shalt thou ever be.
I'll help to still thy sorrow / that thy husband lieth dead."
Then spake she sorrow-stricken: / "Thereof in sooth had Kriemhild
need."
1081
When that the youthful Giselher / such kindly offer made,
Then her mother Ute / and Gernot likewise prayed,
And all her faithful kinsmen, / that she would tarry there:
For that in Siegfried's country / but few of her own blood there were.
1082
"To thee they all are strangers," / did Gernot further say.
Nor lived yet man so mighty / but dead at last he lay.
Bethink thee that, dear sister, / in comfort of thy mood.
Stay thou amid thy kinsmen, / I counsel truly for thy good."
1083
To Giselher she promised / that she would tarry there.
For the men of Siegmund / the horses ready were,
When they thence would journey / to the Nibelungen land:
On carrying-horses laden / the knights' attire did ready stand.

1084
Went the royal Siegmund / unto Kriemhild then;
He spake unto the lady: / "Now do Siegfried's men
Await thee by the horses. / Straight shall we hence away,
For 'mid the men of Burgundy / unwilling would I longer stay."
1085
Then spake the Lady Kriemhild: / "My friends have counselled me,
That by the love I bear them, / here my home shall be,
For that no kinsmen have I / in the Nibelungen land."
Grieved full sore was Siegmund / when he did Kriemhild understand.
1086
Then spake the royal Siegmund: / "To such give not thine ear,
A queen 'mid all my kinsmen, / thou a crown shalt wear
And wield as lordly power / as e'er till now thou hast.
Nor thou a whit shalt forfeit, / that we the hero thus have lost.
1087
"And journey with us thither, / for child's sake eke of thine:
Him shalt thou never, lady, / an orphan leave to pine.
When hath grown thy son to manhood, / he'll comfort thee thy mood.
Meanwhile shall ready serve thee / many a warrior keen and good."
1088
She spake: "O royal Siegmund, / I may not thither ride,
For I here must tarry, / whate'er shall me betide,
'Mid them that are my kinsmen, / who'll help my grief to share."
The knights had sore disquiet / that such tidings they must hear.
1089
"So might we say full truly," / spake they every one,
"That unto us still greater / evil now were done,
Would'st thou longer tarry / here amid our foes:
In sooth were never journey / of knights to court more full of woes."
1090
"Now may ye free from trouble / in God's protection fare:
I'll bid that trusty escort / shall you have in care
Unto Siegmund's country. / My child full dear to me,
Unto your knights' good mercy / let it well commended be."
1091
When that they well perceived / how she would not depart,
Wept all the men of Siegmund / and sad they were at heart.
In what right heavy sorrow / Siegmund then took leave
Of the Lady Kriemhild! / Full sore thereover must he grieve.
1092
"Woe worth this journey hither," / the lofty monarch spake.
"Henceforth from merry meeting / shall nevermore o'ertake

King or his faithful kinsmen / what here our meed hath been.
Here 'mid the men of Burgundy / may we never be more seen."
1093
Then spake the men of Siegfried / in open words and plain:
"An might we right discover / who our lord hath slain,
Warriors bent on vengeance / shall yet lay waste this ground.
Among his kin in plenty / may doughty foemen be found."
1094
Anon he kissed Kriemhild / and spake sorrowfully,
When she there would tarry, / and he the same did see:
"Now ride we joy-forsaken / home unto our land.
First now what 'tis to sorrow / do I rightly understand."
1095
From Worms away sans escort / unto the Rhine they rode:
I ween that they full surely / did go in such grim mood,
That had against them any / aught of evil dared,
Hand of keen Nibelungen / had known full well their life to guard.
1096
Nor parting hand they offered / to any that were there.
Then might ye see how Gernot / and likewise Giselher
Did give him loving greeting. / That as their very own
They felt the wrong he suffered, / by the courteous knights and brave
was shown.
1097
Then spake in words full kindly / the royal knight Gernot:
"God in heaven knoweth / that of guilt I've naught
In the death of Siegfried, / that e'er I e'en did hear
Who here to him were hostile. / Well may I of thy sorrow share."
1098
An escort safe did furnish / the young knight Giselher:
Forth from out that country / he led them full of care,
The monarch with his warriors, / to Netherland their home.
How joyless is the greeting / as thither to their kin they come!
1099
How fared that folk thereafter, / that can I nowise say.
Here heard ye Kriemhild plaining / as day did follow day,
That none there was to comfort / her heart and sorry mood,
Did Giselher not do it; / he faithful was to her and good.
1100
The while the fair Queen Brunhild / in mood full haughty sat,
And weep howe'er did Kriemhild, / but little recked she that,
Nor whit to her of pity / displayed she evermore.
Anon was Lady Kriemhild / eke cause to her of sorrow sore.

NINETEENTH ADVENTURE: How the Nibelungen Hoard was Brought to Worms

1101
When that the noble Kriemhild / thus did widowed stand,
Remained there with his warriors / by her in that land
Eckewart the margrave, / and served her ever true.
And he did help his mistress / oft to mourn his master too.
1102
At Worms a house they built her / the minster high beside,
That was both rich and spacious, / full long and eke full wide,
Wherein with her attendants / joyless did she dwell.
She sought the minster gladly, / —that to do she loved full well.
1103
Seldom undone she left it, / but thither went alway
In sorry mood where buried / her loved husband lay.
God begged she in his mercy / his soul in charge to keep,
And, to the thane right faithful, / for him full often did she weep.
1104
Ute and her attendants / all times a comfort bore,
But yet her heart was stricken / and wounded all so sore
That no whit might avail it / what solace e'er they brought.
For lover taken from her / with such grief her heart was fraught,
1105
As ne'er for spouse belovéd / a wife did ever show.
Thereby how high in virtue / she stood ye well might know.
She mourned until her ending / and while did last her life.
Anon a mighty vengeance / wreaked the valiant Siegfried's wife.
1106
And so such load of sorrow / for her dead spouse she bore,
The story sayeth truly, / for years full three or more,
Nor ever unto Gunther / any word spake she,
And meantime eke her enemy / Hagen never might she see.
1107
Then spake of Tronje Hagen: / "Now seek'st thou such an end,
That unto thee thy sister / be well-disposéd friend?
Then Nibelungen treasure / let come to this country:
Thereof thou much might'st win thee, / might Kriemhild friendly-minded be."
1108
He spake: "Be that our effort. / My brothers' love hath she:

Them shall we beg to win her / that she our friend may be,
And that she gladly see it / that we do share her store."
"I trow it well," spake Hagen, / "may such thing be nevermore."
1109
Then did he Ortwein / unto the court command
And the margrave Gere. / When both were found at hand,
Thither brought they Gernot / and eke young Giselher.
In friendly manner sought they / to win the Lady Kriemhild there.
1110
Then spake of Burgundy / Gernot the warrior strong:
"Lady, the death of Siegfried / thou mournest all too long.
Well will the monarch prove thee / that him he ne'er hath slain.
'Tis heard how that right sorely / thou dost for him unending plain."
1111
She spake: "The king none chargeth: / t'was Hagen's hand that slew.
When Hagen me did question / where might one pierce him through,
How might e'er thought come to me / that hate his heart did bear?
Then 'gainst such thing to guard me," / spake she, "had I ta'en good
care.
1112
"And kept me from betraying / to evil hands his life,
Nor cause of this my weeping / had I his poor lorn wife.
My heart shall hate forever / who this foul deed have done."
And further to entreat her / young Giselher had soon begun.
1113
When that to greet the monarch / a willing mind spake she,
Him soon with noble kinsmen / before her might ye see.
Yet dare might never Hagen / unto her to go:
On her he'd wrought sore evil, / as well his guilty mind did know.
1114
When she no hatred meted / unto Gunther as before,
By Hagen to be greeted / were fitting all the more.
Had but by his counsel / no ill to her been done,
So might he all undaunted / unto Kriemhild have gone.
1115
Nor e'er was peace new offered / kindred friends among
Sealed with tears so many. / She brooded o'er her wrong.
To all she gave her friendship / save to one man alone.
Nor slain her spouse were ever, / were not the deed by Hagen done.
1116
Small time it was thereafter / ere they did bring to pass
That with the Lady Kriemhild / the mighty treasure was,
That from Nibelungen country / she brought the Rhine unto.

It was her bridal portion / and 'twas fairly now her due.

1117

For it did journey thither / Gernot and Giselher.
Warriors eighty hundred / Kriemhild commanded there
That they should go and fetch it / where hidden it did lie,
And where the good thane Alberich / with friends did guard it faithfully.

1118

When saw they coming warriors / from Rhine the hoard to take,
Alberich the full valiant / to his friends in this wise spake:
"We dare not of the treasure / aught from them withhold:
It is her bridal portion, / —thus the noble queen hath told.

1119

"Yet had we never granted," / spake Alberich, "this to do,
But that in evil manner / the sightless mantle too
With the doughty Siegfried / we alike did lose,
The which did wear at all times / the fair Kriemhild's noble spouse.

1120

"Now alas hath Siegfried / had but evil gain
That from us the sightless mantle / the hero thus hath ta'en,
And so hath forced to serve him / all these lands around."
Then went forth the porter / where full soon the keys he found.

1121

There stood before the mountain / ready Kriemhild's men,
And her kinsmen with them. / The treasure bore they then
Down unto the water / where the ships they sought:
To where the Rhine flowed downward / across the waves the hoard
they brought.

1122

Now of the treasure further / may ye a wonder hear:
Heavy wains a dozen / scarce the same might bear
In four days and nights together / from the mountain all away,
E'en did each one of them / thrice the journey make each day.

1123

In it was nothing other / than gold and jewels rare.
And if to every mortal / on earth were dealt a share,
Ne'er 'twould make the treasure / by one mark the less.
Not without good reason / forsooth would Hagen it possess.

1124

The wish-rod lay among them, / of gold a little wand.
Whosoe'er its powers / full might understand,
The same might make him master / o'er all the race of men.
Of Alberich's kin full many / with Gernot returned again.

1125

When they did store the treasure / in King Gunther's land,
And to royal Kriemhild / 'twas given 'neath her hand,
Storing-rooms and towers / could scarce the measure hold.
Nevermore such wonder / might of wealth again be told.
1126
And had it e'en been greater, / yea a thousandfold,
If but again might Kriemhild / safe her Siegfried hold,
Fain were she empty-handed / of all the boundless store.
Spouse than she more faithful / won a hero nevermore.
1127
When now she had the treasure, / she brought into that land
Knights many from far distance. / Yea, dealt the lady's hand
So freely that such bounty / ne'er before was seen.
High in honor held they / for her goodly heart the queen.
1128
Unto both rich and needy / began she so to give
That fearful soon grew Hagen, / if that she would live
Long time in such high power, / lest she of warriors true
Such host might win to serve her, / that cause would be her strength
to rue.
1129
Spake Gunther then: / "The treasure is hers and freedom too.
Wherefore shall I prevent her, / whate'er therewith she do?
Yea, nigh she did her friendship / from me evermore withhold.
Now reck we not who shareth / or her silver or her gold."
1130
Unto the king spake Hagen: / "No man that boasteth wit
Should to any woman / such hoard to hold permit.
By gifts she yet will bring it / that will come the day
When valiant men of Burgundy / rue it with good reason may."
1131
Then spake the monarch Gunther: / "To her an oath I swore,
That I would cause of evil / to her be nevermore,
Whereof henceforth I'll mind me: / sister she is to me."
Then spake further Hagen: / "Let me bear the guilt for thee."
1132
Many they were that kept not / there their plighted word:
From the widow took they / all that mighty hoard:
Every key had Hagen / known to get in hand.
Rage filled her brother Gernot / when he the thing did understand.
1133
Then spake the knight Giselher: / "Hagen here hath wrought
Sore evil to my sister: / permit this thing I'll not.

And were he not my kinsman, / he'd pay it with his life."
Anew did fall aweeping / then the doughty Siegfried's wife.

1134

Then spake the knight Gernot: / "Ere that forever we
Be troubled with this treasure, / let first commanded be
Deep in the Rhine to sink it, / that no man have it more."
In sad manner plaining / Kriemhild stood Giselher before.

1135

She spake: "Belovéd brother, / be mindful thou of me:
What life and treasure toucheth / shalt thou my protector be."
Then spake he to the lady: / "That shall sure betide,
When we again come hither: / now called we are away to ride."

1136

The monarch and his kinsmen / rode from out the land,
And in his train the bravest / ye saw on any hand:
Went all save Hagen only, / and there he stayed for hate,
That he did bear to Kriemhild, / and full gladly did he that.

1137

Ere that the mighty monarch / was thither come again,
In that while had Hagen / all that treasure ta'en.
Where Loch is by the river / all in the Rhine sank he.
He weened thereof to profit, / yet such thing might never be.

1138

The royal knights came thither / again with many a man.
Kriemhild with her maidens / and ladies then began
To mourn the wrong they suffered, / that pity was to hear.
Fain had the faithful Giselher / been unto her a comforter.

1139

Then spake they all together: / "Done hath he grievous wrong."
But he the princes' anger / avoided yet so long
At last to win their favor. / They let him live sans scathe.
Then filled thereat was Kriemhild / as ne'er before with mickle wrath.

1140

Ere that of Tronje Hagen / had hidden thus the hoard,
Had they unto each other / given firm plighted word,
That it should lie concealéd / while one of them might live.
Thereof anon nor could they / to themselves nor unto other give.

1141

With renewéd sorrows / heavy she was of heart
That so her dear-loved husband / perforce from life must part,
And that of wealth they reft her. / Therefor she mourned alway,
Nor ever ceased her plaining / until was come her latest day.

1142

After the death of Siegfried / dwelt she in sorrow then,
—Saith the tale all truly— / full three years and ten,
Nor in that time did ever / for the knight mourn aught the less.
To him she was right faithful, / must all the folk of her confess.

TWENTIETH ADVENTURE: How King Etzel sent to Burgundy for Kriemhild

1143
In that same time when ended / was Lady Helke's life,
And that the monarch Etzel / did seek another wife,
To take a highborn widow / of the land of Burgundy
Hun his friends did counsel: / Lady Kriemhild hight was she.

1144
Since that was ended / the fair Helke's life,
Spake they: "Wilt thou ever / win for thee noble wife,
The highest and the fairest / that ever king did win,
Take to thee this same lady / that doughty Siegfried's spouse hath been."

1145
Then spake the mighty monarch: / "How might that come to pass
Since that I am a heathen, / nor named with sign of cross?
The lady is a Christian, / thereto she'll ne'er agree.
Wrought must be a wonder, / if the thing may ever be."

1146
Then spake again his warriors: / "She yet may do the same.
For sake of thy great power / and thy full lofty name
Shalt thou yet endeavor / such noble wife to gain.
To woo the stately lady / might each monarch high be fain."

1147
Then spake the noble monarch: / "Who is 'mong men of mine,
That knoweth land and people / dwelling far by Rhine?"
Spake then of Bechelaren / the trusty Ruediger:
"I have known from childhood / the noble queen that dwelleth there.

1148
"And Gunther and Gernot, / the noble knights and good,
And hight the third is Giselher: / whatever any should
That standeth high in honor / and virtue, doth each one:
Eke from eld their fathers / have in like noble manner done."

1149

Then spake again Etzel: / "Friend, now shalt thou tell,
If she within my country / crown might wear full well—
For be she fair of body / as hath been told to me,
My friends for this their counsel / shall ever full requited be."

1150

"She likeneth in beauty / well my high lady,
Helke that was so stately. / Nor forsooth might be
In all this world a fairer / spouse of king soe'er.
Whom taketh she for wooer, / glad of heart and mind he were."

1151

He spake: "Make trial, Ruediger, / as thou hold'st me dear.
And if by Lady Kriemhild / e'er I lie full near,
Therefor will I requite thee / as in best mode I may:
So hast thou then fulfilled / all my wish in fullest way.

1152

"Stores from out my treasure / I'll bid to thee to give,
That thou with thy companions / merry long shalt live,
Of steeds and rich apparel / what thou wilt have to share.
Thereof unto thy journey / I'll bid in measure full prepare."

1153

Thereto did give him answer / the margrave Ruediger:
"Did I thy treasure covet / unworthy thing it were.
Gladly will I thy messenger / be unto the Rhine,
From my own store provided: / all have I e'en from hand of thine."

1154

Then spake the mighty monarch: / "When now wilt thou fare
To seek the lovely lady? / God of thee have care
To keep thee on thy journey / and eke a wife to me.
Therein good fortune help me, / that she to us shall gracious be."

1155

Then again spake Ruediger: / "Ere that this land we quit,
Must we first prepare us / arms and apparel fit,
That we may thus in honor / in royal presence stand.
To the Rhine I'll lead five hundred / warriors, a doughty band.

1156

"Wherever they in Burgundy / me and my men may see,
Shall they all and single / then confess of thee
That ne'er from any monarch / so many warriors went
As now to bear thy message / thou far unto the Rhine hast sent.

1157

"May it not, O mighty monarch, / thee from thy purpose move:
Erstwhile unto Siegfried / she gave her noble love,

Who scion is of Siegmund: / him thou here hast seen.
Worthy highest honor / verily the knight had been."

1158
Then answered him King Etzel: / "Was she the warrior's wife,
So worthy was of honor / the noble prince in life,
That I the royal lady / therefor no whit despise.
'Tis her surpassing beauty / that shall be joy unto mine eyes."

1159
Then further spake the margrave: / "Hear then what I do say:
After days four-and-twenty / shall we from hence away.
Tidings to Gotelinde / I'll send, my spouse full dear,
That I to Lady Kriemhild / myself will be thy messenger."

1160
Away to Bechelaren / sent then Ruediger.
Both sad his spouse and joyous / was the news to hear.
He told how for the monarch / a wife he was to woo:
With love she well remembered / the fair Lady Helke too.

1161
When that the margravine / did the message hear,
In part 'twas sorrow to her, / and weep she must in fear
At having other mistress / than hers had been before.
To think on Lady Helke / did grieve her inmost heart full sore.

1162
Ruediger from Hunland / in seven days did part,
Whereat the monarch Etzel / merry was of heart.
When at Vienna city / all was ready for the way,
To begin the journey / might he longer not delay.

1163
At Bechelaren waited / Gotelinde there,
And eke the young margravine, / daughter of Ruediger,
Was glad at thought her father / and all his men to see.
And many a lovely maiden / looked to the coming joyfully.

1164
Ere that to Bechelaren / rode noble Ruediger
From out Vienna city, / was rich equipment there
For them in fullest measure / on carrying-horses brought,
That went in such wise guarded / that robber hand disturbed them not.

1165
When they at Bechelaren / within the town did stand,
His fellows on the journey / did the host command
To lead to fitting quarters / and tend carefully.
The stately Gotelinde, / glad she was her spouse to see.

1166

Eke his lovely daughter / the youthful margravine,—
To her had nothing dearer / than his coming been.
The warriors too from Hunland, / what joy for her they make!
With a laughing spirit / to all the noble maiden spake:

1167

"Be now to us right welcome, / my father and all his men."
Fairest thanks on all sides / saw ye offered then
Unto the youthful margravine / by many a valiant knight.
How Ruediger was minded / knew Gotelinde aright.

1168

When then that night she / by Ruediger lay,
Questioned him the margravine / in full loving way,
Wherefore had sent him thither / the king of Hunland.
He spake: "My Lady Gotelinde, / that shalt thou gladly understand.

1169

"My master now hath sent me / to woo him other wife,
Since that by death was ended / the fair Helke's life.
Now will I to Kriemhild / ride unto the Rhine:
She shall here in Hunland / be spouse to him and stately queen."

1170

"God will it," spake Gotelinde, / "and well the same might be,
Since that so high in honor / ever standeth she.
The death of my good mistress / we then may better bear;
Eke might we grant her gladly / among the Huns a crown to wear."

1171

Then spake to her the margrave: / "Thou shalt, dear lady mine,
To them that shall ride with me / thither unto the Rhine,
In right bounteous manner / deal out a goodly share.
Good knights go lighter-hearted / when they well provided fare."

1172

She spake: "None is among them, / an he would take from me,
But I will give whatever / to him may pleasing be,
Ere that ye part thither, / thou and thy good men."
Thereto spake the margrave: / "So dost thou all my wishes then."

1173

Silken stuffs in plenty / they from her chamber bore,
And to the knights full noble / dealt out in goodly store,
Mantles lined all richly / from collar down to spur.
What for the journey pleased him / did choose therefrom Sir Ruediger.

1174

Upon the seventh morning / from Bechelaren went
The knight with train of warriors. / Attire and armament

Bore they in fullest measure / through the Bavarian land,
And ne'er upon the journey / dared assail them robber band.
1175
Unto the Rhine then came they / ere twelve days were flown,
And there were soon the tidings / of their coming known.
'Twas told unto the monarch / and with him many a man,
How strangers came unto him. / To question then the king began,
1176
If any was did know them, / for he would gladly hear.
They saw their carrying-horses / right heavy burdens bear:
That they were knights of power / knew they well thereby.
Lodgings they made them ready / in the wide city speedily.
1177
When that the strangers / had passed within the gate
Every eye did gaze on / the knights that came in state,
And mickle was the wonder / whence to the Rhine they came.
Then sent the king for Hagen, / if he perchance might know the same.
1178
Then spake he of Tronje: / "These knights I ne'er have seen,
Yet when we now behold them / I'll tell thee well, I ween,
From whence they now ride hither / unto this country.
An I not straightway know them, / from distant land in sooth they be."
1179
For the guests fit lodgings / now provided were.
Clad in rich apparel / came the messenger,
And to the court his fellows / did bear him company.
Sumptuous attire / wore they, wrought full cunningly.
1180
Then spake the doughty Hagen: / "As far as goes my ken,
For that long time the noble / knight I not have seen,
Come they in such manner / as were it Ruediger,
The valiant thane from Hunland, / that leads the stately riders here."
1181
Then straightway spake the monarch: / "How shall I understand
That he of Bechelaren / should come unto this land?"
Scarce had King Gunther / his mind full spoken there,
When saw full surely Hagen / that 'twas the noble Ruediger.
1182
He and his friends then hastened / with warmest welcoming.
Then saw ye knights five hundred / adown from saddle spring,
And were those knights of Hunland / received in fitting way.
Messengers ne'er beheld ye / attired in so fine array.

1183

Hagen of Tronje, / with voice full loud spake he:
"Unto these thanes full noble / a hearty welcome be,
To the lord of Bechelaren / and his men every one."
Thereat was fitting honor / done to every valiant Hun.

1184

The monarch's nearest kinsmen / went forth the guests to meet.
Of Metz the knight Sir Ortwein / Ruediger thus did greet:
"The while our life hath lasted, / never yet hath guest
Here been seen so gladly: / be that in very truth confessed."

1185

For that greeting thanked they / the brave knights one and all.
With train of high attendants / they passed unto the hall,
Where valiant men a many / stood round the monarch's seat.
The king arose from settle / in courteous way the guests to greet.

1186

Right courteously he greeted / then the messenger.
Gunther and Gernot, / full busy both they were
For stranger and companions / a welcome fit to make.
The noble knight Sir Ruediger / by the hand the king did take.

1187

He led him to the settle / where himself he sat:
He bade pour for the strangers / (a welcome work was that)
Mead the very choicest / and the best of wine,
That e'er ye might discover / in all the lands about the Rhine.

1188

Giselher and Gere / joined the company too,
Eke Dankwart and Volker, / when that they knew
The coming of the strangers: / glad they were of mood,
And greeted 'fore the monarch / fair the noble knights and good.

1189

Then spake unto his master / of Tronje the knight:
"Let our thanes seek ever / fully to requite
What erstwhile the margrave / in love to us hath done:
Fair Gotelinde's husband / our gratitude full well hath won."

1190

Thereto spake King Gunther: / "Withhold it not I may.
How they both do bear them, / tell me now, I pray,
Etzel and Helke / afar in Hunland."
Then answered him the margrave: / "Fain would I have thee understand."

1191

Then rose he from the settle / and his men every one.

He spake unto the monarch: / "An may the thing be done,
And is't thy royal pleasure, / so will I naught withhold,
But the message that I bring thee / shall full willingly be told."
1192
He spake: "What tale soever, / doth this thy message make,
I grant thee leave to tell it, / nor further counsel take.
Now shalt thou let us hear it, / me and my warriors too,
For fullest leave I grant thee / thy high purpose to pursue."
1193
Then spake the upright messenger: / "Hither to thee at Rhine
Doth faithful service tender / master high of mine;
To all thy kinsmen likewise, / as many as may be:
Eke is this my message / borne in all good will to thee.
1194
"To thee the noble monarch / bids tell his tale of need.
His folk 's forlorn and joyless; / my mistress high is dead,
Helke the full stately / my good master's wife,
Whereby now is orphaned / full many a fair maiden's life,
1195
"Children of royal parents / for whom hath cared her hand:
Thereby doth the country / in plight full sorry stand.
Alack, nor is there other / that them with love may tend.
I ween the time long distant / eke when the monarch's grief shall end."
1196
"God give him meed," spake Gunther, / "that he so willingly
Doth offer thus good service / to my kinsmen and to me—
I joy that I his greeting / here have heard this day—
The which with glad endeavor / my kinsmen and my men shall pay."
1197
Thereto the knight of Burgundy, / the valiant Gernot, said:
"The world may ever rue it / that Helke fair lies dead,
So manifold the virtues / that did her life adorn."
A willing testimony / by Hagen to the words was borne.
1198
Thereto again spake Ruediger / the noble messenger:
"Since thou, O king, dost grant it, / shalt thou now further hear
What message 'tis my master / beloved hath hither sent,
For that since death of Helke / his days he hath in sorrow spent.
1199
"'Tis told my lord that Kriemhild / doth widowed live alone,
And dead is doughty Siegfried. / May now such thing be done,
And wilt thou grant that favor, / a crown she then shall wear
Before the knights of Etzel: / this message from my lord I bear."

1200

Then spake the mighty monarch / —a king he was of grace—
"My will in this same matter / she'll hear, an so she please.
Thereof will I instruct thee / ere three days are passed by—
Ere I her mind have sounded, / wherefore to Etzel this deny?"

1201

Meanwhile for the strangers / bade they make cheer the best
In sooth so were they tended / that Ruediger confessed
He had 'mong men of Gunther / of friends a goodly store.
Hagen full glad did serve him, / as he had Hagen served of yore.

1202

Thus there did tarry Ruediger / until the third day.
The king did counsel summon / —he moved in wisest way—
If that unto his kinsmen / seemed it fitting thing,
That Kriemhild take unto her / for spouse Etzel the king.

1203

Together all save Hagen / did the thing advise,
And unto King Gunther / spake he in this wise:
"An hast thou still thy senses, / of that same thing beware,
That, be she ne'er so willing, / thou lend'st thyself her will to share."

1204

"Wherefore," spake then Gunther, / "should I allow it not?
Whene'er doth fortune favor / Kriemhild in aught,
That shall I gladly grant her, / for sister dear is she.
Yea, ought ourselves to seek it, / might it but her honor be."

1205

Thereto gave answer Hagen: / "Now such words give o'er.
Were Etzel known unto thee / as unto me of yore,
And did'st thou grant her to him, / as 'tis thy will I hear,
Then wouldst thou first have reason / for thy later weal to fear."

1206

"Wherefore?" spake then Gunther. / "Well may I care for that,
E'er to thwart his temper / that so I aught of hate
At his hands should merit, / an if his wife she be."
Thereto gave answer Hagen: / "Such counsel hast thou ne'er of me."

1207

Then did they bid for Gernot / and Giselher to go,
For wished they of the royal / twain their mind to know,
If that the mighty monarch / Kriemhild for spouse should take.
Yet Hagen and none other / thereto did opposition make.

1208

Then spake of Burgundy / Giselher the thane:
"Well may'st thou now, friend Hagen, / show upright mind again:

For sorrows wrought upon her / may'st thou her well requite.
Howe'er she findeth fortune, / ne'er should it be in thy despite."
1209
"Yea, hast thou to my sister / so many sorrows done,"
So spake further Giselher, / the full noble thane,
"That fullest reason hath she / to mete thee naught but hate.
In sooth was never lady / than she bereft of joy more great."
1210
"What I do know full certain, / that known to all I make:
If e'er shall come the hour / that she do Etzel take,
She'll work us yet sore evil, / howe'er the same she plan.
Then in sooth will serve her / full many a keen and doughty man."
1211
In answer then to Hagen / the brave Gernot said:
"With us doth lie to leave it / until they both be dead,
Ere that we ride ever / unto Etzel's land.
That we be faithful to her / doth honor meantime sure command."
1212
Thereto again spake Hagen: / "Gainsay me here may none.
And shall the noble Kriemhild / e'er sit 'neath Helke's crown,
Howe'er she that accomplish, / she'll do us grievous hurt.
Good knights, therefrom to keep you / doth better with your weal consort."
1213
In anger spake then Giselher / the son of Ute the fair:
"None shall yet among us / himself like traitor bear.
What honor e'er befall her, / rejoice thereat should we.
Whate'er thou sayest, Hagen, / true helper shall she find in me."
1214
When that heard it Hagen / straightway waxed he wroth.
Gernot and Giselher / the knights high-minded both,
And Gunther, mighty monarch, / did counsel finally,
If that did wish it Kriemhild, / by them 'twould unopposéd be.
1215
Then spake the margrave Gere: / "That lady will I tell
How that of royal Etzel / she may think full well.
In fear are subject to him / brave warriors many a one:
Well may he recompense her / for wrong that e'er to her was done."
1216
Then went the knight full valiant / where he did Kriemhild find,
And straightway spake unto her / upon her greeting kind:
"Me may'st thou gladly welcome / with messengers high meed.
Fortune hath come to part thee / now from all thy bitter need.

1217

"For sake of love he bears thee, / lady, doth seek thy hand
One of all the highest / that e'er o'er monarch's land
Did rule in fullest honor, / or ever crown might wear:
High knights do bring the message, / which same thy brother bids
thee hear."

1218

Then spake she rich in sorrow: / "Now God forbid to thee
And all I have of kinsmen / that aught of mockery
They do on me, poor woman. / What were I unto one,
Who e'er at heart the joyance / of a noble wife hath known?"

1219

Much did she speak against it. / Anon as well came there
Gernot her brother / and the young Giselher.
In loving wise they begged her / her mourning heart to cheer:
An would she take the monarch, / verily her weal it were.

1220

Yet might not then by any / the lady's mind be bent,
That any man soever / to love she would consent.
Thereon the thanes besought her: / "Now grant the thing to be,
An dost thou nothing further, / that the messenger thou deign'st to
see."

1221

"That will I not deny you," / spake the high lady,
"That the noble Ruediger / I full gladly see,
Such knightly grace adorns him. / Were he not messenger,
And came there other hither / by him I all unspoken were."

1222

She spake: "Upon the morrow / bid him hither fare
Unto this my chamber. / Then shall he fully hear
How that do stand my wishes, / the which I'll tell him true."
Of her full grievous sorrow / was she minded thus anew.

1223

Eke not else desired / the noble Ruediger
Than that by the lady / leave thus granted were:
He knew himself so skilful, / might he such favor earn,
So should he her full certain / from her spoken purpose turn.

1224

Upon the morrow early / when that the mass was sung
Came the noble messengers, / whereof a mickle throng.
They that should Sir Ruediger / to court bear company,
Many a man full stately / in rich apparel might ye see.

1225

Kriemhild, dame high-stated, / —full sad she was of mood—
There Ruediger awaited, / the noble knight and good.
He found her in such raiment / as daily she did wear:
The while were her attendants / in dresses clad full rich and rare,
1226
Unto the threshold went she / the noble guest to meet,
And the man of Etzel / did she full kindly greet.
Twelve knights there did enter, / himself and eleven more,
And well were they received: / to her such guests came ne'er before.
1227
The messenger to seat him / and his men they gave command.
The twain valiant margraves / saw ye before her stand,
Eckewart and Gere, / the noble knights and keen,
Such was the lady's sorrow, / none saw ye there of cheerful mien.
1228
They saw before her sitting / full many a lady fair,
And yet the Lady Kriemhild / did naught but sorrow there.
The dress upon her bosom / was wet with tears that fell,
And soon the noble margrave / perceived her mickle grief full well.
1229
Then spake the lofty messenger: / "Daughter of king full high,
To me and these my fellows / that bear me company
Deign now the grace to grant us / that we before thee stand
And tell to thee the tidings / wherefore we rode unto thy land."
1230
"That grace to thee is granted," / spake the lofty queen;
"Whate'er may be thy message, / I'll let it now be seen
That I do hear it gladly: / thou'rt welcome messenger."
That fruitless was their errand / deemed the others well to hear.
1231
Then spake of Bechelaren / the noble Ruediger:
"Pledge of true love unto thee / from lofty king I bear,
Etzel who bids thee, lady, / here royal compliment:
He hath to woo thy favor / knights full worthy hither sent.
1232
"His love to thee he offers / full heartily and free:
Fidelity that lasteth / he plighteth unto thee,
As erst to Lady Helke / who o'er his heart held sway.
Yea, thinking on her virtues / hath he full oft had joyless day."
1233
Then spake the royal lady: / "O Margrave Ruediger,
If that known to any / my sharp sorrows were,
Besought then were I never / again to take me spouse.

Such ne'er was won by lady / as the husband I did lose."
1234
"What is that sootheth sorrow," / the valiant knight replied,
"An be't not loving friendship / whene'er that may betide,
And that each mortal choose him / who his delight shall be?
Naught is that so availeth / to keep the heart from sorrow free.
1235
"Wilt thou minded be to love him, / this noble master mine,
O'er mighty crowns a dozen / the power shall be thine.
Thereto of princes thirty / my lord shall give thee land,
The which hath all subdued / the prowess of his doughty hand.
1236
"O'er many a knight full worthy / eke mistress shalt thou be
That my Lady Helke / did serve right faithfully,
And over many a lady / that served amid her train,
Of high and royal lineage," / spake the keen and valiant thane.
1237
"Thereto my lord will give thee / —he bids to thee make known—
If that beside the monarch / thou deign'st to wear a crown,
Power in fullest measure / that Helke e'er might boast:
The same in lordly manner / shalt thou wield o'er Etzel's host."
1238
Then spake the royal lady: / "How might again my life
Have thereof desire / to be a hero's wife?
Hath death in one already / wrought me such sorrows sore,
That joyless must my days be / from this time for evermore."
1239
Then spake the men of Hunland: / "O royal high lady,
Thy life shall there by Etzel / so full of honor be
Thy heart 'twill ever gladden / if but may be such thing:
Full many a thane right stately / doth homage to the mighty king.
1240
"Might but Helke's maidens / and they that wait on thee
E'er be joined together / in one royal company,
Well might brave knights to see them / wax merry in their mood.
Be, lady, now persuaded / —'tis verily thy surest good."
1241
She spake in courteous manner: / "Let further parley be
Until doth come the morrow. / Then hither come to me.
So will I give my answer / to bear upon your way."
The noble knights and worthy / must straight therein her will obey.
1242
When all from thence were parted / and had their lodgings sought,

Then bade the noble lady / that Giselher be brought,
And eke with him her mother. / To both she then did tell
That meet for her was weeping, / and naught might fit her mood so well.

1243

Then spake her brother Giselher: / "Sister, to me 'tis told—
And well may I believe it— / that thy grief manifold
Etzel complete will scatter, / an tak'st thou him for man.
Whate'er be other's counsel, / meseems it were a thing well done."

1244

Further eke spake Giselher: / "Console thee well may he.
From Rhone unto Rhine river, / from Elbe unto the sea,
King there is none other / that holds so lordly sway.
An he for spouse do take thee, / gladden thee full well he may."

1245

"Brother loved full dearly, / wherefore dost counsel it?
To mourn and weep forever / doth better me befit.
How may I 'mid warriors / appear in royal state?
Was ever fair my body, / of beauty now 'tis desolate."

1246

Then spake the Lady Ute / her daughter dear unto:
"The thing thy brother counsels, / my loving child, that do.
By thy friends be guided, / then with thee well 'twill be.
Long time it now hath grieved me / thee thus disconsolate to see."

1247

Then prayed she God with fervor / that he might her provide
With store of gold and silver / and raiment rich beside,
As erstwhile when her husband / did live a stately thane:
Since then so happy hour / never had she known again.

1248

In her own bosom thought she: / "An shall I not deny
My body to a heathen / —a Christian lady I—
So must I while life lasteth / have shame to be my own.
An gave he realms unnumbered, / such thing by me might ne'er be done."

1249

And there withal she left it. / The night through until day,
Upon her couch the lady / with mind full troubled lay.
Nor yet her eyes full shining / of tears at all were free,
Until upon the morrow / forth to matins issued she.

1250

When for mass was sounded, / came there the kings likewise.
Again did they their sister / by faithful word advise

To take for spouse unto her / of Hunland the king.
All joyless was the visage / they saw the lady thither bring.

1251
They bade the men of Etzel / thither lead again,
Who unto their country / fain their leave had ta'en,
Their message won or fruitless, / how that soe'er might be.
Unto the court came Ruediger. / Full eager were his company

1252
By the knight to be informéd / how the thing befell,
And if betimes they knew it / 'twould please them all full well,
For weary was the journey / and long unto their land.
Soon did the noble Ruediger / again in Kriemhild's presence stand.

1253
In full earnest manner / then the knight gan pray
The high royal lady / that she to him might say
What were from her the message / to Etzel he should bear.
Naught but denial only / did he from the lady hear,

1254
For that her love might never / by man again be won.
Thereto spake the margrave: / "Ill such thing were done.
Wherefore such fair body / wilt thou to ruin give?
Spouse of knight full worthy / may'st thou yet in honor live."

1255
Naught booted how they besought her, / till that Ruediger
Spake in secret manner / in the high lady's ear,
How Etzel should requite her / for ills she e'er did know.
Then gan her mickle sorrow / milder at the thought to grow.

1256
Unto the queen then spake he: / "Let now thy weeping be.
If 'mong the Huns hadst thou / other none than me
And my faithful kinsmen / and my good men alone,
Sorely must he repay it / who hath aught to thee of evil done."

1257
Thereat apace all lighter / the lady's sorrow grew,
She spake: "So swear thou truly, / what any 'gainst me do,
That thou wilt be the foremost / my sorrows to requite."
Thereto spake the margrave: / "Lady, to thee my word I plight."

1258
With all his men together / sware then Ruediger
Faithfully to serve her, / and in all things whatsoe'er
Naught would e'er deny her / the thanes from Etzel's land,
Whereof she might have honor: / thereto gave Ruediger his hand.

1259

Then thought the faithful lady: / "Since I thus have won
Band of friends so faithful, / care now have I none
How shall speak the people / in my sore need of me.
The death of my loved husband / perchance shall yet avengéd be."
1260
Thought she: "Since hath Etzel / so many knights and true,
An shall I but command them, / whate'er I will I do.
Eke hath he such riches / that free may be my hand:
Bereft of all my treasure / by Hagen's faithless art I stand."
1261
Then spake she unto Ruediger: / "Were it not, as I do know,
The king is yet a heathen, / so were I fain to go
Whithersoe'er he willed it, / and take him for my lord."
Thereto spake the margrave: / "Lady, no longer hold such word.
1262
"Such host he hath of warriors / who Christians are as we,
That beside the monarch / may care ne'er come to thee.
Yea, may he be baptized / through thee to Christian life:
Well may'st thou then rejoice thee / to be the royal Etzel's wife."
1263
Then spake again her brother: / "Sister, thy favor lend,
That now all thy sorrow / thereby may have an end."
And so long they besought her / that full of sadness she
Her word at length had plighted / the monarch Etzel's wife to be.
1264
She spake: "You will I follow, / I most lorn lady,
That I fare to Hunland, / as soon as it may be
That I friends have ready / to lead me to his land."
Before the knights assembled / fair Kriemhild pledged thereto her hand.
1265
Then spake again the margrave: / "Two knights do serve thee true,
And I thereof have many: / 'tis easy thing to do,
That thee with fitting honor / across the Rhine we guide.
Nor shalt thou, lady, longer / here in Burgundy abide.
1266
"Good men have I five hundred, / and eke my kinsmen stand
Ready here to serve thee / and far in Etzel's land,
Lady, at thy bidding. / And I do pledge the same,
Whene'er thou dost admonish, / to serve thee without cause for shame.
1267
"Now bid with full equipment / thy horses to prepare:
Ruediger's true counsel / will bring thee sorrow ne'er;

And tell it to thy maidens / whom thou wilt take with thee.
Full many a chosen warrior / on the way shall join our company."
1268
They had full rich equipment / that once their train arrayed
The while that yet lived Siegfried, / so might she many a maid
In honor high lead with her, / as she thence would fare.
What steeds all rich caparisoned / awaited the high ladies there!
1269
If till that time they ever / in richest dress were clad,
Thereof now for their journey / full store was ready made,
For that they of the monarch / had such tidings caught.
From chests longtime well bolted / forth the treasures rich were brought.
1270
Little were they idle / until the fifth day,
But sought rich dress that folded / secure in covers lay.
Kriemhild wide did open / all her treasure there,
And largess great would give she / unto the men of Ruediger.
1271
Still had she of the treasure / of Nibelungenland,
(She weened the same in Hunland / to deal with bounteous hand)
So great that hundred horses / ne'er the whole might bear.
How stood the mind of Kriemhild, / came the tidings unto Hagen's ear.
1272
He spake: "Since Kriemhild never / may me in favor hold,
E'en so here must tarry / Siegfried's store of gold.
Wherefore unto mine enemies / such mickle treasure go?
What with the treasure Kriemhild / intendeth, that full well I know.
1273
"Might she but take it thither, / in sooth believe I that,
'Twould be dealt out in largess / to stir against me hate.
Nor own they steeds sufficient / the same to bear away.
'Twill safe be kept by Hagen / —so shall they unto Kriemhild say."
1274
When she did hear the story, / with grief her heart was torn.
Eke unto the monarchs / all three the tale was borne.
Fain would they prevent it: / yet when that might not be,
Spake the noble Ruediger / in this wise full joyfully:
1275
"Wherefore, queen full stately, / weep'st thou o'er this gold?
For thee will King Etzel / in such high favor hold
When but his eyes behold thee, / to thee such store he'll give

That ne'er thou may'st exhaust it: / that, lady, by my word believe."
1276
Thereto the queen gave answer: / "Full noble Ruediger,
Greater treasure never / king's daughter had for share
Than this that Hagen from me / now hath ta'en away."
Then went her brother Gernot / to the chamber where the treasure lay.
1277
With force he stuck the monarch's / key into the door,
And soon of Kriemhild's treasure / they from the chamber bore
Marks full thirty thousand / or e'en more plenteously.
He bade the guests to take it, / which pleased King Gunther well to see.
1278
Then Gotelinde's husband / of Bechelaren spake:
"An if my Lady Kriemhild / with her complete might take
What treasure e'er came hither / from Nibelungenland,
Ne'er a whit would touch it / mine or my royal lady's hand.
1279
"Now bid them here to keep it, / for ne'er the same I'll touch.
Yea brought I from my country / of mine own wealth so much,
That we upon our journey / may be full well supplied,
And ne'er have lack in outlay / as in state we homeward ride."
1280
Chests well filled a dozen / from the time of old
Had for their own her maidens, / of the best of gold
That e'er ye might discover: / now thence away 'twas borne,
And jewels for the ladies / upon the journey to be worn.
1281
Of the might she yet was fearful / of Hagen grim and bold.
Still had she of mass-money / a thousand marks in gold,
That gave she for the soul's rest / of her husband dear.
Such loving deed and faithful / did touch the heart of Ruediger.
1282
Then spake the lady mournful: / "Who now that loveth me,
And for the love they bear me / may willing exiles be,
Who with me to Hunland / now away shall ride?
Take they of my treasure / and steeds and meet attire provide."
1283
Then did the margrave Eckewart / answer thus the queen:
"Since I from the beginning / of thy train have been,
Have I e'er right faithful / served thee," spake the thane,
"And to the end I'll ever / thus faithful unto thee remain.
1284
"Eke will I lead with me / five hundred of my men,

Whom I grant to serve thee / in faithful way again.
Nor e'er shall we be parted / till that we be dead."
Low bowing thanked him Kriemhild, / as verily might be his meed.
1285
Forth were brought the horses, / for that they thence would fare.
Then was a mickle weeping / of friends that parted there.
Ute, queen full stately, / and many a lady more
Showed that from Lady Kriemhild / to part did grieve their hearts full sore.
1286
A hundred stately maidens / with her she led away,
And as for them was fitting, / full rich was their array.
Many a bitter tear-drop / from shining eye fell down:
Yet joys knew they full many / eke in Etzel's land anon.
1287
Thither came Sir Giselher / and Gernot as well,
And with them train of followers, / as duty did compel.
Safe escort would they furnish / for their dear sister then,
And with them led of warriors / a thousand brave and stately men.
1288
Then came the valiant Gere, / and Ortwein eke came he:
Rumold the High Steward / might not absent be.
Unto the Danube did they / night-quarters meet provide.
Short way beyond the city / did the royal Gunther ride.
1289
Ere from the Rhine they started / had they forward sent
Messengers that full quickly / unto Hunland went,
And told unto the monarch / how that Ruediger
For spouse at length had won him / the high-born queen beyond compare.

TWENTY-FIRST ADVENTURE: How Kriemhild fared to the Huns

1290
The messengers leave we riding. / Now shall ye understand
How did the Lady Kriemhild / journey through the land,
And where from her were parted / Gernot and Giselher.
Upon her had they waited / as faithful unto her they were.
1291
As far as to the Danube / at Vergen did they ride,
Where must be the parting / from their royal sister's side,

For that again they homeward / would ride unto the Rhine.
No eye but wet from weeping / in all the company was seen.
1292
Giselher the valiant / thus to his sister said:
"If that thou ever, lady, / need hast of my aid,
And fronts thee aught of trouble, / give me to understand,
And straight I'll ride to serve thee / afar unto King Etzel's land."
1293
Upon the mouth then kissed she / all her friends full dear.
The escort soon had taken / eke leave of Ruediger
And the margrave's warriors / in manner lovingly.
With the queen upon her journey / went many a maid full fair to see.
1294
Four beyond a hundred / there were, all richly clad
In silk of cunning pattern. / Many a shield full broad
On the way did guard the ladies / in hand of valiant thane.
Full many a stately warrior / from thence did backward turn again.
1295
Thence away they hastened / down through Bavarian land.
Soon were told the tidings / how that was at hand
A mickle host of strangers, / where a cloister stands from yore
And where the Inn its torrent / doth into Danube river pour.
1296
At Passau in the city / a lordly bishop bode.
Empty soon each lodging / and bishop's palace stood:
To Bavarian land they hastened / the high guests to meet,
And there the Bishop Pilgrim / the Lady Kriemhild fair did greet.
1297
The warriors of that country / no whit grieved they were
Thus to see follow with her / so many a maiden fair.
Upon those high-born ladies / their eyes with joy did rest,
Full comfortable quarters / prepared they for each noble guest.
1298
With his niece the bishop / unto Passau rode.
When among the burghers / the story went abroad,
That thither was come Kriemhild, / the bishop's niece full fair,
Soon did the towns-people / reception meet for her prepare.
1299
There to have them tarry / was the bishop fain.
To him spake Sir Eckewart: / "Here may we not remain.
Unto Ruediger's country / must we journey down.
Thanes many there await us, / to whom our coming well is known."

1300
The tidings now knew likewise / Lady Gotelinde fair.
Herself and noble daughter / did them quick prepare.
Message she had from Ruediger / that he well pleased would be,
Should she unto Lady / Kriemhild show such courtesy,

1301
That she ride forth to meet her, / and bring his warriors true
Upward unto the Ense. / When they the tidings knew,
Saw ye how on all sides / they thronged the busy way.
Forth to meet the strangers / rode and eke on foot went they.

1302
As far as Everdingen / meanwhile was come the queen:
In that Bavarian country / on the way were never seen
Robbers seeking plunder, / as e'er their custom was:
Of fear from such a quarter / had the travellers little cause.

1303
'Gainst that had well provided / the noble margrave:
A band he led that numbered / good thousand warriors brave.
There was eke come Gotelinde, / spouse of Ruediger,
And bearing her high company / full many noble knights there were.

1304
When came they o'er the Traune / by Ense on the green,
There full many an awning / outstretched and tent was seen,
Wherein that night the strangers / should find them welcome rest.
Well was made provision / by Ruediger for each high guest.

1305
Not long fair Gotelinde did in her quarters stay,
But left them soon behind her. / Then coursed upon the way
With merry jingling bridle / many a well-shaped steed.
Full fair was the reception: / whereat was Ruediger right glad.

1306
On one side and the other / did swell the stately train
Knights that rode full gaily, / many a noble thane.
As they in joust disported, / full many a maid looked on,
Nor to the queen unwelcome / was the riders' service done.

1307
As rode there 'fore the strangers / the men of Ruediger,
From shaft full many a splinter / saw ye fly in air
In hand of doughty warrior / that jousted lustily.
Them might ye 'fore the ladies / pricking in stately manner see.

1308
Anon therefrom they rested. / Knights many then did greet
Full courteously each other. / Then forth Kriemhild to meet

Went the fair Gotelinde, / by gallant warriors led.
Those skilled in lady's service, / —little there the rest they had.
1309
The lord of Bechelaren / unto his lady rode.
Soon the noble margravine / her high rejoicing showed,
That all safe and sound he / from the Rhine was come again.
The care that filled her bosom / by mickle joy from her was ta'en.
1310
When him she had receivéd, / her on the green he bade
Dismount with all the ladies / that in her train she led.
There saw ye all unidle / many a knight of high estate,
Who with full ready service / upon the ladies then did wait.
1311
Then saw the Lady Kriemhild / the margravine where she stood
Amid her fair attendants: / nearer not she rode.
Upon the steed that bore her / the rein she drew full tight,
And bade them straightway help her / adown from saddle to alight.
1312
The bishop saw ye leading / his sister's daughter fair,
And with him eke went Eckewart / to Gotelinde there.
The willing folk on all sides / made way before their feet.
With kiss did Gotelinde / the dame from land far distant greet.
1313
Then spake in manner kindly / the wife of Ruediger;
"Right glad am I, dear lady, / that I thy visage fair
Have in this our country / with mine own eyes seen.
In these times might never / greater joy to me have been."
1314
"God give thee meed," spake Kriemhild, / "Gotelinde, for this grace.
If with son of Botelung / happy may be my place,
May it henceforth be thy profit / that me thou here dost see."
Yet all unknown to either / was that which yet anon must be.
1315
With curtsy to each other / went full many a maid,
The knights a willing service / unto the ladies paid.
After the greeting sat they / adown upon the green;
Knew many then each other / that hitherto had strangers been.
1316
For the ladies they poured refreshment. / Now was come mid-day,
And did those high attendants / there no longer stay,
But went where found they ready / many a spreading tent.
Full willing was the service / unto the noble guests they lent.

1317
The night through until morning / did they rest them there.
They of Bechelaren / meanwhile did prepare
That into fitting quarters / each high guest be brought.
'Twas by the care of Ruediger / that never one did want for aught.

1318
Open ye saw the windows / the castle walls along,
And the burgh at Bechelaren / its gates wide open flung,
As through the guests went pricking, / that there full welcome were.
For them the lord full noble / had bidden quarters meet prepare.

1319
Ruediger's fair daughter / with her attendant train
Came forth in loving manner / to greet the lofty queen.
With her was eke her mother / the stately margravine;
There full friendly greeting / of many a maiden fair was seen.

1320
By the hand they took each other / and thence did pass each pair
Into a Hall full spacious, / the which was builded fair,
And 'neath its walls the Danube / flowed down with rushing tide.
As breezes cool played round them, / might they full happy there abide.

1321
What they there did further, / tell it not I can.
That they so long did tarry, / heard ye the knights complain
That were of Kriemhild's company, / who unwilling there abode.
What host of valiant warriors / with them from Bechelaren rode!

1322
Full kindly was the service / did render Ruediger,
Likewise gave Lady Kriemhild / twelve golden armbands rare
To Gotelinde's daughter, / and dress so richly wrought
That finer was none other / that into Etzel's land she brought.

1323
Though Nibelungen treasure / from her erstwhile was ta'en,
Good-will of all that knew her / did she e'er retain
With such little portion / as yet she did command.
Unto her host's attendants / dealt she thereof with bounteous hand.

1324
The Lady Gotelinde / such honors high again
Did pay in gracious manner / to the guests afar from Rhine
That of all the strangers / found ye never one
That wore not rich attire / from her, and many a precious stone.

1325
When they their fast had broken / and would thence depart,
The lady of the castle / did pledge with faithful heart

Unto the wife of Etzel / service true to bear.
Kriemhild caressed full fondly / the margravine's young daughter fair.

1326

To the queen then spake the maiden: / "If e'er it pleaseth thee,
Well know I that my father / dear full willingly
Unto thee will send me / where thou livest in Hunland."
That faithful was the maiden, / full well did Kriemhild understand.

1327

Now ready were the horses / the castle steps before,
And soon the queen full stately / did take her leave once more
Of the lovely daughter / and spouse of Ruediger.
Eke parted with fair greeting / thence full many a maiden fair.

1328

Each other they full seldom / thereafter might behold.
From Medelick were carried / beakers rich of gold
In hand and eke full many, / wherein was sparkling wine:
Upon the way were greeted / thus the strangers from the Rhine.

1329

High there a lord was seated, / Astold the name he bore,
Who that into Osterland / did lead the way before
As far as to Mautaren / adown the Danube's side.
There did they fitting service / for the lofty queen provide.

1330

Of his niece the bishop / took leave in loving wise.
That she well should bear her, / did he oft advise,
And that she win her honor / as Helke erst had done.
Ah, how great the honor / anon that 'mid the Huns she won!

1331

Unto the Traisem brought they / forth the strangers then.
Fair had they attendance / from Ruediger's men,
Till o'er the country riding / the Huns came them to meet.
With mickle honor did they / then the royal lady greet.

1332

For had the king of Hunland, / Traisem's stream beside,
A full mighty castle, / known afar and wide,
The same hight Traisenmauer: / Dame Helke there before
Did sit, such bounteous mistress / as scarce ye ever might see more,

1333

An it were not Kriemhild / who could such bounty show,
That after days of sorrow / the pleasure she might know,
To be held in honor / by Etzel's men each one:
That praise in fullest measure / had she amid those thanes anon.

1334
Afar the might of Etzel / so well was known around,
That at every season / within his court were found
Knights of all the bravest, / whereof ye e'er did hear
In Christian lands or heathen: / with him all thither come they were.

1335
By him at every season, / as scarce might elsewhere be,
Knights both of Christian doctrine / and heathen use saw ye.
Yet in what mind soever / did each and every stand,
To all in fullest measure / dealt the king with bounteous hand.

TWENTY-SECOND ADVENTURE: How Etzel kept the Wedding-feast with Kriemhild

1336
At Traisenmauer she tarried / until the fourth day.
Upon the road the dust-clouds / meanwhile never lay.
But rose like smoke of fire / around on every side:
Onward then through Austria / King Etzel's warriors did ride.

1337
Then eke unto the monarch / such tidings now were told,
That at the thought did vanish / all his grief of old,
In what high manner Kriemhild / should in his land appear.
Then gan the monarch hasten / where he did find the lady fair.

1338
Of many a tongue and varied / upon the way were seen
Before King Etzel riding / full many warriors keen,
Of Christians and of heathen / a spreading company.
To greet their coming mistress / forth they rode in fair array.

1339
Of Reuss men and Greeks there / great was the tale,
And rapid saw ye riding / the Wallach and the Pole
On chargers full of mettle / that they did deftly guide.
Their own country's custom / did they in no wise lay aside.

1340
From the land of Kief / rode there full many a thane,
And the wild Petschenegers. / Full many a bow was drawn,
As at the flying wild-fowl / through air the bolt was sped.
With might the bow was bended / as far as to the arrow's head.

1341
A city by the Danube / in Osterland doth stand,
Hight the same is Tulna: / of many a distant land

Saw Kriemhild there the customs, / ne'er yet to her were known.
To many there did greet her / sorrow befell through her anon.
1342
Before the monarch Etzel / rode a company
Of merry men and mighty, / courteous and fair to see,
Good four-and-twenty chieftains, / mighty men and bold.
Naught else was their desire / save but their mistress to behold.
1343
Then the Duke Ramung / from far Wallachia
With seven hundred warriors / dashed forth athwart her way:
Their going might ye liken / unto birds in flight.
Then came the chieftain Gibeke, / with his host a stately sight.
1344
Eke the valiant Hornbog / with full thousand men
From the king went forward / to greet his mistress then.
After their country's custom / in joy they shouted loud;
The doughty thanes of Hunland / likewise in merry tourney rode.
1345
Then came a chief from Denmark, / Hawart bold and keen,
And the valiant Iring, / in whom no guile was seen,
And Irnfried of Thuringia, / a stately knight to see:
Kriemhild they greeted / that honor high therefrom had she,
1346
With good knights twelve hundred / whom led they in their train.
Thither with three thousand / came Bloedel eke, the thane
That was King Etzel's brother / out of Hunland:
Unto his royal mistress / led he then his stately band.
1347
Then did come King Etzel / and Dietrich by his side
With all his doughty fellows. / In state there saw ye ride
Many a knight full noble, / valiant and void of fear.
The heart of Lady Kriemhild / did such host of warriors cheer.
1348
Then to his royal mistress / spake Sir Ruediger:
"Lady, now give I greeting / to the high monarch here.
Whom to kiss I bid thee, / grant him such favor then:
For not to all like greeting / may'st thou give 'mid Etzel's men."
1349
They lifted then from saddle / the dame of royal state.
Etzel the mighty monarch / might then no longer wait,
But sprang from off his charger / with many a warrior keen:
Unto Kriemhild hasting / full joyously he then was seen.

1350
As is to us related, / did there high princes twain
By the lady walking / bear aloft her train,
As the royal Etzel / went forward her to meet,
And she the noble monarch / with kiss in kindly wise did greet.

1351
Aside she moved her wimple, / whereat her visage fair
Gleamed 'mid the gold around it. / Though many a knight stood there,
They deemed that Lady Helke / did boast not fairer face.
Full close beside the monarch / his brother Bloedel had his place.

1352
To kiss him then Margrave / Ruediger her did tell,
And eke the royal Gibeke / and Sir Dietrich as well.
Of highest knights a dozen / did Etzel's spouse embrace;
Other knights full many / she greeted with a lesser grace.

1353
All the while that Etzel / stood by Kriemhild so,
Did the youthful riders / as still they're wont to do:
In varied tourney saw ye / each 'gainst the other pass,
Christian knights and heathen, / as for each the custom was.

1354
From men that followed Dietrich / saw ye in kindly wise
Splinters from the lances / flying high arise
Aloft above their bucklers, / from hand of good knight sent!
By the German strangers / pierced was many a shield and rent.

1355
From shaft of lances breaking / did far the din resound.
Together came the warriors / from all the land around,
Eke the guests of the monarch / and many a knight there was.
Thence did the mighty monarch / then with Lady Kriemhild pass.

1356
Stretched a fair pavilion / beside them there was seen:
With tents as well was covered / all around the green,
Where they now might rest them / all that weary were.
By high-born knights was thither / led full many a lady fair.

1357
With their royal mistress, / where in rich cushioned chair
Sat the queen full stately. / 'Twas by the margrave's care
That well had been provided, / with all that seeméd good,
A worthy seat for Kriemhild: / thereat was Etzel glad of mood.

1358
What was by Etzel spoken, / may I not understand.
In his right hand resting / lay her fair white hand.

They sat in loving fashion, / nor Ruediger would let
The king have secret converse / with Lady Kriemhild as yet.

1359
'Twas bidden that the jousting / on all sides they give o'er.
The din of stately tourney / heard ye then no more.
All the men of Etzel / unto their tents did go,
For every warrior present / did they full spacious lodging show.

1360
And now the day was ended / and they did rest the night
Until beheld they shining / once more the morning light.
Soon on charger mounted / again was many a man:
Heigho, what merry pastime, / the king to honor, they began!

1361
By the Huns the monarch / bade honors high be shown.
Soon rode they forth from Tulna / unto Vienna town,
Where found they many a lady / decked out in fair array:
The same the monarch Etzel's / wife received in stately way.

1362
In very fullest measure / upon them there did wait
Whate'er they might desire. / Of knights the joy was great,
Looking toward the revel. / Lodging then sought each one.
The wedding of the monarch / was in merry wise begun.

1363
Yet not for all might lodging / within the town be had.
All that were not strangers, / Ruediger them bade
That they find them lodgings / beyond the city's bound.
I ween that at all seasons / by Lady Kriemhild's side was found

1364
The noble Sir Dietrich / and many another thane,
Who amid their labors / but little rest had ta'en,
That the guests they harbored / of merry mood should be.
For Ruediger and his companions / went the time full pleasantly.

1365
The wedding time was fallen / upon a Whitsuntide,
When the monarch Etzel / lay Kriemhild beside
In the town at Vienna. / So many men I ween
Through her former husband / had not in her service been.

1366
Many that ne'er had seen her / did her rich bounty take,
And many a one among them / unto the strangers spake:
"We deemed that Lady Kriemhild / of wealth no more had aught
Now hath she by her giving / here full many a wonder wrought."

1367
The wedding-feast it lasted / for days full seventeen.
Ne'er of other monarch / hath any told, I ween,
That wedded with more splendor: / of such no tale we hear.
All that there were present, / new-made apparel did they wear.

1368
I ween that far in Netherland / sat she ne'er before
Amid such host of warriors. / And this believe I more:
Was Siegfried rich in treasure, / that yet he ne'er did gain,
As here she saw 'fore Etzel, / so many a high and noble thane.

1369
Nor e'er gave any other / at his own wedding-tide
So many a costly mantle / flowing long and wide,
Nor yet so rich apparel / —so may ye well believe—
As here from hand of Kriemhild / did they one and all receive.

1370
Her friends and eke the strangers / were of a single mind,
That they would not be sparing / of treasure in any kind:
What any from them desired, / they gave with willing hand.
Many a thane from giving / himself of clothing reft did stand.

1371
How by her noble husband / at the Rhine a queen she sat,
Of that she still was minded, / and her eye grew wet thereat.
Yet well she kept it hidden / that none the same might mark.
Now had she wealth of honor / after long years of sorrow dark.

1372
What any did with bounty, / 'twas but an idle wind
By side of Dietrich's giving: / what Etzel's generous mind
Before to him had given, / complete did disappear.
Eke wrought there many a wonder / the hand of bounteous Ruediger.

1373
Bloedelein the chieftain / that came from Hunland,
Full many a chest to empty / did he then command,
Of gold and eke of silver. / That did they freely give.
Right merrily the warriors / of the monarch saw ye live.

1374
Likewise the monarch's minstrels / Werbel and Schwemmelein,
Won they at the wedding / each alone, I ween,
Marks a good thousand / or even more than that,
Whenas fair Lady Kriemhild / 'neath crown by royal Etzel sat.

1375
Upon the eighteenth morning / from Vienna town they went.
Then in knightly pastime / many a shield was rent

By spear full well directed / by doughty rider's hand.
So came the royal Etzel / riding into Hunland.
1376
At Heimburg's ancient castle / they tarried over night.
Tell the tale of people / no mortal ever might,
And the number of good warriors / did o'er the country come.
Ah, what fairest women / were gathered unto Etzel's home!
1377
By Miesenburg's majestic / towers did they embark.
With horses eke and riders / the water all was dark,
As if 'twere earth they trod on, / as far as eye might see.
The way-worn ladies rested / now on board right pleasantly.
1378
Now was lashed together / many a boat full good,
That no harm they suffered / from the waves and flood.
Many a stately awning / likewise above them spread,
Just as if beneath them / had they land and flowery mead.
1379
When to Etzelburg the tidings / soon were borne along,
Therein of men and women / were seen a merry throng.
Who once the Lady Helke / as mistress did obey,
Anon by Lady Kriemhild / lived they many a gladsome day.
1380
There did stand expectant / full many a maid high-born,
That since the death of Helke / had pined all forlorn.
Daughters of seven monarchs / Kriemhild there waiting found,
That were the high adornment / of all King Etzel's country round.
1381
Herrat, a lofty princess, / did all the train obey,
Sister's child to Helke, / in whom high virtues lay,
Betrothéd eke of Dietrich, / of royal lineage born,
Daughter of King Nentwein; / her did high honors eft adorn.
1382
Against the strangers' coming / her heart with joy flowed o'er:
Eke was thereto devoted / of wealth a mickle store.
Who might e'er give the picture, / how the king eft sat on throne?
Nor had with any mistress / the Huns such joyous living known.
1383
As with his spouse the monarch / up from the river came,
Unto the noble Kriemhild / of each they told the name
'Mong them that she did find there: / she fairer each did greet.
Ah, how mighty mistress / she long did sit in Helke's seat!
1384

Ready and true the service / to her was offered there.
The queen dealt out in plenty / gold and raiment rare,
Silver eke and jewels. / What over Rhine she brought
With her unto Hunland, / soon thereof retained she naught.
1385
Eke in faithful service / she to herself did win
All the king's warriors / and all his royal kin,
—So that ne'er did Lady Helke / so mighty power wield
As until death to Kriemhild / such host did willing service yield.
1386
Thus stood so high in honor / the court and country round,
That there at every season / was pleasant pastime found
By each, whithersoever / his heart's desire might stand:
That wrought the monarch's favor / and the queen's full bounteous
hand.

TWENTY-THIRD ADVENTURE: How Kriemhild thought to avenge her Wrong

1387
In full lordly honor, / —truth is that ye hear—
Dwelt they with each other / until the seventh year.
Meanwhile Lady Kriemhild / a son to Etzel bore,
Nor gladder might the monarch / be o'er aught for evermore.
1388
Yet would she not give over, / nor with aught be reconciled,
But that should be baptizéd / the royal Etzel's child
After Christian custom: / Ortlieb they did him call.
Thereat was mickle joyance / over Etzel's borders all.
1389
Whate'er of highest virtues / in Lady Helke lay,
Strove the Lady Kriemhild / to rival her each day.
Herrat the stranger maiden / many a grace she taught,
Who yet with secret pining / for her mistress Helke was distraught.
1390
To stranger and to native / full well she soon was known,
Ne'er monarch's country, said they, / did royal mistress own
That gave with freer bounty, / that held they without fear.
Such praise she bore in Hunland, / until was come the thirteenth year.
1391
Now had she well perceivéd / how all obeyed her will,
As service to royal mistress / king's knights do render still,

And how at every season / twelve kings 'fore her were seen.
She thought of many a sorrow / that wrought upon her once had been.
1392
Eke thought she of lordly power / in Nibelungenland
That she erstwhile had wielded, / and how that Hagen's hand
Of it all had reft her / with her lord Siegfried dead;
She thought for so great evil / how might he ever be repaid.
1393
"'Twould be, might I but bring him / hither into this land."
She dreamed that fondly led her / full often by the hand
Giselher her brother, / full oft in gentle sleep
Thought she to have kissed him, / wherefrom he sorrow soon must reap.
1394
I ween the evil demon / was Kriemhild's counsellor
That she her peace with Gunther / should sacred keep no more,
Whom she kissed in friendly token / in the land of Burgundy.
Adown upon her bosom / the burning tears fell heavily.
1395
On her heart both late and early / lay the heavy thought,
How that, herself all guiltless, / thereto she had been brought,
That she must share in exile / a heathen monarch's bed.
Through Hagen eke and Gunther / come she was to such sore need.
1396
From her heart such longing / seldom might she dismiss.
Thought she: "A queen so mighty / I am o'er wealth like this,
That I upon mine enemies / may yet avenge me well.
Fain were I that on Hagen / of Tronje yet my vengeance fell.
1397
"For friends that once were faithful / full oft my heart doth long.
Were they but here beside me / that wrought on me such wrong,
Then were in sooth avengéd / my lover reft of life;
Scarce may I bide that hour," / spake the royal Etzel's wife.
1398
Kriemhild they loved and honored, / the monarch's men each one,
As they that came there with her: / well might the same be done.
The treasure wielded Eckewart, / and won good knights thereby.
The will of Lady Kriemhild might / none in all that land deny.
1399
She mused at every season: / "The king himself I'll pray,"—
That he to her the favor / might grant in friendly way,
To bring her kinsmen hither / unto Hunland.
What vengeful thought she cherished / might none soever understand.

1400
As she in stillest night-time / by the monarch lay
(In his arms enclosed he held her, / as he was wont alway
To caress the noble lady: / she was to him as life),
Again unto her enemies / turned her thoughts his stately wife.

1401
She spake unto the monarch: / "My lord full dear to me,
Now would I pray a favor, / if with thy grace it be,
That thou wilt show unto me / if merit such be mine
That unto my good kinsmen / truly doth thy heart incline."

1402
The mighty monarch answered / (from guile his heart was free):
"Of a truth I tell thee, / if aught of good may be
The fortune of thy kinsmen, / —of that I were full fain,
For ne'er through love of woman / might I friends more faithful gain."

1403
Thereat again spake Kriemhild: / "That mayst thou well believe,
Full high do stand my kinsmen; / the more it doth me grieve
That they deign so seldom / hither to take their way.
That here I live a stranger, / oft I hear the people say."

1404
Then spake the royal Etzel: / "Beloved lady mine,
Seemed not too far the journey, / I'd bid from yond the Rhine
Whom thou wouldst gladly welcome / hither unto my land."
Thereat rejoiced the lady / when she his will did understand.

1405
Spake she: "Wilt thou true favor / show me, master mine,
Then shall thou speed thy messengers / to Worms across the Rhine.
Were but my friends acquainted / what thing of them I would,
Then to this land came hither / full many a noble knight and good."

1406
He spake: "Whene'er thou biddest, / straight the thing shall be.
Thyself mightst ne'er thy kinsmen / here so gladly see,
As I the sons of Ute, / high and stately queen.
It grieveth me full sorely / that strangers here so long they've been.

1407
"If this thing doth please thee, / beloved lady mine,
Then gladly send I thither / unto those friends of thine
As messengers my minstrels / to the land of Burgundy."
He bade the merry fiddlers / lead before him presently.

1408
Then hastened they full quickly / to where they found the king
By side of Kriemhild sitting. / He told them straight the thing,

How they should be his messengers / to Burgundy to fare.
Full stately raiment bade he / for them straightway eke prepare.
1409
Four and twenty warriors / did they apparel well.
Likewise did the monarch / to them the message tell,
How that they King Gunther / and his men should bid aright.
Them eke the Lady Kriemhild / to secret parley did invite.
1410
Then spake the mighty monarch: / "Now well my words attend.
All good and friendly greeting / unto my friends I send,
That they may deign to journey / hither to my country.
Few be the guests beside them / that were so welcome unto me.
1411
"And if they be so minded / to meet my will in aught,
Kriemhild's lofty kinsmen, / that they forego it not
To come upon the summer / here where I hold hightide,
For that my joy in living / doth greatly with my friends abide."
1412
Then spake the fiddle-player, / Schwemmelein full bold:
"When thinkst thou in this country / such high feast to hold,
That unto thy friends yonder / tell the same we may?"
Thereto spake King Etzel: / "When next hath come midsummer day."
1413
"We'll do as thou commandest," / spake then Werbelein.
Unto her own chamber / commanded then the queen
To bring in secret manner / the messengers alone.
Thereby did naught but sorrow / befall full many a thane anon.
1414
She spake unto the messengers: / "Mickle wealth I give to you,
If my will in this matter / right faithfully ye do,
And bear what tidings send I / home unto our country.
I'll make you rich in treasure / and fair apparelled shall ye be.
1415
"And friends of mine so many / as ever see ye may
At Worms by Rhine river, / to them ye ne'er shall say
That any mood of sorrow / in me ye yet have seen.
Say ye that I commend me / unto the knights full brave and keen."
1416
"Pray them that to King Etzel's / message they give heed,
Thereby to relieve me / of all my care and need,
Else shall the Huns imagine / that I all friendless am.
If I but a knight were, / oft would they see me at their home.

1417
"Eke say ye unto Gernot, / brother to me full dear,
To him might never any / disposéd be more fair;
Pray him that he bring hither / unto this country
All our friends most steadfast, / that we thereby shall honored be.

1418
"Say further eke to Giselher / that he do have in mind,
That by his guilt I never / did cause for sorrow find;
Him therefore would I gladly / here with mine own eyes see,
And give him warmest welcome, / so faithful hath he been to me.

1419
"How I am held in honor, / to my mother eke make plain.
And if of Tronje Hagen / hath mind there to remain,
By whom might they in coming / through unknown lands be shown?
The way to Hunland hither / from youth to him hath well been known."

1420
No whit knew the messengers / wherefore she did advise
That they of Tronje Hagen / should not in any wise
Leave by the Rhine to tarry. / That was anon their bane:
Through him to dire destruction / was doomed full many a doughty thane.

1421
Letters and kindly greeting / now to them they give;
They fared from thence rich laden, / and merrily might live.
Leave then they took of Etzel / and eke his lady fair,
And parted on their journey / dight in apparel rich and rare.

TWENTY-FOURTH ADVENTURE: How Werbel and Schwemmel brought the Message

1422
When to the Rhine King Etzel / his messengers had sent,
With hasty flight fresh tidings / from land to land there went:
With messengers full quickly / to his high festival
He bade them, eke and summoned. / To many thereby did death befall.

1423
The messengers o'er the borders / of Hunland thence did fare
Unto the land of Burgundy; / thither sent they were
Unto three lordly monarchs / and eke their mighty men.
To Etzel's land to bid them / hastily they journeyed then.

1424
Unto Bechelaren / rode they on their way,
Where found they willing service. / Nor did aught delay
Ruediger to commend him / and Gotelinde as well
And eke their fairest daughter / to them that by the Rhine did dwell.

1425
They let them not unladen / with gifts from thence depart,
So did the men of Etzel / fare on with lighter heart.
To Ute and to her household / sent greeting Ruediger,
That never margrave any / to them more well disposéd were.

1426
Unto Brunhild also / did they themselves commend
With willing service offered / and steadfast to the end.
Bearing thus fair greeting / the messengers thence did fare,
And prayed the noble margravine / that God would have them in his care.

1427
Ere the messengers had fully / passed o'er Bavarian ground,
Had the nimble Werbel / the goodly bishop found.
What greetings to his kinsmen / unto the Rhine he sent,
That I cannot tell you; / the messengers yet from him went

1428
Laden with gold all ruddy, / to keep his memory.
Thus spake the Bishop Pilgrim: / "'Twere highest joy to me
Might I my sister's children / here see in home of mine,
For that I may but seldom / go unto them to the Rhine."

1429
What were the ways they followed / as through the lands they fared,
That can I nowise tell you. / Yet never any dared
Rob them of wealth or raiment, / for fear of Etzel's hand:
A lofty king and noble, / mighty in sooth was his command.

1430
Before twelve days were over / came they unto the Rhine,
And rode into Worms city / Werbel and Schwemmelein.
Told were soon the tidings / to the kings and their good men,
How that were come strange messengers. / Gunther the king did question then.

1431
And spake the monarch further: / "Who here may understand
Whence do come these strangers / riding unto our land?"
Yet was never any / might answer to him make,
Until of Tronje Hagen / thus unto King Gunther spake:

1432

"To us hath come strange tidings / to hand this day, I ween,
For Etzel's fiddlers riding / hither have I seen.
The same have by thy sister / unto the Rhine been sent:
For sake of their high master / now give we them fair compliment."

1433

E'en then did ride the messengers / unto the castle door,
And never royal minstrels / more stately went before.
By the monarch's servants / well received they were:
They gave them fitting lodging / and for their raiment had a care.

1434

Rich and wrought full deftly / was the travelling-dress they wore,
Wherein they well with honor / might go the king before;
Yet they at court no longer / would the same garments wear.
The messengers inquired / if any were might wish them there.

1435

In sooth in such condition / many eke were found,
Who would receive them gladly; / to such they dealt around.
Then decked themselves the strangers / in garments richer far,
Such as royal messengers / beseemeth well at court to wear.

1436

By royal leave came forward / to where the monarch sat
The men that came from Etzel, / and joy there was thereat.
Hagen then to meet them / in courteous manner went,
And heartily did greet them, / whereat they gave fair compliment.

1437

To know what were the tidings, / to ask he then began
How did find him Etzel / and each valiant man.
Then answer gave the fiddler: / "Ne'er higher stood the land,
Nor the folk so joyous: / that shall ye surely understand."

1438

They went unto the monarch. / Crowded was the hall.
There were received the strangers / as of right men shall
Kindly greeting offer / in other monarch's land.
Many a valiant warrior / saw Werbel by King Gunther stand.

1439

Right courteously the monarch / began to greet them then:
"Now be ye both right welcome, / Hunland's merry men,
And knights that give you escort. / Hither sent are ye
By Etzel mighty monarch / unto the land of Burgundy?"

1440

They bowed before the monarch; / then spake Werbelein:
"My dear lord and master, / and Kriemhild, sister thine,

Hither to thy country / give fairest compliment.
In faith of kindly welcome / us unto you they now have sent."

1441
Then spake the lofty ruler: / "I joy o'er this ye bring.
How liveth royal Etzel," / further spake the king,
"And Kriemhild, my sister, / afar in Hunland?"
Then answered him the fiddler: / "That shalt thou straightway understand.

1442
"That never any people / more lordly life might show
Than they both do joy in, / —that shalt thou surely know,—
Wherein do share their kinsmen / and all their doughty train.
When from them we parted, / of our journey were they fain."

1443
"My thanks for these high greetings / ye bring at his command
And from my royal sister. / That high in joy they stand,
The monarch and his kinsmen, / rejoiceth me to hear.
For, sooth to say, the tidings / asked I now in mickle fear."

1444
The twain of youthful princes / were eke come thitherward,
As soon as they the tidings / from afar had heard.
Right glad were seen the messengers / for his dear sister's sake
By the young Giselher, / who in such friendly manner spake:

1445
"Right hearty were your welcome / from me and brother mine,
Would ye but more frequent / ride hither to the Rhine;
Here found ye friends full many / whom glad ye were to see,
And naught but friendly favors / the while that in this land ye be."

1446
"To us how high thy favor," / spake Schwemmel, "know we well;
Nor with my best endeavor / might I ever tell
How kindly is the greeting / we bear from Etzel's hand
And from your noble sister, / who doth in highest honor stand.

1447
"Your sometime love and duty / recalleth Etzel's queen,
And how to her devoted / in heart we've ever been,
But first to royal Gunther / do we a message bear,
And pray it be your pleasure / unto Etzel's land to fare.

1448
"To beg of you that favor / commanded o'er and o'er
Etzel mighty monarch / and bids you know the more,
An will ye not your sister / your faces give to see,
So would he know full gladly / wherein by him aggrieved ye be,

1449
"That ye thus are strangers / to him and all his men.
If that his spouse so lofty / to you had ne'er been known,
Yet well he thought to merit / that him ye'd deign to see;
In sooth could naught rejoice him / more than that such thing might
be."

1450
Then spake the royal Gunther: / "A sennight from this day
Shall ye have an answer, / whereon decide I may
With my friends in counsel. / The while shall ye repair
Unto your place of lodging, / and right goodly be your fare."

1451
Then spake in answer Werbel: / "And might such favor be
That we the royal mistress / should first have leave to see,
Ute, the lofty lady, / ere that we seek our rest?"
To him the noble Giselher / in courteous wise these words addressed.

1452
"That grace shall none forbid you. / Will ye my mother greet,
Therein do ye most fully / her own desire meet.
For sake of my good sister / fain is she you to see,
For sake of Lady Kriemhild / ye shall to her full welcome be."

1453
Giselher then led him / unto the lofty dame,
Who fain beheld the messengers / from Hunland that came.
She greeted them full kindly / as lofty manner taught,
And in right courteous fashion / told they to her the tale they brought.

1454
"Pledge of loyal friendship / sendeth unto thee
Now my lofty mistress," / spake Schwemmel. "Might it be,
That she should see thee often, / then shalt thou know full well,
In all the world there never / a greater joy to her befell."

1455
Replied the royal lady: / "Such thing may never be.
Gladly as would I oft-times / my dearest daughter see,
Too far, alas, is distant / the noble monarch's wife.
May ever yet full happy / with King Etzel be her life.

1456
"See that ye well advise me, / ere that ye hence are gone,
What time shall be your parting; / for messengers I none
Have seen for many seasons / as glad as greet I you."
The twain gave faithful promise / such courtesy full sure to do.

1457
Forthwith to seek their lodgings / the men of Hunland went,

The while the mighty monarch / for trusted warriors sent,
Of whom did noble Gunther / straightway question make,
How thought they of the message. / Whereupon full many spake

1458
That he might well with honor / to Etzel's land be bound,
The which did eke advise him / the highest 'mongst them found,
All save Hagen only, / whom sorely grieved such rede.
Unto the king in secret / spake he: "Ill shall be thy meed.

1459
"What deed we twain compounded / art thou full well aware,
Wherefor good cause we ever / shall have Kriemhild to fear,
For that her sometime husband / I slew by my own hand.
How dare we ever journey / then unto King Etzel's land?"

1460
Replied the king: "My sister / no hate doth harbor more.
As we in friendship kissed her, / vengeance she forswore
For evil that we wrought her, / ere that from hence she rode,—
Unless this message, Hagen, / ill for thee alone forebode."

1461
"Now be thou not deceived," / spake Hagen, "say what may
The messengers from Hunland. / If thither be thy way,
At Kriemhild's hands thou losest / honor eke and life,
For full long-avenging / is the royal Etzel's wife."

1462
Added then his counsel / the princely Gernot there:
"Though be it thou hast reason / thine own death to fear
Afar in Hunnish kingdom, / should we for that forego
To visit our high sister, / that were in sooth but ill to do."

1463
Unto that thane did likewise / Giselher then say:
"Since well thou know'st, friend Hagen, / what guilt on thee doth weigh,
Then tarry here behind us / and of thyself have care,
And let who dares the journey / with us unto my sister fare."

1464
Thereat did rage full sorely / Tronje's doughty thane:
"So shall ye ne'er find any / that were to go more fain,
Nor who may better guide you / than I upon your way.
And will ye not give over, / know then my humor soon ye may."

1465
Then spake the Kitchen Master, / Rumold a lofty thane:
"Here might ye guests and kinsmen / in plenty long maintain
After your own pleasure, / for ye have goodly store.

I ween ye ne'er found Hagen / traitor to you heretofore.

1466

"If heed ye will not Hagen, / still Rumold doth advise
—For ye have faithful service / from me in willing wise—
That here at home ye tarry / for the love of me,
And leave the royal Etzel / afar with Kriemhild to be.

1467

"Where in the world might ever / ye more happy be
Than here where from danger / of every foeman free,
Where ye may go as likes you / in goodliest attire,
Drink wine the best, and stately / women meet your heart's desire.

1468

"And daily is your victual / the best that ever knew
A king of any country. / And were the thing not true,
At home ye yet should tarry / for sake of your fair wife
Ere that in childish fashion / ye thus at venture set your life.

1469

"Thus rede I that ye go not. / Mighty are your lands,
And at home more easy may ye / be freed from hostile hands
Than if ye pine in Hunland. / How there it is, who knows?
O Master, go not thither, / —such is the rede that Rumold owes."

1470

"We'll ne'er give o'er the journey," / Gernot then did say,
"When thus our sister bids us / in such friendly way
And Etzel, mighty monarch. / Wherefore should we refrain?
Who goes not gladly thither, / here at home may he remain."

1471

Thereto gave answer Hagen: / "Take not amiss, I pray,
These my words outspoken, / let befall what may.
Yet do I counsel truly, / as ye your safety prize,
That to the Huns ye journey / armed full well in warlike guise.

1472

"Will ye then not give over, / your men together call,
The best that ye may gather / from districts one and all.
From out them all I'll choose you / a thousand knights full good,
Then may ye reck but little / the vengeful Kriemhild's angry mood."

1473

"I'll gladly heed thy counsel," / straight the king replied,
And bade the couriers traverse / his kingdom far and wide.
Soon they brought together / three thousand men or more,
Who little weened what mickle / sorrow was for them in store.

1474

Joyful came they riding / to King Gunther's land.

Steeds and equipment for them / all he did command,
Who should make the journey / thence from Burgundy.
Warriors many were there / to serve the king right willingly.

1475
Hagen then of Tronje / to Dankwart did assign
Of their warriors eighty / to lead unto the Rhine.
Equipped in knightly harness / were they soon at hand.
Riding in gallant fashion / unto royal Gunther's land.

1476
Came eke the doughty Volker, / a noble minstrel he,
With thirty goodly warriors / to join the company,
Who wore so rich attire / 'twould fit a monarch well.
That he would fare to Hunland, / bade he unto Gunther tell.

1477
Who was this same Volker / that will I let you know:
He was a knight full noble, / to him did service owe
Many a goodly warrior / in the land of Burgundy.
For that he well could fiddle, / named the Minstrel eke was he.

1478
Thousand men chose Hagen, / who well to him were known.
What things in storm of battle / their doughty arm had done,
Or what they wrought at all times, / that knew he full well.
Nor of them might e'er mortal / aught but deeds of valor tell.

1479
The messengers of Kriemhild, / full loath they were to wait,
For of their master's anger / stood they in terror great.
Each day for leave to journey / more great their yearning grew,
But daily to withhold it / crafty Hagen pretext knew.

1480
He spake unto his master: / "Well shall we beware
Hence to let them journey / ere we ourselves prepare
In seven days thereafter / to ride to Etzel's land:
If any mean us evil, / so may we better understand.

1481
"Nor may the Lady Kriemhild / ready make thereto,
That any by her counsel / scathe to us may do.
Yet if such wish she cherish, / evil shall be her meed,
For many a chosen warrior / with us shall we thither lead."

1482
Shields well-wrought and saddles, / with all the mickle gear
That into Etzel's country / the warriors should wear,
The same was now made ready / for many a knight full keen.
The messengers of Kriemhild / before King Gunther soon were seen.

1483
When were come the messengers, / Gernot them addressed:
"King Gunther now is minded / to answer Etzel's quest.
Full gladly go we thither / with him to make high-tide
And see our lofty sister, / —of that set ye all doubt aside."

1484
Thereto spake King Gunther: / "Can ye surely say
When shall be the high-tide, / or upon what day
We shall there assemble?" / Spake Schwemmel instantly:
"At turn of sun in summer / shall in sooth the meeting be."

1485
The monarch leave did grant them, / ere they should take their way,
If that to Lady Brunhild / they would their homage pay,
His high pleasure was it / they unto her should go.
Such thing prevented Volker, / and did his mistress' pleasure so.

1486
"In sooth, my Lady Brunhild / hath scarce such health to-day
As that she might receive you," / the gallant knight did say.
"Bide ye till the morrow, / may ye the lady see."
When thus they sought her presence, / might their wish not granted be.

1487
To the messengers right gracious / was the mighty king,
And bade he from his treasure / on shields expansive bring
Shining gold in plenty / whereof he had great store.
Eke richest gifts received they / from his lofty kinsmen more.

1488
Giselher and Gernot, / Gere and Ortwein,
That they were free in giving / soon full well was seen.
So costly gifts were offered / unto each messenger
That they dared not receive them, / for Etzel's anger did they fear.

1489
Then unto King Gunther / Werbel spake again:
Sire, let now thy presents / in thine own land remain.
The same we may not carry, / my master hath decreed
That we accept no bounty. / Of that in sooth we've little need."

1490
Thereat the lord of Rhineland / was seen in high displeasure,
That they should thus accept not / so mighty monarch's treasure?
In their despite yet took they / rich dress and gold in store,
The which moreover with them / home to Etzel's land they bore.

1491
Ere that they thence departed / they Lady Ute sought,

Whereat the gallant Giselher / straight the minstrels brought
Unto his mother's presence. / Kind greetings sent the dame,
And wish that high in honor / still might stand her daughter's name.

1492
Then bade the lofty lady / embroidered silks and gold
For the sake of Kriemhild, / whom loved she as of old,
And eke for sake of Etzel, / unto the minstrels give.
What thus so free was offered / might they in sooth right fain receive.

1493
Soon now had ta'en departure / the messengers from thence,
From knight and fairest lady, / and joyous fared they hence
Unto Suabian country; / Gernot had given behest
Thus far for armed escort, / that none their journey might molest.

1494
When these had parted from them, / safe still from harm were they,
For Etzel's might did guard them / wherever led their way.
Nor ever came there any / that aught to take would dare,
As into Etzel's country / they in mickle haste did fare.

1495
Where'er they friends encountered, / to all they straight made known
How that they of Burgundy / should follow after soon
From Rhine upon their journey / unto the Huns' country.
The message brought they likewise / unto Bishop Pilgrim's see.

1496
As down 'fore Bechelaren / they passed upon their way,
The tidings eke to Ruediger / failed they not to say,
And unto Gotelinde, / the margrave's wife the same.
At thought so soon to see them / was filled with joy the lofty dame.

1497
Hasting with the tidings / each minstrel's courser ran,
Till found they royal Etzel / within his burgh at Gran.
Greeting upon greeting, / which they must all bestow,
They to the king delivered; / with joy his visage was aglow.

1498
When that the lofty Kriemhild / did eke the tidings hear,
How that her royal brothers / unto the land would fare,
In sooth her heart was gladdened; / on the minstrels she bestowed
Richest gifts in plenty, / as she to her high station owed.

1499
She spake: "Now shall ye, Werbel / and Schwemmel, tell to me
Who cometh of my kinsmen / to our festivity,
Who of all were bidden / this our land to seek?
Now tell me, when the message / heard he, what did Hagen speak?"

1500
Answered: "He came to council / early upon a day,
But little was of pleasant / in what he there did say.
When learned he their intention, / in wrath did Hagen swear,
To death 'twere making journey, / to country of the Huns to fare.

1501
"Hither all are coming, / thy royal brothers three,
And they right high in spirit. / Who more shall with them be,
The tale to tell entire / were more than I might do.
To journey with them plighted / Volker the valiant fiddler too."

1502
"'Twere little lost, full truly," / answered then the queen,
"If by my eyes never / Volker here were seen.
'Tis Hagen hath my favor, / a noble knight is he,
And mickle is my pleasure / that him full soon we here may see."

1503
Her way the Lady Kriemhild / then to the king did take,
And in right joyous manner / unto her consort spake:
"How liketh thee the tidings, / lord full dear to me?
What aye my heart hath yearned for, / that shall now accomplished be."

1504
"Thy will my joy was ever," / the lofty monarch said.
"In sooth for my own kinsmen / I ne'er have been so glad,
To hear that they come hither / unto my country.
To know thy friends are coming, / hath parted sadness far from me."

1505
Straight did the royal provosts / give everywhere decree
That hall and stately palace / well prepared should be
With seats, that unprovided / no worthy guest be left.
Anon by them the monarch / should be of mickle joy bereft.

TWENTY-FIFTH ADVENTURE: How the Knights all fared to the Huns

1506
Tell we now no further / how they here did fare.
Knights more high in spirit / saw ye journey ne'er
In so stately fashion / to the land of e'er a king.
Of arms and rich attire / lacked they never anything.

1507
At Rhine the lordly monarch / equipped his warriors well,

A thousand knights and sixty, / as I did hear tell,
And eke nine thousand squires / toward the festivity.
Whom they did leave behind them / anon must mourn full grievously.
1508
As at Worms across the courtyard / equipment full they bore
Spake there of Speyer / a bishop old and hoar
Unto Lady Ute: / "Our friends have mind to fare
Unto the festivity; / may God their honor have in care."
1509
Then spake unto her children / Ute the noble dame:
"At home ye here should tarry, / ye knights full high in fame.
Me dreamt but yester even / a case of direst need,
How that in this country / all the feathered fowl were dead."
1510
"Who recketh aught of dreamings," / Hagen then replied,
"Distraught is sure his counsel / when trouble doth betide,
Or he would of his honor / have a perfect care.
I counsel that my master / straight to take his leave prepare.
1511
"Gladly shall we journey / into Etzel's land;
There at their master's service / may good knights ready stand,
For that we there shall witness / Kriemhild's festivity."
That Hagen gave such counsel, / rue anon full sore did he.
1512
Yet in sooth far other / than this had been his word,
Had not with bitter mocking / Gernot his anger stirred.
He spake to him of Siegfried / whom Kriemhild loved so,
And said: "Therefore the journey / would Hagen willingly forego."
1513
Then spake of Tronje Hagen: / "Through fear I nothing do.
Whenever will ye, Masters, / set straight your hand thereto,
With you I'll gladly journey / unto Etzel's land."
Many a shield and helmet / there hewed anon his mighty hand.
1514
The ships stood ready waiting, / whereunto ample store
Of clothing for the journey / men full many bore,
Nor had they time for resting / till shades of even fell.
Anon in mood full joyous / bade they friends at home farewell.
1515
Tents full large and many / arose upon the green,
Yonder side Rhine river. / But yet the winsome queen
Caressed the doughty monarch / that night, and still did pray
That far from Etzel's country / among his kinsmen might he stay.

1516

When sound of flute and trumpet / arose at break of day,
A signal for their parting, / full soon they took their way.
Each lover to his bosom / did friend more fondly press:
King Etzel's wife full many / did part anon in dire distress.

1517

The sons of stately Ute, / a good knight had they,
A brave man and a faithful. / When they would thence away,
Apart unto the monarch / did he his mind reveal,
And spake: "That ye will journey, / may I naught but sorrow feel."

1518

Hight the same was Rumold, / a man of doughty hand.
He spake: "To whom now leave ye / people here and land?
O that never any / might alter your intent!
Small good, methinks, may follow / message e'er by Kriemhild sent."

1519

"The land to thee entrusted / and eke my child shall be,
And tender care of ladies, / —so hast command from me.
Whene'er thou seest weeping, / do there thy comfort give.
Yea, trust we free from sorrow / at hand of Etzel's wife to live."

1520

For knight and royal master / the chargers ready were,
As with fond embracing / parted many there,
Who long in joy together / a merry life had led.
By winsome dame full many / therefor must bitter tear be shed.

1521

As did those doughty warriors / into the saddle spring,
Might full many a lady / be seen there sorrowing;
For told them well their spirit / that thus so long to part
Did bode a dire peril, / the which must ever cloud the heart.

1522

As mounted stood the valiant / thanes of Burgundy,
Might ye a mickle stirring / in that country see,
Both men and women weeping / on either riverside.
Yet pricked they gaily forward, / let what might their folk betide.

1523

The Nibelungen warriors / in hauberks bright arrayed
Went with them, a thousand, / while at home behind them stayed
Full many a winsome lady, / whom saw they nevermore.
The wounds of doughty Siegfried / still grieved the Lady Kriemhild
sore.

1524

Their journey they directed / onward to the Main,

Up through East Frankish country, / the men of Gunther's train
Thither led by Hagen, / who well that country knew;
Marshal to them was Dankwart, / a knight of Burgundy full true.

1525
On from East Frankish country / to Schwanefeld they went,
A train of valiant warriors / of high accomplishment,
The monarchs and their kinsmen, / all knights full worthy fame.
Upon the twelfth morning / the king unto the Danube came.

1526
The knight of Tronje, Hagen, / the very van did lead,
Ever to the Nibelungen / a surest help in need.
First the thane full valiant / down leapt upon the ground,
And straightway then his charger / fast unto a tree he bound.

1527
Flooded were the waters / and ne'er a boat was near,
Whereat began the Nibelungen / all in dread to fear
They ne'er might cross the river, / so mighty was the flood.
Dismounted on the shore, / full many a stately knight then stood.

1528
"Ill may it," spake then Hagen, / "fare here with thee,
Lord of Rhine river. / Now thyself mayst see
How flooded are the waters, / and swift the current flows.
I ween, before the morrow / here many a goodly knight we lose."

1529
"How wilt reproach me, Hagen?" / the lofty monarch spake.
I pray thee yet all comfort / not from our hearts to take.
The ford shalt thou discover / whereby we may pass o'er,
Horse and equipment bringing / safely unto yonder shore."

1530
"In sooth, not I," quoth Hagen, / "am yet so weary grown
Of life, that in these waters / wide I long to drown.
Ere that, shall warriors sicken / in Etzel's far country
Beneath my own arm stricken: / —'tis my intent full certainly.

1531
"Here tarry by the water, / ye gallant knights and good,
The while I seek the boatmen / myself along the flood,
Who will bring us over / into Gelfrat's land."
With that the doughty Hagen / took his trusty shield in hand.

1532
He cap-a-pie was arméd, / as thus he strode away,
Upon his head a helmet / that gleamed with brilliant ray,
And o'er his warlike harness / a sword full broad there hung,
That on both its edges / did fiercely cut, in battle swung.

1533
He sought to find the boatmen / if any might be near,
When sound of falling waters / full soon upon his ear.
Beside a rippling fountain, / where ran the waters cool,
A group of wise mermaidens / did bathe themselves within the pool.

1534
Ware of them soon was Hagen / and stole in secret near,
But fast away they hurried / when they the sound did hear.
That they at all escaped him, / filled they were with glee.
The knight did take their clothing, / yet wrought none other injury.

1535
Then spake the one mermaiden, / Hadburg that hight:
"Hagen, knight full noble, / tell will we thee aright,
An wilt thou, valiant warrior, / our garments but give o'er,
What fortune may this journey / to Hunland have for thee in store."

1536
They hovered there before him / like birds above the flood,
Wherefore did think the warrior / that tell strange things they could,
And all the more believed he / what they did feign to say,
As to his eager question / in ready manner answered they.

1537
Spake one: "Well may ye journey / to Etzel's country.
Thereto my troth I give thee / in full security
That ne'er in any kingdom / might high guests receive
Such honors as there wait you, / —this may ye in sooth believe."

1538
To hear such speech was Hagen / in sooth right glad of heart;
He gave to them their garments, / and straightway would depart.
But when in strange attire / they once more were dight,
Told they of the journey / into Etzel's land aright.

1539
Spake then the other mermaid, / Siegelind that hight:
"I warn thee, son of Aldrian, / Hagen valiant knight,
'Twas but to gain her clothing / my cousin falsely said,
For, comest thou to Hunland, / sorely shalt thou be betrayed.

1540
"Yea, that thou turnest backward / is fitter far, I ween;
For but your death to compass / have all ye warriors keen
Receivéd now the bidding / unto Etzel's land.
Whose doth thither journey, / death leadeth surely by the hand."

1541
Thereto gave answer Hagen: / "False speech hath here no gain.
How might it ever happen / that we all were slain

Afar in Etzel's country / through hate of any man?"
To tell the tale more fully / unto him she then began.

1542
Spake again the other: / "The thing must surely be,
That of you never any / his home again shall see,
Save only the king's chaplain; / well do we understand
That he unscathed returneth / unto royal Gunther's land."

1543
Then spake the valiant Hagen / again in angry way:
"Unto my royal masters / 'twere little joy to say
That we our lives must forfeit / all in Hunland.
Now show us, wisest woman, / how pass we safe to yonder strand."

1544
She spake: "Since from thy purposed / journey thou wilt not turn,
Where upward by the water / a cabin stands, there learn
Within doth dwell a boatman, / nor other find thou mayst."
No more did Hagen question, / but strode away from there in haste.

1545
As went he angry-minded / one from afar did say:
"Now tarry still, Sir Hagen; / why so dost haste away?
Give ear yet while we tell thee / how thou reachest yonder strand.
Master here is Else, / who doth rule this borderland.

1546
"Hight is his brother Gelfrat, / and is a thane full rare,
Lord o'er Bavarian country. / Full ill with you 'twill fare,
Will ye pass his border. / Watchful must ye be,
And eke with the ferryman / 'twere well to walk right modestly.

1547
"He is so angry-minded / that sure thy bane 'twill be,
Wilt thou not show the warrior / all civility.
Wilt thou that he transport thee, / give all the boatman's due.
He guardeth well the border / and unto Gelfrat is full true.

1548
"If he be slow to answer, / then call across the flood
That thy name is Amelrich. / That was a knight full good,
Who for a feud did sometime / go forth from out this land.
The ferryman will answer, / when he the name doth understand.

1549
Hagen high of spirit / before those women bent,
Nor aught did say, but silent / upon his way he went.
Along the shore he wandered / till higher by the tide
On yonder side the river / a cabin standing he espied.

1550
He straight began a calling / across the flood amain.
"Now fetch me over, boatman," / cried the doughty thane.
"A golden armband ruddy / I'll give to thee for meed.
Know that to make this crossing / I in sooth have very need."

1551
Not fitting 'twas high ferryman / his service thus should give,
And recompense from any / seldom might he receive;
Eke were they that served him / full haughty men of mood.
Still alone stood Hagen / on the hither side the flood.

1552
Then cried he with such power / the wave gave back the sound,
For in strength far-reaching / did the knight abound:
"Fetch me now, for Amelrich, / Else's man, am I,
That for feud outbroken / erstwhile from this land did fly."

1553
Full high upon his sword-point / an armband did he hold,
Fair and shining was it / made of ruddy gold,
The which he offered to him / for fare to Gelfrat's land.
The ferryman high-hearted / himself did take the oar in hand.

1554
To do with that same boatman / was ne'er a pleasant thing;
The yearning after lucre / yet evil end doth bring.
Here where thought he Hagen's / gold so red to gain,
Must he by the doughty / warrior's fierce sword be slain.

1555
With might across the river / his oar the boatman plied,
But he who there was naméd / might nowhere be espied.
His rage was all unbounded / when he did Hagen find,
And loud his voice resounded / as thus he spake his angry mind:

1556
"Thou mayst forsooth be calléd / Amelrich by name:
Whom I here did look for, / no whit art thou the same.
By father and by mother / brother he was to me.
Since me thou thus hast cozened, / so yet this side the river be."

1557
"Nay, by highest Heaven," / Hagen did declare.
"Here am I a stranger / that have good knights in care.
Now take in friendly manner / here my offered pay,
And guide me o'er the ferry; / my favor hast thou thus alway."

1558
Whereat replied the boatman: / "The thing may never be.
There are that to my masters / do bear hostility;

Wherefore I never stranger / do lead into this land.
As now thy life thou prizest, / step straightway out upon the strand."
1559
"Deny me not," quoth Hagen, / "for sad in sooth my mood.
Take now for remembrance / this my gold so good,
And carry men a thousand / and horses to yonder shore."
Quoth in rage the boatman: / "Such thing will happen nevermore."
1560
Aloft he raised an oar / that mickle was and strong,
And dealt such blow on Hagen, / (but rued he that ere long,)
That in the boat did stumble / that warrior to his knee.
In sooth so savage boatman / ne'er did the knight of Tronje see.
1561
With thought the stranger's anger / the more to rouse anew,
He swung a mighty boat-pole / that it in pieces flew
Upon the crown of Hagen;— / he was a man of might.
Thereby did Else's boatman / come anon to sorry plight.
1562
Full sore enraged was Hagen, / as quick his hand he laid
Upon his sword where hanging / he found the trusty blade.
His head he struck from off him / and flung into the tide.
Known was soon the story / to the knights of Burgundy beside.
1563
While the time was passing / that he the boatman slew,
The waters bore him downward, / whereat he anxious grew.
Ere he the boat had righted / began his strength to wane,
So mightily was pulling / royal Gunther's doughty thane.
1564
Soon he yet had turned it, / so rapid was his stroke,
Until the mighty oar / beneath his vigor broke.
As strove he his companions / upon the bank to gain,
No second oar he found him. / Yet soon the same made fast again.
1565
With quickly snatched shield-strap, / a fine and narrow band.
Downward where stood a forest / he sought again the land,
And there his master found he / standing upon the shore.
In haste came forth to meet him / many a stately warrior more.
1566
The gallant knight they greeted / with right hearty mood.
When in the boat perceived they / reeking still the blood
That from the wound had issued / where Hagen's sword did swing,
Scarce could his companions / bring to an end their questioning.

1567
When that royal Gunther / the streaming blood did see
Within the boat there running, / straightway then spake he:
"Where is now the ferryman, / tell me, Hagen, pray?
By thy mighty prowess / his life, I ween, is ta'en away."

1568
Thereto replied he falsely: / "When the boat I found
Where slopeth a wild meadow, / I the same unbound.
Hereabout no ferryman / I to-day have seen,
Nor ever cause of sorrow / unto any have I been."

1569
The good knight then of Burgundy, / the gallant Gernot, spake:
"Dear friends full many, fear I, / the flood this day will take,
Since we of the boatmen / none ready here may find
To guide us o'er the current. / 'Tis mickle sorrow to my mind."

1570
Full loudly cried then Hagen: / "Lay down upon the grass,
Ye squires, the horse equipments. / I ween a time there was,
Myself was best of boatmen / that dwelt the Rhine beside.
To Gelfrat's country trow I / to bring you safely o'er the tide."

1571
That they might come the sooner / across the running flood,
Drove they in the horses. / Their swimming, it was good,
For of them never any / beneath the waves did sink,
Though many farther downward / must struggle sore to gain the brink.

1572
Their treasure and apparel / unto the boat they bore,
Since by no means the journey / thought they to give o'er.
Hagen was director, / and safely reached the strand
With many a stalwart warrior / bound unto the unknown land.

1573
Gallant knights a thousand / first he ferried o'er,
Whereafter came his own men. / Of others still were more,
For squires full nine thousand / he led unto that land.
That day no whit was idle / that valiant knight of Tronje's hand.

1574
When he them all in safety / o'er the flood had brought,
Of that strange story / the valiant warrior thought,
Which erstwhile had told him / those women of the sea.
Lost thereby the chaplain's / life well-nigh was doomed to be.

1575
Beside his priestly baggage / he saw the chaplain stand,
Upon the holy vestments / resting with his hand.

No whit was that his safety; / when Hagen him did see,
Must the priest full wretched / suffer sorest injury.

1576
From out the boat he flung him / ere might the thing be told,
Whereat they cried together: / "Hold, O Master, hold!"
Soon had the youthful Giselher / to rage thereat begun,
And mickle was his sorrow / that Hagen yet the thing had done.

1577
Then outspake Sir Gernot, / knight of Burgundy:
"What boots it thee, Sir Hagen, / that thus the chaplain die?
Dared any else to do it, / thy wrath 'twould sorely stir.
Wherein the priest's offending, / thus thy malice to incur?"

1578
To swim the chaplain struggled. / He thought him yet to free,
If any but would help him. / Yet such might never be,
For that the doughty Hagen / full wrathful was of mood,
He sunk him to the bottom, / whereat aghast each warrior stood.

1579
When that no help forthcoming / the wretched priest might see,
He sought the hither shore, / and fared full grievously.
Though failed his strength in swimming, / yet helped him God's own hand,
That he came securely / back again unto the land.

1580
Safe yonder stood the chaplain / and shook his dripping dress.
Thereby perceived Hagen / how true was none the less
The story that did tell him / the strange women of the sea.
Thought he: "Of these good warriors / soon the days must ended be."

1581
When that the boat was emptied, / and complete their store
All the monarch's followers / had borne upon the shore,
Hagen smote it to pieces / and cast it on the flood,
Whereat in mickle wonder / the valiant knights around him stood.

1582
"Wherefore dost this, brother," / then Sir Dankwart spake;
"How shall we cross the river / when again we make
Our journey back from Hunland, / riding to the Rhine?"
Behold how Hagen bade him / all such purpose to resign.

1583
Quoth the knight of Tronje: / "This thing is done by me,
That if e'er coward rideth / in all our company,
Who for lack of courage / from us away would fly,
He beneath these billows / yet a shameful death must die."

1584
One there journeyed with them / from the land of Burgundy,
That was a knight of valor, / Volker by name was he.
He spake in cunning manner / whate'er might fill his mind,
And aught was done by Hagen / did the Fiddler fitting find.

1585
Ready stood their chargers, / the carriers laden well;
At passage of the river / was there naught to tell
Of scathe to any happened, / save but the king's chaplain.
Afoot must he now journey / back unto the Rhine again.

TWENTY-SIXTH ADVENTURE: How Gelfrat was Slain by Dankwart

1586
When now they all were gathered / upon the farther strand,
To wonder gan the monarch: / "Who shall through this land
On routes aright direct us, / that not astray we fare?"
Then spake the doughty Volker: / "Thereof will I alone have care."

1587
"Now hark ye all," quoth Hagen, / "knight and squire too,
And list to friendly counsel, / as fitting is to do.
Full strange and dark the tidings / now ye shall hear from me:
Home nevermore return we / unto the land of Burgundy.

1588
"Thus mermaids twain did tell me, / who spake to me this morn,
That back we come not hither. / You would I therefore warn
That arméd well ye journey / and of all ills beware.
To meet with doughty foemen / well behooveth us prepare.

1589
"I weened to turn to falsehood / what those wise mermaids spake,
Who said that safe this journey / none again should make
Home unto our country / save the chaplain alone:
Him therefore was I minded / to-day beneath the flood to drown."

1590
From company to company / quickly flew the tale,
Whereon grew many a doughty / warrior's visage pale,
As gan he think in sorrow / how death should snatch away
All ere the journey ended; / and very need for grief had they.

1591
By Moeringen was it / they had the river crossed,
Where also Else's boatman / thus his life had lost.

There again spake Hagen: / "Since in such wise by me
Wrath hath been incurréd, / assailed full surely shall we be.
1592
"Myself that same ferryman / did this morning slay.
Far bruited are the tidings. / Now arm ye for the fray,
That if Gelfrat and Else / be minded to beset
Our train to-day, they surely / with sore discomfiture be met.
1593
"So keen they are, well know I / the thing they'll not forego.
Your horses therefore shall ye / make to pace more slow,
That never man imagine / we flee away in fear."
"That counsel will I follow," / spake the young knight Giselher.
1594
"Who will guide our vanguard / through this hostile land?"
"Volker shall do it," spake they, / "well doth he understand
Where leadeth path and highway, / a minstrel brave and keen."
Ere full the wish was spoken, / in armor well equipped was seen
1595
Standing the doughty Fiddler. / His helmet fast he bound,
And from his stately armor / shot dazzling light around.
Eke to a staff he fastened / a banner, red of hue.
Anon with royal masters / came he to sorest sorrow too.
1596
Unto Gelfrat meanwhile / had sure tidings flown,
How that was dead his boatman; / the story eke was known
Unto the doughty Else, / and both did mourn his fate.
Their warriors they summoned, / nor must long time for answer wait.
1597
But little space it lasted / —that would I have you know—
Ere that to them hasted / who oft a mickle woe
Had wrought in stress of battle / and injury full sore;
To Gelfrat now came riding / seven hundred knights or more.
1598
When they their foes to follow / so bitterly began,
Led them both their masters. / Yet all too fast they ran
After the valiant strangers / vengeance straight to wreak.
Ere long from those same leaders / did death full many a warrior take.
1599
Hagen then of Tronje / the thing had ordered there,
—How of his friends might ever / knight have better care?—
That he did keep the rearguard / with warriors many a one,
And Dankwart eke, his brother; / full wisely the thing was done.

1600
When now the day was over / and light they had no more,
Injury to his followers / gan he to dread full sore.
They shield in hand rode onward / through Bavarian land,
And ere they long had waited / beset they were by hostile band.
1601
On either side the highway / and close upon their rear
Of hoofs was heard the clatter; / too keen the chasers were.
Then spake the valiant Dankwart: / "The foe is close at hand.
Now bind we on the helmet, / —wisdom doth the same command."
1602
Upon the way they halted, / nor else they safe had been.
Through the gloom perceived they / of gleaming shields the sheen.
Thereupon would Hagen / longer not delay:
"Who rideth on the highway?"— / That must Gelfrat tell straight-way.
1603
Of Bavaria the margrave / thereupon replied:
"Our enemies now seek we, / and swift upon them ride.
Fain would I discover / who hath my boatman slain.
A knight he was of valor, / whose death doth cause me grievous pain."
1604
Then spake of Tronje Hagen: / "And was the boatman thine
That would not take us over? / The guilt herein is mine.
Myself did slay the warrior, / and had, in sooth, good need,
For that beneath his valor / I myself full nigh lay dead.
1605
"For pay I rich attire / did bid, and gold a store,
Good knight, that to thy country / he should us ferry o'er.
Thereat he raged full sorely / and on me swung a blow
With a mighty boat-pole, / whereat I eke did angry grow.
1606
"For my sword then reached I / and made his rage to close
With a wound all gaping: / so thou thy knight didst lose.
I'll give thee satisfaction / as to thee seemeth good."
Straightway began the combat, / for high the twain in valor stood.
1607
"Well know I," spake Gelfrat, / "when Gunther with his train
Rode through this my country / that we should suffer bane
From Hagen, knight of Tronje. / No more shall he go free,
But for my boatman's slaying / here a hostage must he be."
1608
Against their shields then lowered / for the charge the spear
Gelfrat and Hagen; / eager to close they were.

Else and Dankwart / spurred eke in stately way,
Scanning each the other; / then both did valorous arm display.
1609
How might ever heroes / show doughty arm so well?
Backward from off his charger / from mighty tilt there fell
Hagen the valiant, / by Gelfrat's hand borne down.
In twain was rent the breast-piece: / to Hagen thus a fall was known.
1610
Where met in charge their followers, / did crash of shafts resound.
Risen eke was Hagen, / who erst unto the ground
Was borne by mighty lance-thrust, / prone upon the grass.
I ween that unto Gelfrat / nowise of gentle mood he was.
1611
Who held their horses' bridles / can I not recount,
But soon from out their saddles / did they all dismount.
Hagen and Gelfrat / straightway did fierce engage,
And all their men around them / did eke a furious combat wage.
1612
Though with fierce onslaught Hagen / upon Gelfrat sprung,
On his shield the noble margrave / a sword so deftly swung
That a piece from off the border / 'mid flying sparks it clave.
Well-nigh beneath its fury / fell dead King Gunther's warrior brave.
1613
Unto Dankwart loudly / thereat he gan to cry:
"Help! ho! my good brother! / Encountered here have I
A knight of arm full doughty, / from whom I come not free."
Then spake the valiant Dankwart: / "Myself thereof the judge will be."
1614
Nearer sprang the hero / and smote him such a blow
With a keen-edged weapon / that he in death lay low.
For his slain brother Else / vengeance thought to take,
But soon with all his followers / 'mid havoc swift retreat must make.
1615
Slain was now his brother, / wound himself did bear,
And of his followers eighty / eke had fallen there,
By grim death snatched sudden. / Then must the doughty knight,
From Gunther's men to save him, / turn away in hasty flight.
1616
When that they of Bavaria / did from the carnage flee,
The blows that followed after / resounded frightfully;
For close the knights of Tronje / upon their enemies chased,
Who to escape the fury / did quit the field in mickle haste.

1617

Then spake upon their fleeing / Dankwart the doughty thane:
"Upon our way now let us / backward turn again,
And leave them hence to hasten / all wet with oozing blood.
Unto our friends return we, / this verily meseemeth good."

1618

When back they were returnéd / where did the scathe befall,
Outspake of Tronje Hagen: / "Now look ye, warriors all,
Who of our tale is lacking, / or who from us hath been
Here in battle riven / through the doughty Gelfrat's spleen."

1619

Lament they must for warriors / four from them were ta'en.
But paid for were they dearly, / for roundabout lay slain
Of their Bavarian foemen / a hundred or more.
The men of Tronje's bucklers / with blood were wet and tarnished o'er.

1620

From out the clouds of heaven / a space the bright moon shone.
Then again spake Hagen: / "Bear report let none
To my beloved masters / how we here did fare.
Let them until the morrow / still be free from aught of care."

1621

When they were back returnéd / who bore the battle's stress,
Sore troubled was their company / from very weariness.
"How long shall we keep saddle?" / was many a warrior's quest.
Then spake the valiant Dankwart: / "Not yet may we find place of rest,

1622

"But on ye all must journey / till day come back again."
Volker, knight of prowess, / who led the foremost train,
Bade to ask the marshal: / "This night where shall we be,
That rest them may our chargers, / and eke my royal masters three?"

1623

Thereto spake valiant Dankwart: / "The same I ne'er can say,
Yet may we never rest us / before the break of day.
Where then we find it fitting / we'll lay us on the grass."
When they did hear his answer, / what source of grief to all it was!

1624

Still were they unbetrayéd / by reeking blood and red,
Until the sun in heaven / its shining beams down shed
At morn across the hill-tops, / that then the king might see
How they had been in battle. / Spake he then full angrily:

1625

"How may this be, friend Hagen? / Scorned ye have, I ween,
That I should be beside you, / where coats of mail have been

Thus wet with blood upon you. / Who this thing hath done?"
Quoth he: "The same did Else, / who hath this night us set upon.
1626
"To avenge his boatman / did they attack our train.
By hand of my brother / hath Gelfrat been slain.
Then fled Else before us, / and mickle was his need.
Ours four, and theirs a thousand, / remained behind in battle dead."
1627
Now can we not inform you / where resting-place they found.
But cause to know their passing / had the country-folk around,
When there the sons of Ute / to court did fare in state.
At Passau fit reception / did presently the knights await.
1628
The noble monarchs' uncle, / Bishop Pilgrim that was,
Full joyous-hearted was he / that through the land did pass
With train of lusty warriors / his royal nephews three.
That willing was his service, / waited they not long to see.
1629
To greet them on their journey / did friends lack no device,
Yet not to lodge them fully / might Passau's bounds suffice.
They must across the water / where spreading sward they found,
And lodge and tent erected / soon were stretching o'er the ground.
1630
Nor from that spot they onward / might journey all that day,
And eke till night was over, / for pleasant was their stay.
Next to the land of Ruediger / must they in sooth ride on,
To whom full soon the story / of their coming eke was known.
1631
When fitting rest had taken / the knights with travel worn,
And of Etzel's country / they had reached the bourn,
A knight they found there sleeping / that ne'er should aught but wake,
From whom of Tronje Hagen / in stealth a mighty sword did take.
1632
Hight in sooth was Eckewart / that same valiant knight.
For what was there befallen / was he in sorry plight,
That by those heroes' passing / he had lost his sword.
At Ruediger's marches / found they meagre was the guard.
1633
"O, woe is me dishonored," / Eckewart then cried;
"Yea, rueth me fully sorely, / this Burgundian ride.
What time was taken Siegfried, / did joy depart from me.
Alack, O Master Ruediger, / how ill my service unto thee!"

1634
Hagen, full well perceiving / the noble warrior's plight,
Gave him again his weapon / and armbands six full bright.
"These take, good knight, in token / that thou art still my friend.
A valiant warrior art thou, / though dost thou lone this border tend."

1635
"May God thy gifts repay thee," / Eckewart replied,
"Yet rueth me full sorely / that to the Huns ye ride.
Erstwhile slew ye Siegfried / and vengeance have to fear;
My rede to you is truly: / "Beware ye well of danger here."

1636
"Now must God preserve us," / answered Hagen there.
"In sooth for nothing further / have these thanes a care
Than for place of shelter, / the kings and all their band,
And where this night a refuge / we may find within this land.

1637
"Done to death our horses / with the long journey are,
And food as well exhausted," / Hagen did declare.
"Nor find we aught for purchase; / a host we need instead,
Who would in kindness give us, / ere this evening, of his bread."

1638
Thereto gave answer Eckewart: / "I'll show you such a one,
That so warm a welcome / find ye never none
In country whatsoever / as here your lot may be,
An if ye, thanes full gallant, / the noble Ruediger will see.

1639
He dwelleth by the highway / and is most bounteous host
That house e'er had for master. / His heart may graces boast,
As in the lovely May-time / the flowrets deck the mead.
To do good thanes a service / is for his heart most joyous deed."

1640
Then spake the royal Gunther: / "Wilt thou my messenger be,
If will my dear friend Ruediger, / as favor done to me,
His hospitable shelter / with all my warriors share,
Therefor full to requite thee / shall e'er hereafter be my care."

1641
"Thy messenger am I gladly," / Eckewart replied,
And in right willing manner / straight away did ride,
The message thus receivéd / to Ruediger to bear.
Nor did so joyous tidings / for many a season greet his ear.

1642
Hasting to Bechelaren / was seen a noble thane.
The same perceivéd Ruediger, / and spake: "O'er yonder plain

Hither hastens Eckewart, / who Kriemhild's might doth own."
He weened that by some foemen / to him had injury been done.

1643

Then passed he forth the gateway / where the messenger did stand.
His sword he loosed from girdle / and laid from out his hand.
The message that he carried / might he not long withhold
From the master and his kinsmen; / full soon the same to them was told.

1644

He spake unto the margrave: / "I come at high command
Of the lordly Gunther / of Burgundian land,
And Giselher and Gernot, / his royal brothers twain.
In service true commends him / unto thee each lofty thane.

1645

"The like hath Hagen bidden / and Volker as well
With homage oft-times proffered. / And more have I to tell,
The which King Gunther's marshal / to thee doth send by me:
How that the valiant warriors / do crave thy hospitality."

1646

With smiling visage Ruediger / made thereto reply:
"Now joyeth me the story / that the monarchs high
Do deign to seek my service, / that ne'er refused shall be.
Come they unto my castle, / 'tis joy and gladness unto me."

1647

"Dankwart the marshal / hath bidden let thee know
Who seek with them thy shelter / as through thy land they go:
Three score of valiant leaders / and thousand knights right good,
With squires eke nine thousand." / Thereat was he full glad of mood.

1648

"To me 'tis mickle honor," / Ruediger then spake,
"That through my castle's portals / such guests will entry make,
For ne'er hath been occasion / my service yet to lend.
Now ride ye, men and kinsmen, / and on these lofty knights attend."

1649

Then to horse did hasten / knight and willing squire,
For glad they were at all times / to do their lord's desire,
And keen that thus their service / should not be rendered late.
Unwitting Lady Gotelinde / still within her chamber sate.

TWENTY-SEVENTH ADVENTURE: How they came to Bechelaren

1650
Then went forth the margrave / where two ladies sate,
His wife beside his daughter, / nor longer did he wait
To tell the joyful tidings / that unto him were brought,
How Kriemhild's royal brothers / his hospitality had sought.
1651
"Dearly lovéd lady," / spake then Ruediger,
"Full kind be thy reception / to lordly monarchs here,
That now with train of warriors / to court do pass this way.
Fair be eke thy greeting / to Hagen, Gunther's man, this day.
1652
"One likewise with them cometh, / Dankwart by name,
Volker hight the other, / a knight of gallant fame.
Thyself and eke thy daughter / with kiss these six shall greet;
Full courteous be your manner / as ye the doughty thanes shall meet."
1653
Gave straight their word the ladies, / and willing were thereto.
From out great chests they gorgeous / attire in plenty drew,
Which they to meet the lofty / strangers thought to wear,
Mickle was the hurry / there of many a lady fair.
1654
On ne'er a cheek might any / but nature's hue be seen.
Upon their head they carried / band of golden sheen,
That was a beauteous chaplet, / that so their glossy hair
By wind might not be ruffled: / that is truth as I declare.
1655
At such employment busy / leave we those ladies now.
Here with mickle hurry / across the plain did see
Friends of noble Ruediger / the royal guests to meet,
And them with warmest welcome / unto the margrave's land did greet.
1656
When coming forth the margrave / saw their forms appear,
How spake with heart full joyous / the valiant Ruediger!
"Welcome be ye, Sires, / and all your gallant band.
Right glad am I to see you / hither come unto my land."
1657
Then bent the knights before him / each full courteously.
That he good-will did bear them / might they full quickly see.
Hagen had special greeting, / who long to him was known;

To Volker eke of Burgundy / was like highest honor shown.
1658
Thus Dankwart eke he greeted, / when spake the doughty thane:
"While we thus well are harbored, / who then for all the train
Of those that follow with us / shall meet provision make?"
"Yourselves this night right easy / shall rest," the noble margrave
spake.
1659
"And all that follow with you, / with equipment whatsoe'er
Ye bring into my country / of steed or warlike gear,
So sure shall it be guarded / that of all the sum,
E'en to one spur's value, / to you shall never damage come.
1660
"Now stretch aloft, my squires, / the tents upon the plain.
What here ye have of losses / will I make good again.
Unbridle now the horses / and let them wander free."
Upon their way they seldom / did meet like hospitality.
1661
Thereat rejoiced the strangers. / When thus it ordered was,
Rode the high knights forward. / All round upon the grass
Lay the squires attendant / and found a gentle rest.
I ween, upon their journey / was here provision costliest.
1662
Out before the castle / the noble margravine
Had passed with her fair daughter. / In her train were seen
A band of lovely women / and many a winsome maid,
Whose arms with bracelets glittered, / and all in stately robes arrayed.
1663
The costly jewels sparkled / with far-piercing ray
From out their richest vestments, / and buxom all were they.
Now came the strangers thither / and sprang upon the ground.
How high in noble courtesy / the men of Burgundy were found!
1664
Six and thirty maidens / and many a fair lady,
—Nor might ye ever any / more winsome wish to see—
Went then forth to meet them / with many a knight full keen.
At hands of noble ladies / fairest greeting then was seen.
1665
The margrave's youthful daughter / did kiss the kings all three
As eke had done her mother. / Hagen stood thereby.
Her father bade her kiss him; / she looked the thane upon,
Who filled her so with terror, / she fain had left the thing undone.

1666
When she at last must do it, / as did command her sire,
Mingled was her color, / both pale and hue of fire.
Likewise kissed she Dankwart / and the Fiddler eke anon:
That he was knight of valor / to him was such high favor shown.
1667
The margrave's youthful daughter / took then by the hand
The royal knight Giselher / of Burgundian land.
E'en so led forth her mother / the gallant Gunther high.
With those guests so lofty / walked they there full joyfully.
1668
The host escorted Gernot / to a spacious hall and wide,
Where knights and stately ladies / sate them side by side.
Then bade they for the strangers / pour good wine plenteously:
In sooth might never heroes / find fuller hospitality.
1669
Glances fond and many / saw ye directed there
Upon Ruediger's daughter, / for she was passing fair.
Yea, in his thoughts caressed her / full many a gallant knight;
A lady high in spirit, / well might she every heart delight.
1670
Yet whatsoe'er their wishes, / might none fulfilléd be.
Hither oft and thither / glanced they furtively
On maidens and fair ladies, / whereof were many there.
Right kind the noble Fiddler / disposéd was to Ruediger.
1671
They parted each from other / as ancient custom was,
And knights and lofty ladies / did separating pass
When tables were made ready / within the spacious hall.
There in stately manner / they waited on the strangers all.
1672
To do the guests high honor / likewise the table sought
With them the lofty margravine. / Her daughter led she not,
But left among the maidens, / where fitting was she sat.
That they might not behold her, grieved were the guests in sooth
thereat.
1673
The drinking and the feasting, / when 'twas ended all,
Escorted was the maiden / again into the hall.
Then of merry jesting / they nothing lacked, I ween,
Wherein was busy Volker, / a thane full gallant and keen.
1674
Then spake the noble Fiddler / to all in lofty tone:

"Great mercy, lordly margrave, / God to thee hath shown,
For that he hath granted / unto thee a wife
Of so surpassing beauty, / and thereto a joyous life.
1675
"If that I were of royal / birth," the Fiddler spake,
"And kingly crown should carry, / to wife I'd wish to take
This thy lovely daughter, / —my heart thus prompteth me.
A noble maid and gentle / and fair to look upon is she."
1676
Then outspake the margrave: / "How might such thing be,
That king should e'er desire / daughter born to me?
Exiled from my country / here with my spouse I dwell:
What avails the maiden, / be she favored ne'er so well?"
1677
Thereto gave answer Gernot, / a knight of manner kind:
"If to my desire / I ever spouse would find,
Then would I of such lady / right gladly make my choice."
In full kindly manner / added Hagen eke his voice:
1678
"Now shall my master Giselher / take to himself a spouse.
The noble margrave's daughter / is of so lofty house,
That I and all his warriors / would glad her service own,
If that she in Burgundy / should ever wear a royal crown."
1679
Glad thereat full truly / was Sir Ruediger,
And eke Gotelinde: / they joyed such words to hear.
Anon arranged the heroes / that her as bride did greet
The noble knight Giselher, / as was for any monarch meet.
1680
What thing is doomed to happen, / who may the same prevent?
To come to the assembly / they for the maidens sent,
And to the knight they plighted / the winsome maid for wife,
Pledge eke by him was given, / his love should yet endure with life.
1681
They to the maid allotted / castles and spreading land,
Whereof did give assurance / the noble monarch's hand
And eke the royal Gernot, / 'twould surely so be done.
Then spake to them the margrave: / "Lordly castles have I none,
1682
"Yet true shall be my friendship / the while that I may live.
Unto my daughter shall I / of gold and silver give
What hundred sumpter-horses / full laden bear away,
That her husband's lofty kinsmen / find honor in the fair array."

1683
They bade the knight and maiden / within a ring to stand,
As was of old the custom. / Of youths a goodly band,
That all were merry-hearted, / did her there confront,
And thought they on her beauty / as mind of youth is ever wont.
1684
When they began to question / then the winsome maid,
Would she the knight for husband, / somewhat she was dismayed,
And yet forego she would not / to have him for her own.
She blushed to hear the question, / as many another maid hath done.
1685
Her father Ruediger prompted / that Yes her answer be,
And that she take him gladly. / Unto her instantly
Sprang the young Sir Giselher, / and in his arm so white
He clasped her to his bosom. / —Soon doomed to end was her delight.
1686
Then spake again the margrave: / "Ye royal knights and high,
When that home ye journey / again to Burgundy
I'll give to you my daughter, / as fitting is to do,
That ye may take her with you." / They gave their plighted word thereto.
1687
What jubilation made they / yet at last must end.
The maiden then was bidden / unto her chamber wend,
And guests to seek their couches / and rest until the day.
For them the host provided / a feast in hospitable way.
1688
When they had feasted fully / and to the Huns' country
Thence would onward journey, / "Such thing shall never be,"
Spake the host full noble, / "but here ye still shall rest.
Seldom hath my good fortune / welcomed yet so many a guest."
1689
Thereto gave answer Dankwart: / "In sooth it may not be.
Bread and wine whence hast thou / and food sufficiently,
Over night to harbor / of guests so great a train?"
When the host had heard it, / spake he: "All thy words are vain.
1690
"Refuse not my petition, / ye noble lords and high.
A fortnight's full provision / might I in sooth supply,
For you and every warrior / that journeys in your train.
Till now hath royal Etzel / small portion of my substance ta'en."
1691
Though fain they had declined it, / yet they there must stay

E'en to the fourth morning. / Then did the host display
So generous hand and lavish / that it was told afar.
He gave unto the strangers / horses and apparel rare.

1692

The time at last was over / and they must journey thence.
Then did the valiant Ruediger / with lavish hand dispense
Unto all his bounty, / refused he unto none
Whate'er he might desire. / Well-pleased they parted every one.

1693

His courteous retainers / to castle gateway brought
Saddled many horses, / and soon the place was sought
Eke by the gallant strangers / each bearing shield in hand,
For that they thence would journey / onward into Etzel's land.

1694

The host had freely offered / rich presents unto all,
Ere that the noble strangers / passed out before the hall.
High in honor lived he, / a knight of bounty rare.
His fair daughter had he / given unto Giselher.

1695

Eke gave he unto Gunther, / a knight of high renown,
What well might wear with honor / the monarch as his own,
—Though seldom gift received he— / a coat of harness rare.
Thereat inclined King Gunther / before the noble Ruediger.

1696

Then gave he unto Gernot / a good and trusty blade,
Wherewith anon in combat / was direst havoc made.
That thus the gift was taken / rejoiced the margrave's wife:
Thereby the noble Ruediger / was doomed anon to lose his life.

1697

Gotelinde proffered Hagen, / as 'twas a fitting thing,
Her gifts in kindly manner. / Since scorned them not the king,
Eke he without her bounty / to the high festivity
Should thence not onward journey. / Yet loath to take the same was he.

1698

"Of all doth meet my vision," / Hagen then spake,
"Would I wish for nothing / with me hence to take
But alone the shield that hanging / on yonder wall I see.
The same I'd gladly carry / into Etzel's land with me."

1699

When the stately margravine / Hagen's words did hear,
Brought they to mind her sorrow, / nor might she stop a tear.
She thought again full sadly / how her son Nudung fell,

Slain by hand of Wittich; / and did her breast with anguish swell.

1700
She spake unto the hero: / "The shield to thee I'll give.
O would to God in heaven / that he still did live,
Whose hand erstwhile did wield it! / In battle fell he low,
And I, a wretched mother, / must weep with never-ending woe.

1701
Thereat the noble lady / up from the settle rose,
And soon her arms all snow-white / did the shield enclose.
She bore it unto Hagen, / who made obeisance low;
The gift she might with honor / upon so valiant thane bestow.

1702
O'er it, to keep its color, / a shining cover lay
With precious stones all studded, / nor ever shone the day
Upon a shield more costly; / if e'er a longing eye
Did covet to possess it, / scarce thousand marks the same might buy.

1703
The shield in charge gave Hagen / thence away to bear.
Before his host then Dankwart / himself presented there,
On whom the margrave's daughter / did costly dress bestow.
Wherein anon in Hunland / arrayed full stately he did go.

1704
Whate'er of gifts by any / was accepted there,
Them had his hand ne'er taken, / but that intent all were
To do their host an honor / who gave with hand so free.
By his guests in combat / soon doomed was he slain to be.

1705
Volker the valiant / to Gotelinde came
And stood in courteous manner / with fiddle 'fore the dame.
Sweet melodies he played her / and sang his songs thereby,
For thought he from Bechelaren / to take departure presently.

1706
The margravine bade to her / a casket forth to bear.
And now of presents given / full freely may ye hear.
Therefrom she took twelve armbands / and drew them o'er his hand.
"These shall thou with thee carry, / as ridest thou to Etzel's land,

1707
"And for my sake shalt wear them / when at court thou dost appear,
That when thou hither comest / I may the story hear
How thou hast done me honor / at the high festival."
What did wish the lady, / faithfully performed he all.

1708
Thus to his guests the host spake: / "That ye more safely fare,

Myself will give you escort / and bid them well beware
That upon the highway / no ill on you be wrought."
Thereat his sumpter horses / straightway laden forth were brought

1709
The host was well prepared / with five hundred men
With horse and rich attire. / These led he with him then
In right joyous humor / to the high festival.
Alive to Bechelaren / again came never one of all.

1710
Thence took his leave Sir Ruediger / with kiss full lovingly;
As fitting was for Giselher, / likewise the same did he.
With loving arms enfolding / caressed they ladies fair.
To many a maid the parting / did bring anon full bitter tear.

1711
On all sides then the windows / were open wide flung,
As with his train of warriors / the host to saddle sprung.
I ween their hearts did tell them / how they should sorrow deep.
For there did many a lady / and many a winsome maiden weep.

1712
For dear friends left behind him / grieved many a knight full sore.
Whom they at Bechelaren / should behold no more.
Yet rode they off rejoicing / down across the sand
Hard by the Danube river / on their way to Etzel's land.

1713
Then spake to the Burgundians / the gallant knight and bold,
Ruediger the noble: / "Now let us not withhold
The story of our coming / unto the Hun's country.
Unto the royal Etzel / might tidings ne'er more welcome be."

1714
Down in haste through Austria / the messenger did ride,
Who told unto the people / soon on every side,
From Worms beyond Rhine river / were high guests journeying.
Nor unto Etzel's people / gladder tidings might ye bring.

1715
Onward spurred the messengers / who did the message bear,
How now in Hunnish country / the Nibelungen were.
"Kriemhild, lofty lady, / warm thy welcome be;
In stately manner hither / come thy loving brothers three."

1716
Within a lofty casement / the Lady Kriemhild stood,
Looking for her kinsmen, / as friend for friend full good.
From her father's country / saw she many a knight;
Eke heard the king the tidings, / and laughed thereat for sheer delight.

1717

"Now well my heart rejoiceth," / spake Lady Kriemhild.
"Hither come my kinsmen / with many a new-wrought shield
And brightly shining hauberk: / who gold would have from me,
Be mindful of my sorrow; / to him I'll ever gracious be."

TWENTY-EIGHTH ADVENTURE: How the Burgundians came to Etzel's Castle

1718

When that the men of Burgundy / were come into the land,
He of Bern did hear it, / the agéd Hildebrand.
He told it to his master, / who sore thereat did grieve;
The knight so keen and gallant / bade he in fitting way receive.

1719

Wolfhart the valiant / bade lead the heroes forth.
In company with Dietrich / rode many a thane of worth,
As out to receive them / across the plain he went,
Where might ye see erected / already many a stately tent.

1720

When that of Tronje Hagen / them far away espied,
Unto his royal masters / full courteously he said:
"Now shall ye, doughty riders, / down from the saddle spring,
And forward go to meet them / that here to you a welcome bring.

1721

"A train there cometh yonder, / well knew I e'en when young.
Thanes they are full doughty / of the land of Amelung.
He of Bern doth lead them, / and high of heart they are;
To scorn their proffered greeting / shall ye in sooth full well beware."

1722

Dismounted then with Dietrich, / (as was meet and right,)
Attended by his squire / many a gallant knight.
They went unto the strangers / and greeted courteously
The knights that far had ridden / from the land of Burgundy.

1723

When then Sir Dietrich / saw them coming near,
What words the thane delivered, / now may ye willing hear,
Unto Ute's children. / Their journey grieved him sore.
He weened that Ruediger knowing / had warned what lay for them in store.

1724

"Welcome be ye, Masters, / Gunther and Giselher,

Gernot and Hagen, / welcome eke Volker
And the valiant Dankwart. / Do ye not understand?
Kriemhild yet sore bemoaneth / the hero of Nibelungen land."
1725
"Long time may she be weeping," / Hagen spake again;
"In sooth for years a many / dead he lies and slain.
To the monarch now of Hunland / should she devoted be:
Siegfried returneth never, / buried now long time is he."
1726
"How Siegfried's death was compassed, / let now the story be:
While liveth Lady Kriemhild, / look ye for injury."
Thus did of Bern Sir Dietrich / unto them declare:
"Hope of the Nibelungen, / of her vengeance well beware."
1727
"Whereof shall I be fearful?" / the lofty monarch spake:
"Etzel hath sent us message, / (why further question make?)
That we should journey hither / into his country.
Eke hath my sister Kriemhild / oft wished us here as guests to see.
1728
"I give thee honest counsel," / Hagen then did say,
"Now shalt thou here Sir Dietrich / and his warriors pray
To tell thee full the story, / if aught may be designed,
And let thee know more surely / how stands the Lady Kriemhild's
mind."
1729
Then went to speak asunder / the lordly monarchs three,
Gunther and Gernot, / and Dietrich went he.
"Now tell us true, thou noble / knight of Bern and kind,
If that perchance thou knowest / how stands thy royal mistress' mind."
1730
The lord of Bern gave answer: / "What need to tell you more?
I hear each day at morning / weeping and wailing sore
The wife of royal Etzel, / who piteous doth complain
To God in heaven that Siegfried / her doughty spouse from her was
ta'en."
1731
"Then must we e'en abide it," / was the fearless word
Of Volker the Fiddler, / "what we here have heard.
To court we yet shall journey / and make full clear to all,
If that to valiant warriors / may aught amid the Huns befall."
1732
The gallant thanes of Burgundy / unto court then rode,
And went in stately manner / as was their country's mode.

Full many a man in Hunland / looked eagerly to see
Of what manner Hagen, / Tronje's doughty thane, might be.
1733
For that was told the story / (and great the wonder grew)
How that of Netherland / Siegfried he slew,
That was the spouse of Kriemhild, / in strength without a peer,
Hence a mickle questioning / after Hagen might ye hear.
1734
Great was the knight of stature, / may ye know full true,
Built with breast expansive; / mingled was the hue
Of his hair with silver; / long he was of limb;
As he strode stately forward / might ye mark his visage grim.
1735
Then were the thanes of Burgundy / unto quarters shown,
But the serving-man of Gunther / by themselves alone.
Thus the queen did counsel, / so filled she was with hate.
Anon where they were harbored / the train did meet with direst fate.
1736
Dankwart, Hagen's brother, / marshal was he.
To him the king his followers / commended urgently,
That he provide them plenty / and have of them good care.
The noble knight of Burgundy / their safety well in mind did bear.
1737
By her train attended, / Queen Kriemhild went
To greet the Nibelungen, / yet false was her intent.
She kissed her brother Giselher / and took him by the hand:
Thereat of Tronje Hagen / did tighter draw his helmet's band.
1733
"After such like greeting," / the doughty Hagen spake,
"Let all watchful warriors / full precaution take:
Differs wide the greeting / on masters and men bestowed.
Unhappy was the hour / when to this festival we rode."
1739
She spake: "Now be ye welcome / to whom ye welcome be.
For sake of friendship never / ye greeting have from me.
Tell me now what bring ye / from Worms across the Rhine,
That ye so greatly welcome / should ever be to land of mine?"
1740
"An I had only known it," / Hagen spake again,
"That thou didst look for present / from hand of every thane,
I were, methinks, so wealthy / —had I me bethought—
That I unto this country / likewise to thee my gift had brought."
1741

"Now shall ye eke the story / to me more fully say:
The Nibelungen treasure, / where put ye that away?
My own possession was it, / as well ye understand.
That same ye should have brought me / hither unto Etzel's land."

1742
"In sooth, my Lady Kriemhild, / full many a day hath flown
Since of the Nibelungen / hoard I aught have known.
Into the Rhine to sink it / my lords commanded me:
Verily there must it / until the day of judgment be."

1743
Thereto the queen gave answer: / "Such was e'en my thought.
Thereof right little have ye / unto me hither brought,
Although myself did own it / and once o'er it held sway.
'Tis cause that I for ever / have full many a mournful day."

1744
"The devil have I brought thee," / Hagen did declare.
"My shield it is so heavy / that I have to bear,
And my plaited armor; / my shining helmet see,
And sword in hand I carry, / —so might I nothing bring for thee."

1745
Then spake the royal lady / unto the warriors all:
"Weapon shall not any / bear into the hall.
To me now for safe keeping, / ye thanes shall give them o'er."
"In sooth," gave answer Hagen, / "such thing shall happen nevermore.

1746
"Such honor ne'er I covet, / royal lady mild,
That to its place of keeping / thou shouldst bear my shield
With all my other armor, / —for thou art a queen.
Such taught me ne'er my sire: / myself will be my chamberlain."

1747
"Alack of these my sorrows!" / the Lady Kriemhild cried;
"Wherefore will now my brother / and Hagen not confide
To me their shields for keeping? / Some one did warning give.
Knew I by whom 'twas given, / brief were the space that he might live."

1748
Thereto the mighty Dietrich / in wrath his answer gave:
"'Tis I who now these noble / lords forewarnéd have,
And Hagen, knight full valiant / of the land of Burgundy.
Now on! thou devil's mistress, / let not the deed my profit be."

1749
Great shame thereat did Kriemhild's / bosom quickly fill;
She feared lest Dietrich's anger / should work her grievous ill.
Naught she spake unto them / as thence she swiftly passed,

But fierce the lightning glances / that on her enemies she cast.
1750
By hand then grasped each, other / doughty warriors twain:
Hight the one was Dietrich, / with Hagen, noble thane.
Then spake in courteous manner / that knight of high degree:
"That ye are come to Hunland, / 'tis very sorrow unto me;
1751
"For what hath here been spoken / by the lofty queen."
Then spake of Tronje Hagen: / "Small cause to grieve, I ween."
Held converse thus together / those brave warriors twain,
King Etzel which perceiving / thus a questioning began:
1752
"I would learn full gladly," / —in such wise spake he—
"Who were yonder warrior, / to whom so cordially
Doth greeting give Sir Dietrich. / Meseemeth high his mood.
Whosoe'er his sire, / a thane he is of mettle good."
1753
Unto the king gave answer / of Kriemhild's train a knight:
"Born he was of Tronje, / Aldrian his sire hight.
How merry here his bearing, / a thane full grim is he.
That I have spoken truly, / shalt thou anon have cause to see."
1754
"How may I then perceive it / that fierce his wrath doth glow?"
Naught of basest treachery / yet the king did know,
That anon Queen Kriemhild / 'gainst her kinsmen did contrive,
Whereby returned from Hunland / not one of all their train alive.
1755
"Well knew I Aldrian, / he once to me was thane:
Praise and mickle honor / he here by me did gain.
Myself a knight did make him, / and gave him of my gold.
Helke, noble lady, / did him in highest favor hold.
1756
"Thereby know I fully / what Hagen since befell.
Two stately youths as hostage / at my court did dwell,
He and Spanish Walter, / from youth to manhood led.
Hagen sent I homeward; / Walter with Hildegunde fled."
1757
He thought on ancient story / that long ago befell.
His doughty friend of Tronje / knew he then right well,
Whose youthful valor erstwhile / did such assistance lend.
Through him in age he must be / bereft of many a dearest friend.

TWENTY-NINTH ADVENTURE: How He arose not before Her

1758
Then parted from each other / the noble warriors twain,
Hagen of Tronje / and Dietrich, lofty thane.
Then did King Gunther's warrior / cast a glance around,
Seeking a companion / the same he eke full quickly found.

1759
As standing there by Giselher / he did Volker see,
He prayed the nimble Fiddler / to bear him company,
For that full well he knew it / how grim he was of mood,
And that in all things was he / a knight of mettle keen and good.

1760
While yet their lords were standing / there in castle yard
Saw ye the two knights only / walking thitherward
Across the court far distant / before the palace wide.
The chosen thanes recked little / what might through any's hate betide.

1761
They sate them down on settle / over against a hall,
Wherein dwelt Lady Kriemhild, / beside the palace wall.
Full stately their attire / on stalwart bodies shone.
All that did look upon them / right gladly had the warriors known.

1762
Like unto beasts full savage / were they gaped upon,
The two haughty heroes, / by full many a Hun.
Eke from a casement Etzel's / wife did them perceive:
Once more to behold them / must fair Lady Kriemhild grieve.

1763
It called to mind her sorrow, / and she to weep began,
Whereat did mickle wonder / many an Etzel's man,
What grief had thus so sudden / made her sad of mood.
Spake she: "That hath Hagen, / ye knights of mettle keen and good."

1764
They to their mistress answered: / "Such thing, how hath it been?
For that thee right joyous / we but now have seen.
Ne'er lived he so daring / that, having wrought thee ill,
His life he must not forfeit, / if but to vengeance point thy will."

1765
"I live but to requite him / that shall avenge my wrong;
Whate'er be his desire / shall unto him belong.
Prostrate I beseech you," / —so spake the monarch's wife—

"Avenge me upon Hagen, / and forfeit surely be his life."
1766
Three score of valiant warriors / made ready then straightway
To work the will of Kriemhild / and her best obey
By slaying of Sir Hagen, / the full valiant thane,
And eke the doughty Fiddler; / by shameful deed thus sought they
gain.
1767
When the queen beheld there / so small their company,
In full angry humor / to the warriors spake she:
"What there ye think to compass, / forego such purpose yet:
So small in numbers never / dare ye Hagen to beset.
1768
"How doughty e'er be Hagen, / and known his valor wide,
A man by far more doughty / that sitteth him beside,
Volker the Fiddler: / a warrior grim is he.
In sooth may not so lightly / the heroes twain confronted be."
1769
When that she thus had spoken, / ready soon were seen
Four hundred stalwart warriors; / for was the lofty queen
Full intent upon it / to work them evil sore.
Therefrom for all the strangers / was mickle sorrow yet in store.
1770
When that complete attiréd / were here retainers seen,
Unto the knights impatient / in such wise spake the queen:
"Now bide ye yet a moment / and stand ye ready so,
While I with crown upon me / unto my enemies shall go.
1771
"And list while I accuse him / how he hath wrought me bane,
Hagen of Tronje, / Gunther's doughty thane.
I know his mood so haughty, / naught he'll deny of all.
Nor reck I what of evil / therefrom may unto him befall."
1772
Then saw the doughty Fiddler / —he was a minstrel keen—
Adown the steps descending / the high and stately queen
Who issued from the castle. / When he the queen espied,
Spake the valiant Volker / to him was seated by his side:
1773
"Look yonder now, friend Hagen, / how that she hither hies
Who to this land hath called us / in such treacherous wise.
No monarch's wife I ever / saw followed by such band
Of warriors armed for battle, / that carry each a sword in hand.
1774

"Know'st thou, perchance, friend Hagen, / if hate to thee they bear?
Then would I well advise thee / of them full well beware
And guard both life and honor. / That methinks were good,
For if I much mistake not, / full wrathful is the warriors' mood.
1775
"Of many eke among them / so broad the breasts do swell,
That who would guard him 'gainst them / betimes would do it well.
I ween that 'neath their tunics / they shining mail-coats wear:
Yet might I never tell thee, / 'gainst whom such evil mind they bear."
1776
Then spake all wrathful-minded / Hagen the warrior keen:
"On me to vent their fury / is their sole thought, I ween,
That thus with brandished weapons / their onward press we see.
Despite them all yet trow I / to come safe home to Burgundy.
1777
"Now tell me, friend Volker, / wilt thou beside me stand,
If seek to work me evil / here Kriemhild's band?
That let me hear right truly, / as I am dear to thee.
By thy side forever / shall my service faithful be."
1778
"Full surely will I help thee," / the minstrel straight replied;
"And saw I e'en a monarch / with all his men beside
Hither come against us, / the while a sword I wield
Not fear shall ever prompt me / from thy side one pace to yield."
1779
"Now God in heaven, O Volker, / give thy high heart its meed.
Will they forsooth assail me, / whereof else have I need?
Wilt thou thus stand beside me / as here is thy intent,
Let come all armed these warriors, / on whatsoever purpose bent."
1780
"Now rise we from this settle," / the minstrel spake once more,
"While that the royal lady / passeth here before.
To her be done this honor / as unto lady high.
Ourselves in equal manner / shall we honor eke thereby."
1781
"Nay, nay! as me thou lovest," / Hagen spake again,
"For so would sure imagine / here each hostile thane
That 'twere from fear I did it, / should I bear me so.
For sake of never any / will I from this settle go.
1782
"Undone we both might leave it / in sooth more fittingly.
Wherefore should I honor / who bears ill-will to me?
Such thing will I do never, / the while I yet have life.

Nor reck I aught how hateth / me the royal Etzel's wife."
1783
Thereat defiant Hagen / across his knee did lay
A sword that shone full brightly, / from whose knob did play
The light of glancing jasper / greener than blade of grass.
Well perceivéd Kriemhild / that it erstwhile Siegfried's was.
1784
When she the sword espiéd, / to weep was sore her need.
The hilt was shining golden, / the sheath a band of red.
As it recalled her sorrow, / her tears had soon begun;
I ween for that same purpose / 'twas thus by dauntless Hagen done.
1785
Eke the valiant Volker / a fiddle-bow full strong
Unto himself drew nearer; / mickle it was and long,
Like unto a broad-sword / full sharp that was and wide.
So sat they all undaunted / the stately warriors side by side.
1786
There sat the thanes together / in such defiant wise
That would never either / from the settle rise
Through fear of whomsoever. / Then strode before their feet
The lofty queen, and wrathful / did thus the doughty warriors greet.
1787
Quoth she: "Now tell me, Hagen, / upon whose command
Barest thou thus to journey / hither to this land,
And knowest well what sorrow / through thee my heart must bear.
Wert thou not reft of reason, / then hadst thou kept thee far from here."
1788
"By none have I been summoned," / Hagen gave reply.
"Three lofty thanes invited / were to this country:
The same I own as masters / and service with them find.
Whene'er they make court journey / 'twere strange should I remain behind."
1789
Quoth she: "Now tell me further, / wherefore didst thou that
Whereby thou hast deservéd / my everlasting hate?
'Twas thou that slewest Siegfried, / spouse so dear to me,
The which, till life hath ended, / must ever cause for weeping be."
1790
Spake he: "Why parley further, / since further word were vain?
E'en I am that same Hagen / by whom was Siegfried slain,
That deft knight of valor. / How sore by him 'twas paid
That the Lady Kriemhild / dared the fair Brunhild upbraid!

1791

"Beyond all cavil is it, / high and royal dame,
Of all the grievous havoc / I do bear the blame.
Avenge it now who wisheth, / woman or man tho't be.
An I unto thee lie not, / I've wrought thee sorest injury."

1792

She spake: "Now hear, ye warriors, / how denies he not at all
The cause of all my sorrow. / Whate'er may him befall
Reck I not soever, / that know ye, Etzel's men."
The overweening warriors / blank gazed upon each other then.

1793

Had any dared the onset, / seen it were full plain
The palm must be awarded / to the companions twain,
Who had in storm of battle / full oft their prowess shown.
What that proud band designed / through fear must now be left undone.

1794

Outspake one of their number: / "Wherefore look thus to me?
What now I thought to venture / left undone shall be,
Nor for reward of any / think I my life to lose;
To our destruction lures us / here the royal Etzel's spouse."

1795

Then spake thereby another: / "Like mind therein have I.
Though ruddy gold were offered / like towers piléd high,
Yet would I never venture / to stir this Fiddler's spleen.
Such are the rapid glances / that darting from his eyes I've seen.

1796

"Likewise know I Hagen / from youthful days full well,
Nor more about his valor / to me need any tell.
In two and twenty battles / I the knight have seen,
Whereby sorest sorrow / to many a lady's heart hath been.

1797

"When here they were with Etzel, / he and the knight of Spain
Bore storm of many a battle / in many a warlike train
For sake of royal honor, / so oft thereof was need.
Wherefore of right are honors / high the valiant Hagen's meed.

1798

"Then was yet the hero / but a child in years;
Now how hoary-headed / who were his youthful feres,
To wisdom now attainéd, / a warrior grim and strong,
Eke bears he with him Balmung, / the which he gained by mickle wrong."

1799
Therewith the matter ended, / and none the fight dared start,
Whereat the Lady Kriemhild / full heavy was of heart.
Her warriors thence did vanish, / for feared they death indeed
At hands of the Fiddler, / whereof right surely was there need.

1800
Outspake then the Fiddler: / "Well we now have seen,
That enemies here do greet us, / as we forewarned have been.
Back unto the monarchs / let us straight repair,
That none against our masters / to raise a hostile hand may dare.

1801
"How oft from impious purpose / doth fear hold back the hand,
Where friend by friend doth only / firm in friendship stand,
Until right sense give warning / to leave the thing undone.
Thus wisdom hath prevented / the harm of mortals many a one."

1802
"Heed I will thy counsel," / Hagen gave reply.
Then passed they where / the monarchs found they presently
In high state received / within the palace court.
Loud the valiant Volker / straight began after this sort

1803
Unto his royal masters: / "How long will ye stand so,
That foes may press upon you? / To the king ye now shall go,
And from his lips hear spoken / how is his mind to you."
The valiant lords and noble / consorted then by two and two.

1804
Of Bern the lofty Dietrich / took by the hand
Gunther the lordly monarch / of Burgundian land;
Irnfried escorted Gernot, / a knight of valor keen,
And Ruediger with Giselher / going unto the court was seen.

1805
Howe'er with fere consorted / there any thane might be,
Volker and Hagen / ne'er parted company,
Save in storm of battle / when they did reach life's bourne,
'Twas cause that highborn ladies / anon in grievous way must mourn.

1806
Unto the court then passing / with the kings were seen.
Of their lofty retinue / a thousand warriors keen,
And threescore thanes full valiant / that followed in their train;
The same from his own country / had doughty Hagen with him ta'en.

1807
Hawart and eke Iring, / chosen warriors twain,
Saw ye walk together / in the royal train.

By Dankwart and Wolfhart, / a thane of high renown,
Was high courtly bearing / there before the others shown.
1808
When the lord of Rhineland / passed into the hall,
Etzel mighty monarch / waited not at all,
But sprang from off his settle / when he beheld him nigh.
By monarch ne'er was given / greeting so right heartily.
1809
"Welcome be, Lord Gunther, / and eke Sir Gernot too,
And your brother Giselher. / My greetings unto you
I sent with honest purpose / to Worms across the Rhine;
And welcome all your followers / shall be unto this land of mine.
1810
"Right welcome be ye likewise, / doughty warriors twain,
Volker the full valiant, / and Hagen dauntless thane,
To me and to my lady / here in my country.
Unto the Rhine to greet you / many a messenger sent she."
1811
Then spake of Tronje Hagen: / "Thereof I'm well aware,
And did I with my masters / not thus to Hunland fare,
To do thee honor had I / ridden unto thy land."
Then took the lofty monarch / the honored strangers by the hand.
1812
He led them to the settle / whereon himself he sat,
Then poured they for the strangers / —with care they tended that—
In goblets wide and golden / mead and mulberry wine,
And bade right hearty welcome / unto the knights afar from Rhine.
1813
Then spake the monarch Etzel: / "This will I freely say:
Naught in this world might happen / to bring my heart more joy,
Than that ye lofty heroes / thus are come to me.
The queen from mickle sadness / thereby make ye likewise free.
1814
"To me 'twas mickle wonder / wherein had I transgressed,
That I for friends had won me / so many a noble guest,
Yet ye had never deignéd / to come to my country.
'Tis now turned cause of gladness / that you as guests I here may see."
1815
Thereto gave answer Ruediger, / a knight of lofty mind:
"Well mayst thou joy to see them; / right honor shalt thou find
And naught but noble bearing / in my high mistress' kin.
With them for guest thou likewise / many a stately thane dost win."

1816

At turn of sun in summer / were the knights arrived
At mighty Etzel's palace. / Ne'er hath monarch lived
That lordly guests did welcome / with higher compliment.
When come was time of eating, / the king with them to table went.

1817

Amid his guests more stately / a host was seated ne'er.
They had in fullest measure / of drink and goodly fare;
Whate'er they might desire, / they ready found the same.
Tales of mickle wonder / had spread abroad the heroes' fame.

THIRTIETH ADVENTURE: How they kept Guard

1818

And now the day was ended / and nearing was the night.
Came then the thought with longing / unto each way-worn knight,
When that they might rest them / and to their beds be shown.
'Twas mooted first by Hagen / and straight was answer then made known.

1819

To Etzel spake then Gunther: / "Fair days may God thee give!
To bed we'll now betake us, / an be it by thy leave;
We'll come betimes at morning, / if so thy pleasure be."
From his guests the monarch / parted then full courteously.

1820

Upon the guests on all sides / the Huns yet rudely pressed,
Whereat the valiant Volker / these words to them addressed:
"How dare ye 'fore these warriors / thus beset the way?
If that ye desist not, / rue such rashness soon ye may.

1821

"Let fall will I on some one / such stroke of fiddle-bow,
That eyes shall fill with weeping / if he hath friend to show.
Why make not way before us, / as fitting were to do!
Knights by name ye all are, / but knighthood's ways unknown to you."

1822

When outspake the Fiddler / thus so wrathfully
Backward glanced bold Hagen / to see what this might be.
Quoth he: "He redes you rightly, / this keen minstrel knight.
Ye followers of Kriemhild, / now pass to rest you for the night.

1823

"The thing whereof ye're minded / will none dare do, I ween.

If aught ye purpose 'gainst us, / on the morrow be that seen,
And let us weary strangers / the night in quiet pass;
I ween, with knights of honor / such evermore the custom was."
1824
Then were led the strangers / into a spacious hall
Where they found prepared / for the warriors one and all
Beds adorned full richly, / that were both wide and long.
Yet planned the Lady Kriemhild / to work on them the direst wrong.
1825
Rich quilted mattress covers / of Arras saw ye there
Lustrous all and silken, / and spreading sheets there were
Wrought of silk of Araby, / the best might e'er be seen.
O'er them lay rich embroidered / stuffs that cast a brilliant sheen.
1826
Coverlets of ermine / full many might ye see,
With sullen sable mingled, / whereunder peacefully
They should rest the night through / till came the shining day.
A king with all retinue / ne'er, I ween, so stately lay.
1827
"Alack for these night-quarters!" / quoth young Giselher,
"Alack for my companions / who this our journey share!
How kind so e'er my sister's / hospitality,
Dead by her devising, / I fear me, are we doomed to be."
1828
"Let now no fears disturb you," / Hagen gave reply;
"Through the hours of sleeping / keep the watch will I.
I trust full well to guard you / until return the day,
Thereof be never fearful; / let then preserve him well who may."
1829
Inclined they all before him / threat to give him grace.
Then sought they straight their couches; / in sooth 'twas little space
Until was softly resting / every stately man.
But Hagen, valiant hero, / the while to don his armor gan.
1830
Spake then to him the Fiddler, / Volker a doughty thane:
"I'll be thy fellow, Hagen, / an wilt thou not disdain,
While watch this night thou keepest, / until do come the morn."
Right heartily the hero / to Volker then did thanks return.
1831
"God in heaven requite thee, / Volker, trusty fere.
In all my time of trouble / wished I none other near,
None other but thee only, / when dangers round me throng.
I'll well repay that favor, / if death withhold its hand so long."

1832
Arrayed in glittering armor / both soon did ready stand;
Each did take unto him / a mighty shield in hand,
And passed without the portal / there to keep the way.
Thus were the strangers guarded, / and trusty watchers eke had they.

1833
Volker the valiant, / as he sat before the hall,
Leaned his trusty buckler / meanwhile against the wall,
Then took in hand his fiddle / as he was wont to do:
All times the thane would render / unto his friends a service true.

1834
Beneath the hall's wide portal / he sat on bench of stone;
Than he a bolder fiddler / was there never none.
As from his chords sweet echoes / resounded through the hall,
Thanks for glad refreshment / had Volker from the warriors all.

1835
Then from the strings an echo / the wide hall did fill,
For in his fiddle-playing / the knight had strength and skill.
Softer then and sweeter / to fiddle he began
And wiled to peaceful slumber / many an anxious brooding man.

1836
When they were wrapped in slumber / and he did understand,
Then took again the warrior / his trusty shield in hand
And passed without the portal / to guard the entrance tower,
And safe to keep his fellows / where Kriemhild's crafty men did lower.

1837
About the hour of midnight, / or earlier perchance,
The eye of valiant Volker / did catch a helmet's glance
Afar from out the darkness: / the men of Kriemhild sought
How that upon the strangers / might grievous scathe in stealth be wrought.

1838
Quoth thereat the Fiddler: / "Friend Hagen, 'tis full clear
That we do well together / here this watch to share.
I see before us yonder / men arméd for the fight;
I ween they will attack us, / if I their purpose judge aright."

1839
"Be silent, then," spake Hagen, / "and let them come more nigh.
Ere that they perceive us / shall helmets sit awry,
By good swords disjointed / that in our hands do swing.
Tale of vigorous greeting / shall they back to Kriemhild bring."

1840
Amid the Hunnish warriors / one full soon did see,

That well the door was guarded; / straightway then cried he:
"The thing we here did purpose / 'tis need we now give o'er,
For I behold the Fiddler / standing guard before the door.
1841
"Upon his head a helmet / of glancing light is seen,
Welded strong and skilful, / dintless, of clearest sheen.
The mail-rings of his armor / do sparkle like the fire,
Beside him stands eke Hagen; / safe are the strangers from our ire."
1842
Straightway they back returned. / When Volker that did see,
Unto his companion / wrathfully spake he:
"Now let me to those caitiffs / across the court-yard go;
What mean they by such business, / from Kriemhild's men I fain
would know."
1843
"No, as thou dost love me," / Hagen straight replied;
"If from this hall thou partest, / such ill may thee betide
At hands of these bold warriors / and from the swords they bear,
That I must haste to help thee, / though here our kinsmen's bane it
were.
1844
"Soon as we two together / have joined with them in fight,
A pair or two among them / will surely hasten straight
Hither to this hall here, / and work such havoc sore
Upon our sleeping brethren, / as must be mournéd evermore."
1845
Thereto gave answer Volker: / "So much natheless must be,
That they do learn full certain / how I the knaves did see,
That the men of Kriemhild / hereafter not deny
What they had wrought full gladly / here with foulest treachery."
1846
Straightway then unto them / aloud did Volker call:
"How go ye thus in armor, / ye valiant warriors all?
Or forth, perchance, a-robbing, / Kriemhild's men, go ye?
Myself and my companion / shall ye then have for company."
1847
Thereto no man gave answer. / Wrathful grew his mood:
"Fie, ye caitiff villains," / spake the hero good,
"Would ye us so foully / have murdered while we slept?
With knights so high in honor / full seldom thus hath faith been kept."
1848
Then unto Queen Kriemhild / were the tidings borne,
How her men did fail their purpose: / 'twas cause for her to mourn.

Yet otherwise she wrought it, / for grim she was of mood:
Anon through her must perish / full many a valorous knight and good.

THIRTY-FIRST ADVENTURE: How they went to Mass

1849
"So cool doth grow my armor," / Volker made remark,
"I ween but little longer / will endure the dark.
By the air do I perceive it, / that soon will break the day."
Then waked they many a warrior / who still in deepest slumber lay.

1850
When brake the light of morning / athwart the spacious hall,
Hagen gan awaken / the stranger warriors all,
If that they to the minster / would go to holy mass.
After the Christian custom, / of bells a mickle ringing was.

1851
There sang they all uneven, / that plainly might ye see
How Christian men and heathen / did not full well agree.
Each one of Gunther's warriors / would hear the service sung,
So were they all together / up from their night-couches sprung.

1852
Then did the warriors lace them / in so goodly dress,
That never heroes any, / that king did e'er possess,
More richly stood attired; / that Hagen grieved to see.
Quoth he: "Ye knights, far other / here must your attire be.

1853
"Yea, know among you many / how here the case doth stand.
Bear ye instead of roses / your good swords in hand,
For chaplets all bejewelled / your glancing helmets good,
Since we have well perceivéd / how is the angry Kriemhild's mood.

1854
"To-day must we do battle, / that will I now declare.
Instead of silken tunic / shall ye good hauberks wear,
And for embroidered mantle / a trusty shield and wide,
That ye may well defend you, / if ye must others' anger bide.

1855
"My masters well belovéd, / knights and kinsmen true,
'Tis meet that ye betake you / unto the minster too,
That God do not forsake you / in peril and in need,
For certain now I make you / that death is nigh to us indeed.

1856
"Forget ye not whatever / wrong ye e'er have done,
But there 'fore God right meekly / all your errors own;
Thereto would I advise you, / ye knights of high degree,
For God alone in heaven / may will that other mass ye see."
1857
Thus went they to the minster, / the princes and their men.
Within the holy churchyard / bade them Hagen then
Stand all still together / that they part not at all.
Quoth he: "Knows not any / what may at hands of Huns befall.
1858
"Let stand, good friends, all ready, / your shields before your feet,
That if ever any / would you in malice greet,
With deep-cut wound ye pay him; / that is Hagen's rede,
That from men may never / aught but praises be your meed."
1859
Volker and Hagen, / the twain thence did pass
Before the broad minster. / Therein their purpose was
That the royal Kriemhild / must meet them where they stood
There athwart her pathway. / In sooth full grim she was of mood.
1860
Then came the royal Etzel / and eke his spouse full fair.
Attired were the warriors / all in raiment rare
That following full stately / with her ye might see;
The dust arose all densely / round Kriemhild's mickle company.
1861
When the lofty monarch / thus all armed did see
The kings and their followers, / straightway then cried he:
"How see I in this fashion / my friends with helm on head?
By my troth I sorrow / if ill to them have happenéd.
1862
"I'll gladly make atonement / as doth to them belong.
Hath any them affronted / or done them aught of wrong,
To me 'tis mickle sorrow, / well may they understand.
To serve them am I ready, / in whatsoever they command."
1863
Thereto gave answer Hagen: / "Here hath wronged us none.
'Tis custom of my masters / to keep their armor on
Till full three days be over, / when high festival they hold.
Did any here molest us, / to Etzel would the thing be told."
1864
Full well heard Kriemhild likewise / how Hagen gave reply.
Upon him what fierce glances / flashed furtively her eye!

Yet betray she would not / the custom of her country,
Though well she long had known it / in the land of Burgundy.
1865
How grim soe'er and mighty / the hate to them she bore,
Had any told to Etzel / how stood the thing before,
Well had he prevented / what there anon befell.
So haughty were they minded / that none to him the same would tell.
1866
With the queen came forward / there a mighty train,
But no two handbreadths yielded / yet those warriors twain
To make way before her. / The Huns did wrathful grow,
That their mistress passing / should by them be jostled so.
1867
Etzel's highborn pages / were sore displeased thereat,
And had upon the strangers / straightway spent their hate,
But that they durst not do it / their high lord before.
There was a mickle pressing, / yet naught of anger happened more.
1868
When they thence were parting / from holy service done,
On horse came quickly prancing / full many a nimble Hun.
With the Lady Kriemhild / went many a maiden fair,
And eke to make her escort / seven thousand knights rode there.
1869
Kriemhild with her ladies / within the casement sat
By Etzel, mighty monarch, / —full pleased he was thereat.
They wished to view the tourney / of knights beyond compare.
What host of strangers riding / thronged the court before them there!
1870
The marshal with the squires / not in vain ye sought,
Dankwart the full valiant: / with him had he brought
His royal master's followers / of the land of Burgundy.
For the valiant Nibelungen / the steeds well saddled might ye see.
1871
When their steeds they mounted, / the kings and all their men,
Volker thane full doughty, / gave his counsel then,
That after their country's fashion / they ride a mass mellay.
His rede the heroes followed / and tourneyed in full stately way.
1872
The knight had counsel given / in sooth that pleased them well;
The clash of arms in mellay / soon full loud did swell.
Many a valiant warrior / did thereto resort,
As Etzel and Kriemhild / looked down upon the spacious court.

1873
Came there unto the mellay / six hundred knights of those
That followed Dietrich's bidding, / the strangers to oppose.
Pastime would they make them / with the men of Burgundy,
And if he leave had granted. / had done the same right willingly.

1874
In their company rode there / how many a warrior bold!
When unto Sir Dietrich / then the thing was told,
Forbade he that 'gainst Gunther's / men they join the play.
He feared lest harm befall them, / and well his counsel did he weigh.

1875
When of Bern the warriors / thence departed were,
Came they of Bechelaren, / the men of Ruediger,
Bearing shield five hundred, / and rode before the hall;
Rather had the margrave / that they came there not at all.

1876
Prudently then rode he / amid their company
And told unto his warriors / how they might plainly see,
That the men of Gunther / were in evil mood:
Did they forego the mellay, / please him better far it would.

1877
When they were thence departed, / the stately knights and bold,
Came they of Thuringia, / as hath to us been told,
And of them of Denmark / a thousand warriors keen.
From crash of spear up-flying / full frequent were the splinters seen.

1878
Irnfried and Hawart / rode into the mellay,
Whom the gallant men of Rhineland / received in knightly play:
Full oft the men of Thuringia / they met in tournament,
Whereby the piercing lance-point / through many a stately shield was sent.

1879
Eke with three thousand warriors / came Sir Bloedel there.
Etzel and Kriemhild / were of his coming ware,
As this play of chivalry / before them they did see.
Now hoped the queen that evil / befall the men of Burgundy.

1880
Schrutan and Gibecke / rode into the mellay,
Eke Ramung and Hornbog / after the Hunnish way;
Yet must they come to standstill / 'fore the thanes of Burgundy.
High against the palace / wall the splintered shafts did fly.

1881
How keen soe'er the contest, / 'twas naught but knightly sport.

With shock of shields and lances / heard ye the palace court
Loud give back the echo / where Gunther's men rode on.
His followers in the jousting / on every side high honor won.

1882

So long they held such pastime / and with so mickle heat
That through the broidered trappings / oozed clear drops of sweat
From the prancing chargers / whereon the knights did ride.
In full gallant manner / their skill against the Huns they tried.

1883

Then outspake the Fiddler, / Volker deft of hand:
"These knights, I ween, too timid / are 'gainst us to stand.
Oft did I hear the story / what hate to us they bore;
Than this a fairer season / to vent it, find they nevermore."

1884

"Lead back unto the stables," / once more spake Volker then,
"Now our weary chargers; / we'll ride perchance again
When comes the cool of evening, / if fitting time there be.
Mayhap the queen will honor / award to men of Burgundy."

1885

Beheld they then prick hither / one dressed in state so rare
That of the Huns none other / might with him compare.
Belike from castle tower / did watch his fair lady;
So gay was his apparel / as it some knight's bride might be.

1886

Then again quoth Volker: / "How may I stay my hand?
Yonder ladies' darling / a knock shall understand.
Let no man here deter me, / I'll give him sudden check.
How spouse of royal Etzel / thereat may rage, I little reck."

1887

"Nay, as thou dost love me," / straight King Gunther spake;
"All men will but reproach us / if such affront we make.
The Huns be first offenders, / for such would more befit."
Still did the royal Etzel / in casement by Queen Kriemhild sit.

1888

"I'll add unto the mellay," / Hagen did declare;
"Let now all these ladies / and knights be made aware
How we can ride a charger; / 'twere well we make it known,
For, come what may, small honor / shall here to Gunther's men be shown."

1889

Once more the nimble Volker / into the mellay spurred,
Whereat full many a lady / soon to weep was heard.
His lance right through the body / of that gay Hun he sent:

'Twas cause that many a woman / and maiden fair must sore lament.
1890
Straight dashed into the mellay / Hagen and his men.
With three score of his warriors / spurred he quickly then
Forward where the Fiddler / played so lustily.
Etzel and Kriemhild / full plainly might the passage see.
1891
Then would the kings their minstrel / —that may ye fairly know—
Leave not all defenceless / there amid the foe.
With them a thousand heroes / rode forth full dexterously,
And soon had gained their purpose / with show of proudest chivalry.
1892
When in such rude fashion / the stately Hun was slain,
Might ye hear his kinsmen / weeping loud complain.
Then all around did clamor: / "Who hath the slayer been?"
"None but the Fiddler was it, / Volker the minstrel keen."
1893
For swords and for shields then / called full speedily
That slain margrave's kinsmen / of the Hun's country.
To avenge him sought they / Volker in turn to slay.
In haste down from the casement / royal Etzel made his way.
1894
Arose a mighty clamor / from the people all;
The kings and men of Burgundy / dismounted 'fore the hall,
And likewise their chargers / to the rear did send.
Came then the mighty Etzel / and sought to bring the strife to end.
1895
From one of that Hun's kinsmen / who near by him did stand
Snatched he a mighty weapon / quick from out his hand,
And therewith backward smote them, / for fierce his anger wrought.
"Shall thus my hospitality / unto these knights be brought to naught?"
1896
"If ye the valiant minstrel / here 'fore me should slay,"
Spake the royal Etzel, / "it were an evil day.
When he the Hun impaléd / I did observe full well,
That not through evil purpose / but by mishap it so befell.
1897
"These my guests now must ye / ne'er disturb in aught."
Himself became their escort. / Away their steeds were brought
Unto the stables / by many a waiting squire,
Who ready at their bidding / stood to meet their least desire.
1898
The host with the strangers / into the palace went,

Nor would he suffer any / further his wrath to vent.
Soon were the tables ready / and water for them did wait.
Many then had gladly / on them of Rhineland spent their hate.
1899
Not yet the lords were seated / till some time was o'er.
For Kriemhild o'er her sorrow / meantime did trouble sore.
She spake: "Of Bern, O Master, / thy counsel grant to me,
Thy help and eke thy mercy, / for here in sorry plight I be."
1900
To her gave answer Hildebrand, / a thane right praiseworthy:
"Who harms the Nibelungen / shall ne'er have help of me,
How great soe'er the guerdon. / Such deed he well may rue,
For never yet did any / these gallant doughty knights subdue."
1901
Eke in courteous manner / Sir Dietrich her addressed:
"Vain, O lofty mistress, / unto me thy quest.
In sooth thy lofty kinsmen / have wronged me not at all,
That I on thanes so valorous / should thus with murderous purpose fall.
1902
"Thy prayer doth thee small honor, / O high and royal dame,
That upon thy kinsmen / thou so dost counsel shame.
Thy grace to have they deeméd / when came they to this land.
Nevermore shall Siegfried / avengéd be by Dietrich's hand."
1903
When she no guile discovered / in the knight of Bern,
Unto Bloedel straightway / did she hopeful turn
With promise of wide marches / that Nudung erst did own.
Slew him later Dankwart / that he forgot the gift full soon.
1904
Spake she: "Do thou help me, / Sir Bloedel, I pray.
Yea, within the palace / are foes of mine this day,
Who erstwhile slew Siegfried, / spouse full dear to me.
Who helps me to avenge it, / to him I'll e'er beholden be."
1905
Thereto gave answer Bloedel: / "Lady, be well aware,
Ne'er to do them evil / 'fore Etzel may I dare,
For to thy kinsmen, lady, / beareth he good will.
Ne'er might the king me pardon, / wrought I upon them aught of ill."
1906
"But nay, Sir Bloedel, my favor / shall thou have evermore.
Yea, give I thee for guerdon / silver and gold in store,
And eke a fairest lady, / that Nudung erst should wed:

By her fond embraces / may'st thou well be comforted.
1907
"The land and eke the castles, / all to thee I'll give;
Yea, may'st thou, knight full noble, / in joyance ever live,
Call'st thou thine the marches, / wherein did Nudung dwell.
Whate'er this day I promise, / fulfil it all I will full well."
1908
When understood Sir Bloedel / what gain should be his share,
And pleased him well the lady / for that she was so fair,
By force of arms then thought he / to win her for his wife.
Thereby the knight aspirant / was doomed anon to lose his life.
1909
"Unto the hall betake thee," / quoth he unto the queen,
"Alarum I will make thee / ere any know, I ween.
Atone shall surely Hagen / where he hath done thee wrong:
To thee I'll soon give over / King Gunther's man in fetters strong."
1910
"To arms, to arms!" quoth Bloedel, / "my good warriors all:
In their followers' quarters / upon the foe we'll fall.
Herefrom will not release me / royal Etzel's wife.
To win this venture therefore / fear not each one to lose his life."
1911
When at length Queen Kriemhild / found Bloedel well content
To fulfil her bidding, / she to table went
With the monarch Etzel / and eke a goodly band.
Dire was the treason / she against the guests had planned.
1912
Since in none other manner / she knew the strife to start,
(Kriemhild's ancient sorrow / still rankled in her heart),
Bade she bring to table / Etzel's youthful son:
By woman bent on vengeance / how might more awful deed be done?
1913
Went upon the instant / four of Etzel's men,
And soon came bearing Ortlieb, / the royal scion, then
Unto the princes' table, / where eke grim Hagen sate.
The child was doomed to perish / by reason of his deadly hate.
1914
When the mighty monarch / then his child did see,
Unto his lady's kinsmen / in manner kind spake he:
"Now, my good friends, behold ye / here my only son,
And child of your high sister: / may it bring you profit every one.
1915
"Grow he but like his kindred, / a valiant man he'll be,

A mighty king and noble, / doughty and fair to see.
Live I but yet a little, / twelve lands shall he command;
May ye have faithful service / from the youthful Ortlieb's hand.

1916
"Therefore grant me favor, / ye good friends of mine;
When to your country ride ye / again unto the Rhine,
Shall ye then take with you / this your sister's son,
And at your hands may ever / by the child full fair be done.

1917
"Bring him up in honor / until to manhood grown.
If then in any country / hath wrong to you been done,
He'll help you by his valor / vengeance swift to wreak."
Eke heard the Lady Kriemhild / royal Etzel thus to speak.

1918
"Well might these my masters / on his faith rely,
Grew he e'er to manhood," / Hagen made reply:
"Yet is the prince, I fear me, / more early doomed of fate.
'Twere strange did any see me / ever at court on Ortlieb wait."

1919
The monarch glanced at Hagen, / sore grieved at what he heard;
Although the king full gallant / thereto spake ne'er a word,
Natheless his heart was saddened / and heavy was his mind.
Nowise the mood of Hagen / was to merriment inclined.

1920
It grieved all the princes / and the royal host
That of his child did Hagen / make such idle boast.
That they must likewise leave it / unanswered, liked they not:
They little weaned what havoc / should by the thane anon be wrought.

THIRTY-SECOND ADVENTURE: How Bloedel was Slain

1921
The knights by Bloedel summoned / soon armed and ready were,
A thousand wearing hauberks / straightway did repair
Where Dankwart sat at table / with many a goodly squire.
Soon knight on knight was seeking / in fiercest way to vent his ire.

1922
When there Sir Bloedel / strode unto the board,
Dankwart the marshal / thus spoke courteous word:
"Unto this hall right welcome / good Sir Bloedel be.
What business hast thou hither / is cause of wonder yet to me."

1923
"No greeting here befits thee," / spake Bloedel presently,
"For that this my coming / now thy end must be,
Through Hagen's fault, thy brother, / who Siegfried erstwhile slew
To the Huns thou mak'st atonement, / and many another warrior too."

1924
"But nay, but nay, Sir Bloedel," / Dankwart spake thereto,
"For so should we have reason / our coming here to rue.
A child I was and little / when Siegfried lost his life,
Nor know I why reproacheth / me the royal Etzel's wife."

1925
"In sooth I may the story / never fully tell.
Gunther and Hagen was it / by whom the deed befell.
Now guard you well, ye strangers, / for doomed in sooth are ye,
Unto Lady Kriemhild / must your lives now forfeit be."

1926
"An so thou wilt desist not," / Dankwart declared,
"Regret I my entreaty, / my toil were better spared."
The nimble thane and valiant / up from the table sprung,
And drew a keen-edged weapon, / great in sooth that was and long.

1927
Then smote he with it Bloedel / such a sudden blow
That his head full sudden / before his feet lay low.
"Be that thy wedding-dower," / the doughty Dankwart spake,
"Along with bride of Nudung / whom thou would'st to thy bosom take.

1928
"To-morrow may she marry, / but some other one:
Will he have bridal portion, / e'en so to him be done."
A Hun that liked not treason / had given him to know
How that the queen upon him / thought to work so grievous woe.

1929
When the men of Bloedel / saw thus their master slain,
To fall upon the strangers / would they longer not refrain.
With swords swung high above them / upon the squires they flew
In a grimmest humor. / Soon many must that rashness rue.

1930
Full loudly cried then Dankwart / to all his company:
"Behold ye, noble squires, / the fate that ours must be.
Now quit yourselves with valor, / for evil is our pass,
Though fair to us the summons / hither from Lady Kriemhild was!"

1931
They, too, reached down before them, / who no weapons bore,
And each a massive footstool / snatched from off the floor,

For the Burgundian squires / no whit were they dismayed;
And by the selfsame weapons / was many a dint in helmet made.
1932
How fierce they fought to shield them / the strangers one and all!
E'en their arméd foemen / drove they from the hall.
Or smote dead within it / hundreds five or more;
All the valiant fighters / saw ye drenched with ruddy gore.
1933
Ere long the wondrous tidings / some messenger did tell
Unto Etzel's chieftain / —fierce did their anger swell—
How that slain was Bloedel / and knights full many a one;
The which had Hagen's brother / with his lusty squires done.
1934
The Huns, by anger driven, / ere Etzel was aware,
Two thousand men or over, / did quick themselves prepare.
They fell upon those squires / —e'en so it had to be—
And never any living / they left of all that company.
1935
A mickle host they faithless / unto those quarters brought,
But lustily the strangers / 'gainst their assailants fought.
What booted swiftest valor? / Soon must all lie dead.
A dire woe thereafter / on many a man was visited.
1936
Now may ye hear a wondrous / tale of honor told:
Of squires full nine thousand / soon in death lay cold,
And eke good knights a dozen / there of Dankwart's band.
Forlorn ye saw him only / the last amid his foemen stand.
1937
The din at last was ended / and lulled the battle-sound,
When the valiant Dankwart / did cast a glance around.
"Alack for my companions," / cried he, "now from me reft.
Alack that I now only / forlorn amid my foes am left."
1938
The swords upon his body / fell full thick and fast,
Which rashness many a warrior's / widow mourned at last.
His shield he higher lifted / and drew the strap more low:
Down coats of ring-made armor / made he the ebbing blood to flow.
1939
"O woe is me!" spake Dankwart, / the son of Aldrian.
"Now back, ye Hunnish fighters, / let me the open gain,
That the air give cooling / to me storm-weary wight."
In splendid valor moving / strode forward then anew the knight.

1940

As thus he battle-weary / through the hall's portal sprang,
What swords of new-come fighters / upon his helmet rang!
They who not yet had witnessed / what wonders wrought his hand,
Rashly rushed they forward / to thwart him of Burgundian land.

1941

"Now would to God," quoth Dankwart, / "I found a messenger
Who to my brother Hagen / might the tidings bear,
That 'fore host of foemen / in such sad case am I!
From hence he'd surely help me, / or by my side he slain would lie."

1942

Then Hunnish knights gave answer: / "Thyself the messenger
Shalt be, when to thy brother / thee a corse we bear.
So shall that thane of Gunther / first true sorrow know.
Upon the royal Etzel / here hast thou wrought so grievous woe."

1943

Quoth he: "Now leave such boasting / and yield me passage free,
Else shall mail-rings a many / with blood bespattered be.
Myself will tell the tidings / soon at Etzel's court,
And eke unto my masters / of this my travail make report."

1944

Etzel's men around him / belabored he so sore
That they at sword-point / durst not withstand him more.
Spears shot into his shield he / so many there did stop
That he the weight unwieldy / must from out his hand let drop.

1945

Then thought they to subdue him / thus of his shield bereft,
But lo! the mighty gashes / wherewith he helmets cleft!
Must there keen knights full many / before him stagger down,
High praise the valiant Dankwart / thereby for his valor won.

1946

On right side and on left side / they still beset his way,
Yet many a one too rashly / did mingle in the fray.
Thus strode he 'mid the foemen / as doth in wood the boar
By yelping hounds beleaguered; / more stoutly fought he ne'er before.

1947

As there he went, his pathway / with reeking blood was wet.
Yea, never any hero / more bravely battled yet
When by foes surrounded, / than he did might display.
To court did Hagen's brother / with splendid valor make his way.

1948

When stewards and cup-bearers / heard how sword-blades rung,
Many a brimming goblet / from their hands they flung

And eke the viands ready / that they to table bore;
Thus many doughty foemen / withstood him where he sought the door.

1949
"How now, ye stewards?" / cried the weary knight;
"'Twere better that ye tended / rather your guests aright,
Bearing to lords at table / choice food that fitteth well,
And suffered me these tidings / unto my masters dear to tell."

1950
Whoe'er before him rashly / athwart the stairway sprung,
On him with blow so heavy / his mighty sword he swung,
That soon faint heart gave warning / before his path to yield.
Mickle wonder wrought he / where sword his doughty arm did wield.

THIRTY-THIRD ADVENTURE: How the Burgundians fought with the Huns

1951
Soon as the valiant Dankwart / stood beneath the door,
Bade he Etzel's followers / all make way before.
With blood from armor streaming / did there the hero stand;
A sharp and mighty weapon / bore he naked in his hand.

1952
Into the hall then Dankwart / cried with voice full strong:
"At table, brother Hagen, / thou sittest all too long.
To thee and God in heaven / must I sore complain:
Knights and squires also / lie within their lodging slain."

1953
Straight he cried in answer: / "Who hath done such deed?"
"That hath done Sir Bloedel / and knights that he did lead.
Eke made he meet atonement, / that may'st thou understand:
His head from off his body / have I struck with mine own hand."

1954
"'Tis little cause for sorrow," / Hagen spake again,
"When they tell the story / of a valiant thane,
That he to death was smitten / by knight of high degree.
The less a cause for weeping / to winsome women shall it be.

1955
"Now tell me, brother Dankwart, / how thou so red may'st be;
From thy wounds thou sufferest, / I ween, full grievously.
Lives he within this country / who serves thee in such way,
Him must the devil shelter, / or for the deed his life shall pay."

1956

"Behold me here all scatheless. / My gear is wet with blood,
From wounds of others, natheless, / now hath flowed that flood,
Of whom this day so many / beneath my broadsword fell:
Must I make solemn witness, / ne'er knew I full the tale to tell."

1957

He answered: "Brother Dankwart, / now take thy stand before,
And Huns let never any / make passage by the door.
I'll speak unto these warriors, / as needs must spoken be:
Dead lie all our followers, / slain by foulest treachery."

1958

"Must I here be chamberlain," / replied the warrior keen,
"Well know I such high monarchs / aright to serve, I ween.
So will I guard the stairway / as sorts with honor well."
Ne'er to the thanes of Kriemhild / so sorry case before befell.

1959

"To me 'tis mickle wonder," / Hagen spake again,
"What thing unto his neighbor / whispers each Hunnish thane.
I ween they'd forego the service / of him who keeps the door,
And who such high court tidings / to his friends of Burgundy bore.

1960

"Long since of Lady Kriemhild / the story I did hear,
How unavenged her sorrow / she might no longer bear.
A memory-cup now quaff we / and pay for royal cheer!
The youthful lord of Hunland / shall make the first instalment here."

1961

Thereat the child Ortlieb / doughty Hagen slew,
That from the sword downward / the blood to hand-grip flew,
And into lap of Kriemhild / the severed head down rolled.
Then might ye see 'mid warriors / a slaughter great and grim unfold.

1962

By both hands swiftly wielded, / his blade then cut the air
And smote upon the tutor / who had the child in care,
That down before the table / his head that instant lay:
It was a sorry payment / wherewith he did the tutor pay.

1963

His eye 'fore Etzel's table / a minstrel espied:
To whom in hasty manner / did wrathful Hagen stride,
Where moved it on the fiddle / his right hand off smote he;
"Have that for thy message / unto the land of Burgundy."

1964

"Alack my hand!" did Werbel / that same minstrel moan;
"What, Sir Hagen of Tronje, / have I to thee done?

I bore a faithful message / unto thy master's land.
How may I more make music / thus by thee bereft of hand?"
1965
Little in sooth recked Hagen, / fiddled he nevermore.
Then in the hall all wrathful / wrought he havoc sore
Upon the thanes of Etzel / whereof he many slew;
Ere they might find exit, / to death then smote he not a few.
1966
Volker the full valiant / up sprang from board also:
In his hand full clearly / rang out his fiddle-bow,
For mightily did fiddle / Gunther's minstrel thane.
What host of foes he made him / because of Hunnish warriors slain!
1967
Eke sprang from the table / the lofty monarchs three,
Who glad had stilled the combat / ere greater scathe might be.
Yet all their art availed not / their anger to assuage,
When Volker and Hagen / so mightily began to rage.
1968
When the lord of Rhineland / saw how his toil was vain,
Gaping wounds full many / himself did smite amain
Through rings of shining mail-coats / there upon the foe.
He was a valiant hero, / as he full gallantly did show.
1969
Strode eke into the combat / Gernot a doughty thane;
By whom of Hunnish warriors / full many a one was slain
With a sword sharp-edgéd / he had of Ruediger;
Oft sent to dire ruin / by him the knights of Etzel were.
1970
The youthful son of Ute / eke to the combat sprang,
And merrily his broadsword / upon the helmets rang
Of many a Hunnish warrior / there in Etzel's land;
Feasts of mickle wonder / wrought Giselher with dauntless hand.
1971
How bold soe'er was any, / of kings and warrior band,
Saw ye yet the foremost / Giselher to stand
There against the foemen, / a knight of valor good;
Wounded deep full many / made he to fall in oozing blood.
1972
Eke full well defend them / did Etzel's warriors too.
There might ye see the strangers / their gory way to hew
With swords all brightly gleaming / adown that royal hall;
Heard ye there on all sides / loudly ring the battle-call.
1973

Join friends within beleaguered / would they without full fain,
Yet might they at the portal / but little vantage gain.
Eke they within had gladly / gained the outer air;
Nor up nor down did Dankwart / suffer one to pass the stair.

1974
There before the portal / surged a mighty throng,
And with a mickle clangor / on helm the broadsword rung.
Thus on the valiant Dankwart / his foes did sorely press,
And soon his trusty brother / was anxious grown o'er his distress.

1975
Full loudly cried then Hagen / unto Volker:
"Trusty fere, behold'st thou / my brother standing there,
Where on him Hunnish warriors / their mighty blows do rain?
Good friend, save thou my brother / ere we do lose the valiant thane."

1976
"That will I do full surely," / thereat the minstrel spake.
Adown the hall he fiddling / gan his way to make;
In his hand full often / a trusty sword rang out,
While grateful knights of Rhineland / acclaimed him with a mickle shout.

1977
Soon did the valiant Volker / Dankwart thus address:
"Hard this day upon thee / hath weighed the battle's stress.
That I should come to help thee / thy brother gave command;
Keep thou without the portal, / I inward guarding here will stand."

1978
Dankwart, thane right valiant, / stood without the door
And guarded so the stairway / that none might pass before.
There heard ye broadswords ringing, / swung by warrior's hand,
While inward in like manner / wrought Volker of Burgundian land.

1979
There the valiant Fiddler / above the press did call:
"Securely now, friend Hagen, / closed is the hall.
Yea, so firmly bolted / is King Etzel's door
By hands of two good warriors, / as thousand bars were set before,"

1980
When Hagen thus of Tronje / the door did guarded find,
The warrior far renownéd / swung his shield behind;
He first for harm receivéd / revenge began to take,
Whereat all hope of living / did soon his enemies forsake.

1981
When of Bern Sir Dietrich / rightly did perceive
How the doughty Hagen / did many a helmet cleave,

The king of Amelungen / upon a bench leaped up;
Quoth he: "Here poureth Hagen / for us exceeding bitter cup."
1982
Great fear fell eke on Etzel, / as well might be the case,
(What trusty followers snatched they / to death before his face!)
For well nigh did his enemies / on him destruction bring.
There sat he all confounded. / What booted him to be a king?
1983
Cried then aloud to Dietrich / Kriemhild, the high lady:
"Now help me, knight so noble, / that hence with life I flee,
By princely worth, I pray thee, / thou lord of Amelung's land;
If here do reach me Hagen, / straight find I death beneath his hand."
1984
"How may my help avail thee, / noble queen and high?"
Answered her Sir Dietrich, / "Fear for myself have I.
Too sorely is enraged / each knight in Gunther's band,
To no one at this season / may I lend assisting hand."
1985
"But nay, but nay, Sir Dietrich, / full noble knight and keen,
What maketh thy bright chivalry, / let it this day be seen,
And bring me hence to safety, / else am I death's sure prey."
Good cause was that on Kriemhild's / bosom fear so heavy lay.
1986
"So will I here endeavor / to help thee as I may;
Yet shalt thou well believe me, / hath passed full many a day
Since saw I goodly warriors / of so bitter mood.
'Neath swords behold I flowing / through helmets plenteously the blood."
1987
Lustily then cried he, / the warrior nobly born,
That his voice rang loudly / like blast from bison's horn,
That all around the palace / gave back the lusty sound;
Unto the might of Dietrich / never limit yet was found.
1988
When did hear King Gunther / how called the doughty man
Above the storm of combat, / to hearken he began.
Quoth he: "The voice of Dietrich / hath fallen upon mine ear;
I ween some of his followers / before our thanes have fallen here.
1989
"High on the board I see him; / he beckons with the hand.
Now my good friends and kinsmen / of Burgundian land,
Stay ye your hands from conflict, / let us hear and see
If done upon the chieftain / aught by my men of scathe there be."

1990
When thus King Gunther / did beg and eke command,
With swords in stress of battle / stayed they all the hand.
'Twas token of his power / that straight the strife did pause.
Then him of Bern he questioned / what of his outcry were the cause.

1991
He spake: "Full noble Dietrich, / what here on thee is wrought
By any of my warriors? / For truly is my thought
To make a full atonement / and amends to thee.
If here hath wronged thee any, / 'twere cause of mickle grief to me."

1992
Then answered him Sir Dietrich: / "Myself do nothing grieve.
Grant me with thy protection / but this hall to leave
And quit the dire conflict, / with them that me obey.
Then surely will I ever / seek thy favor to repay."

1993
"How plead'st thou thus so early?" / Wolfhart was heard;
"The Fiddler so securely / the door not yet hath barred,
But it so wide we'll open / to pass it through, I trow."
"Now hold thy peace," quoth Dietrich, / "wrought but little here hast
thou."

1994
Then spake the royal Gunther: / "That grant I thee to do,
Forth from the hall lead many / or lead with thee few,
An if my foes it be not; / here stay they every one.
Upon me here in Hunland / hath grievous wrong by them been done."

1995
When heard he Gunther's answer / he took beneath his arm
The noble Queen Kriemhild, / who dreaded mickle harm.
On the other side too led he / Etzel with him away;
Eke went thence with Dietrich / six hundred knights in fair array.

1996
Then outspake the margrave, / the noble Ruediger:
"If leave to any others / be granted forth to fare,
Of those who glad would serve you, / give us the same to see.
Yea, peace that's never broken / 'twixt friends 'tis meet should ever
be."

1997
Thereto gave answer Giselher / of the land of Burgundy:
"Peace and unbroken friendship / wish we e'er with thee,
With thee and all thy kinsmen, / as true thou ever art.
We grant thee all untroubled / with thy friends from hence to part."

1998
When thus Sir Ruediger / from the hall did pass,
A train of knights five hundred / or more with him there was,
Of them of Bechelaren, / kinsmen and warriors true,
Whose parting gave King Gunther / anon full mickle cause to rue.

1999
When did a Hunnish warrior / Etzel's passing see
'Neath the arm of Dietrich, / to profit him thought he.
Smote him yet the Fiddler / such a mighty blow,
That 'fore the feet of Etzel / sheer on the floor his head fell low.

2000
When the country's monarch / had gained the outer air,
Turned he looking backward / and gazed on Volker.
"Alack such guests to harbor! / Ah me discomfited!
That all the knights that serve me / shall before their might lie dead.

2001
"Alack their coming hither!" / spake the king once more.
"Within, a warrior fighteth / like to wild forest boar;
Hight the same is Volker, / and a minstrel is also;
To pass the demon scatheless / I to fortune's favor owe.

2002
"Evil sound his melodies, / his strokes of bow are red,
Yea, beneath his music / full many a knight lies dead.
I know not what against us / hath stirred that player's ire,
For guests ne'er had I any / whereby to suffer woe so dire."

2003
None other would they suffer / to pass the door than those.
Then 'neath the hall's high roof-tree / a mighty din arose.
For evil wrought upon them / those guests sore vengeance take.
Volker the doughty Fiddler, / what shining helmets there he brake!

2004
Gunther, lofty monarch, / thither turned his ear.
"Hear'st thou the music, Hagen, / that yonder Volker
Doth fiddle for the Hun-men, / when near the door they go?
The stroke is red of color, / where he doth draw the fiddle-bow."

2005
"Mickle doth it rue me," / Hagen spake again,
"That in the hall far severed / I am from that bold thane.
I was his boon companion / and he sworn friend to me:
Come we hence ever scatheless, / trusty feres we yet shall be.

2006
"Behold now, lofty sire, / the faith of Volker bold!
With will he seeks to win him / thy silver and thy gold.

With fiddle-bow he cleaveth / e'en the steel so hard,
Bright-gleaming crests of helmets / are scattered by his mighty sword.
2007
"Never saw I fiddler / so dauntless heart display,
As the doughty Volker / here hath done this day.
Through shield and shining helmet / his melodies ring clear;
Give him to ride good charger / and eke full stately raiment wear."
2008
Of all the Hunnish kindred / that in the hall had been,
None now of all their number / therein to fight was seen.
Hushed was the din of battle / and strife no more was made:
From out their hands aweary / their swords the dauntless warriors laid.

THIRTY-FOURTH ADVENTURE: How they cast out the Dead

2009
From toil of battle weary / rested the warriors all.
Volker and Hagen / passed out before the hall,
And on their shields did lean them, / those knights whom naught could daunt.
Then with full merry converse / gan the twain their foes to taunt.
2010
Spake meanwhile of Burgundy / Giselher the thane:
"Not yet, good friends, may ye / think to rest again.
Forth from the hall the corses / shall ye rather bear.
Again we'll be assailéd, / that would I now in sooth declare.
2011
"Beneath our feet no longer / here the dead must lie.
But ere in storm of battle / at hand of Huns to die,
We'll deal such wounds around us / as 'tis my joy to see.
Thereon," spake Giselher, / "my heart is fixed right steadfastly."
2012
"I joy in such a master," / Hagen spake again:
"Such counsel well befitteth / alone so valiant thane
As my youthful master / hath shown himself this day.
Therefor, O men of Burgundy, / every one rejoice ye may."
2013
Then followed they his counsel / and from the hall they bore
Seven thousand bodies / and cast them from the door.
Adown the mounting stairway / all together fell,

Whereat a sound of wailing / did from mourning kinsmen swell.

2014
Many a man among them / so slight wound did bear
That he were yet recovered / had he but gentle care,
Who yet falling headlong / now surely must be dead.
Thereat did grieve their kinsmen / as verily was sorest need.

2015
Then outspake the Fiddler, / Volker a hero bold:
"Now do I find how truly / hath to me been told
That cowards are the Hun-men / who do like women weep.
Rather should be their effort / their wounded kin alive to keep."

2016
These words deemed a margrave / spoken in kindly mood.
He saw one of his kinsmen / weltering in his blood.
In his arms he clasped him / and thought him thence to bear,
But as he bent above him / pierced him the valiant minstrel's spear.

2017
When that beheld the others / all in haste they fled,
Crying each one curses / on that same minstrel's head.
From the ground then snatched he / a spear with point full keen,
That 'gainst him up the stairway / by a Hun had hurléd been.

2018
Across the court he flung it / with his arm of might
Far above the people. / Then did each Hunnish knight
Seek him safer quarters / more distant from the hall.
To see his mighty prowess / did fill with fear his foemen all.

2019
As knights full many thousand / far 'fore the palace stood,
Volker and Hagen / gan speak in wanton mood
"Unto King Etzel, / nor did they aught withhold;
Wherefrom anon did sorrow / o'ertake those doughty warriors bold.

2020
"'Twould well beseem," quoth Hagen, / "the people's lofty lord
Foremost in storm of battle / to swing the cutting sword,
As do my royal masters / each fair example show.
Where hew they through the helmets / their swords do make the blood
to flow."

2021
To hear such words brave Etzel / snatched in haste his shield.
"Now well beware of rashness," / cried Lady Kriemhild,
"And offer to thy warriors / gold heaped on shield full high:
If yonder Hagen reach thee, / straightway shalt thou surely die."

2022
So high was the king's mettle / that he would not give o'er,
Which case is now full seldom / seen in high princes more;
They must by shield-strap tugging / him perforce restrain.
Grim of mood then Hagen / began him to revile again.

2023
"It was a distant kinship," / spake Hagen, dauntless knight,
"That Etzel unto Siegfried / ever did unite,
And husband he to Kriemhild / was ere thee she knew.
Wherefore, O king faint-hearted, / seek'st thou such thing 'gainst me to do?"

2024
Thereto eke must listen / the noble monarch's spouse,
And grievously to hear it / did Kriemhild's wrath arouse.
That he 'fore men of Etzel / durst herself upbraid;
To urge them 'gainst the strangers / she once more her arts essayed.

2025
Cried she: "Of Tronje Hagen / whoso for me will slay,
And his head from body severed / here before me lay,
For him the shield of Etzel / I'll fill with ruddy gold,
Eke lands and lordly castles / I'll give him for his own to hold."

2026
"I wot not why they tarry," / —thus the minstrel cried;
"Ne'er saw I heroes any / so their courage hide,
When to them was offered, / like this, reward so high.
'Tis cause henceforth that Etzel / for aye to them goodwill deny."

2027
"Who in such craven manner / do eat their master's bread,
And like caitiffs fail him / in time of greatest need,
Here see I standing many / of courage all forlorn,
Yet would be men of valor; / all time be they upheld to scorn."

THIRTY-FIFTH ADVENTURE: How Iring was Slain

2028
Cried then he of Denmark, / Iring the margrave:
"Fixed on things of honor / my purpose long I have,
And oft in storm of battle, / where heroes wrought, was I.
Bring hither now my armor, / with Hagen I'll the combat try."

2029
"I counsel thee against it," / Hagen then replied,

"Or bring a goodly company / of Hun-men by thy side.
If peradventure any / find entrance to the hall,
I'll cause that nowise scatheless / down the steps again they fall."

2030
"Such words may not dissuade me," / Iring spake once more;
"A thing of equal peril / oft have I tried before.
Yea, will I with my broadsword / confront thee all alone.
Nor aught may here avail thee / thus to speak in haughty tone."

2031
Soon the valiant Iring / armed and ready stood,
And Irnfried of Thuringia / a youth of mettle good,
And eke the doughty Hawart, / with thousand warriors tried.
Whate'er his purpose, Iring / should find them faithful by his side.

2032
Advancing then with Iring / did the Fiddler see
All clad in shining armor / a mighty company,
And each a well-made helmet / securely fastened wore.
Thereat the gallant Volker / began to rail in anger sore.

2033
"Seest thou, friend Hagen, / yonder Iring go,
Who all alone to front thee / with his sword did vow?
Doth lying sort with honor? / Scorned the thing must be.
A thousand knights or over / here bear him arméd company."

2034
"Now make me not a liar," / cried Hawart's man aloud,
"For firm is still my purpose / to do what now I vowed,
Nor will I turn me from it / through any cause of fear.
Alone I'll stand 'fore Hagen, / awful howsoe'er he were."

2035
On ground did throw him Iring / before his warriors' feet,
That they leave might grant him / alone the knight to meet.
Loath they were to do it; / well known to them might be
The haughty Hagen's prowess / of the land of Burgundy.

2036
Yet so long besought he / that granted was their leave;
When they that followed with him / did his firm mind perceive,
And how 'twas bent on honor, / they not restrained him.
Then closed the two chieftains / together in a combat grim.

2037
Iring of Denmark / raised his spear on high,
And with the shield he covered / himself full skilfully;
He upward rushed on Hagen / unto the hall right close,
When round the clashing fighters / soon a mighty din arose.

2038

Each hurled upon the other / the spear with arm of might,
That the firm shields were piercéd / e'en to their mail-coats bright,
And outward still projecting / the long spear-shafts were seen.
In haste then snatched their broadswords / both the fighters grim and keen.

2039

In might the doughty Hagen / and prowess did abound,
As Iring smote upon him / the hall gave back the sound.
The palace all and towers / re-echoed from their blows,
Yet might that bold assailant / with victory ne'er the combat close.

2040

On Hagen might not Iring / wreak aught of injury.
Unto the doughty Fiddler / in haste then turnéd he.
Him by his mighty sword-strokes / thought he to subdue,
But well the thane full gallant / to keep him safe in combat knew.

2041

Then smote the doughty Fiddler / so lustily his shield
That from it flew its ornaments / where he the sword did wield.
Iring must leave unconquered / there the dauntless man;
Next upon King Gunther / of Burgundy in wrath he ran.

2042

There did each in combat / show him man of might;
Howe'er did Gunther and Iring / yet each the other smite,
From wounds might never either / make the blood to flow,
So sheltered each his armor, / well wrought that was and strong enow.

2043

Gunther left he standing, / upon Gernot to dash,
And when he smote ring-armor / the fire forth did flash.
But soon had he of Burgundy, / Gernot the doughty thane,
Well nigh his keen assailant / Iring of Denmark slain.

2044

Yet from the prince he freed him, / for nimble was he too.
Four of the men of Burgundy / the knight full sudden slew
Of those that followed with them / from Worms across the Rhine.
Thereupon might nothing / the wrath of Giselher confine.

2045

"God wot well, Sir Iring," / young Giselher then cried,
"Now must thou make requital / for them that here have died
'Neath thy hand so sudden." / He rushed upon him so
And smote the knight of Denmark / that he might not withstand the blow.

2046
Into the blood down fell he / staggering 'neath its might,
That all who there beheld it / might deem the noble knight
Sword again would never / wield amid the fray.
Yet 'neath the stroke of Giselher / Iring all unwounded lay.

2047
Bedazed by helmet's sounding / where ringing sword swung down,
Full suddenly his senses / so from the knight were flown:
That of his life no longer / harbored he a thought.
That the doughty Giselher / by his mighty arm had wrought.

2048
When somewhat was subsided / the din within his head
From mighty blow so sudden / on him was visited,
Thought he: "I still am living / and bear no mortal wound.
How great the might of Giselher, / till now unwitting, have I found."

2049
He hearkened how on all sides / his foes around did stand;
Knew they what he did purpose, / they had not stayed their hand.
He heard the voice of Giselher / eke in that company,
As cunning he bethought him / how yet he from his foes might flee.

2050
Up from the blood he started / with fierce and sudden bound;
By grace alone of swiftness / he his freedom found.
With speed he passed the portal / where Hagen yet did stand,
And swift his sword he flourished / and smote him with his doughty hand.

2051
To see such sight quoth Hagen: / "To death thou fall'st a prey;
If not the Devil shield thee, / now is thy latest day."
Yet Iring wounded Hagen / e'en through his helmet's crown.
That did the knight with Waske, / a sword that was of far renown.

2052
When thus Sir Hagen / the smart of wound did feel,
Wrathfully he brandished / on high his blade of steel.
Full soon must yield before him / Hawart's daring man,
Adown the steps pursuing / Hagen swiftly after ran.

2053
O'er his head bold Iring / his shield to guard him swung,
And e'en had that same stairway / been full three times as long,
Yet had he found no respite / from warding Hagen's blows.
How plenteously the ruddy / sparks above his helm arose!

2054
Unscathed at last came Iring / where waited him his own.
Soon as was the story / unto Kriemhild known,
How that in fight on Hagen / he had wrought injury,
Therefor the Lady Kriemhild / him gan to thank full graciously.

2055
"Now God requite thee, Iring, / thou valiant knight and good,
For thou my heart hast comforted / and merry made my mood.
Red with blood his armor, / see I yonder Hagen stand."
For joy herself did Kriemhild / take his shield from out his hand.

2056
"Small cause hast thou to thank him," / thus wrathful Hagen spake;
"For gallant knight 'twere fitting / trial once more to make.
If then returned he scatheless, / a valiant man he were.
The wound doth boot thee little / that now from his hand I bear.

2057
"That here from wound upon me / my mail-coat see'st thou red,
Shall bring woful reprisal / on many a warrior's head.
Now is my wrath aro`sed / in full 'gainst Hawart's thane.
As yet in sooth hath Iring / wrought on me but little bane."

2058
Iring then of Denmark / stood where fanned the wind.
He cooled him in his armor / and did his helm unbind.
Then praised him all the people / and spoke him man of might,
Whereat the margrave's bosom / swelled full high with proud delight.

2059
"Now hearken friends unto me," / Iring once more spake;
"Make me straightway ready, / new trial now to make
If I this knight so haughty / may yet perchance subdue."
New shield they brought, for Hagen / did his erstwhile asunder hew.

2060
Soon stood again the warrior / in armor all bedight.
In hand a spear full massy / took the wrathful knight,
Wherewith on yonder Hagen / he thought to vent his hate.
With grim and fearful visage / on him the vengeful thane did wait.

2061
Yet not abide his coming / might Hagen longer now.
Adown he rushed upon him / with many a thrust and blow,
Down where the stairway ended / for fierce did burn his ire.
Soon the might of Iring / must 'neath his furious onset tire,

2062
Their shields they smote asunder / that the sparks began
To fly in ruddy showers. / Hawart's gallant man

Was by sword of Hagen / wounded all so sore
Through shield and shining cuirass, / that whole he found him never more.
2063
When how great the wound was / Iring fully knew,
Better to guard his helm-band / his shield he higher drew.
The scathe he first receivéd / he deemed sufficient quite,
Yet injury far greater / soon had he from King Gunther's knight.
2064
From where it lay before him / Hagen a spear did lift
And hurled it upon Iring / with aim so sure and swift,
It pierced his head, and firmly / fixed the shaft did stand;
Full grim the end that met him / 'neath the doughty Hagen's hand.
2065
Backward Iring yielded / unto his Danish men.
Ere for the knight his helmet / they undid again,
From his head they drew the spear-point; / to death he was anigh.
Wept thereat his kinsmen, / and sore need had verily.
2066
Came thereto Queen Kriemhild / and o'er the warrior bent,
And for the doughty Iring / gan she there lament.
She wept to see him wounded, / and sorely grieved the queen.
Then spake unto his kinsmen / the warrior full brave and keen.
2067
"I pray thee leave thy moaning, / royal high lady.
What avails thy weeping? / Yea, soon must ended be
My life from wounds outflowing / that here I did receive.
To serve thyself and Etzel / will death not longer grant me leave."
2068
Eke spake he to them of Thuringia / and to them of Danish land:
"Of you shall never any / receive the gift in hand
From your royal mistress / of shining gold full red.
Whoe'er withstandeth Hagen / death calleth down upon his head."
2069
From cheek the color faded, / death's sure token wore
Iring the gallant warrior: / thereat they grieved full sore.
Nor more in life might tarry / Hawart's valiant knight:
Enraged the men of Denmark / again did arm them for the fight.
2070
Irnfried and Hawart / before the hall then sprang
Leading thousand warriors. / Full furious a clang
Of weapons then on all sides / loud and great ye hear.
Against the men of Burgundy / how hurled they many a mighty spear!

2071
Straight the valiant Irnfried / the minstrel rushed upon,
But naught but grievous injury / 'neath his hand he won:
For the noble Fiddler / did the landgrave smite
E'en through the well-wrought helmet; / yea, grim and savage was the knight.

2072
Sir Irnfried then in answer / the valiant minstrel smote,
That must fly asunder / the rings of his mailed coat
Which showered o'er his cuirass / like sparks of fire red.
Soon must yet the landgrave / fall before the Fiddler dead.

2073
Eke were come together / Hawart and Hagen bold,
And saw he deeds of wonder / who did the sight behold.
Swift flew the sword and fiercely / swung by each hero's hand.
But soon lay Hawart prostrate / before him of Burgundian land.

2074
When Danish men and Thuringians / beheld their masters fall,
Fearful was the turmoil / that rose before the hall
As to the door they struggled, / on dire vengeance bent.
Full many a shield and helmet / was there 'neath sword asunder rent.

2075
"Now backward yield," cried Volker / "and let them pass within;
Thus only are they thwarted / of what they think to win.
When but they pass the portals / are they full quickly slain.
With death shall they the bounty / of their royal mistress gain."

2076
When thus with pride o'erweening / they did entrance find,
The head of many a warrior / was so to earth inclined,
That he must life surrender / 'neath blows that thickly fell.
Well bore him valiant Gernot / and eke Sir Giselher as well.

2077
Four knights beyond a thousand / were come into the house;
The light from sword-blades glinted, / swift swung with mighty souse.
Not one of all their number / soon might ye living see;
Tell might ye mickle wonders / of the men of Burgundy.

2078
Thereafter came a stillness, / and ceased the tumult loud.
The blood in every quarter / through the leak-holes flowed,
And out along the corbels / from men in death laid low.
That had the men of Rhineland / wrought with many a doughty blow.

2079
Then sat again to rest them / they of Burgundian land,

281

Shield and mighty broadsword / they laid from out the hand.
But yet the valiant Fiddler / stood waiting 'fore the door,
If peradventure any / would seek to offer combat more.
2080
Sorely did King Etzel / and eke his spouse lament,
Maidens and fair ladies / did sorrow sore torment.
Death long since upon them, / I ween, such ending swore.
To fall before the strangers / was doomed full many a warrior more.

THIRTY-SIXTH ADVENTURE: How the Queen bade set fire to the Hall

2081
"Now lay ye off the helmets," / the words from Hagen fell:
"I with a boon companion / will be your sentinel.
And seek the men of Etzel / to work us further harm,
For my royal masters / full quickly will I cry alarm."
2082
Then freed his head of armor / many a warrior good.
They sate them on the corses, / that round them in the blood
Of wounds themselves had dealt them, / prostrate weltering lay.
Now to his guests so lofty / scant courtesy did Etzel pay.
2083
Ere yet was come the even, / King Etzel did persuade,
And eke the Lady Kriemhild, / that once more essayed
The Hunnish knights to storm them. / Before them might ye see
Good twenty thousand warriors, / who soon for fight must ready be.
2084
Then with a furious onset / the strangers they attacked.
Dankwart, Hagen's brother, / who naught of courage lacked,
Sprang out 'mid the besiegers / to ward them from the door.
'Twas deemed a deadly peril, / yet scatheless stood he there before.
2085
Fierce the struggle lasted / till darkness brought an end.
Themselves like goodly heroes / the strangers did defend
Against the men of Etzel / all the long summer day.
What host of valiant warriors / before them fell to death a prey!
2086
At turn of sun in summer / that havoc sore was wrought,
When the Lady Kriemhild / revenge so dire sought
Upon her nearest kinsmen / and many a knight beside,
Wherefore with royal Etzel / never more might joy abide.

2087
As day at last was ending / sad they were of heart.
They deemed from life 'twere better / in sudden death to part
Than be thus long tormented / by great o'erhanging dread.
That respite now be granted, / the knights so proud and gallant prayed.

2088
They prayed to lead the monarch / hither to them there.
As heroes blood-bespotted, / and stained from battle-gear,
Forth from the hall emergéd / the lofty monarchs three.
They wist not to whom complainéd / might their full grievous sorrows be.

2089
Etzel and Kriemhild / they soon before them found,
And great was now their company / from all their lands around.
Spake Etzel to the strangers: / "What will ye now of me?
Ye hope for end of conflict, / but hardly may such favor be.

2090
"This so mighty ruin / that ye on me have wrought,
If death thwart not my purpose, / shall profit you in naught.
For child that here ye slew me / and kinsmen dear to me,
Shall peace and reconcilement / from you withheld forever be."

2091
Thereto gave answer Gunther: / "To that drove sorest need.
Lay all my train of squires / before thy warriors dead
Where they for night assembled. / How bore I so great blame?
Of friendly mind I deemed thee, / as trusting in thy faith I came."

2092
Then spake eke of Burgundy / the youthful Giselher:
"Ye knights that still are living / of Etzel, now declare
Whereof ye may reproach me! / How hath you harmed my hand?
For in right friendly manner / came I riding to this land."

2093
Cried they: "Well is thy friendship / in burgh and country known
By sorrow of thy making. / Gladly had we foregone
The pleasure of thy coming / from Worms across the Rhine.
Our country hast thou orphaned, / thou and brother eke of thine."

2094
In angry mood King Gunther / unto them replied:
"An ye this mighty hatred / appeased would lay aside,
Borne 'gainst us knights here homeless, / to both a gain it were
For Etzel's wrath against us / we in sooth no guilt do bear."

2095
The host then to the strangers: / "Your sorrow here and mine

Are things all unequal. / For now must I repine
With honor all bespotted / and 'neath distress of woe.
Of you shall never any / hence from my country living go."
2096
Then did the doughty Gernot / unto King Etzel say:
"God then in mercy move thee / to act in friendly way.
Slay us knights here homeless, / yet grant us down to go
To meet thee in the open: / thine honor biddeth thus to do.
2097
"Whate'er shall be our portion, / let that straightway appear.
Men hast thou yet so many / that, should they banish fear,
Not one of us storm-weary / might keep his life secure.
How long shall we here friendless / this woeful travail yet endure?"
2098
By the warriors of Etzel / their wish nigh granted was,
And leave well nigh was given / that from the hall they pass.
When Kriemhild knew their purpose, / high her anger swelled,
And straightway such a respite / was from the stranger knights
withheld.
2099
"But nay, ye Hunnish warriors! / what ye have mind to do,
Therefrom now desist ye, / —such is my counsel true;
Nor let foes so vengeful / pass without the hall,
Else must in death before them / full many of your kinsmen fall.
2100
"If of them lived none other / but Ute's sons alone,
My three noble brothers, / and they the air had won
Where breeze might cool their armor, / to death ye were a prey.
In all this world were never / born more valiant thanes than they."
2101
Then spake the youthful Giselher: / "Full beauteous sister mine,
When to this land thou bad'st me / from far beside the Rhine,
I little deemed such trouble / did here upon me wait.
Whereby have I deservéd / from the Huns such mortal hate?
2102
"To thee I ever faithful / was, nor wronged thee e'er.
In such faith confiding / did I hither fare,
That thou to me wert gracious, / O noble sister mine.
Show mercy now unto us, / we must to thee our lives resign."
2103
"No mercy may I show you, / —unmerciful I'll be.
By Hagen, knight of Tronje, / was wrought such woe to me,
That ne'er is reconcilement / the while that I have life.

That must ye all atone for," / —quoth the royal Etzel's wife.

2104

"Will ye but Hagen only / to me as hostage give,
Then will I not deny you / to let you longer live.
Born are ye of one mother / and brothers unto me,
So wish I that compounded / here with these warriors peace may be."

2105

"God in heaven forfend it," / Gernot straightway said;
"E'en though we were a thousand, / lay we all rather dead,
We who are thy kinsmen, / ere that warrior one
Here we gave for hostage. / Never may such thing be done."

2106

"Die must we all," quoth Giselher, / "for such is mortal's end.
Till then despite of any, / our knighthood we'll defend.
Would any test our mettle, / here may he trial make.
For ne'er, when help he needed, / did I a faithful friend forsake."

2107

Then spake the valiant Dankwart, / a knight that knew no fear;
"In sooth stands not unaided / my brother Hagen here.
Who here have peace denied us / may yet have cause to rue.
I would that this ye doubt not, / for verily I tell you true."

2108

The queen to those around her: / "Ye gallant warriors, go
Now nigher to the stairway / and straight avenge my woe.
I'll ever make requital / therefor, as well I may.
For his haughty humor / will I Hagen full repay.

2109

"To pass without the portal / let not one at all,
For at its four corners / I'll bid ignite the hall.
So will I fullest vengeance / take for all my woe."
Straightway the thanes of Etzel / ready stood her hest to do.

2110

Who still without were standing / were driven soon within
By sword and spear upon them, / that made a mighty din.
Yet naught might those good warriors / from their masters take,
By their faith would never / each the other's side forsake.

2111

To burn the hall commanded / Etzel's wife in ire,
And tortured they those warriors / there with flaming fire;
Full soon with wind upon it / the house in flames was seen.
To any folk did never / sadder plight befall, I ween.

2112

Their cries within resounded: / "Alack for sorest need!

How mickle rather lay we / in storm of battle dead.
'Fore God 'tis cause for pity, / for here we all must die!
Now doth the queen upon us / vengeance wreak full grievously."
2113
Among them spake another: / "Our lives we here must end.
What now avails the greeting / the king to us did send?
So sore this heat oppresseth / and parched with thirst my tongue,
My life from very anguish / I ween I must resign ere long."
2114
Then quoth of Tronje Hagen: / "Ye noble knights and good,
Whoe'er by thirst is troubled, / here let him drink the blood.
Than wine more potent is it / where such high heat doth rage,
Nor may we at this season / find us a better beverage."
2115
Where fallen knight was lying, / thither a warrior went.
Aside he laid his helmet, / to gaping wound he bent,
And soon was seen a-quaffing / therefrom the flowing blood.
To him though all unwonted, / yet seemed he there such drinking good.
2116
"Now God reward thee, Hagen," / the weary warrior said,
"That I so well have drunken, / thus by thy teaching led.
Better wine full seldom / hath been poured for me,
And live I yet a season / I'll ever faithful prove to thee."
2117
When there did hear the others / how to him it seeméd good,
Many more beheld ye / eke that drank the blood.
Each thereby new vigor / for his body won,
And eke for lover fallen / wept many a buxom dame anon.
2118
The flaming brands fell thickly / upon them in the hall,
With upraised shields they kept them / yet scatheless from their fall,
Though smoke and heat together / wrought them anguish sore.
Beset were heroes never, / I ween, by so great woe before.
2119
Then spake of Tronje Hagen: / "Stand nigh unto the wall,
Let not the brands all flaming / upon your helmets fall.
Into the blood beneath you / tread them with your feet.
In sooth in evil fashion / us doth our royal hostess greet."
2120
In trials thus enduréd / ebbed the night away.
Still without the portal / did the keen Fiddler stay
And Hagen his good fellow, / o'er shield their bodies leant;

They deemed the men of Etzel / still on further mischief bent.

2121

Then was heard the Fiddler: / "Pass we into the hall,
For so the Huns shall fondly / deem we are perished all
Amid the mickle torture / we suffer at their hand.
Natheless shall they behold us / boun for fight before them stand."

2122

Spake then of Burgundy / the young Sir Giselher:
"I ween 'twill soon be dawning, / for blows a cooler air.
To live in fuller joyance / now grant us God in heaven.
To us dire entertainment / my sister Kriemhild here hath given."

2123

Spake again another: / "Lo! how I feel the day.
For that no better fortune / here await us may,
So don, ye knights, your armor, / and guard ye well your life.
Full soon, in sooth, we suffer / again at hands of Etzel's wife."

2124

Fondly Etzel fancied / the strangers all were dead,
From sore stress of battle / and from the fire dread;
Yet within were living / six hundred men so brave,
That never thanes more worthy / a monarch for liegemen might have.

2125

The watchers set to watch them / soon full well had seen
How still lived the strangers, / spite what wrought had been
Of harm and grievous evil, / on the monarchs and their band.
Within the hall they saw them / still unscathed and dauntless stand.

2126

Told 'twas then to Kriemhild / how they from harm were free.
Whereat the royal lady / quoth, such thing ne'er might be
That any still were living / from that fire dread.
"Nay, believe I rather / that within they all lie dead."

2127

Gladly yet the strangers / would a truce compound,
Might any grace to offer / amid their foes be found.
But such appeared not any / in them of Hunnish land.
Well to avenge their dying / prepared they then with willing hand.

2128

About the dawn of morning / greeted they were again
With a vicious onslaught, / that paid full many a thane.
There was flung upon them / many a mighty spear,
While gallantly did guard them / the lofty thanes that knew not fear.

2129

The warriors of Etzel / were all of eager mood,

And Kriemhild's promised bounty / win for himself each would;
To do the king's high bidding / did likewise urge their mind.
'Twas cause full soon that many / were doomed swift death in fight to find.

2130
Of store of bounty promised / might wonders great be told,
She bade on shields to carry / forth the ruddy gold,
And gave to him that wished it / or would but take her store;
In sooth a greater hire / ne'er tempted 'gainst the foe before.

2131
A mickle host of warriors / went forth in battle-gear.
Then quoth the valiant Volker: / "Still may ye find us here.
Ne'er saw I move to battle / warriors more fain,
That to work us evil / the bounty of the king have ta'en."

2132
Then cried among them many: / "Hither, ye knights, more nigh!
Since all at last must perish, / 'twere better instantly;
And here no warrior falleth / but who fore-doomed hath been."
With well-flung spears all bristling / full quickly then their shields were seen.

2133
What need of further story? / Twelve hundred stalwart men,
Repulsed in onset gory, / still returned again;
But dealing wounds around them / the strangers cooled their mood,
And there stood all unvanquished. / Flowing might ye see the blood

2134
From deep wounds and mortal, / whereof were many slain.
For friends in battle fallen / heard ye loud complain;
Slain were all those warriors / that served the mighty king,
Whereat from loving kinsmen / arose a mickle sorrowing.

THIRTY-SEVENTH ADVENTURE: How the Margrave Ruediger was Slain

2135
At morning light the strangers / had wrought high deed of fame,
When the spouse of Gotelinde / unto the courtyard came.
To behold on both sides / such woe befallen there,
Might not refrain from weeping / sorely the faithful Ruediger.

2136
"O woe is me!" exclaimed he, / "that ever I was born.
Alack that this great sorrow / no hand from us may turn!

Though I be ne'er so willing, / the king no peace will know,
For he beholds his sorrow / ever great and greater grow."

2137
Then did the kindly Ruediger / unto Dietrich send,
If to the lofty monarchs / they yet might truce extend.
The knight of Bern gave message: / "How might such thing be?
For ne'er the royal Etzel / granteth to end it peacefully."

2138
When a Hunnish warrior / saw standing Ruediger
As from eyes sore weeping / fell full many a tear,
To his royal mistress spake he: / "Behold how stands he there
With whom here by Etzel / none other may in might compare,

2139
"And who commandeth service / of lands and people all.
How many lordly castles / Ruediger his own doth call,
That unto him hath given / the bounty of the king!
Not yet in valorous conflict / saw'st thou here his sword to swing.

2140
"Methinks, but little recks he, / what may here betide,
Since now in fullest measure / his heart is satisfied.
'Tis told he is, surpassing / all men, forsooth, so keen,
But in this time of trials / his valor ill-displayed hath been."

2141
Stood there full of sorrow / the brave and faithful man,
Yet whom he thus heard speaking / he cast his eyes upon.
Thought he: "Thou mak'st atonement, / who deem'st my mettle cold.
Thy thought here all too loudly / hast thou unto the people told."

2142
His fist thereat he doubled / and upon him ran,
And smote with blow so mighty / there King Etzel's man
That prone before him straightway / fell that mocker dead.
So came but greater sorrow / on the royal Etzel's head.

2143
"Hence thou basest caitiff," / cried then Ruediger;
"Here of pain and sorrow / enough I have to bear.
Wherefore wilt thou taunt me / that I the combat shun?
In sooth had I the utmost / of harm upon the strangers done,

2144
"For that good reason have I / to bear them hate indeed,
But that myself the warriors / as friends did hither lead.
Yea, was I their safe escort / into my master's land;
So may I, man most wretched, / ne'er raise against them hostile hand."

2145
Then spake the lofty Etzel / unto the margrave:
"What aid, O noble Ruediger, / here at thy hands we have!
Our country hath so many / already doomed to die,
We need not any other: / now hast thou wrought full wrongfully."

2146
Returned the knight so noble: / "My heart he sore hath grieved,
And reproached me for high honors / at thy hand received
And eke for gifts unto me / by thee so freely made;
Dearly for his slander / hath the base traducer paid."

2147
When had the queen come hither / and had likewise seen
How on the Hunnish warrior / his wrath had vented been,
Incontinent she mourned it, / and tears bedimmed her sight.
Spake she unto Ruediger: / "How dost thou now our love requite,

2148
"That for me and thy master / thou bring'st increase of woe?
Now hast thou, noble Ruediger, / ever told us so,
How that thou life and honor / for our sake wouldst dare.
Eke heard I thanes full many / proclaim thee knight beyond compare.

2149
"Of the oath I now remind thee / that thou to me didst swear,
When counsel first thou gavest / to Etzel's land to fare,
That thou wouldst truly serve me / till one of us were dead:
Of that I wretched woman / never stood so sore in need."

2150
"Nor do I, royal mistress, / deny that so I sware
That I for thy well-being / would life and honor dare:
But eke my soul to forfeit, / —that sware I not indeed.
'Tis I thy royal brothers / hither to this land did lead."

2151
Quoth she: "Bethink thee, Ruediger, / of thy fidelity
And oath once firmly plighted / that aught of harm to me
Should ever be avengéd, / and righted every ill."
Replied thereto the margrave: / "Ne'er have I failed to work thy will."

2152
Etzel the mighty monarch / to implore him then began,
And king and queen together / down knelt before their man,
Whereat the good margrave / was seen in sorest plight,
And gan to mourn his station / in piteous words the faithful knight.

2153
"O woe is me most wretched," / he sorrow-stricken cried,
"That forced I am my honor / thus to set aside,

And bonds of faith and friendship / God hath imposed on me.
O Thou that rul'st in heaven! / come death, I cannot yet be free.

2154
"Whate'er it be my effort / to do or leave undone,
I break both faith and honor / in doing either one;
But leave I both, all people / will cry me worthy scorn.
May He look down in mercy / who bade me wretched man be born!"

2155
With many a prayer besought him / the king and eke his spouse,
Wherefore was many a warrior / soon doomed his life to lose
At hand of noble Ruediger, / when eke did die the thane.
Now hear ye how he bore him, / though filled his heart with sorest pain.

2156
He knew how scathe did wait him / and boundless sorrowing,
And gladly had refuséd / to obey the king
And eke his royal mistress. / Full sorely did he fear,
That if one stranger slew he, / the scorn of all the world he'd bear.

2157
Then spake unto the monarch / the full gallant thane:
"O royal sire, whatever / thou gavest, take again,
The land and every castle, / that naught remain to me.
On foot a lonely pilgrim / I'll wander to a far country."

2158
Thereto replied King Etzel: / "Who then gave help to me?
My land and lordly castles / give I all to thee,
If on my foes, O Ruediger, / revenge thou wilt provide.
A mighty monarch seated, / shalt thou be by Etzel's side."

2159
Again gave answer Ruediger: / "How may that ever be?
At my own home shared they / my hospitality.
Meat and drink I offered / to them in friendly way,
And gave them of my bounty: / how shall I seek them here to slay ?

2160
"The folk belike will fancy / that I a coward be.
Ne'er hath faithful service / been refused by me
Unto the noble princes / and their warriors too;
That e'er I gained their friendship, / now 'tis cause for me to rue.

2161
"For spouse unto Sir Giselher / gave I a daughter mine,
Nor into fairer keeping / might I her resign,
Where truth were sought and honor / and gentle courtesy:
Ne'er saw I thane so youthful / virtuous in mind as he."

2162
Again gave answer Kriemhild: / "O noble Ruediger,
To me and royal Etzel / in mercy now give ear
For sorrows that o'erwhelm us. / Bethink thee, I implore,
That monarch never any / harbored so evil guests before."
2163
Spake in turn the margrave / unto the monarch's wife:
"Ruediger requital / must make to-day with life
For that thou and my master / did me so true befriend.
Therefore must I perish; / now must my service find an end.
2164
"E'en this day, well know I, / my castles and my land
Must surely lose their master / beneath a stranger's hand.
To thee my wife and children / commend I for thy care,
And with all the lorn ones / that wait by Bechelaren's towers fair."
2165
"Now God reward thee, Ruediger," / thereat King Etzel quoth.
He and the queen together, / right joyful were they both.
"To us shall all thy people / full commended be;
Eke trow I by my fortune / no harm shall here befall to thee."
2166
For their sake he ventured / soul and life to lose.
Thereat fell sore to weeping / the royal Etzel's spouse.
He spake: "I must unto you / my plighted word fulfil.
Alack! beloved strangers, / whom to assail forbids my will."
2167
From the king there parting / ye saw him, sad of mood,
And passed unto his warriors / who at small distance stood.
"Don straightway now your armor, / my warriors all," quoth he.
"Alas! must I to battle / with the valiant knights of Burgundy."
2168
Then straightway for their armor / did the warriors call.
A shining helm for this one, / for that a shield full tall
Soon did the nimble squires / before them ready hold.
Anon came saddest tidings / unto the stranger warriors bold.
2169
With Ruediger there saw ye / five hundred men arrayed,
And noble thanes a dozen / that came unto his aid,
Thinking in storm of battle / to win them honor high.
In sooth but little knew they / how death awaited them so nigh.
2170
With helm on head advancing / saw ye Sir Ruediger.
Swords that cut full keenly / the margrave's men did bear,

And eke in hand each carried / a broad shield shining bright.
Boundless was the Fiddler's / sorrow to behold the sight.
2171
When saw the youthful Giselher / his bride's sire go
Thus with fastened helmet, / how might he ever know
What he therewith did purpose / if 'twere not only good?
Thereat the noble monarchs / right joyous might ye see of mood.
2172
"I joy for friends so faithful," / spake Giselher the thane,
"As on our journey hither / we for ourselves did gain.
Full great shall be our vantage / that I found spouse so dear,
And high my heart rejoiceth / that plighted thus to wed we were."
2173
"Small cause I see for comfort," / thereto the minstrel spake.
"When saw ye thanes so many / come a truce to make
With helmet firmly fastened / and bearing sword in hand?
By scathe to us will Ruediger / service do for tower and land."
2174
The while that thus the Fiddler / had spoken to the end,
His way the noble Ruediger / unto the hall did wend.
His trusty shield he rested / on the ground before his feet,
Yet might he never offer / his friends in kindly way to greet.
2175
Loudly the noble margrave / cried into the hall:
"Now guard you well, ye valiant / Nibelungen all.
From me ye should have profit: / now have ye harm from me.
But late we plighted friendship: / broken now these vows must be."
2176
Then quailed to hear such tidings / those knights in sore distress,
For none there was among them / but did joy the less
That he would battle with them / for whom great love they bore.
At hand of foes already / had they suffered travail sore.
2177
"Now God in heaven forfend it," / there King Gunther cried,
"That from mercy to us / thou so wilt turn aside,
And the faithful friendship / whereof hope had we.
I trow in sooth that never / may such thing be done by thee."
2178
"Desist therefrom I may not," / the keen knight made reply,
"But now must battle with you, / for vow thereto gave I.
"Now guard you, gallant warriors, / as fear ye life to lose:
From plighted vow release me / will nevermore King Etzel's spouse."

2179
"Too late thou turnst against us," / spake King Gunther there.
"Now might God requite thee, / O noble Ruediger,
For the faith and friendship / thou didst on us bestow,
If thou a heart more kindly / even to the end wouldst show.
2180
"We'd ever make requital / for all that thou didst give,—
I and all my kinsmen, / wouldst thou but let us live,—
For thy gifts full stately, / as faithfully thou here
To Etzel's land didst lead us: / know that, O noble Ruediger."
2181
"To me what pleasure were it," / Ruediger did say,
"With full hand of my treasure / unto you to weigh
And with a mind right willing / as was my hope to do!
Thus might no man reproach me / with lack of courtesy to you."
2182
"Turn yet, O noble Ruediger." / Gernot spake again,
"For in so gracious manner / did never entertain
Any host the stranger, / as we were served by thee;
And live we yet a little, / shall thou well requited be."
2183
"O would to God, full noble / Gernot," spake Ruediger,
"That ye were at Rhine river / and that dead I were
With somewhat saved of honor, / since I must be your foe!
Upon good knights was never / wrought by friends more bitter woe."
2184
"Now God requite thee, Ruediger," / Gernot gave reply,
"For gifts so fair bestowéd. / I rue to see thee die,
For that in thee shall perish / knight of so gentle mind.
Here thy sword I carry, / that gav'st thou me in friendship kind.
2185
"It never yet hath failed me / in this our sorest need,
And 'neath its cutting edges / many a knight lies dead.
'Tis strong and bright of lustre, / cunning wrought and well.
I ween, whate'er was given / by knight it doth in worth excel.
2186
"An wilt thou not give over / upon us here to fall,
And if one friend thou slayest / here yet within this hall,
With this same sword thou gavest, / I'll take from thee thy life.
I sorrow for thee Ruediger, / and eke thy fair and stately wife."
2187
"Would God but give, Sir Gernot, / that such thing might be,
That thou thy will completely / here fulfilled mightst see,

And of thy friends not any / here his life should lose!
Yea, shalt thou live to comfort / both my daughter and my spouse."
2188
Then out spake of Burgundy / the son of Ute fair:
"How dost thou so, Sir Ruediger? / All that with me are
To thee are well disposéd. / Thou dost an evil thing,
And wilt thine own fair daughter / to widowhood too early bring.
2189
"If thou with arméd warriors / wilt thus assail me here,
In what unfriendly manner / thou makest to appear
How that in thee I trusted / beyond all men beside,
When thy fairest daughter / erstwhile I won to be my bride."
2190
"Thy good faith remember, / O Prince of virtue rare,
If God from hence do bring thee," / —so spake Ruediger:
"Forsake thou not the maiden / when bereft of me,
But rather grant thy goodness / be dealt to her more graciously."
2191
"That would I do full fairly," / spake Giselher again.
"But if my lofty kinsmen, / who yet do here remain,
Beneath thy hand shall perish, / severed then must be
The friendship true I cherish / eke for thy daughter and for thee."
2192
"Then God to us give mercy," / the knight full valiant spake.
Their shields in hand then took they, / as who perforce would make
Their passage to the strangers / into Kriemhild's hall.
Adown the stair full loudly / did Hagen, knight of Tronje, call:
2193
"Tarry yet a little, / O noble Ruediger,
For further would we parley," / —thus might ye Hagen hear—
"I and my royal masters, / as presseth sorest need.
What might it boot to Etzel / that we strangers all lay dead.
2194
"Great is here my trouble," / Hagen did declare:
"The shield that Lady Gotelinde / gave to me to bear
Hath now been hewn asunder / by Hun-men in my hand.
With friendly thought I bore it / hither into Etzel's land.
2195
"Would that God in heaven / might grant in kindliness,
That I a shield so trusty / did for my own possess
As in thy hand thou bearest, / O noble Ruediger!
In battle-storm then need I / never hauberk more to wear."

2196
"Full glad I'd prove my friendship / to thee with mine own shield,
Dared I the same to offer / before Lady Kriemhild.
But take it, natheless, Hagen, / and bear it in thy hand.
Would that thou mightst take it / again unto Burgundian land!"

2197
When with mind so willing / he offered him his shield,
Saw ye how eyes full many / with scalding tears were filled;
For the last gift was it / that was offered e'er
Unto any warrior / by Bechelaren's margrave, Ruediger.

2198
How grim soe'er was Hagen / and stern soe'er of mind,
That gift to pity moved him / that there the chieftain kind,
So near his latest moment, / did on him bestow.
From eyes of many another / began likewise the tears to flow.

2199
"Now God in heaven requite thee, / O noble Ruediger!
Like unto thee none other / warrior was there e'er,
Unto knights all friendless / so bounteously to give.
God grant in his mercy / thy virtue evermore to live.

2200
"Woe's me to hear such tiding," / Hagen did declare.
"Such load of grief abiding / already do we bear,
If we with friends must struggle, / to God our plaint must be."
Thereto replied the margrave: / "'Tis cause of sorrow sore to me."

2201
"To pay thee for thy favor, / O noble Ruediger,
Howe'er these lofty warriors / themselves against thee bear,
Yet never thee in combat / here shall touch my hand,
E'en though complete thou slayest / them from out Burgundian land."

2202
Thereat the lofty Ruediger / 'fore him did courteous bend.
On all sides was lamenting / that no man might end
These so great heart-sorrows / that sorely they must bear.
The father of all virtue / fell with noble Ruediger.

2203
Then eke the minstrel Volker / from hall down glancing said:
"Since Hagen thus, my comrade, / peace with thee hath made,
Lasting truce thou likewise / receivest from my hand.
Well hast thou deserved it / as fared we hither to this land.

2204
"Thou, O noble margrave, / my messenger shalt be.
These arm-bands ruddy golden / thy lady gave to me,

That here at this high festival / I the same should wear.
Now mayst thyself behold them / and of my faith a witness bear."
2205
"Would God but grant," / spake Ruediger, "who ruleth high in heaven,
That to thee by my lady / might further gift be given!
I'll gladly tell thy tidings / to spouse full dear to me,
An I but live to see her: / from doubt thereof thou mayst be free."
2206
When thus his word was given, / his shield raised Ruediger.
Nigh to madness driven / bode he no longer there,
But ran upon the strangers / like to a valiant knight.
Many a blow full rapid / smote the margrave in his might.
2207
Volker and Hagen / made way before the thane,
As before had promised / to him the warriors twain.
Yet found he by the portal / so many a valiant man
That Ruediger the combat / with mickle boding sore began.
2208
Gunther and Gernot / with murderous intent
Let him pass the portal, / as knights on victory bent.
Backward yielded Giselher, / with sorrow all undone;
He hoped to live yet longer, / and therefore Ruediger would shun.
2209
Straight upon their enemies / the margrave's warriors sprung,
And following their master / was seen a valiant throng.
Swords with cutting edges / did they in strong arm wield,
'Neath which full many a helmet / was cleft, and many a fair wrought shield.
2210
The weary strangers likewise / smote many a whirring slash,
Wherefrom the men of Bechelaren / felt deep and long the gash
Through the shining ring-mail / e'en to their life's core.
In storm of battle wrought they / glorious deeds a many more.
2211
All his trusty followers / now eke had gained the hall,
On whom Volker and Hagen / did soon in fury fall,
And mercy unto no man / save Ruediger they showed.
The blood adown through helmets, / where smote their swords, full plenteous flowed.
2212
How right furiously / were swords 'gainst armor driven!
On shields the well-wrought mountings / from their wards were riven,
And fell their jewelled facings / all scattered in the blood.

Ne'er again might warriors / show in fight so grim a mood.
2213
The lord of Bechelaren / through foemen cut his way,
As doth each doughty warrior / in fight his might display.
On that day did Ruediger / show full plain that he
A hero was undaunted, / full bold and eke full praiseworthy.
2214
Stood there two knights right gallant, / Gunther and Gernot,
And in the storm of battle / to death full many smote.
Eke Giselher and Dankwart, / never aught recked they
How many a lusty fighter / saw 'neath their hand his latest day.
2215
Full well did show him Ruediger / a knight of mettle true,
Doughty in goodly armor. / What warriors there he slew!
Beheld it a Burgundian, / and cause for wrath was there.
Not longer now was distant / the death of noble Ruediger.
2216
Gernot, knight full doughty, / addressed the margrave then,
Thus speaking to the hero: / "Wilt thou of all my men
Living leave not any, / O noble Ruediger?
That gives me grief unmeasured; / the sight I may not longer bear.
2217
"Now must thy gift unto me / prove thy sorest bane,
Since of my friends so many / thou from me hast ta'en.
Now hither turn to front me, / thou bold and noble knight:
As far as might may bear me / I trust to pay thy gift aright."
2218
Ere that full the margrave / might make his way to him,
Must rings of glancing mail-coats / with flowing blood grow dim.
Then sprang upon each other / those knights on honor bent,
And each from wounds deep cutting / sought to keep him all unshent.
2219
Their swords cut so keenly / that might withstand them naught.
With mighty arm Sir Ruediger / Gernot then smote
Through the flint-hard helmet, / that downward flowed the blood.
Therefor repaid him quickly / the knight of keen and valiant mood.
2220
The gift he had of Ruediger / high in hand he swung,
And though to death was wounded / he smote with blow so strong
That the good shield was cloven / and welded helmet through.
The spouse of fair Gotelinde, / then his latest breath he drew.
2221
In sooth so sad requital / found rich bounty ne'er.

Slain fell they both together, / Gernot and Ruediger,
Alike in storm of battle, / each by the other's hand.
Sore was the wrath of Hagen / when he the harm did understand.
2222
Cried there the lord of Tronje: / "Great is here our loss.
In death of these two heroes / such scathe befalleth us,
Wherefor land and people / shall repine for aye.
The warriors of Ruediger / must now to us the forfeit pay."
2223
"Alack for this my brother, / snatched by death this day!
What host of woes unbidden / encompass me alway!
Eke must I moan it ever / that noble Ruediger fell.
Great is the scathe to both sides / and great the sorrowing as well."
2224
When then beheld Sir Giselher / his lover's sire dead,
Must all that with him followed / suffer direst need.
There Death was busy seeking / to gather in his train,
And of the men of Bechelaren / came forth not one alive again.
2225
Gunther and Giselher / and with them Hagen too,
Dankwart and Volker, / doughty thanes and true,
Went where found they lying / the two warriors slain,
Nor at the sight the heroes / might their grief and tears restrain.
2226
"Death robbeth us right sorely," / spake young Sir Giselher:
"Yet now give o'er your weeping / and let us seek the air,
That the ringed mail grow cooler / on us storm-weary men.
God in sooth will grant us / not longer here to live, I ween."
2227
Here sitting, and there leaning / was seen full many a thane,
Resting once more from combat, / the while that all lay slain
The followers of Ruediger. / Hushed was the battle's din.
At length grew angry Etzel, / that stillness was so long within.
2228
"Alack for such a service!" / spake the monarch's wife;
"For never 'tis so faithful / that our foes with life
Must to us make payment / at Ruediger's hand.
He thinks in sooth to lead them / again unto Burgundian land.
2229
"What boots it, royal Etzel, / that we did ever share
With him what he desired? / The knight doth evil there.
He that should avenge us, / the same a truce doth make."
Thereto the stately warrior / Volker in answer spake:

2230
"Alas 'tis no such case here, / O high and royal dame.
Dared I but give the lie to / one of thy lofty name,
Thou hast in fiendish manner / Ruediger belied.
He and all his warriors / have laid all thoughts of truce aside.
2231
"With so good heart obeyed he / his royal master's will
That he and all his followers / here in death lie still.
Look now about thee, Kriemhild, / who may thy hests attend.
Ruediger the hero / hath served thee faithful to the end.
2232
"Wilt thou my words believe not, / to thee shall clear be shown."
To cause her heart a sorrow, / there the thing was done.
Wound-gashed they bore the hero / where him the king might see.
Unto the thanes of Etzel / ne'er might so great sorrow be.
2233
When did they the margrave / a corse on bier behold,
By chronicler might never / written be nor told
All the wild lamenting / of women and of men,
As with grief all stricken / out-poured they their hearts' sorrow then.
2234
Royal Etzel's sorrow / there did know no bound.
Like to the voice of lion / echoing rang the sound
Of the king's loud weeping, / wherein the queen had share.
Unmeasured they lamented / the death of noble Ruediger.

THIRTY-EIGHTH ADVENTURE: How all Sir Dietrich's Knights were Slain

2235
On all sides so great sorrow / heard ye there around,
That palace and high tower / did from the wail resound.
Of Bern a man of Dietrich / eke the same did hear,
And speedily he hastened / the tidings to his lord to bear.
2236
Spake he unto his master: / "Sir Dietrich give me ear.
What yet hath been my fortune, / never did I hear
Lamenting past all measure, / as at this hour hath been.
Scathe unto King Etzel / himself hath happenéd, I ween.
2237
"Else how might they ever / all show such dire need?
The king himself or Kriemhild, / one of them lieth dead,

By the doughty strangers / for sake of vengeance slain.
Unmeasured is the weeping / of full many a stately thane."
2238
Then spake of Bern Sir Dietrich: / "Ye men to me full dear,
Now haste ye not unduly. / The deeds performéd here
By the stranger warriors / show sore necessity.
That peace with them I blighted, / let it now their profit be."
2239
Then spake the valiant Wolfhart: / "Thither will I run
To make question of it / what they now have done,
And straight will tidings bring thee, / master full dear to me,
When yonder I inform me, / whence may so great lamenting be."
2240
Answer gave Sir Dietrich: / "Fear they hostility,
The while uncivil questioning / of their deed there be,
Lightly are stirred to anger / good warriors o'er the thing.
Yea, 'tis my pleasure, Wolfhart, / thou sparest them all such
questioning.
2241
Helfrich he then commanded / thither with speed to go
That from men of Etzel / he might truly know,
Or from the strangers straightway, / what thing there had been.
As that, so sore lamenting / of people ne'er before was seen.
2242
Questioned then the messenger: / "What hath here been wrought?"
Answered one among them: / "Complete is come to naught
What of joy we cherished / here in Hunnish land.
Slain here lieth Ruediger, / fallen 'neath Burgundian hand.
2243
"Of them that entered with him / not one doth longer live."
Naught might ever happen / Helfrich more to grieve,
Nor ever told he tidings / so ruefully before.
Weeping sore the message / unto Dietrich then he bore.
2244
"What the news thou bringst us?" / Dietrich spake once more;
"Yet, O doughty Helfrich, / wherefore dost weep so sore?"
Answered the noble warrior: / "With right may I complain:
Yonder faithful Ruediger / lieth by the Burgundians slain."
2245
The lord of Bern gave answer: / "God let not such thing be!
That were a mighty vengeance, / and eke the Devil's glee.
Whereby had ever Ruediger / from them deserved such ill?
Well know I to the strangers / was ever well disposed his will."

2246

Thereto gave answer Wolfhart: / "In sooth have they this done,
Therefor their lives shall forfeit / surely, every one.
And make we not requital, / our shame for aye it were;
Full manifold our service / from hand of noble Ruediger."

2247

Then bade the lord of Amelungen / the case more full to learn.
He sat within a casement / and did full sadly mourn.
He prayed then that Hildebrand / unto the strangers go,
That he from their own telling / of the case complete might know.

2248

The warrior keen in battle, / Master Hildebrand,
Neither shield nor weapon / bore he in his hand,
But would in chivalrous manner / unto the strangers go.
His sister's son reviled him / that he would venture thus to do.

2249

Spake in anger Wolfhart: / "Goest thou all weaponless,
Must I of such action / free my thought confess:
Thou shalt in shameful fashion / hither come again;
Goest thou arméd thither, / will all from harm to thee refrain."

2250

So armed himself the old man / at counsel of the young.
Ere he was ware of it, / into their armor sprung
All of Dietrich's warriors / and stood with sword in hand.
Grieved he was, and gladly / had turned them Master Hildebrand.

2251

He asked them whither would they. / "Thee company we'll bear,
So may, perchance, less willing / Hagen of Tronje dare,
As so oft his custom, / to give thee mocking word."
The thane his leave did grant them / at last when he their speech had heard.

2252

Keen Volker saw approaching, / in armor all arrayed,
Of Bern the gallant warriors / that Dietrich's word obeyed,
With sword at girdle hanging / and bearing shield in hand.
Straight he told the tidings / to his masters of Burgundian land.

2253

Spake the doughty Fiddler: / "Yonder see I come near
The warriors of Dietrich / all clad in battle gear
And decked their heads with helmets, / as if our harm they mean.
For us knights here homeless / approacheth evil end, I ween."

2254

Meanwhile was come anigh them / Master Hildebrand.

Before his foot he rested / the shield he bore in hand,
And soon began to question / the men of Gunther there:
"Alack, ye gallant warriors, / what harm hath wrought you Ruediger?
2255
"Me did my master Dietrich / hither to you command:
If now the noble margrave / hath fallen 'neath the hand
Of any knight among you, / as word to us is borne,
Such a mighty sorrow / might we never cease to mourn."
2256
Then spake of Tronje Hagen: / "True is the tale ye hear.
Though glad I were, if to you / had lied the messenger,
And if the faithful Ruediger / still his life might keep,
For whom both man and woman / must ever now in sorrow weep!"
2257
When they for sooth the passing / of the hero knew,
Those gallant knights bemoaned him / like faithful friends and true;
On Dietrich's lusty warriors / saw ye fall the tear
Adown the bearded visage, / for sad of heart in truth they were.
2258
Of Bern then a chieftain, / Siegstab, further cried:
"Of all the mickle comfort / now an end is made,
That Ruediger erst prepared us / after our days of pain.
The joy of exiled people / here lieth by you warriors slain."
2259
Then spake of Amelungen / the thane Wolfwein:
"If that this day beheld I / dead e'en sire of mine,
No more might be my sorrow / than for this hero's life.
Alack! who bringeth comfort / now to the noble margrave's wife?"
2260
Spake eke in angry humor / Wolfhart a stalwart thane:
"Who now shall lead our army / on the far campaign,
As full oft the margrave / of old hath led our host?
Alack! O noble Ruediger, / that in such manner thee we've lost!"
2261
Wolfbrand and Helfrich / and Helmnot with warriors all
Mournéd there together / that he in death must fall.
For sobbing might not further / question Hildebrand.
He spake: "Now do, ye warriors, / according to my lord's command.
2262
"Yield unto us Ruediger's / corse from out the hall,
In whose death to sorrow / hath passed our pleasure all;
And let us do him service / for friendship true of yore
That e'er for us he cherished / and eke for many a stranger more.

2263
"We too from home are exiles / like unto Ruediger.
Why keep ye us here waiting? / Him grant us hence to bear,
That e'en though death hath reft him / our service he receive,
Though fairer had we paid it / the while the hero yet did live."
2264
Thereto spake King Gunther: / "No service equal may
That which, when death hath reft him, / to friend a friend doth pay.
Him deem I friend right faithful, / whoe'er the same may do.
Well make ye here requital / for many a service unto you."
2265
"How long shall we beseech you," / spake Wolfhart the thane;
"Since he that best consoled us / by you now lieth slain,
And we, alas, no longer / his living aid may have,
Grant us hence to bear him / and lay the hero in his grave."
2266
Thereto answered Volker: / "Thy prayer shall all deny.
From out the hall thou take him, / where doth the hero lie
'Neath deep wounds and mortal / in blood now smitten down.
So may by thee best service / here to Ruediger be shown."
2267
Answered Wolfhart boldly: / "Sir Fiddleman, God wot
Thou shalt forbear to stir us, / for woe on us thou'st wrought.
Durst I despite my master, / uncertain were thy life;
Yet must we here keep silence, / for he did bid us shun the strife."
2268
Then spake again the Fiddler: / "'Tis all too much of fear,
For that a thing's forbidden, / meekly to forbear.
Scarce may I deem it valor / worthy good knight to tell."
What said his faithful comrade, / did please the doughty Hagen well.
2269
"For proof be not o'er-eager," / Wolfhart quick replied,
"Else so I'll tune thy fiddle / that when again ye ride
Afar unto Rhine river, / sad tale thou tellest there.
Thy haughty words no longer / may I now with honor bear."
2270
Spake once more the Fiddler: / "If e'er the harmony
Of my fiddle-strings thou breakest, / thy helmet's sheen shall be
Made full dim of lustre / by stroke of this my hand,
Howe'er fall out my journey / homeward to Burgundian land."
2271
Then would he rush upon him / but that him did restrain
Hildebrand his uncle / who seizéd him amain.

"I ween thou would'st be witless, / by youthful rage misled.
My master's favor had'st thou / evermore thus forfeited."
2272
"Let loose the lion, Master, / that doth rage so sore.
If but my sword may reach him," / spake Volker further more,
"Though he the world entire / by his own might had slain,
I'll smite him that an answer / never may he chant again."
2273
Thereat with anger straightway / the men of Bern were filled.
Wolfhart, thane right valiant, / grasped in haste his shield,
And like to a wild lion / out before them sped.
By friends a goodly number / full quickly was he followéd.
2274
Though by the hall went striding / ne'er so swift the thane,
O'ertook him Master Hildebrand / ere he the steps might gain,
For nowise would he let him / be foremost in the fray.
In the stranger warriors / worthy foemen soon found they.
2275
Straight saw ye upon Hagen / rush Master Hildebrand,
And sword ye heard give music / in each foeman's hand.
Sore they were enragéd, / as ye soon were ware,
For from their swinging broadswords / whirred the ruddy sparks in air.
2276
Yet soon the twain were parted / in the raging fight:
The men of Bern so turned it / by their dauntless might.
Ere long then was Hildebrand / from Hagen turned away,
While that the doughty Wolfhart / the valiant Volker sought to slay.
2277
Upon the helm the Fiddler / he smote with blow so fierce
That the sword's keen edges / unto the frame did pierce.
With mighty stroke repaid him / the valiant minstrel too,
And so belabored Wolfhart / that thick the sparks around him flew.
2278
Hewing they made the fire / from mail-rings scintillate,
For each unto the other / bore a deadly hate.
Of Bern the thane Wolfwein / at length did part the two,—
Which thing might none other / than man of mickle prowess do.
2279
Gunther, knight full gallant, / received with ready hand
There the stately warriors / of Amelungen land.
Eke did young Giselher / of many a helmet bright,
With blood all red and reeking, / cause to grow full dim the light.

2280
Dankwart, Hagen's brother, / was a warrior grim.
What erstwhile in combat / had been wrought by him
Against the men of Etzel / seemed now as toying vain,
As fought with flaming ire / the son of valiant Aldrian.

2281
Ritschart and Gerbart, / Helfrich and Wichart
Had oft in storm of battle / with valor borne their part,
As now 'fore men of Gunther / they did clear display.
Likewise saw ye Wolfbrand / glorious amid the fray.

2282
There old Master Hildebrand / fought as he were wode.
Many a doughty warrior / was stricken in the blood
By the sword that swinging / in Wolfhart's hand was seen.
Thus took dire vengeance / for Ruediger those knights full keen.

2283
Havoc wrought Sir Siegstab / there with might and main.
Ho! in the hurly-burly / what helms he cleft in twain
Upon the crowns of foemen, / Dietrich's sister's son!
Ne'er in storm of battle / had he more feats of valor done.

2284
When the doughty Volker / there aright had seen
How many a bloody rivulet / was hewn by Siegstab keen
From out the well-wrought mail-rings, / the hero's ire arose.
Quick he sprang toward him, / Siegstab then his life must lose.

2285
Ere long time was over, / 'neath the Fiddler's hand,
Who of his art did give him / such share to understand
That beneath his broadsword / smitten to death he lay.
Old Hildebrand avenged him / as bade his mighty arm alway.

2286
"Alack that knight so loved," / spake Master Hildebrand,
"Here should thus lie fallen / 'neath Volker's hand.
Now lived his latest hour / in sooth this Fiddler hath."
Filled was the hero Hildebrand / straightway with a mighty wrath.

2287
With might smote he Volker / that severed flew the band
E'en to the hall's wide limit / far on either hand
From shield and eke from helmet / borne by the Fiddler keen;
Therewith the doughty Volker / reft of life at last had been.

2288
Pressed eager to the combat / Dietrich's warriors true,
Smiting that the mail-rings / afar from harness flew,

And that the broken sword-points / soaring aloft ye saw,
The while that reeking blood-stains / did they from riven helmets draw.

2289

There of Tronje Hagen / beheld Volker dead.
In that so bloody carnage / 'twas far the sorest need
Of all that did befall him / in death of friend and man.
Alack! for him what vengeance / Hagen then to wreak began!

2290

"Therefrom shall profit never / Master Hildebrand.
Slain hath been here my helper / 'neath the warrior's hand,
The best of feres in battle / that fortune ever sent."
His shield upraised he higher / and hewing through the throng he went.

2291

Next saw ye Dankwart / by doughty Helfrich slain,
Gunther and Giselher / did full sorely plain,
When they beheld him fallen / where fiercely raged the fray.
For his death beforehand / dearly did his foemen pay.

2292

The while coursed Wolfhart / thither and back again,
Through Gunther's men before him / hewing wide a lane.
Thrice in sooth returning / strode he down the hall,
And many a lusty warrior / 'neath his doughty hand must fall.

2293

Soon the young Sir Giselher / cried aloud to him:
"Alack, that I should ever / find such foeman grim!
Sir knight, so bold and noble, / now turn thee here to me.
I trow to end thy coursing, / the which will I no longer see."

2294

To Giselher then turned him / Wolfhart in the fight,
And gaping wounds full many / did each the other smite.
With such a mighty fury / he to the monarch sped
That 'neath his feet went flying / the blood e'en high above his head.

2295

With rapid blows and furious / the son of Ute fair
Received the valiant Wolfhart / as came he to him there.
How strong soe'er the thane was, / his life must ended be.
Never king so youthful / might bear himself more valiantly.

2296

Straight he smote Wolfhart / through well-made cuirass,
That from the wound all gaping / the flowing blood did pass.
Unto death he wounded / Dietrich's liegeman true,

Which thing in sooth might never / any save knight full gallant do.
2297
When the valiant Wolfhart / of the wound was ware,
His shield flung he from him / and high with hand in air
Raised he a mighty weapon / whose keen edge failéd not.
Through helmet and through mail-rings / Giselher with might he smote.
2298
Grimly each the other / there to death had done.
Of Dietrich's men no longer / lived there ever one.
When old Master Hildebrand / Wolfhart's fall had seen,
In all his life there never / such sorrow him befell, I ween.
2299
Fallen now were Gunther's / warriors every one,
And eke the men of Dietrich. / Hildebrand the while had gone
Where Wolfhart had fallen / down in pool of blood.
In his arms then clasped he / the warrior of dauntless mood.
2300
Forth from the hall to bear him / vainly did he try:
But all too great the burden / and there he still must lie.
The dying knight looked upward / from his bloody bed
And saw how that full gladly / him his uncle thence had led.
2301
Spake he thus mortal wounded: / "Uncle full dear to me,
Now mayst thou at such season / no longer helpful be.
To guard thee well from Hagen / indeed me seemeth good,
For bears he in his bosom / a heart in sooth of grimmest mood.
2302
"And if for me my kinsmen / at my death would mourn,
Unto the best and nearest / by thee be message borne
That for me they weep not, / —of that no whit is need.
At hand of valiant monarch / here lie I gloriously dead.
2303
"Eke my life so dearly / within this hall I've sold,
That have sore cause for weeping / the wives of warriors bold.
If any make thee question, / then mayst thou freely say
That my own hand nigh hundred / warriors hath slain to-day."
2304
Now was Hagen mindful / of the minstrel slain,
From whom the valiant Hildebrand / erstwhile his life had ta'en.
Unto the Master spake he: / "My woes shalt thou repay.
Full many a warrior gallant / thou hast ta'en from us hence away."
2305

He smote upon Hildebrand / that loud was heard the tone
Of Balmung resounding / that erst did Siegfried own,
But Hagen bold did seize it / when he the hero slew.
The old warrior did guard him, / as he was knight of mettle true.
2306
Dietrich's doughty liegeman / with broadsword did smite
That did cut full sorely, / upon Tronje's knight;
Yet had the man of Gunther / never any harm.
Through his cuirass well-jointed / Hagen smote with mighty arm.
2307
Soon as his wound perceivéd / the aged Hildebrand,
Feared he more of damage / to take from Hagen's hand;
Across his back full deftly / his shield swung Dietrich's man,
And wounded deep, the hero / in flight 'fore Hagen's fury ran.
2308
Now longer lived not any / of all that goodly train
Save Gunther and Hagen, / doughty warriors twain.
With blood from wound down streaming / fled Master Hildebrand,
Whom soon in Dietrich's presence, / saw ye with saddest tidings stand.
2309
He found the chieftain sitting / with sorrow all distraught,
Yet mickle more of sadness / unto him he brought.
When Dietrich saw how Hildebrand / cuirass all blood-red wore,
With fearful heart he questioned, / what the news to him he bore.
2310
"Now tell me, Master Hildebrand, / how thus wet thou be
From thy life-blood flowing, / or who so harmeth thee.
In hall against the strangers / thou'st drawn thy sword, I ween.
'Twere well my straight denial / here by these had honored been."
2311
Replied he to his master: / "From Hagen cometh all.
This deep wound he smote me / there within the hall
When I from his fury / thought to turn away.
'Tis marvel that I living / saved me from the fiend this day."
2312
Then of Bern spake Dietrich: / "Aright hast thou thy share,
For thou didst hear me friendship / unto these knights declare,
And now the peace hast broken, / that I to them did give.
If my disgrace it were not, / by this hand no longer shouldst thou live."
2313
"Now be not, Master Dietrich, / so sorely stirred to wrath.
On me and on my kinsmen / is wrought too great a scathe.
Thence sought we Ruediger / to bear all peacefully,

The which by men of Gunther / to us no whit would granted be."
2314
"Ah, woe is me for sorrow! / Is Ruediger then dead,
In all my need there never / such grief hath happenéd.
The noble Gotelinde / is cousin fair to me.
Alack for the poor orphans / that there in Bechelaren must be!"
2315
Grief and anguish filled him / o'er Ruediger thus slain,
Nor might at all the hero / the flowing tears restrain.
"Alack for faithful helper / that death from me hath torn.
King Etzel's trusty liegeman / never may I cease to mourn.
2316
"Canst thou, Master Hildebrand, / true the tidings say,
Who might be the warrior / that Ruediger did slay?"
"That did the doughty Gernot / with mighty arm," he said:
"Eke at hand of Ruediger / lieth the royal hero dead."
2317
Spake he again to Hildebrand: / "Now let my warriors know,
That straightway they shall arm them, / for thither will I go.
And bid to fetch hither / my shining mail to me.
Myself those knights will question / of the land of Burgundy."
2318
"Who here shall do thee service?" / spake Master Hildebrand;
"All that thou hast yet living, / thou seest before thee stand.
Of all remain I only; / the others, they are dead."
As was in sooth good reason, / filled the tale his soul with dread,
2319
For in his life did never / such woe to him befall.
He spake: "Hath death so reft me / of my warriors all,
God hath forsaken Dietrich, / ah me, a wretched wight!
Sometime a lofty monarch / I was, high throned in wealth and might."
2320
"How might it ever happen?" / Dietrich spake again,
"That so worthy heroes / here should all be slain
By the battle-weary / strangers thus beset?
Ill fortune me hath chosen, / else death had surely spared them yet.
2321
"Since that fate not further / to me would respite give,
Then tell me, of the strangers / doth any longer live?"
Answered Master Hildebrand: / "God wot, never one
Save Hagen, and beside him / Gunther lofty king alone."
2322
"Alack, O faithful Wolfhart, / must I thy death now mourn,

Soon have I cause to rue me / that ever I was born.
Siegstab and Wolfwein / and eke Wolfbrand!
Who now shall be my helpers / in the Amelungen land?
2323
"Helfrich, thane full valiant, / and is he likewise slain?
For Gerbart and Wichart / when shall I cease to plain?
Of all my life's rejoicing / is this the latest day.
Alack that die for sorrow / never yet a mortal may!"

THIRTY-NINTH ADVENTURE: How Gunther and Hagen and Kriemhild were Slain

2324
Himself did then Sir Dietrich / his armor take in hand,
To don the which did help him / Master Hildebrand.
The doughty chieftain meanwhile / must make so loud complain
That from high palace casement / oft came back the sound again.
2325
Natheless his proper humor / soon he did regain,
And arméd full in anger / stood the worthy thane;
A shield all wrought full firmly / took he straight in hand,
And forth they strode together, / he and Master Hildebrand.
2326
Spake then of Tronje Hagen: / "Lo, where doth hither wend
In wrath his way Sir Dietrich. / 'Tis plain he doth intend
On us to wreak sore vengeance / for harm befallen here.
To-day be full decided / who may the prize for valor bear!
2327
"Let ne'er of Bern Sir Dietrich / hold him so high of might
Nor deem his arm so doughty / and terrible in fight
That, will he wreak his anger / on us for sorest scathe,"—
Such were the words of Hagen, / —"I dare not well withstand his wrath."
2328
Upon these words defiant / left Dietrich Hildebrand,
And to the warriors hither / came where both did stand
Without before the palace, / and leaning respite found.
His shield well proved in battle / Sir Dietrich lowered to the ground.
2329
Addressed to them Sir Dietrich / these words of sorrowing:

"Wherefore hast thou such evil, / Gunther mighty king,
Wrought 'gainst me a stranger? / What had I done to thee,
Of my every comfort / in such manner reft to be?
2330
"Seemed then not sufficient / the havoc unto you
When from us the hero / Ruediger ye slew,
That now from me ye've taken / my warriors one and all?
Through me did so great sorrow / ne'er to you good knights befall.
2331
"Of your own selves bethink you / and what the scathe ye bore,
The death of your companions / and all your travail sore,
If not your hearts, good warriors, / thereat do heavy grow.
That Ruediger hath fallen, / —ah me! how fills my heart with woe!
2332
"In all this world to any / more sorrow ne'er befell,
Yet have ye minded little / my loss and yours as well.
Whate'er I most rejoiced in / beneath your hands lies slain;
Yea, for my kinsmen fallen / never may I cease to plain."
2333
"No guilt lies here upon us," / Hagen in answer spake.
"Unto this hall hither / your knights their way did take,
With goodly train of warriors / full arméd for the fight.
Meseemeth that the story / hath not been told to thee aright."
2334
"What shall I else believe in? / To me told Hildebrand
How, when the knights that serve me / of Amelungenland
Did beg the corse of Ruediger / to give them from the hall,
Nought offered ye but mockings / unto the valiant warriors all."
2335
Then spake the King of Rhineland: / "Ruediger to bear away
Came they in company hither; / whose corse to them deny
I bade, despiting Etzel, / nor with aught malice more,
Whereupon did Wolfhart / begin to rage thereat full sore."
2336
Then spake of Bern the hero: / "'Twas fated so to be.
Yet Gunther, noble monarch, / by thy kingly courtesy
Amends make for the sorrow / thou here on me hast wrought,
That so thy knightly honor / still unsullied be in aught.
2337
"Then yield to me as hostage / thyself and eke thy man;
So will I surely hinder, / as with best might I can,
That any here in Hunland / harm unto thee shall do:
Henceforward shalt thou find me / ever well disposed and true."

2338
"God in heaven forfend it," / Hagen spake again,
"That unto thee should yield them / ever warriors twain
Who in their strength reliant / all armed before thee stand,
And yet 'fore foes defiant / may freely swing a blade in hand."

2339
"So shall ye not," spake Dietrich, / "proffered peace forswear,
Gunther and Hagen. / Misfortune such I bear
At both your hands, 'tis certain / ye did but do aright,
Would ye for so great sorrow / now my heart in full requite.

2340
"I give you my sure promise / and pledge thereto my hand
That I will bear you escort / home unto your land;
With honors fit I'll lead you, / thereon my life I set,
And for your sake sore evil / suffered at your hands forget."

2341
"Ask thou such thing no longer," / Hagen then replied.
"For us 'twere little fitting / the tale be bruited wide,
That twain of doughty warriors / did yield them 'neath thy hand.
Beside thee is none other / now but only Hildebrand."

2342
Then answered Master Hildebrand: / "The hour may come, God wot,
Sir Hagen, when thus lightly / disdain it thou shalt not
If any man such offer / of peace shall make to thee.
Welcome might now my master's / reconciliation be."

2343
"I'd take in sooth his friendship," / Hagen gave reply,
"Ere that I so basely / forth from a hall would fly.
As thou hast done but lately, / O Master Hildebrand.
I weened with greater valor / couldst thou 'fore a foeman stand."

2344
Thereto gave answer Hildebrand: / "From thee reproach like that?
Who was then on shield so idle / 'fore the Waskenstein that sat,
The while that Spanish Walter / friend after friend laid low?
Such valor thou in plenty / hast in thine own self to show."

2345
Outspake then Sir Dietrich: / "Ill fits it warriors bold
That they one another / like old wives should scold.
Thee forbid I, Hildebrand, / aught to parley more.
Ah me, most sad misfortune / weigheth on my heart full sore.

2346
"Let me hear, Sir Hagen," / Dietrich further spake,
"What boast ye doughty warriors / did there together make,

When that ye saw me hither / come with sword in hand?
Thought ye then not singly / me in combat to withstand?"
2347
"In sooth denieth no one," / bold Sir Hagen spake,
"That of the same with sword-blow / I would trial make,
An but the sword of Niblung / burst not within my hand.
Yea, scorn I that to yield us / thus haughtily thou mak'st demand."
2348
When Dietrich now perceivéd / how Hagen raged amain,
Raise his shield full quickly / did the doughty thane.
As quick upon him Hagen / adown the perron sprang,
And the trusty sword of Niblung / full loud on Dietrich's armor rang.
2349
Then knew full well Sir Dietrich / that the warrior keen
Savage was of humor, / and best himself to screen
Sought of Bern the hero / from many a murderous blow,
Whereby the valiant Hagen / straightway came he well to know.
2350
Eke fear he had of Balmung, / a strong and trusty blade.
Each blow meanwhile Sir Dietrich / with cunning art repaid,
Till that he dealt to Hagen / a wound both deep and long,
Whereat give o'er the struggle / must the valiant knight and strong.
2351
Bethought him then Sir Dietrich: / "Through toil thy strength has fled,
And little honor had I / shouldst thou lie before me dead.
So will I yet make trial / if I may not subdue
Thee unto me as hostage." / Light task 'twas not the same to do.
2352
His shield down cast he from him / and with what strength he found
About the knight of Tronje / fast his arms he wound.
In such wise was subduéd / by him the doughty knight;
Gunther the noble monarch / did weep to see his sorry plight.
2353
Bind Hagen then did Dietrich, / and led him where did stand
Kriemhild the royal lady, / and gave into her hand
Of all the bravest warrior / that ever weapon bore.
After her mickle sorrow / had she merry heart once more.
2354
For joy before Sir Dietrich / bent royal Etzel's wife:
"Blessed be thou ever / in heart while lasteth life.
Through thee is now forgotten / all my dire need;
An death do not prevent me, / from me shall ever be thy meed."
2355

Then spake to her Sir Dietrich, / "Take not his life away,
High and royal lady, / for full will he repay
Thee for the mickle evil / on thee have wrought his hands.
Be it not his misfortune / that bound before thee here he stands."
2356
Then bade she forth lead Hagen / to dungeon keep near by,
Wherein he lay fast bolted / and hid from every eye.
Gunther, the noble monarch, / with loudest voice did say:
"The knight of Bern who wrongs me, / whither hath he fled away?"
2357
Meanwhile back towards him / the doughty Dietrich came,
And found the royal Gunther / a knight of worthy name.
Eke he might bide longer / but down to meet him sprang,
And soon with angry clamor / their swords before the palace rang.
2358
How famed soe'er Sir Dietrich / and great the name he bore,
With wrath was filled King Gunther, / and eke did rage full sore
At thought of grievous sorrow / suffered at his hand:
Still tell they as high wonder / how Dietrich might his blows withstand.
2359
In store of doughty valor / each did nothing lack.
From palace and from tower / the din of blows came back
As on well-fastened helmets / the lusty swords came down,
And royal Gunther's valor / in the fight full clear was shown.
2360
The knight of Bern yet tamed him / as Hagen erst befell,
And oozing through his armor / the blood was seen to swell
From cut of sharpest weapon / in Dietrich's arm that swung.
Right worthily King Gunther / had borne him after labors long.
2361
Bound was then the monarch / by Sir Dietrich's hand,
Albeit bonds should suffer / ne'er king of any land.
But deemed he, if King Gunther / and Hagen yet were free,
Secure might never any / from their searching vengeance be.
2362
When in such manner Dietrich / the king secure had bound
By the hand he led him / where Kriemhild he found.
At sight of his misfortune / did sorrow from her flee:
Quoth she: "Welcome Gunther / from out the land of Burgundy."
2363
He spake: "Then might I thank thee, / sister of high degree,
When that some whit more gracious / might thy greeting be.
So angry art thou minded / ever yet, O queen,

Full spare shall be thy greeting / to Hagen and to me, I ween."
2364
Then spake of Bern the hero: / "Ne'er till now, O queen,
Given o'er as hostage / have knights so worthy been,
As I, O lofty lady, / in these have given to thee:
I pray thee higher evils / to spare them now for sake of me."
2365
She vowed to do it gladly. / Then forth Sir Dietrich went
With weeping eyes to see there / such knights' imprisonment.
In grimmest ways thereafter / wreaked vengeance Etzel's wife:
Beneath her hand those chosen / warriors twain must end their life.
2366
She let them lie asunder / the less at ease to be,
Nor did each the other / thenceforward ever see
Till that unto Hagen / her brother's head she bore.
In sooth did Kriemhild vengeance / wreak upon the twain full sore.
2367
Forth where she should find Hagen / the queen her way did take,
And in right angry manner / she to the warrior spake:
"An thou wilt but restore me / that thou hast ta'en from me,
So may'st thou come yet living / home to the land of Burgundy."
2368
Answered thereto grim Hagen: / "'Twere well thy breath to save,
Full high and royal lady. / Sworn by my troth I have
That I the hoard will tell not; / the while that yet doth live
Of my masters any, / the treasure unto none I'll give."
2369
"Then ended be the story," / the noble lady spake.
She bade them from her brother / straightway his life to take.
His head they struck from off him, / which by the hair she bore
Unto the thane of Tronje. / Thereat did grieve the knight full sore.
2370
When that he in horror / his master's head had seen,
Cried the doughty warrior / unto Kriemhild the queen:
"Now is thy heart's desire / at length accomplishéd.
And eke hath all befallen / as my foreboding heart hath said.
2371
"Dead lieth now the noble / king of Burgundy,
Also youthful Giselher / and Sir Gernot eke doth he.
The treasure no one knoweth / but God and me alone,
Nor e'er by thee, she-devil, / shall its hiding-place be known."
2372
Quoth she: "But ill requital / hast thou made to me.

Yet mine the sword of Siegfried / now henceforth shall be,
The which when last I saw him, / my loved husband bore,
In whom on me such sorrow / through guilt of thine doth weigh full
sore."

2373

She drew it from the scabbard, / nor might he say her nay,
Though thought she from the warrior / his life to take away.
With both hands high she raised it / and off his head struck she,
Whereat did grieve King Etzel / full sore the sorry sight to see.

2374

"To arms!" cried then the monarch: / "here lieth foully slain
Beneath the hand of woman / of all the doughtiest thane
That e'er was seen in battle / or ever good shield bore!
Though foeman howsoever, / yet grieveth this my heart full sore."

2375

Quoth then the aged Hildebrand: / "Reap no gain she shall,
That thus she dared to slay him. / Whate'er to me befall,
And though myself in direst / need through him have been,
By me shall be avengéd / the death of Tronje's knight full keen."

2376

In wrathful mood then Hildebrand / unto Kriemhild sprung,
And 'gainst the queen full swiftly / his massy blade he swung.
Aloud she then in terror / 'fore Hildebrand did wail,
Yet that she shrieked so loudly, / to save her what might that avail?

2377

So all those warriors fated / by hand of death lay strewn,
And e'en the queen full lofty / in pieces eke was hewn.
Dietrich and royal Etzel / at length to weep began,
And grievously they mournéd / kinsmen slain and many a man.

2378

Who late stood high in honor / now in death lay low,
And fate of all the people / weeping was and woe.
To mourning now the monarch's / festal tide had passed,
As falls that joy to sorrow / turneth ever at the last.

2379

Nor can I tell you further / what later did befall,
But that good knights and ladies / saw ye mourning all,
And many a noble squire, / for friends in death laid low.
Here hath the story ending, / —that is the Nibelungen woe.

CPSIA information can be obtained
at www.ICGtesting.com
Printed in the USA
LVHW051158060121
675685LV00006B/138